STAR TREK® 101

STAR TREK® 101

A Practical Guide to Who, What, Where, and Why

Terry J. Erdmann & Paula M. Block

Star Trek and *Star Trek: The Next Generation*®
created by Gene Roddenberry

Star Trek: Deep Space Nine®
created by Rick Berman & Michael Piller

Star Trek: Voyager®
created by Rick Berman & Michael Piller & Jeri Taylor

Star Trek: Enterprise®
created by Rick Berman & Brannon Braga

POCKET BOOKS
New York   London   Toronto   Sydney

Pocket Books
A Division of Simon & Schuster, Inc.
1230 Avenue of the Americas
New York, NY 10020

Copyright © 2008 by
Paramount Pictures Corporation.
All Rights Reserved.

™, ® and © 2008 by CBS Studios Inc. All Rights Reserved.
STAR TREK and related marks are trademarks of CBS Studios Inc.

●CBS CONSUMER PRODUCTS

CBS, the CBS EYE logo, and related marks are trademarks of CBS Broadcasting Inc.
™ & © CBS Broadcasting Inc. All Rights Reserved.

This book is published by Pocket Books, a division of Simon & Schuster, Inc., under exclusive license from CBS Studios Inc.

First Pocket Books trade paperback edition September 2008

POCKET and colophon are registered trademarks of Simon & Schuster, Inc.

For information about special discounts for bulk purchases, please contact Simon & Schuster Special Sales at 1-800-456-6798 or business@simonandschuster.com.

Designed by Richard Oriolo

Manufactured in the United States of America

10 9 8 7 6 5 4 3 2 1

ISBN-13: 978-0-7434-9723-7
ISBN-10:   0-7434-9723-6

This one's for the fans—

past, present, and future

A USER-FRIENDLY INTRODUCTION

Maybe you've heard of a guy named Spock, but you're not really sure if he's a baby doctor or a spaceman. Or maybe you've heard, "Beam me up, Scotty," but you don't quite know what it means. If so, then this book is for you.

Or maybe you know a *lot* about Spock, and all about beaming up. If so, then this book is for you, too.

For those of you with little or no *Trek* experience, we have only one instruction: *Don't be intimidated.* (The rest of you already know that.)

If you're wondering whether you can really understand all this . . . stuff, just remember that *Star Trek* has far fewer facts than they threw at you in high school and it's a lot more fun. Plus, you don't have to take Phys Ed.

Lesson One: A writer, Gene Roddenberry, created a science-fiction television show called *Star Trek* in 1966. (It became one of the most successful entertainment franchises in history.)

The rest is recess.

We've broken this book into seven chapters because there are six *Star Trek* television shows, one of which is animated (one chapter each), and ten *Star Trek* motion pictures (all in one chapter).

As you read, you'll come across references to specific page numbers, marked in parentheses. These point you to relevant tidbits of information regarding the character or incident that you've been reading about, and help to identify which episode to watch if it sounds interesting (or which rerun to catch, since *Star Trek* is always airing somewhere).

As this book points out, some of the stories are real clinkers, and you'll likely find them entertaining for all the wrong reasons.

You'll also find an assortment of "sidebars"—tidbits of information that we've highlighted because we think they're important, unique, or just plain fun.

As you peruse the *Star Trek* television shows (all seven hundred and thirty-four of them) and films, you'll find comedies, dramas, war stories, romances, morality tales, and action-adventures. If you're new to all of this, you are about to enter an entertaining realm. If you're already an expert, we hope you'll have fun revisiting old friends.

On your mark . . . get set . . . engage!

—Terry J. Erdmann & Paula M. Block
Los Angeles, 2008

CONTENTS

STAR TREK® 101

The *U.S.S. Enterprise*'s mandate to seek out new life and new civilizations sometimes leads to uneasy gatherings of visitors with differing agendas.

ONE

STAR TREK

"Wagon Train to the Stars"

79 hour-long episodes, 1966–1969

SERIES PREMISE

A FEW HUNDRED YEARS IN THE FUTURE, A HEROIC CAPTAIN AND HIS CREW explore the galaxy in a really fast spacecraft known as the *Starship Enterprise*. The crew's standing orders from Starfleet are recited by the captain at the beginning of each episode:

> Space, the final frontier. These are the voyages of the *Starship Enterprise*. Its five-year mission: to explore strange new worlds, to seek out new life and new civilizations, to boldly go where no man has gone before.

THE SHIP

The *U.S.S. Enterprise* NCC-1701 is an interstellar spacecraft with a crew complement of 430 men and women. The ship is powered by warp-drive engines that allow it to travel many times faster than the speed of light, covering great distances within a practical time frame. (You don't really need to know this to enjoy the show; just assume you'll be visiting an average of one planet per week.)

Because the ship is large and a bit ungainly, the *Enterprise* never lands. It wasn't designed for it. Whenever the ship arrives at a strange new world, it stays in orbit while a "landing party" either pilots a small craft down to the surface or uses the transporter to "beam" there (this will be explained later). The transporter, like warp drive, is a great time-saving device; Starfleet clearly employs a lot of efficiency experts.

THE MAIN CHARACTERS

JAMES T. KIRK (William Shatner), captain

> Risk is our business. That's what this starship is all about. That's why we're aboard her.
> —"RETURN TO TOMORROW"

Kirk is the quintessential Starfleet officer, a man among men and a hero for the ages. His adventures are legendary. He has earned the admiration of his peers, the grudging respect of his opponents, and a chest full of commendations for valor. Cunning, courageous, and confident, Kirk is renowned for his ability to think outside the box, manipulating seemingly impossible situations like a master chess player. If he has one flaw, it is his tendency to ignore Starfleet regulations when he feels the end justifies the means. Kirk's unique style of "cowboy diplomacy" has served him well in countless close encounters.

Kirk was born on Earth in Iowa. He proved a very serious student at Starfleet Academy, remembered by a classmate as a "stack of books with legs." As a Starfleet officer, he is a study in contrasts. He depends on the state-of-the-art twenty-third-century technology that surrounds him but prefers resolving difficult situations with a hands-on approach—bare-knuckle brawling or bamboozling sophisticated alien computers with his glib tongue. Kirk openly deplores humankind's ancient instinct for war and killing but has a deep-seated distrust of apparent peace and tranquillity. He dreams of "a beach to walk on" with a beautiful woman but firmly believes that man wasn't meant to live in paradise. Although Kirk has quite a reputation as a ladies' man, no woman has ever come between him and his career; his passion for the *Enterprise* always comes first. His most serious relationship was with Edith Keeler, a forward-thinking but ill-fated social worker whom Kirk met when he traveled into Earth's past.

Key Kirk Episodes
- "The Enemy Within"
- "Court Martial"
- "Shore Leave"
- "The City on the Edge of Forever"

"You keep wondering if man was meant to be out here—you keep wondering and you keep signing on." —Kirk, "The Naked Time"

officer, and the only man Kirk trusts to second-guess him on all major decisions. Why? Well, for one thing, Spock is probably the smartest man in Starfleet—quite possibly the galaxy. His cerebral abilities are so renowned that they once inspired a group of aliens to invade the *Enterprise* to steal his brain. (He got it back.)

Like must Vulcans, Spock worships at the altar of logic. His decisions are always "flawlessly logical." Kirk feels safer about Spock's guesses than he does about most other people's facts. That's because Spock doesn't let emotions cloud his judgment. In fact, Spock has no emotions. Or so he says.

Spock is only half Vulcan. His father, Sarek, was a Vulcan diplomat; his mother, Amanda, a human schoolteacher from Earth. He was raised on his father's world, where the inhabitants are trained from birth to lock away their feelings and lose the key.

Growing up, Spock was torn between the stern discipline of his father's Vulcan teachings and the free-range emotions of his mother. The Vulcan children tormented Spock at school. His father didn't speak to him for eighteen years because Spock opted to join Starfleet rather than attend the Vulcan Science Academy. And Spock's fiancée, T'Pring, spurned him at the altar in favor of a more traditional Vulcan.

Spock is married to his career, which is just as well since he claims to be immune to the charms of women. He has experienced romantic yearnings only under unusual circumstances triggered by alien spores and *Pon farr*.

SPOCK (Leonard Nimoy), first officer

I have a human half . . . as well as an alien half, submerged, constantly at war with each other . . . I survive it because my intelligence wins out over both, makes them live together.
—"THE ENEMY WITHIN"

The first Vulcan to enlist in Starfleet, Spock (he has a first name, but it's unpronounceable) is the *Enterprise*'s science officer as well as its first

Key Spock Episodes

- "The Naked Time"
- "This Side of Paradise"
- "Amok Time"
- "Journey to Babel"

LEONARD "BONES" McCOY (DeForest Kelley), chief medical officer

He's dead, Jim.
—"THE ENEMY WITHIN"

Given half a chance, Leonard McCoy is far more likely to explain what he *isn't* than what he *is*. He's not a bricklayer, psychiatrist, escalator, engineer, coal miner, or moon-shuttle conduc-

tor. He's "just an old country doctor" who happens to know a lot about twenty-third-century medicine. Born in Georgia, on Earth, McCoy still retains a touch of the charming Southern gentleman about him, which balances out his often cantankerous nature.

More than a little old-fashioned, McCoy isn't convinced that humankind should be gallivanting across the galaxy in a warp-powered starship. He loathes having his atoms "scattered back and forth across space" via the transporter, and he is disturbed by the fact that neither computers nor Vulcans have a clue about compassion. As might be expected, Spock's slavish devotion to technology, logic, and statistics drives McCoy crazy, and he's constantly trying to punch holes in Spock's cool Vulcan reserve. However, Spock is just as good at getting a rise out of McCoy, playing the good doctor's emotions like a concert pianist.

If Kirk represents the soul of the *Enterprise* and Spock the mind, then McCoy is undoubtedly the heart. The good doctor's insight provides the captain with a touchstone to his own humanity. He's the guy Kirk seeks out when he needs to let his hair down, generally over a drink.

Key McCoy Episodes
- "Shore Leave"
- "The City on the Edge of Forever"
- "Friday's Child"
- "For the World Is Hollow and I Have Touched the Sky"

"I signed aboard this ship to practice medicine, not to have my atoms scattered back and forth across space by this gadget."
—McCoy, "Space Seed"

MONTGOMERY SCOTT (James Doohan), chief engineer

> I can't change the laws of physics.
>
> —"THE NAKED TIME"

Montgomery Scott—known to one and all as "Scotty"—is the ship's miracle worker. He's also its chief engineer, but those titles might as well be one and the same when you have a fellow like Scotty keeping your starship shipshape. There's no one you'd rather have at the controls of the transporter when you're ready to beam up.

Born in Scotland, Scott retains a bit of the highlanders' Gaelic lilt in his dialect. He refers to the ship's engines as his "bairns" (children) and is prone to calling junior personnel "laddie" or "lass." Scott's affection for the *Enterprise* may be a bit stronger than his devotion to the captain. He once started a brawl because someone likened the NCC-1701 to a "garbage scow." The fact that earlier Kirk was described as "a swaggering, overbearing, tin-plated dictator with delusions of godhood" hadn't bothered him.

Although he enjoys an occasional nip of Scotch, Scott generally prefers an evening with a technical manual to a night on the town.

Key Scott Episodes

- "Wolf in the Fold"
- "The Trouble With Tribbles"
- "The Lights of Zetar"

"Fool me once, shame on you—fool me twice, shame on me." —Scott, "Friday's Child"

SULU (George Takei), helm officer

Richelieu, beware!

—"THE NAKED TIME"

Sulu is a Renaissance man, counting among his passions botany, fencing, ancient handguns . . . and a subconscious desire to emulate Alexandre Dumas's swashbuckling literary hero D'Artagnan. He's the ship's main helmsman, which essentially means he's the driver.

Key Sulu Episodes
- "The Naked Time"
- "Mirror, Mirror"

UHURA (Nichelle Nichols), communications officer

Hailing frequencies still open, sir.

—"THE CORBOMITE MANEUVER"

As the ship's communications officer, Uhura spends much of her workday sending transmissions to Starfleet Command and responding to Captain Kirk's requests to open hailing frequencies to new life and new civilizations. Still, there are probably worse jobs on a starship, and Uhura is the only female permanently assigned to the bridge. Her name means "freedom" in Swahili. When she's off duty, Uhura enjoys singing for her fellow crew members.

Key Uhura Episodes
- **"The Changeling"**
- **"The Trouble With Tribbles"**

PAVEL ANDREIEVICH CHEKOV (Walter Koenig), navigator

It's a Russian invention.
—"THE TROUBLE WITH TRIBBLES"

Ensign Pavel Chekov is an excellent navigator, despite the fact that his internal magnetic needle is permanently stuck on his homeland, Russia. He attributes—correctly or incorrectly—most scientific discoveries to that country and praises the virtues of native Russian products over all others. One of the *Enterprise*'s youngest bridge officers, Chekov has a plucky sense of bravado, but he has his limits, particularly when it comes to physical discomfort.

Key Chekov Episodes
- "The Deadly Years"
- "Day of the Dove"

"I transferred the whole kit and kaboodle into their engine room, where they'll be no tribble at all." —Scott, "The Trouble With Tribbles"

CHRISTINE CHAPEL (Majel Barrett), nurse

I'm in love with you, Mister Spock.

—"THE NAKED TIME"

Chapel is the primary nurse in sickbay. She originally signed aboard the *Enterprise* to search for her missing fiancé. When she discovered that he had turned himself into an android, she transferred her attention to Mister Spock (an emotionally lateral move at best).

Key Chapel Episode

- "What Are Little Girls Made Of?"

JANICE RAND (Grace Lee Whitney), yeoman

Captain, look at my legs.

—"MIRI"

As the captain's personal assistant, Yeoman Rand attends to many of Kirk's small needs, bringing him coffee, meals, and reports that he needs to sign. She sports a unique basket-weave hairdo and has a bit of a crush on her boss.

Key Rand Episode

- "Charlie X"

"The most cooperative man in this world is a dead man—and if you don't keep your mouth shut, you're gonna be cooperating."

—Bela Oxmyx, "A Piece of the Action"

KEVIN THOMAS RILEY (Bruce Hyde), navigator

Never fear, O'Riley's here!

—"THE NAKED TIME"

Riley is the relief navigator on the *Enterprise*. As a boy on Tarsus IV, he was one of the few eye-witnesses to a massacre that killed his parents and thousands of other colonists. He fancies himself the descendant of Irish kings and once usurped command of the *Enterprise* while under the intoxicating influence of an alien virus.

Key Riley Episode

- "The Naked Time"

THE FIRST PILOT. "The Cage." Written by Gene Roddenberry. "The Cage" was the original pilot for *Star Trek*. In it, a starship captain is kidnapped by a group of aliens who hope to breed him with a female human for their private zoo. It stars Jeffrey Hunter as Captain Christopher Pike (Kirk's predecessor). Deemed "too intellectual," the episode never aired. A second pilot was commissioned by NBC, with the mandate that it contain "more action." The broadcaster also asked writer Gene Roddenberry to get rid of the guy with the pointy ears, but he refused. Numerous scenes from "The Cage" were later worked into the two-part episode "The Menagerie."

MAJOR ALIENS

Vulcans

A highly intelligent humanoid species native to the planet Vulcan. With the exception of their pointed ears, Vulcans look a great deal like humans. Internally, it's a different story: their hearts are located where a human's liver would be; their blood is green rather than red; and they have an inner eyelid that protects them from the intensity of the sun on their home planet.

Vulcans are much stronger than humans, and they live longer, well past the century mark. They tend to be calmer than humans, having bottled up their emotions. Thousands of years ago, the Vulcans were as violent and passionate as all the other species in the galaxy—that is, until a Vulcan philosopher named Surak taught them to forswear passion and embrace logic.

Vulcans live their lives by logic. They plan their careers with it, pick a mate with it, set their clocks by it. They eat, sleep, and breathe logic. And that leaves zero room for emotions, because emotions, as any Vulcan will tell you, are irrational, unpredictable, and inconvenient.

DID YOU KNOW . . . that Vulcans are strict vegetarians? . . . that most male Vulcan names begin with *S* and most female names with *T* followed by an apostrophe? . . . that "Live long and prosper" is the Vulcan equivalent of "shalom"?

VULCAN NERVE PINCH is a martial arts technique that requires great strength. Applying finger pressure to a cluster of nerves located at the base of the neck instantly renders a person unconscious.

VULCAN MIND-MELD is a mind-reading technique that allows a Vulcan to establish a telepathic link with another individual and share that person's consciousness. Vulcans don't enter into this ritual lightly, because it is a deeply personal, intimate experience. With an unwilling participant, the mind-meld can be highly invasive and psychologically violent, akin to mental rape.

IMPORTANT VULCANS

SURAK (Barry Atwater), father of Vulcan philosophy

Surak's teachings of logic and peace put an end to the destructive civil wars that plagued Vulcan centuries earlier. To modern-day Vulcans, he's Mahatma Gandhi and Abraham Lincoln rolled into one.

SAREK (Mark Lenard), father of Spock and Vulcan ambassador to the Federation

As a scientist and a diplomat, Sarek is unrivaled. He disapproved of Spock's chosen career path but ultimately came to accept it (see "Journey to Babel," p. 32). Sarek is married to Amanda, a human schoolteacher.

T'PAU (Celia Lovsky), big-shot Vulcan political figure

We're never told what office T'Pau holds, but she commands great respect among Vulcans and humans alike. Kirk refers to her as "all of Vulcan in one package." T'Pau presided at Spock's ill-fated wedding ceremony (see "Amok Time," p. 30).

T'PRING (Arlene Martel), Spock's intended mate

T'Pring was telepathically bonded to Spock when they were both seven years old, in a ceremony that was a precursor to the couple's arranged marriage. At the actual ceremony decades later (see "Amok Time," p. 30), T'Pring revealed that she preferred another man.

> *"I've never understood the female capacity to avoid a direct answer to any question."*
> —Spock, "This Side of Paradise"

Klingons

An aggressive, warrior civilization with great military power and immense territorial ambition. They are the Federation's most formidable opponents and the alien species James Kirk is least happy to see when he beams down to any planet.

Klingons are human in appearance, generally with swarthy complexions and distinctive eyebrows. Many of the men sport facial hair, goatees that would have fit right into Genghis Khan's era. Most non-Klingons would say that their personalities also are reminiscent of the Mongol hordes, right down to their thirst for conquest of alien lands. At one point in the twenty-third century, territorial disputes between the Federation and the Klingon Empire became so volatile that the two sides almost went to war. Only the benevolent intervention of the powerful Organians prevented combat (see "Errand of Mercy," p. 29).

KOR (John Colicos), Klingon commander

Kor is an ambitious Klingon who invaded the planet Organia and set himself up as its military governor (see "Errand of Mercy," p. 29). He was unaware that Organia's peaceful inhabitants were actually extremely advanced life-forms.

KOLOTH (William Campbell), Klingon captain

The haughty captain of a Klingon warship encountered by Kirk at Deep Space Station K-7 (see "The Trouble With Tribbles," p. 33). Although Captain Koloth claimed that all he wanted at the station was a little rest and relaxation for his crew, the discovery that a large supply of grain stored on K-7 had been poisoned made everyone suspicious of Koloth's motives.

KANG (Michael Ansara), Klingon captain

A strong captain and a devoted husband, Kang was the victim, along with Kirk, of an energy-based life-form that sought to feed on the hostile emotions generated by both men's crews (see "Day of the Dove," p. 36).

KAHLESS THE UNFORGETTABLE (Robert Herron), a major figure in Klingon history

The Vulcans have Surak and the Klingons have Kahless, the bravest warrior ever and the guy that every Klingon seeks to emulate.

"Man stagnates if he has no ambition, no desire to be more than he is."—Kirk, "This Side of Paradise"

Romulans

They look just like Vulcans—and there's a reason for that. Several thousand years ago, they *were* Vulcans, but they abandoned their home planet. Exactly why and how this diaspora occurred isn't clear, but the most accepted theory is that they didn't embrace the philosophy spread by peace lover Surak.

As in many dysfunctional families, the Vulcans put the memory of their not-so-dearly-departed brethren out of their collective minds. It didn't occur to them that they might one day reappear in another guise. Earth and its allies had fought a bitter war against the Romulan Star Empire in 2160, but because all the fighting was conducted with spaceships, no one knew what the enemy looked like. It was only after Kirk's crew caught a glimpse of them on the view screen during a deadly encounter in 2266 (see "Balance of Terror," p. 27) that everyone discovered that Romulans look *just like Vulcans.*

ROMULAN COMMANDER, MALE (Mark Lenard)

This unnamed commander took his starship into Federation territory to test Federation defenses (see "Balance of Terror," p. 27). Had he succeeded in his mission, a Romulan-Federation war might have transpired, but the *Enterprise* crew managed to best the commander in a dangerous game of cat and mouse. The commander admired Kirk's strategic skills.

ROMULAN COMMANDER, FEMALE (Joanne Linville)

The officer in charge of the Romulan vessel that captured the *Enterprise* when the Federation ship crossed into Romulan territory (see "The *Enterprise* Incident," p. 35). Unaware that the *Enterprise*'s mission was to steal a Romulan cloaking device, the commander inadvertently gave Kirk the opportunity to do just that while she attempted to maneuver Mister Spock into a rather personal Romulan/Vulcan détente.

"A question—since before your sun burned hot in space and before your race was born, I have awaited a question."
—the Guardian, "The City on the Edge of Forever"

DID YOU KNOW that Romulans once were Vulcans? That the Romulans had a brief strategic alliance with the Klingons that allowed them to share technology and ship design?

ROMULAN NEUTRAL ZONE was established as part of the peace treaty following a war between Earth and the Romulans. The Neutral Zone is a region of space that serves as the buffer separating the Romulan Star Empire from Federation space. Entry into the zone by either party is considered an act of war.

ROMULAN BIRD-OF-PREY is a small but powerful starship equipped with a deadly plasma energy weapon and a cloaking device. The ship has two weaknesses: it can't travel very fast, and it must turn its cloaking device off in order to fire its weapons. The belly of the ship is decorated with a painting of a large predatory bird.

ROMULAN CLOAKING DEVICE renders a ship invisible to sensors and the unaided eye. Because it requires a great deal of power, the cloak must be deactivated before the ship can fire its weapons or use its transporter.

"After a time, you may find that having is not so pleasing a thing, after all, as wanting."
—Spock, "Amok Time"

THE MENAGERIE

Mugatos

Ill-tempered, gorilla-like apes with long, white fur, poisonous fangs, and a big horn sticking out of the top of the head (see "A Private Little War," p. 34).

Gorn

Big, green, and mean, these bipedal lizards sport dazzling multifaceted eyes and a bad attitude. The Gorn have little patience with trespassers. After they wipe out a Federation colony over a territorial dispute (see "Arena," p. 28), Kirk is forced to fight one mano a mano, emerging the bare-chested winner.

Tellarites

Tellarites are stubborn and argumentative— one might even say pigheaded (see "Journey to Babel," p. 32). They also *look* pigheaded, with their prominent snouts and vacant eyes.

Horta

An intelligent silicon-based life-form that looks like a cross between a lava flow and an extra-large pepperoni pizza (see "The Devil in the Dark," p. 29). Horta live underground on the planet Janus VI, ingesting minerals as they tunnel through solid rock. Every fifty thousand years, all the adults die off, with the exception of one caretaker, who looks after their eggs and raises the hatchlings.

Andorians

Andorians have baby blue skin, silver-white hair, and pert antennae. They tend to stand out in a crowd, even amid a motley group of Federation ambassadors (see "Journey to Babel," p. 32). They describe themselves as a "passionate, violent" people.

Tholians

Highly territorial—and highly punctual—Tholians don't take kindly to Federation ships passing through their space. Their appearance is a mystery; we don't know if their heads are shaped like multifaceted hunks of crystal, or if they just wear helmets of that shape. While their small ships aren't much of a threat on their own, two ships can create a powerful tractor field, ensnaring their enemies within a deadly web (see "The Tholian Web," p. 36).

Tribbles

They "are the sweetest creatures known to man," at least according to their chief promoter, trader Cyrano Jones (see "The Trouble With Tribbles," p. 33). The more tribbles eat, the more they reproduce. They can produce as many as ten offspring every twelve hours. They seem to like everyone—except Klingons.

TEN ESSENTIAL EPISODES

1. **"Where No Man Has Gone Before" Written by Samuel A. Peeples.**

   After the *Enterprise* passes through a strange energy barrier in space, Crewman Gary Mitchell begins to show signs of superhuman psychokinetic abilities and a dangerous "God complex." Fearing for the lives of his crew, Kirk attempts to strand Mitchell on an uninhabited planet but ultimately is forced to destroy him.

   This was the first episode filmed. It was not, however, the original pilot for Star Trek *(see "The First Pilot," p. 10).*

2. **"The Naked Time" Written by John D. F. Black.**

   The crew of the *Enterprise* contracts a mysterious virus that strips away all inhibitions—an embarrassing problem that quickly becomes catastrophic when Lieutenant Riley shuts down the ship's engines, allowing the *Enterprise* to be dragged out of orbit toward a planet that's about to explode.

   Fans enjoy this episode because it provides rare insight into the characters' subconscious emotions.

3. **"Space Seed" Teleplay by Gene L. Coon and Carey Wilber. Story by Carey Wilber.**

   The *Enterprise* encounters a ship carrying a crew of genetically enhanced humans—refugees from Earth's Eugenics Wars. Kirk prevents their leader, Khan Noonien Singh, from taking over the *Enterprise* and offers Khan a choice: incarceration on Earth or banishment on an uninhabited world. Khan chooses banishment.

   "Space Seed" is the inspiration for the motion picture Star Trek II: The Wrath of Khan, *in which Ricardo Montalban reprises his role as Khan.*

4. **"This Side of Paradise" Teleplay by D. C. Fontana. Story by Nathan Butler and D. C. Fontana.**

   Under the influence of alien spores, the crew abandons the *Enterprise* to take up residence on a beautiful world where everyone is strangely mellow.

   For the first time in his life, Spock is happy.

5. **"The City on the Edge of Forever" Written by Harlan Ellison.**

   Delusional after inadvertently injecting himself with a powerful stimulant, McCoy leaps through a time portal into Earth's 1930s and changes history by altering a crucial event in that era. When Kirk and Spock follow, they learn that they must allow a woman named Edith Keeler to die in order to restore reality as they know it. The complication: Kirk has fallen in love with her.

   This is widely acknowledged as the best episode of the series, a compelling blend of science fiction, humor, and pathos.

6. **"Amok Time" Written by Theodore Sturgeon.**

   On learning that Spock will die if he doesn't return to Vulcan to participate in an ancient mating ritual, Kirk bucks Starfleet orders to escort his friend home. Spock's intended bride chooses the captain, rather than Spock, as her champion in a battle to the death.

   This episode introduces all things Vulcan.

7. **"Mirror, Mirror" Written by Jerome Bixby.**

   During diplomatic negotiations with the Halkans, a transporter malfunction swaps Kirk, McCoy, Scotty, and Uhura for their barbaric counterparts from a parallel, or "mirror," universe. Kirk must find a way to save the Halkans

Time travel is easy; explaining Vulcan ears is difficult.

from subjugation by the Terran Empire and get the foursome back to their own *Enterprise* before their true identities are revealed.

It's the ultimate "evil twin" episode, with delicious doppelgängers for everyone, a sexy mistress for Kirk, and an amoral Mirror Spock.

8. "The Trouble With Tribbles" Written by David Gerrold.
A trip to Space Station K-7 puts Kirk at odds with a group of feisty Klingons, a pompous Federation undersecretary, a shady space trader, and more than 1,771,561 prolific trib-

bles. All of which leads Kirk to ask the burning question: "Who put the tribbles in the quadrotriticale, and what was in the grain that killed them?"

Although "The City on the Edge of Forever" is the critical favorite, "The Trouble With Tribbles" is unquestionably the most popular episode and one of the series's few outright comedies.

9. "Journey to Babel" Written by D. C. Fontana.
Murder and political intrigue plague the *Enterprise* as it ferries a group of Federation ambassadors to an important diplomatic con-

ference. Complicating matters: Spock is duty bound to take charge of the ship after Kirk is critically injured—but his estranged father, the Vulcan ambassador, will die if Spock doesn't relinquish command in order to participate in an incapacitating medical procedure.

10. **"A Piece of the Action" Teleplay by David P. Harmon and Gene L. Coon. Story by David P. Harmon.**

The *Enterprise* visits a planet whose inhabitants have been culturally contaminated by a book about 1920s Chicago mobsters. When feuding mob bosses "put the bag" on members of his crew, Kirk decides to do as the natives do by brandishing a "heater" and demanding "a piece of the action."

How could anyone dislike an episode that features Kirk and Spock in pin-striped suits and fedoras?

WHAT IT IS . . .

OF PHASERS (and Photons)

Think ray gun. One suspects the name "phaser" was used because it sounded like "laser," only a lot cooler.

The most recognizable phaser is a handheld device that fires a visible energy beam. It can be set on a variety of levels, ranging from "stun" to "kill," depending on just how bad the bad guys are.

The *Starship Enterprise* is equipped with much larger phasers capable of causing damage to distant objects, such as planets, enemy starships, and the temples of false gods. And when all else fails, there are always photon torpedoes in the ship's armory—warp-powered, self-propelled missiles that pack quite a punch.

STARFLEET, or IN THE NAVY (but not really)

Kirk and his crew belong to Starfleet, an agency chartered by the United Federation of Planets to conduct exploratory, scientific, diplomatic, and defensive operations in deep space. The *Enterprise* is just one ship in a fleet that regularly sails off on missions to distant lands and travels between established bases. Many Starfleet officers attend a four-year institution, Starfleet Academy, which teaches the cadets to be all that they can be.

Sounds kind of like the navy, doesn't it? Well, it's not.

Star Trek was not conceived as a show about a futuristic branch of the U.S. military, but its creators understood that familiar naval terminology would make the series accessible. All of the *Enterprise*'s details were nautical: the floors were decks, the walls bulkheads; there was forward and aft—not front and rear—and port and starboard rather than left and right. It was commanded by a captain (as opposed to, say, a "space ranger" or a "supreme high commander") and populated by yeomen, ensigns, and assorted officers. All terms were familiar to the twentieth-century ear, even if the uniforms were a little weird.

BEAM ME UP, SCOTTY

Star Trek may have been about a bunch of people traveling through space, but the episodes generally were about what they did when they got to a planet. Obviously they'd want to visit the planet's surface, stretch their legs, meet the locals, and buy a few souvenirs. But how to get down there? They could (and on occasion did) send crew members down in a small landing craft—but that certainly wouldn't be appropriate if they had to get someplace in a hurry or incognito.

Hence the transporter, one of the most brilliant conceits on *Star Trek*. The transporter briefly converts a crewman into particles of energy, then transmits—or "beams"—that energy to the desired destination, where the crewman is reconverted back to original form. That's the concept in a nutshell, and there wasn't really much elaboration on how the thing actually worked. It was as simple as: guy steps onto a platform; guy turns into some sparkles; sparkles turn back into a guy someplace else. Neat. Efficient. Foolproof.

Most of the time, anyway.

GIVE ME WARP 3, MISTER SULU . . .

The *Enterprise* is a faster-than-light spacecraft. In other words, it is capable of traveling faster than the speed of light (186,000 miles per second). Of course, the ship can travel slower than that too, by using its impulse drive—basically, a souped-up version of the type of propulsion system that moves our space shuttles. But on impulse drive, it would take 400,000 years to cross the galaxy. Hence the need for faster-than-light technology: warp drive.

Warp-drive engines allow particles of matter and antimatter to commingle within a reaction chamber. When the particles get together, they destroy each other, giving off a helluva lot of energy in the process, and allowing the ship to "warp" space. The matter and antimatter reaction is regulated by a dilithium crystal. That's why dilithium crystals are so valuable, and why the plots of so many episodes hinge on various species fighting over them.

The *Enterprise* generally moves through space at warp factors ranging from warp 1 to warp 8.

"OPEN HAILING FREQUENCIES"

Once upon a time, if you wanted to make a call, you had to ask someone, generally a phone company employee known as the "operator," to dial the number for you. You can still see this demonstrated on television (in reruns, of course) when Sheriff Andy picks up the phone and says, "Sarah, ring me the sheriff over in Mount Pilot." Or when Radar cranks the handset and shouts, "Sparky, I need to talk to Tokyo." Or when Captain Kirk orders, "Lieutenant Uhura, get me Starfleet." Uhura plugs in her futuristic earpiece, navigates some subspace frequencies, and places the call. When she gets through, Uhura announces, "Hailing frequencies open."

> **WHAT'S IN A NAME?** Although many people assume that the "U.S.S." portion of *U.S.S. Enterprise* stands for "United States Ship," it actually stands for "United Space Ship."

CLASS-M PLANET

Whenever the *Enterprise* arrives at a new world, Science Officer Spock briefs Kirk on the planetary conditions below. Sometimes he'll go into a litany about temperature variables between various continents or about the pollution content of the atmosphere. More often than not, however, he'll simply describe the planet as "Class-M," and Kirk knows that he can safely beam down without wearing a clunky environmental suit that makes him look like Diver Dan.

What is Class-M? It's a designation used to describe a planet capable of supporting life "as we know it," with a breathable oxygen-nitrogen atmosphere and a temperature range that won't boil the crew's blood. Most of the planets the *Enterprise* stops at fit the classification and are very Earth-like. Which is very convenient for filming on location.

THE PRIME DIRECTIVE

The Prime Directive is Starfleet General Order #1, and you'll hear it mentioned in lots of *Star Trek* episodes. It prohibits Starfleet personnel from messing with the normal development of any "less advanced" society.

Violations of the Prime Directive can have serious consequences. Although Kirk is well aware of the pitfalls of violating General Order #1, he's bent or broken it on more than one occasion, generally when he felt that a stagnant society needed a good kick in the pants.

UNITED FEDERATION OF PLANETS

Think United Nations, only bigger. It is an interstellar alliance of planetary governments and colonies, united for trading and for exploratory, scientific, cultural, diplomatic, and defensive endeavors. Governed by a council and led by a president, the Federation exists for the benefit and protection of member planets as well as individual citizens.

PRIMARY COLORS

You can tell who's who and what he or she does on the *Enterprise* by the color of the uniform. Gold indicates that the wearer is in Starfleet's command track. Blue means the sciences, including medicine. A red shirt indicates support services, such as communications, engineering, and security.

Wearing a red shirt can be like wearing a bull's-eye. While on landing party duty, odds are it'll be the "red shirt" who won't be returning to the ship.

STARDATE

How do you keep track of your appointments when you're orbiting Gamma Hydra IV and your date book is calibrated to Earth's revolutions around the sun? Do what Starfleet professionals do—dump that antiquated Gregorian calendar and adopt the stardate system. It's guaranteed to adjust for shifts in relative time that occur due to your vessel's speed and space-warp capability, and compute them against your position in the galaxy.

Sounds good. The producers invented it to let viewers know the show took place in the future (as if seeing a spaceship whipping past some planet didn't do the trick). But the numbers Kirk mentioned in his captain's log each week had about as much relevance to reality as the show's Nielsen ratings.

TRICORDER

This is the best multifunctional tool known to (fictional) humankind. In essence, it's a portable sensing, recording, and computing device all

FAMOUS MISQUOTES THROUGHOUT HISTORY. Humphrey Bogart never said, "Play it again, Sam," and James Kirk never said, "Beam me up, Scotty." He did say, "Two to beam up," or variations of that, a lot of times, but the best "remembered" bit of *Star Trek* dialogue seems to have evolved on its own, somewhere out there in the audience's universe.

wrapped up in one. Like a BlackBerry on steroids. McCoy instantly diagnoses a patient's ailment by scanning him or her with a medical tricorder. Scotty deduces malfunctions by scanning the engines with his engineering tricorder. And so on.

COMMUNICATOR

It's a cell phone, with unlimited minutes, unlimited roaming, and really good reception . . . most of the time.

Of course, when *Star Trek* first aired, there were no cell phones. You may have noticed that the one you now carry looks an awful lot like the one Kirk used to flip open every time he called the ship.

Coincidence?

SHIELDS OR DEFLECTORS

Different terms for an invisible defensive energy barrier that can be deployed to protect the *Enterprise* from any manner of danger. Most of the time, it's pretty darn effective. One drawback: you can't use the transporter while the shields are up.

A shield—or force field—also can be used to secure entrance to (or exit from) a small area, such as the ship's brig.

LANDING PARTY

Members of the crew sent down to a planet's surface. Each landing party generally includes at least one "red shirt" (see Primary Colors, p. 22).

UNIVERSAL TRANSLATOR

This device senses and compares the brain wave patterns of intelligent life-forms, then uses the patterns it recognizes to provide a basis for translation. The result is heard in an approximation of the speaker's voice. This explains why all the aliens in *Star Trek* sound as if they speak English, but it doesn't explain how the translator gets their lips to *look* as if they speak English.

THE BLACK SHEEP IN THE FOLD. "Spock's Brain" ranks as one of *Star Trek*'s most memorable episodes—but not in a good way. An alien woman steals Spock's brain to replace the out-of-warranty controller for her planet's complex environmental system. Kirk races against time to find the missing organ before Spock's brainless body dies. Although ostensibly a "serious" episode, the script is rife with lines that seem lifted from a hokey B movie.

"You are an excellent starship commander, but as a taxi driver, you leave much to be desired."—Spock, "A Piece of the Action"

"You're asking me to work with equipment which is hardly very far ahead of stone knives and bearskins."—Spock, "The City on the Edge of Forever"

Cold adherence to logic may fascinate Vulcan women, but Uhura prefers a romantic moonlit sky.

EPISODE SYNOPSES

Season One

1. The Man Trap

The *Enterprise* stops at planet M-113 to bring supplies to Robert and Nancy Crater, a pair of human archaeologists who are that world's only inhabitants. Although the Craters, who mention that they're particularly short on salt, attempt to convince the crew that everything is fine on M-113, Kirk soon has reason to doubt their claims. For one thing, Nancy Crater appears different to every man she encounters. McCoy sees her as the lovely young woman he dated years earlier, Kirk sees her as a graying middle-aged housewife, and crewman Darnell sees her as a sexy blonde. Then Darnell turns up dead, his body drained of salt. Soon after that, crew members aboard the *Enterprise* begin having their own strange and deadly encounters with the being that Robert Crater claims is his wife, leading Spock to conclude that Nancy is something other than human.

2. Charlie X

Kirk agrees to give passage to orphaned teenager Charlie Evans, the only survivor of a colony ship that crashed on the distant planet Thasus years ago. After being on his own for fourteen years, Charlie is hungry for company, particularly female company, and he misinterprets Yeoman Rand's friendship for something with the potential to become far more intimate. Like most adolescents, Charlie doesn't take rejection very well, and he doesn't like being told what to do. Unlike most adolescents, the powerful mental abilities he learned from the native Thasians make his tantrums deadly to anyone who displeases him.

3. Where No Man Has Gone Before

As the *Enterprise* patrols the perimeter of the galaxy, the crew finds the flight recorder of the *Valiant*, an interstellar vessel that was lost two centuries earlier. According to that ship's record, the *Valiant* sustained damage and casualties after it passed through an unusual energy field at the edge of the galaxy. Not long after, the ship's captain was apparently driven to destroy his own ship. Puzzled, Kirk orders the *Enterprise* to continue its exploration of the region, only to encounter the same bizarre energy field. Exposure to the field injures Lieutenant Commander Gary Mitchell, a longtime friend of Kirk's. When Mitchell recovers, he's a changed man, able to move things with his mind and to listen in on people's thoughts. Spock advises Kirk to kill Mitchell before he becomes too powerful to stop. Unfortunately, that's no longer an option.

4. The Naked Time

The *Enterprise* travels to the dying planet Psi 2000 to pick up a group of research scientists before their world disintegrates. A landing party discovers that the scientists are already dead, apparently the victims of some very bizarre behavior. After the landing party returns to the *Enterprise*, members of the crew begin acting strangely: Sulu chases crewmen down the corridors with a sword, while Riley commandeers engineering and serenades the crew with Irish folk tunes. Even the Vulcan science officer, Mister Spock, is affected, reduced to tears over his inability to tell his mother he loved her. Clearly, whatever affected the scientists on Psi 2000 is contagious, but can McCoy find a cure before the *Enterprise* is destroyed along with the doomed planet?

5. The Enemy Within

A transporter malfunction gives Kirk a split personality—literally. Now there are an "evil" Kirk who's running amok, guzzling brandy, and attacking female crew members, and a "good" Kirk, who's meek, indecisive, and unable to command. To make matters worse, both Kirks are dying—neither half can survive without the other. Meanwhile, on the surface of the planet the *Enterprise* is orbiting, a stranded landing party is slowly freezing to death. It's up to Chief Engineer Scott to figure out a way to repair the transporter and merge the two Kirks before the captain dies.

6. Mudd's Women

Just before his small ship is destroyed in an asteroid field, con man Harry Mudd and his cargo of three alluring women are beamed aboard the *Enterprise*. After the ship's computer reveals a laundry list of legal infractions that Mudd has committed, Kirk sends him to the brig. But the starship's trip into the asteroid field has burned out some of the dilithium crystals required to power the warp engines. Suddenly, Mudd sees a way out of his dilemma: he'll help Kirk obtain the desperately needed crystals— but only if Kirk transports him and his comely cargo to a planet occupied by three exceptionally wealthy dilithium miners.

7. What Are Little Girls Made Of?

The *Enterprise* travels to Exo III to learn the fate of Doctor Roger Korby, the brilliant scientist (and fiancé of Nurse Christine Chapel) who disappeared while on an expedition to the desolate planet. To everyone's surprise, Korby is alive

and well—and he's got company. He's found some ancient machinery that can produce androids—humanoid robots—in whatever configuration he desires. He's so enamored by the technology that he's implanted his own consciousness into an android body. Unfortunately, somewhere along the way, Korby has lost his humanity. He decides the *Enterprise* would be the perfect vehicle to seed the galaxy with his wonderful androids—and if Kirk doesn't want to cooperate, Korby's certain he can count on Kirk's android duplicate to do so.

8. Miri

The *Enterprise* finds an Earth-like planet where the only inhabitants are children who are much older than they look. Some three hundred years ago, their parents experimented with a serum that they thought would prolong life. It worked on the kids, slowing their aging process, but for everyone past the age of puberty, it is an automatic death sentence. As they learn the truth about the children, Kirk and his landing party find that they've contracted the deadly virus that killed the adults centuries ago. McCoy attempts to find a cure, and Kirk enlists the aid of Miri, an adolescent girl who has a crush on him, to negotiate a truce with the pack of hostile preteens.

9. Dagger of the Mind

There's something strange going on at Tantalus V, a "progressive" penal colony. While the *Enterprise* is delivering supplies to the facility, a seemingly deranged inmate escapes to the ship and begs for asylum. But he's no ordinary inmate—he's actually one of the administrators! When Kirk investigates the place, he learns that Doctor Tristan Adams, the director, has developed an overzealous dependence on a new device. The "neural neutralizer" can selectively remove criminal thoughts, but Kirk finds out firsthand that it also has applications that are uncomfortably close to brainwashing.

10. The Corbomite Maneuver

While exploring an uncharted region of space, the *Enterprise* encounters a gigantic spherical spaceship manned by Balok, a sinister-looking alien. Balok accuses Kirk of trespassing and tells the captain that he will destroy the *Enterprise* in ten minutes. Realizing that the big glowing ball is a lot more powerful than his own ship, Kirk opts to use a poker strategy to save his crew. If Balok fires upon the *Enterprise*, the "corbomite" in the ship's hull will self-destruct and take Balok's ship with it. The bluff seems to work—but Kirk doesn't realize that Balok too has a few surprises up his sleeve.

11./12. The Menagerie

After the *Enterprise*'s first commander, Christopher Pike, is severely disabled in an accident, Spock hijacks the *Enterprise* to deliver his former captain to Talos IV, a world that starships are forbidden to visit. The planet is inhabited by a race of powerful telepaths who have the dangerous ability to make illusion seem real. Years earlier, the Talosians had captured Pike, intending to keep him in a kind of zoo. But although they offered Pike the companionship of an appealing female captive, he eventually forced the beings to release him. Now Spock is determined to help the Talosians recapture Pike, and he's risking his career—as well as Kirk's—to do it.

13. The Conscience of the King

Kirk suspects Anton Karidian, the leader of a traveling Shakespearean troupe, of being Kodos the Executioner, the former governor of Tarsus IV. Years earlier, after a fungus destroyed his world's food supply, Kodos declared martial law and executed half of Tarsus's inhabitants, so that others of his choosing could live. Only a few survivors of the massacre can identify Kodos, and when those survivors start dying, Kirk thinks he knows who's to blame.

14. Balance of Terror

A Romulan ship with newly developed cloaking technology destroys several Federation outposts along the Neutral Zone between Federation and Romulan space, then sets course for home. Realizing that the Romulan ship's success will reveal an exploitable vulnerability to the Federation's enemy, Kirk plans to stop it at all costs. But the Romulan commander is as cunning as Kirk, and a game of cat and mouse ensues.

15. Shore Leave

An uninhabited idyllic world appears to be the perfect place for the *Enterprise*'s crew to get some rest and relaxation. Then McCoy encounters a large talking rabbit, Sulu runs into an ancient samurai warrior, and Kirk is floored by the presence of both a former Starfleet Academy nemesis and a beautiful old flame. It all seems like fun and games until a black knight on horseback skewers McCoy with his lance. As other members of the crew become embroiled in encounters of increasing peril, Kirk realizes that the planet is no wonderland.

16. The Galileo Seven

A scientific mission headed by Spock goes wrong when the *Shuttlecraft Galileo* is forced off course, crash-landing on the primitive world of Taurus II. Although the seven occupants of the vehicle are unharmed, they have no way to contact the *Enterprise*, and the brutish, apelike inhabitants of the planet have no love for strangers. As Scott works to repair the craft, the primitives manage to kill two members of the crew, and Spock faces the increasing hostility of the remaining crewmen, who feel that his dependence on cold-blooded logic makes him a questionable leader.

17. The Squire of Gothos

In a supposedly empty sector of space, the *Enterprise* comes across a mysterious uncharted planet inhabited by a powerful entity named Trelane. He possesses the astounding ability to transform energy into matter but has the temperament of a child—and a spoiled child, at that. After transporting various members of the crew to his planet, which he calls Gothos, Trelane tries to get Kirk and the others to participate in his odd fantasy about life on eighteenth-century Earth. When Kirk refuses to play along, he finds himself on trial for his life—with Trelane as his judge and executioner.

18. Arena

Upon discovering that the Starfleet base on Cestus III has been destroyed, the *Enterprise* gives chase to a Gorn spaceship that's responsible for the damage. As the two ships cross into uncharted territory, they are stopped by the powerful Metrons, who accuse both Kirk and the Gorn commander of trespassing. The Metrons decide to settle the conflict between the two species by having Kirk fight his counterpart in single combat on a nearby planet. The winner will go free, while the loser will be destroyed, along with his ship and crew. As Kirk sizes up his Gorn opponent, an immensely strong man-sized reptile, it's clear that hand-to-hand combat won't carry the day. But is Kirk resourceful enough to win?

19. Tomorrow Is Yesterday

The gravitational forces of a black star toss the *Enterprise* back in time, and the crew awakens to find itself orbiting Earth in the twentieth century. Spotting the ship over Nebraska, the U.S. Air Force sends up Captain John Christopher to investigate. The *Enterprise* is forced to beam Christopher aboard after it inadvertently destroys his ship, which leaves the crew with a problem. If Christopher is returned to Earth, he'll report what he's seen—which could change history. Making matters worse, there's footage of the *Enterprise* at the base below, and Spock isn't entirely sure that the ship can make it back to the twenty-third century.

20. Court Martial

Kirk is put on trial after computer records show that when a dangerous ion storm threatened the *Enterprise*, the captain jettisoned an observatory pod that had a crewman inside without giving the man time to escape. Kirk's recollection of the incident is different, but prosecuting attorney Areel Shaw, an old girlfriend of the captain's, seems to have an open-and-shut case. Kirk's exoneration hinges on the courtroom skills of Sam Cogley, an eccentric attorney who prefers books to computers, and Spock's inexplicable ability to repeatedly beat the ship's computer at chess.

21. The Return of the Archons

The *Enterprise* travels to Beta III to learn the fate of the *Archon*, a ship that disappeared while visiting the planet one hundred years earlier. When Sulu returns to the ship in a curiously altered mental state, Kirk decides to check out the planet. The inhabitants seem pathologically tranquil. Everything on the planet is done for the good of "the Body"—the whole of Beta society—but the society is stagnant and nonproductive. "The Body" is under the strict mental control of Landru, an apparently omniscient computer that's been in charge for thousands of years. It was Landru that destroyed the *Archon* and "absorbed" its crew into the populace of Beta III. The same fate awaits the *Enterprise* if Kirk can't find a way to stop Landru.

22. Space Seed

The *Enterprise* comes upon an old "sleeper ship" that carries a crew in suspended animation. It's only after Kirk decides to allow the sleepers to be resuscitated that he realizes his mistake. These are refugees from Earth's violent Eugenics War and their revived leader, Khan Noonien Singh, still has all the ambition, strength, and cunning that allowed him to conquer a large portion of Earth three centuries earlier. Khan and his followers quickly seize control of the *Enterprise* and give Kirk and his crew an ultimatum: yield to his leadership or die.

23. A Taste of Armageddon

At the urging of a Federation ambassador, Kirk attempts to establish diplomatic contact with the planet Eminiar VII. Upon arrival, Kirk learns that the planet has been at war with the neighboring world of Vendikar for more than five hundred years. Despite the fact that there have been thousands of casualties in the conflict, there is no sign of damage on either world. The reason is simple: the two planets are engaged in a virtual war, wherein computers project the weapons strikes and how many victims are killed. Those unlucky inhabitants declared "dead" must willingly report to vaporization booths for actual destruction—and the war's latest victims are the entire crew of the *Enterprise*!

24. This Side of Paradise

The crew of the *Enterprise* arrives at Omicron Ceti III certain that the colonists who settled on the planet are dead, the victims of long-term exposure to deadly berthold radiation. To their surprise, the colonists are hale and hardy. Among them is Leila Kalomi, a former acquaintance of Spock's who has long harbored affection for him. Leila shows Spock the secret of the group's survival: a native plant species that shares a symbiotic relationship with the colonists. The plant's spores immunize them against the radiation while at the same time inducing a feeling of peace and harmony—and the desire to live on the planet forever. Once exposed to the spores, Spock yields to his submerged human emotions and returns Leila's affections. Before long, everyone on the *Enterprise* has been exposed and moved down to the colony. How does Kirk get his mutinous crew to forsake paradise?

25. The Devil in the Dark

The miners of Janus VI ask for the *Enterprise*'s help in locating the creature that is destroying their equipment and attacking their personnel. The silicon-based creature excretes an acid that allows it to tunnel swiftly through solid rock. The miners want it killed so they can get back to work, but Spock is reluctant to comply because he suspects that it may be an intelligent being, with motive behind its mayhem.

26. Errand of Mercy

With relations between the Federation and the Klingon Empire at an all-time low, Kirk is eager to get the inhabitants of Organia to allow the Federation to establish a presence on their strategically located world. The placid Organians, however, are unwilling to cooperate, even when a Klingon occupation force led by Commander Kor invades their planet. As the *Enterprise* and a Klingon ship square off to do battle against each other, the Organians demonstrate why they really don't need help from the Federation—or anyone else—to keep their corner of space conflict free.

27. The Alternative Factor

The *Enterprise*'s instruments detect a moment of "nonexistence," a highly unusual phenomenon experienced at the same time across the entire universe. Noting a life-form reading on the supposedly desolate planet below, Kirk beams down and finds Lazarus, who claims to be hunting a creature bent on the destruction of all life. Lazarus has created an interdimensional door that allows passage between our universe and its antimatter counterpart, where his enemy resides. Passing through that doorway is what triggered the bizarre cosmic effect the *Enterprise* noted. Lazarus requests some of the *Enterprise*'s dilithium crystals to continue his search, but Kirk turns him down. Later, Lazarus's counterpart from the alternative universe—an antimatter duplicate of the man Kirk met—explains that he must prevent Lazarus from fulfilling his quest. If Lazarus succeeds and matter and antimatter interact, the man explains, the universe will be destroyed.

28. The City on the Edge of Forever

While treating Sulu following an accident on the bridge, McCoy inadvertently injects himself with an overdose of a powerful stimulant. In a delusional state, McCoy transports to the planet below, a world that seems to be the source of the mysterious time-distortion waves the *Enterprise* has been investigating. Kirk beams down with a landing party, but he is too late to stop McCoy from leaping through the portal of an ancient living machine that calls itself the Guardian of Forever. At the moment McCoy passes through the Guardian, the *Enterprise* disappears, stranding the landing party on the desolate planet. The Guardian explains that McCoy has traveled to Earth's past and something he's done there has changed history, altering the present. It's up to Kirk and Spock to follow McCoy into the past and prevent him from effecting that change.

29. Operation: Annihilate!

En route to the planet Deneva, home of Kirk's brother, Sam, the *Enterprise* spots a ship that's headed on a suicidal course toward the Denevan sun. Just before the ship is destroyed, its pilot transmits a message that he has freed himself—but from what? Beaming down to the planet, Kirk finds his brother dead and his sister-in-law, Aurelan, and nephew, Peter, near death. Before dying, Aurelan reveals that Deneva has been invaded by strange parasites that attack the human nervous system. They manipulate their hosts by inducing excruciating pain. While investigating the infestation, Spock is attacked by one of the parasites. Thanks to his rigid Vulcan mental discipline, Spock is able to withstand the pain, but he reveals that the creatures want to use the *Enterprise* to spread across the galaxy. With Spock's life in the balance, McCoy searches for a way to defeat the parasites without permanently damaging their human hosts.

Season Two

30. Amok Time

When the normally staid Spock begins behaving erratically, Kirk orders him to undergo a medical exam. McCoy is at a loss; Spock seems to be suffering from enormous physical stress, but the doctor can't determine the cause. Reluctantly, Spock reveals that he has entered the *Pon farr*—an overwhelming biochemical mating urge that periodically compels members of the unemotional Vulcan race to take a mate, or die. Spock's "bride" awaits him on Vulcan. Defying orders, Kirk sets course for the planet, unaware that there are other aspects of the primitive mating drive that will put his own life at peril.

31. Who Mourns for Adonais?

The *Enterprise* encounters an unusual phenomenon: a giant hand that materializes before the starship and holds it motionless. The hand—a manifestation of energy—belongs to a powerful being that claims to be Apollo, the mythical god. Apollo invites members of the crew to join him on the planet below. Once there, they learn that Apollo seeks the blind adoration that he once inspired in the inhabitants of ancient Earth—and he has the power to demand it. Kirk is unwilling to spend the rest of his life paying homage to an alien with delusions of godhood.

32. The Changeling

While trying to determine the cause behind the devastation of the Malurian system, Kirk beams aboard Nomad, a small, self-contained computer/space probe. Nomad is the result of a mechanical union between two space probes with strikingly different agendas: one was designed to seek out alien life, while the other was meant to collect sterilized soil samples. The newly hybridized mechanism determined that its mission was to sterilize (read: eradicate) imperfect life-forms. The four billion inhabitants of the Malurian system were imperfect, Nomad reveals. And so is the crew of the *Enterprise*.

33. Mirror, Mirror

Thanks to a transporter malfunction, Kirk, McCoy, Scott, and Uhura swap places with their counterparts from another universe. They quickly discover that civilization in this universe has evolved along much different lines from their own. *Enterprise* crew members rise in the ranks by practicing intimidation and assassination, and Kirk is expected to execute anyone who challenges his authority, including the peaceful Halkans, who decline to share their

dilithium crystals. As Scotty works on getting the group home, Kirk searches for a way to spare the Halkans without forfeiting his own life.

34. The Apple

The landing party that beams down to beautiful Gamma Trianguli VI discovers that what appears to be a paradise is actually a very dangerous place. The inhabitants of the world are a simple, gentle people who make daily offerings of "food"—actually fuel—to the sophisticated computer they know as their serpent-headed god Vaal. Although Vaal, which has carefully controlled the living conditions on this world for centuries, provides an Eden-like setting for its natives, it's not fond of visitors. When it attacks the *Enterprise*, Captain Kirk decides it's time for Vaal to relinquish its hold on Gamma Trianguli.

35. The Doomsday Machine

En route to investigate the destruction of several planetary systems, the *Enterprise* spots the *U.S.S. Constellation*, a crippled ship with only one person left aboard: Commodore Matt Decker. He reports that both the systemwide destruction *and* the damage to the *Constellation* are due to a gigantic robotic vessel. Decker's entire crew was wiped out when he attempted to save their lives by beaming them to a nearby planet, which subsequently was gobbled up by the planet-killing berserker ship. Before long, Decker—nearly out of his mind with guilt and grief—puts the entire crew of the *Enterprise* in harm's way as he attempts to use Kirk's ship to defeat the berserker.

36. Catspaw

Koroh and Sylvia, a pair of aliens whose species hopes to conquer humankind, disguise their technology in trappings of the supernatural in order to terrorize a landing party from the

Enterprise. They manage to transform several crewmen into "zombies," but they err in their assumption that superstition will triumph over logic, and they overestimate the witchlike Sylvia's ability to charm Kirk. With the safety of the *Enterprise* at stake, Kirk sets Korob and Sylvia against each other as he and Spock seek the true source of their power.

37. I, Mudd

Norman, an android disguised as an *Enterprise* crewman, locks the ship on course for a planet entirely populated by his fellow androids—and one human being, Kirk's former nemesis, Harry Mudd. It was Mudd who arranged for Norman to shanghai the starship. Trapped on the planet since his own ship crash-landed, Mudd hopes to trade Kirk's crew for his own freedom. The androids have been very accommodating, following Mudd's every command and creating feminine companions to his personal specifications. The androids won't let Mudd leave—but not for the reasons he thinks. Now that they have Kirk's ship, they intend to use it to travel throughout the galaxy and protect humankind from its lowest impulses.

38. Metamorphosis

As Kirk, Spock, and McCoy attempt to transport ailing Federation Commissioner Nancy Hedford to the *Enterprise* via the *Shuttlecraft Galileo*, a strange cloudlike entity drags the vessel off course and takes it to planet Gamma Canaris N. There they encounter Zefram Cochrane, the man who, more than a century earlier, invented the warp drive that made travel to distant worlds possible. Although Cochrane appears youthful, he claims that he was an old man when he came to this world, waylaid, like Kirk and company, by the cloud creature, which

he knows as the Companion. The Companion restored his youth and cared for Cochrane. Now, sensing Cochrane's loneliness, it has brought him some human companions—and it doesn't intend to let any of them leave, even though Hedford will die.

39. Journey to Babel

Tensions run high aboard the *Enterprise* as the ship transports delegates to the Babel Conference, where the fate of a planet applying for membership in the Federation will be determined. Among those delegates are Vulcan ambassador Sarek and his human wife, Amanda—Spock's parents. The science officer and his father have not spoken in nearly twenty years, a standoff that seems unlikely to end during the trip to Babel. The ambassador has also earned the animosity of several delegates, including one who is found murdered. Evidence points to Sarek as the killer. Then Sarek suffers a potentially fatal heart attack and Spock is the only one who can provide the blood required for surgery. But when Kirk is stabbed by another delegate, and the *Enterprise* is attacked by an unidentified vessel, Spock cannot leave the bridge.

40. Friday's Child

The crew of the *Enterprise* arrives at Capella IV to negotiate a mining agreement, only to discover that the Klingons got there first. The Klingons have forged an alliance with a rebel faction that seeks to usurp Akaar, the Capellan leader. Akaar is slain, and by Capellan law, the life of his pregnant wife, Eleen, is also forfeit. Kirk refuses to allow that to happen.

41. The Deadly Years

The colonists on Gamma Hydra IV have been afflicted by a radiation-induced illness that triggers highly accelerated aging—and now members of the *Enterprise* landing party are showing signs of the same illness. As Kirk, Spock, McCoy, and Scott grow older by the hour, McCoy puzzles over why Ensign Chekov, who also was on Gamma Hydra, has *not* been affected. Commodore Stocker, temporarily in charge, orders an ill-advised shortcut through Romulan territory.

42. Obsession

When Kirk was a lieutenant on the *Farragut*, half the crew—including Garrovick, the ship's captain—was killed by a cloudlike creature. Kirk felt he could have destroyed it, if only he hadn't hesitated. Now the cloud creature has appeared again, and a crewman—the son of Kirk's former captain—has also hesitated before firing. Kirk's obsession with the creature drives him to punish Garrovick's son and to risk the lives of the rest of his crew in order to hunt the beast down and kill it once and for all.

43. Wolf in the Fold

Kirk and McCoy take Scott to Argelius II, a renowned mecca of hedonism, for a therapeutic leave. After a local woman who was in Scott's company is brutally murdered, the engineer is the main suspect. When two additional murders of females occur, Scott is once again in the vicinity. Could his earlier injury have triggered a pathological hatred of women?

44. The Trouble With Tribbles

The *Enterprise* is diverted to Space Station K-7 to protect an important shipment of grain. There Kirk finds his patience severely taxed by an obnoxious Federation bureaucrat, an arrogant Klingon commander and a slippery trader who deals in questionable merchandise. After the trader gives Uhura a sample of his wares— a tribble—Kirk's troubles escalate rapidly. Tribbles, which eat and reproduce constantly,

quickly infest both the *Enterprise* and the space station, where they eventually find their way into the grain shipment that Kirk promised to protect.

45. The Gamesters of Triskelion

Kirk, Uhura, and Chekov are abducted by a powerful transporter beam that carries them to the distant planet Triskelion. There they learn that they are to be trained as gladiators to fight for the benefit of the Providers, three disembodied brains that rule the planet. As the crew of the *Enterprise* tries to locate its missing comrades, Kirk attempts to get the Providers to change their traditional wagers.

46. A Piece of the Action

The Federation has been negligent in checking on the progress of the civilization of Sigma Iotia II. The *Horizon* was the last Federation ship to visit the distant planet, one hundred years ago. When the *Enterprise* arrives, it finds signs of severe cultural contamination. The Iotian populace has taken to heart a book left behind by the *Horizon*—titled *Chicago Mobs of the Twenties*—and fashioned a society patterned exclusively on the book.

47. The Immunity Syndrome

The *Enterprise* is ordered to investigate the Federation's loss of contact with solar system Gamma 7A and the *U.S.S. Intrepid*, the ship previously assigned to check out the region. The crew of the *Intrepid* is dead, as are the inhabitants of system Gamma 7A, all victims of a gigantic one-celled amoeba-like entity that feeds on the energy of living beings. Learning that the destructive life-form is about to reproduce, Kirk realizes that the *Enterprise* is the only thing that can stop the creature.

48. A Private Little War

The *Enterprise* travels to a primitive world that Kirk visited thirteen years earlier. At the time, Kirk was taken with the peaceful ways of the inhabitants and was befriended by Tyree, the leader of a tribe known as the "hill people." When he beams down with Spock and McCoy, Kirk finds that much has changed. A group of the planet's inhabitants are armed with flintlock rifles, weapons that they shouldn't have at their current stage of development. Before long, Kirk learns that there are Klingons on the planet, and they've been arming the "villagers," a tribe that doesn't get along with the hill people.

49. Return to Tomorrow

The *Enterprise* responds to a mysterious SOS sent from beneath the surface of a long-dead planet. In an underground vault, Kirk finds receptacles that house the consciousness of this civilization's last three survivors: Sargon, the planetary leader; his wife, Thalassa; and his former enemy, Henoch. Sargon asks to temporarily implant his consciousness, as well as that of Thalassa and Henoch, into three crew members' bodies so that they can construct the android shells that will ultimately house their consciousnesses. Kirk agrees. Sargon's mind is placed in Kirk's body, Henoch's into Spock's, and Thalassa's into that of an attractive astrobiologist. What neither Kirk nor Sargon knows is that Henoch plans to keep Spock's body, and he's not above killing both Sargon and Kirk to do it.

50. Patterns of Force

Federation cultural observer John Gill thought he was doing the right thing when he initiated a little social experiment on the planet Ekos. He decided to use the extremely efficient model of Earth's Nazi Germany to centralize Ekos's chaotic political structure. When the *Enterprise* arrives, the crew discovers that Gill's unautho-

rized experiment has worked too well. A dictator is running the planet, and the Ekosians are ruthlessly persecuting the inhabitants of neighboring planet Zeon.

51. By Any Other Name

A group of Kelvan explorers from the Andromeda galaxy have been investigating our own galaxy to determine if it's suitable for colonization. Having lost their ship, they decide to take the *Enterprise* for the three-hundred-year trip home. Knowing that the Kelvans have the ability to literally crush his crew if he tries to confront them, Kirk explores a more subversive way of defeating the Kelvans. With no tactile perceptions or emotions in their natural state, the human form the Kelvans have adopted to utilize the starship has plenty of human weaknesses—which Kirk, Spock, McCoy, and Scotty eagerly exploit.

52. The Omega Glory

The *Enterprise* discovers the *Starship Exeter* in orbit around Omega IV. A landing party of Kirk, Spock, and McCoy discovers that there's no one alive on the ship. The *Exeter*'s crew has been reduced to dust by a mysterious disease that was contracted on the planet below—and now Kirk, Spock, and McCoy have been exposed. Unable to return to the *Enterprise*, the trio beams to the surface, where they encounter Ron Tracey, the *Exeter*'s captain. They learn that the disease stays dormant if the infected person remains on the planet. It is the remnant of bacteriological warfare conducted between the inhabitants, the Yangs and the Kohms. Tracey has chosen to side with the Kohms and use his advanced weapons against the barbarian Yangs.

53. The Ultimate Computer

When the *Enterprise* is assigned to serve as the test ship for the experimental M-5 supercomputer, Kirk fears that Starfleet's need for human beings may end. The M-5 handles the ship flawlessly during its first test, but then it begins to take the war games seriously, imperiling the crews of several starships. After Kirk learns that the computer was programmed with the memory patterns and thought processes of its brilliant but unstable inventor, he realizes that he's facing an even bigger problem.

54. Bread and Circuses

Kirk, Spock, and McCoy observe that the civilization on planet 892-IV resembles Earth's ancient Roman Empire. Proconsul Claudius Marcus, the man in charge, pits hapless citizens against each other in the arena, where a high percentage of them lose their lives in the brutal gladiatorial games. The proconsul already has made short work of the crew of one ship, and he's eager to see how long Kirk's crew will survive in the arena.

55. Assignment: Earth

The *Enterprise* travels back to the year 1968 to learn how Earth managed to avoid a pending nuclear crisis. Once in orbit around Earth, the crew inadvertently beams aboard the mysterious Gary Seven, who claims to be a twentieth-century human trained by aliens to deal with the situation. Kirk isn't inclined to trust Seven, who's in possession of futuristic equipment and accompanied by a strangely intelligent black cat.

Season Three

56. Spock's Brain

A beautiful woman materializes on the *Enterprise* and renders everyone aboard unconscious. When the bridge crew awakens, they discover that Spock is no longer at his post. McCoy locates the Vulcan in sickbay, lying on a diagnostic bed—his brain surgically removed! Reasoning that the mysterious intruder must have had something to do with the theft, Kirk tracks her ship to a distant planet where the primitive males live on the frozen surface and the females live in a high-tech underground facility.

57. The *Enterprise* Incident

An erratic Kirk takes the *Enterprise* into Romulan territory, where it is immediately surrounded by Romulan warships demanding surrender. When Kirk and Spock beam over to the Romulan flagship to meet with its female commander, the captain says that his trespassing was the result of an equipment malfunction. However, Spock contradicts Kirk's explanation, noting that the captain, clearly suffering from diminished mental stability, ordered the crew to enter Romulan space without orders from Starfleet.

58. The Paradise Syndrome

While investigating a beautiful planet threatened by an approaching asteroid, Kirk, Spock, and McCoy discover a mysterious obelisk located near a village of transplanted Native Americans. Kirk inadvertently triggers a trapdoor in the obelisk and falls into the device's interior, where he is rendered unconscious by an alien mechanism. Unable to find Kirk, Spock and McCoy return to the *Enterprise*, which must leave in order to halt the progress of the distant asteroid.

59. And the Children Shall Lead

An *Enterprise* landing party arriving on Triacus discovers that all the adult members of a scientific expedition have committed suicide. Their children seem fine, if strangely unconcerned about their parents' deaths. After beaming the children up to the ship, Kirk attempts to determine what happened to the adults, unaware that the evil entity that triggered their deaths has been summoned to the *Enterprise* by the children.

60. Is There in Truth No Beauty?

Hoping to use the Medusan species's phenomenal mental abilities to improve starship navigational capabilities, the *Enterprise* brings aboard Federation engineer Laurence Marvick, telepath Miranda Jones, and Kollos, the Medusan ambassador to the Federation. Because even a glimpse of the noncorporeal Medusans is so jarring that it induces insanity, Kollos travels within a shielded container. Unfortunately, Marvick, who is infatuated with Jones, attempts to kill his "rival," Kollos, and in the process makes visual contact with the ambassador. In the grip of madness, Marvick programs the *Enterprise* to speed past the galactic barrier.

61. Spectre of the Gun

After Kirk ignores an alien buoy warning the ship away from Melkotian space, the Melkotians subject Kirk and his crew to a surrealistic reenactment of a historical event: the gunfight at the O.K. Corral. Although the Melkotians intend the reenactment to result in the trespassers' deaths, Spock suspects that the entire experience is an illusion.

62. Day of the Dove

Kirk is convinced that the Klingon battle cruiser commanded by Kang is responsible for the deaths of the Federation colonists on planet Beta XII-A. Kang is convinced that Kirk is responsible for badly damaging his battle cruiser and killing most of his crew. In fact, the havoc was caused by a malevolent energy being that feeds on aggressive emotions and goads rational men to irrational thoughts. After

Kang forces Kirk to beam the Klingons aboard the *Enterprise*, the two crews erupt in a frenzy of brutal combat, while the energy creature gorges on a feast of anger and hatred.

63. For the World Is Hollow and I Have Touched the Sky

The *Enterprise* encounters an asteroid-shaped spaceship that carries the inhabitants of the planet Yonada. The spaceship—and, indeed, the remnants of Yonada's civilization—is controlled by a sophisticated computer known as the Oracle, which the people have come to think of as a godlike entity. Unfortunately, the Oracle's programming is no longer functioning properly, and the huge spaceship is on a collision course with an inhabited world. Kirk and Spock attempt to tread the fine line between helping the Yonadans, who are ignorant of the truth about both their "world" and their god, and saving the people in the asteroid ship's path.

64. The Tholian Web

After finding the *U.S.S. Defiant* drifting in space, Kirk leads a landing party to the derelict. The entire crew is dead, apparently killed in a widespread mutiny. But what triggered the bizarre behavior? The landing party then learns that the ship—and indeed space itself—appears to be destabilizing around them. Kirk calls for an immediate beam-out, but Scott can transport only three of the four men, and Kirk disappears along with the *Defiant*. Spock determines that there may be a way to recover the captain. The unstable nature of space in this region appears to be making *Enterprise* crew members violent and irrational, just like *Defiant*'s crew—and an alien species known as the Tholians has arrived, claiming that the *Enterprise* has violated their space.

65. Plato's Stepchildren

A distress call brings the *Enterprise* to the planet Platonius, where the ruler, Parmen, is on the verge of death from an infected leg. The Platonians are powerful telekinetics—they can move things with their minds—but they have no resistance to infection. After McCoy cures Parmen, the grateful Platonians ask him to remain on their world. McCoy refuses, but the Platonians won't take no for an answer. Using the power of their minds, they force Kirk and Spock, and later Uhura and Chapel, into a series of bizarre and humiliating performances in order to force McCoy to change his mind.

66. Wink of an Eye

The *Enterprise* receives a distress call from the planet Scalos, but when the landing party beams down, the planet appears to be uninhabited. Returning to the ship, the crew finds signs that someone has been tampering with its equipment—but there's no sign of an intruder. After Kirk's coffee is spiked with Scalosian water, the captain's metabolism is accelerated and he can see that the ship has been infiltrated by the Scalosians, who sent the distress call. Kirk learns that Scalos has been contaminated by volcanic emissions that, over time, have hyperaccelerated the entire populace and sterilized all the males.

67. The Empath

The *Enterprise* travels to Minara II to pick up two Federation researchers before the Minaran sun goes nova. When Kirk, Spock, and McCoy beam down, they discover that the researchers are dead. However, there are three other humanoids on the planet: a beautiful mute woman with astounding empathic abilities and two highly advanced beings who identify themselves as Vians. The Vians have the ability to save the inhabitants of only one planet within the Minaran system before its sun blows up. They feel that the empath's people are the likeliest candidates, but to make sure, the Vians conduct a brutal experiment. Will she sacrifice her own life to save that of another species?

68. Elaan of Troyius

The neighboring planets Elas and Troyius have been at war for many years, but with the potential incursion of the Klingon Empire into their star system, it is imperative that they make peace. To facilitate a treaty, the *Enterprise* escorts Elaan, the leader of Elas, to Troyius, where she is to wed that world's leader. But temperamental Elaan wants no part of the arranged union.

69. Whom Gods Destroy

When Kirk and Spock arrive at the Elba II rehabilitation facility, they find that the inmates have taken over the asylum. Their leader, Garth, once a brilliant starship captain but now criminally insane, has learned how to change his shape so that he can impersonate anyone. After his attempts to force Kirk to give him control of the *Enterprise* fail, Garth tries a new tack: changing his appearance to resemble Kirk.

70. Let That Be Your Last Battlefield

The *Enterprise* intercepts a stolen shuttlecraft and its sole passenger, Lokai, a native of the planet Cheron. Lokai, who claims to be a victim of racial persecution on his homeworld, asks for political asylum. Bele, an officer of Cheron's Commission on Political Traitors, arrives. To Bele, Lokai's criminal nature is apparent in his appearance: Lokai is black on his left side and white on the right, whereas Bele, a member of the ruling class, is black on the right side and white on the left. The ship soon becomes the battlefield for the two men's deadly feud.

71. The Mark of Gideon

Kirk attempts to beam down to the coordinates of the planet Gideon's ruling council chambers, but he fails to arrive. Spock requests permission to send a search party to look for Kirk, but the council refuses. From Kirk's point of view, he never left the *Enterprise*, which has been inexplicably stripped of crew members. There's only one other person aboard—a beautiful young woman named Odona, who denies knowing anything.

72. That Which Survives

As Kirk, McCoy, Sulu, and geologist D'Amato beam down to an unexplored planet, a beautiful woman appears in the transporter room and kills the transporter operator. When the landing party materializes below, it is unable to contact the *Enterprise*, which has been hurtled nearly a thousand light-years from its prior location. Spock heads back to the planet, where the landing party encounters the mysterious woman they saw on the ship. She kills D'Amato and then disappears. Not long after, she kills an engineer on the *Enterprise* as she attempts to sabotage the ship's return to her world.

73. The Lights of Zetar

Enterprise crew member Mira Romaine has been assigned to supervise the transfer of new equipment to Memory Alpha, the central library facility for the Federation. After a strange energy storm destroys the staff of Memory Alpha, Romaine discovers that she has an unusual mental connection to the energy phenomenon, which is actually a noncorporeal amalgamation of the collective survivors of the planet Zetar. The Zetarians have been searching for a host body for a long time, and they feel that Romaine would make an ideal one.

74. Requiem for Methuselah

An outbreak of deadly Rigelian fever leads the *Enterprise* to Holberg 917-G in search of ryetalyn, the only known cure. On Holberg, Kirk encounters a reclusive man named Flint and his beautiful ward, Rayna. Although Flint isn't happy to receive visitors, he provides help in gathering the ryetalyn and allows Rayna to socialize with the landing party while it waits. Rayna's interest in Kirk, however, provokes an unanticipated emotional showdown between Kirk and Flint.

75. The Way to Eden

After the *Enterprise* apprehends a stolen spacecraft, Kirk discovers that its crew consists of a group of young idealists and Doctor Sevrin, their charismatic leader. Sevrin admits to having taken the ship in order to find the mythical planet Eden, a world reputed to be the embodiment of paradise. Kirk dismisses Sevrin's ideas and has him placed in protective confinement, but a number of crew members give Sevrin's theories some credence, including, surprisingly, Spock.

76. The Cloud Minders

Upon arriving at the planet Ardana for a shipment of valuable zenite, Kirk learns that he's come at an inopportune time. The planet's Troglyte population, which has traditionally mined the substance beneath the planet's surface, is on the verge of a major rebellion against the upper-class inhabitants of the beautiful cloud city known as Stratos. The city dwellers feel the Troglytes are naturally inferior to them, while the Troglytes feel they deserve a better life.

77. The Savage Curtain

After scanning the nearby *Enterprise*, Yarnek, a rocklike inhabitant of the planet Excalbia, decides that he'd like to see a demonstration of the concepts that humans refer to as "good" and "evil." Accordingly, he sends a manifestation of Abraham Lincoln—a hero to Kirk—to invite the captain and Spock to Excalbia. Once there, Yarnek proposes a battle between the forces of good and evil. Good will be represented by Kirk, Spock, Lincoln, and a manifestation of Surak, the father of Vulcan philosophy. Bad will be represented by Genghis Khan; Kahless, founder of the Klingon Empire; Colonel Green, the despotic leader of a genocidal war; and Zora, a scientist who conducted monstrous experiments on the inhabitants of her own world.

78. All Our Yesterdays

Knowing that Sarpeidon will soon be destroyed by the explosion of its sun, Kirk, Spock, and McCoy visit the planet to determine where its inhabitants have gone. There they find the last remaining resident, a librarian named Atoz, who has used the atavachron—an artificial time portal—to send the populace into various eras of their own distant past. As the *Enterprise* trio studies the unique device, they inadvertently slip into Sarpeidon's past—Kirk passing into an era where strangers often were accused of witchcraft, and Spock and McCoy into the planet's ice age.

79. Turnabout Intruder

Janice Lester, an old flame of Kirk's, despises the captain because he was able to achieve what she never could: command of a starship. She lures the *Enterprise* to Camus II, where she has discovered an alien device capable of transferring minds between bodies, and successfully transfers her mind to Kirk's body, and his to hers. When Kirk regains consciousness in Lester's body, he tries to get word to McCoy or Spock, only to be sedated by Lester's loyal assistant. Spock notices a curious change in "Kirk's" demeanor and becomes suspicious enough to conduct a mind-meld on "Lester."

"Once, just once, I'd like to be able to land someplace and say, 'Behold, I am the Archangel Gabriel.'"—McCoy, "Bread and Circuses"

"Logic informed me that under the circumstances the only possible action would have to be one of desperation—a logical decision, logically arrived at."—Spock, "The Galileo Seven"

SIZE MATTERS. The *Enterprise* is 289 meters long. Or, for those of us who went to high school in the Midwest, 317.9 yards, or 953.7 feet. Now, since a football field is 100 yards long, that means the starship is the length of three football fields, plus enough left over for a Beer & Red Hots stand. Pass the mustard.

Early style art, making flesh
and blood into ink and paint.

STAR TREK: THE ANIMATED SERIES

"A Two-Dimensional Wagon Train to the Stars"

22 half-hour episodes, 1973–1974

SERIES PREMISE

A BRAVE CAPTAIN AND HIS CREW EXPLORE THE GALAXY IN A SPACECRAFT known as the *Starship Enterprise*—pretty much the same thing you saw in the live-action version of *Star Trek* (Chapter 1). Captain Kirk's monologue from that show is repeated at the beginning of each animated episode, and the stardates (p. 22) here fit right into the range featured on *Star Trek*. You can surmise that the animated adventures fall within the *Starship Enterprise*'s original five-year mission.

As crude as the 1970s animation may look now, it allowed for more expansive visual effects and elaborate makeup than the 1960s live-action series. The *Enterprise* crew runs into more exotic spaceships and a wide variety of alien life-forms that don't all look like humans.

THE SHIP

The *U.S.S. Enterprise* NCC-1701 essentially is the same, although occasionally you'll hear about features that weren't mentioned in the live-action series, like the automatic bridge defense system, which is pretty self-explanatory. (With only twenty-four minutes to tell a story, the writers don't waste a lot of time with exposition.) There are new variations on shuttlecrafts, including the aquashuttle, which, as you may have guessed, can travel on or under water.

CANON TO THE RIGHT OF THEM, CANON TO THE LEFT . . . Are these cartoons part of the "official" *Star Trek* universe? Depends who you ask. *Star Trek* creator Gene Roddenberry was actively involved with the animated series's conception and production. Years after it aired, Roddenberry expressed some regrets over certain aspects of the series and indicated that he did not consider them to be "canon"—that is, part of the established history for the characters he had created. Some *Star Trek* aficionados like to cite another Roddenberry-attributed statement—"*Star Trek* canon is what appears on screen" (as opposed to, say, what appears in *Star Trek* novels and comic books), which would mean that what happens in the *Animated Series* is as valid as what happens in any episode.

THE MAIN CHARACTERS

All but one of the original seven senior crew members are here: Kirk, Spock, McCoy, Scott, Sulu, and Uhura. Who's missing? Ensign Chekov, who we assume is either working a different shift or has temporarily been assigned elsewhere. Sitting in for him is a multilimbed fellow named Lieutenant Arex.

There are familiar faces in nonstrategic parts of the ship. You'll see Nurse Chapel in several episodes and even Transporter Operator Kyle, who seems to be the first *Enterprise* officer to be allowed to sport facial hair—a handlebar mustache.

You'll also see two familiar faces that Kirk and company would just as soon have avoided: Intergalactic con man Harry Mudd (see "I, Mudd," p. 32) and unctuous trader Cyrano Jones (see "The Trouble With Tribbles," p. 33).

"Due to Chief Engineering Officer Scott's euphoric state of mind, I am assuming command of the Enterprise.*"*
—Uhura, "The Lorelei Signal"

"Two Doctor McCoys just might bring the level of medical efficiency on this ship to acceptable levels." —Spock, "The Survivor"

NEW CHARACTERS

AREX (James Doohan), navigator

Approaching parking orbit, Captain.

—"MUDD'S PASSION"

Arex sits next to Sulu on the bridge and handles the ship's navigational functions. He has a bright red complexion and yellow eyes. Although Arex's planet of origin isn't mentioned in the episodes, the background notes for the show indicate he is from Edos, where the number three obviously is popular. His people have three arms, three legs, and three fingers on each hand.

Key Arex Episode

- "Mudd's Passion"

M'RESS (Majel Barrett), communications officer

You're funny—and very attractive for a human.
—"MUDD'S PASSION"

Lieutenant M'Ress is an attractive feline who serves as the ship's relief communications officer. Like Arex, M'Ress's homeworld was never mentioned on air. However, background notes for the show suggest that she's from the planet Cait, in the Lynx system. Visually, she's a cross between a lioness and a shapely human female. Although Earth's female lions don't sport manes, M'Ress has long flowing locks on her head, which emphasize her femininity. Her voice is soft and sexy, and she tends to use throaty purrs for punctuation.

Key M'Ress Episode
- "Mudd's Passion"

DID YOU KNOW that Vulcans have their own version of a bar mitzvah? It's called the *kahs-wan* ritual, and it's a test of courage and strength in which every Vulcan child must survive a solitary trek across the treacherous desert ("Yesteryear").

MAJOR ALIENS

Vulcans

Yup, they're the same pointy-eared, logical species that viewers first encountered in the live-action *Star Trek* series. We learn a few additional things about them in the animated series, primarily in the episode "Yesteryear." Vulcans go to healers rather than doctors. It's made clear that Vulcan kids can be as cruel as human kids. And, just to clarify any misconceptions, Spock explains that Vulcans do not lack emotion—they simply don't allow it to control them.

IMPORTANT VULCAN

YOUNG SPOCK (Billy Simpson)

Spock was your typical half-breed child. He didn't have any friends other than his fanged bearlike pet *sehlat* named I-Chaya ("Journey to Babel"). When Spock was five, he performed a practical joke. Apparently, it was the scandal of the neighborhood; it's still fresh on the mind of the local healer two years later when Spock attempts to solicit the old man's medical assistance. Spock's cousin Selek was the one who taught him how to utilize the Vulcan neck pinch. But Cousin Selek is actually the adult Spock—which means that Spock learned the Vulcan neck pinch from himself.

Klingons

The warrior species returns in the animated series, and they have a nasty new weapon: a projected stasis field that paralyzes the defenses of their opponents' ships ("More Tribbles, More Troubles"). Unfortunately for them, the field uses far too much energy for the weapon to have much long-term potential. The Klingons still hate the Federation, and they still hate tribbles, so they've developed a nasty new secret weapon just to use against tribbles.

IMPORTANT KLINGONS

KOLOTH (James Doohan), Klingon captain

Kirk's opponent from *Star Trek*'s "The Trouble With Tribbles" returns in "More Tribbles, More Troubles."

KOR (voice, James Doohan), Klingon captain

Kor doesn't like the crew of the *Enterprise* any better in "The Time Trap" than he did in "Errand of Mercy." This time around, he needs Kirk's cooperation to extricate his ship from the Delta Triangle of marooned spaceships. Kirk helps him, and Kor attempts to repay him in typical Klingon fashion.

Romulans

They get a shape-shifting Vendorian to fool the crew into entering the Romulan Neutral Zone, then demand that Kirk turn over the *Enterprise* (see "The Survivor," p. 50). Interestingly, nearly a hundred years later, the Romulans will modify the scheme slightly and trick Captain Picard into entering the Neutral Zone so they can demand that he turn over his *Enterprise* (see "The Defector," p. 86). It doesn't work either time.

THE MENAGERIE

Taureans

A life-draining force prematurely ages male Taureans. The female colonists are all stunning blondes who have developed a biological resistance to the planet's ill effects. It works only if they replenish their energy levels every twenty-seven years by sucking the life force from hapless males aboard passing spaceships (see "The Lorelei Signal," p. 50).

Vendorians

A race of sentient, tentacled shape-shifters. The Federation has quarantined their world because of their culturewide proclivity for deceit (see "The Survivor," p. 50).

Skorr

Once existed as an aggressive warrior race. A great philosopher emerged within Skorr society and changed their lives forever. Today the Skorr are proponents of peace (see "The Jihad," p. 52).

Pandronians

The inhabitants of Pandros look like bipedal Chinese fu dogs but actually are sentient "colony creatures" able to split into various components. Pandronians tend to see themselves as superior to one-piece humans.

Andorians

Per their appearance in *most* incarnations of *Star Trek*, Andorians have light blue skin. But for some reason, Thelin, the Andorian who briefly takes Spock's place as first officer aboard the *Enterprise* (see "Yesteryear," p. 50), has *pink* skin.

Tribbles

Cuddly they may be, but tribbles inherently are problematic (see "The Trouble With Tribbles," p. 33). They love to eat, and the more they eat, the more they reproduce. In "More Tribbles, More Troubles," Cyrano Jones claims to have come up with a safe tribble that doesn't reproduce, but in fact he has created a tribble that gets progressively bigger and fatter as it eats, eventually surpassing the chunkiest sumo wrestler.

> *"We've got tribbles on the ship, quintotriticale in the corridors, Klingons in the quadrant—it can ruin your whole day, sir!"*
> —Scotty, "More Tribbles, More Troubles"

LE MATYA is a very large feline predator that prowls the Vulcan wilderness. It has venomous teeth and claws.

THE ORIONS: A HISTORY OF SNEAKINESS. *Star Trek* introduced viewers to the Orion animal women (see "The Menagerie," p. 27). Later on, we heard about Orion raiders (see "Journey to Babel," p. 32), but the only Orion actually to appear in that episode was passing as an Andorian. The *Animated Series*, however, gives us a bit more (until *Star Trek: Enterprise*). The Orions have a history of neutrality, but the species's predilection for appropriating other people's goods threatens that status in "The Pirates of Orion." We also learn that "all unsuccessful Orion missions end in suicide." As for appearance, here, the Orions wear hooded masks (the better to hide their identities in a police lineup). Underneath those masks they look blue rather than green. Compounding the confusion, for some reason everyone in the episode refers to them as "Or-ee-ans" rather than the more familiar "O-rye-ons."

THE BEST EPISODE

"Yesteryear," written by D. C. Fontana, the same woman who established much of what we know about Vulcans (see "Journey to Babel," p. 32). "Yesteryear" deals with an interesting science fiction premise and carries the emotional significance found in the best *Star Trek* live-action episodes. Although many *Star Trek* fans fondly remember the animated adventures, a number of the episodes are flawed by truncated stories (the result of being twenty-four minutes long) or overly simplistic story lines (the show aired during the Saturday morning children's cartoon block). "Yesteryear" is *the* exception.

THE "SPOCK'S BRAIN" AWARD. "The Lorelei Signal" wins. The beautiful sirens of Taurus II aren't a lot brighter than the females of "Spock's Brain" who conspired to steal Spock's brain. The Taurean women have the technology to transmit a signal powerful enough to lure male victims to their world. But do they ever think of using that signal to summon help? Or to ask a passing starship to take them to a less deadly world?

NOW HEAR THIS! The animated series features some quintessential *Star Trek* minutiae. Ever wonder what the *T* in James T. Kirk stands for? In "Bem," we learn that it stands for "Tiberius."

Star Trek: The Next Generation, produced more than a decade later, would introduce the holodeck (see p. 75). In the animated series we actually saw the precursor in "The Practical Joker," a computer console located in one of the *Enterprise*'s rec rooms. The animated *Enterprise* also came equipped with food synthesizers, foreshadowing *TNG*'s food replicators.

"I can't command a ship from inside an aquarium." —Kirk, "The Ambergris Element"

"Captain, the engines are buckling! We can not keep up at this speed!"
—Scotty, "The Counter-Clock Incident"

WHAT IT IS . . .

SPACE SUITS? WE DON'T NEED NO STINKIN' SPACE SUITS!

On the live-action *Star Trek* that preceded the animated series—and every other version of *Star Trek* that followed—Starfleet crews had to dress up in big, cumbersome space suits to survive in the vacuum of space. But on this show, when one of them wants to take a walk outside the ship, he simply throws on a "life support belt" and pushes a little button. Presto! A glowing force field appears around him and he can traipse through that chilly oxygen-free vacuum of space as if it were a sunny day at the beach. Not only that, but he can have a conversation with the belted crewman standing next to him, despite the absence of atmosphere to conduct the sound waves.

QU'EST-CE QUE C'EST "GLOMMER"?

The glommer is a Klingon "invention," a genetically engineered tribble predator (see "More Tribbles, More Troubles," p. 50). With its oddly placed spiky teeth, beady eyestalks, and knobby-jointed multiple limbs, the glommer is endearing in a so-ugly-it's-cute kind of way. The glommer is no match for Cyrano Jones's jumbo tribbles.

EPISODE SYNOPSES

1. Beyond the Farthest Star

The *Enterprise* is dragged off course by the gravitational pull of a dying star. Trapped in orbit around the star, along with the *Enterprise*, is the wreckage of an ancient ship. That ship's crew permanently incapacitated its vessel rather than allow a malevolent entity to commandeer it. Unfortunately, the entity is still alive—and it has plans for the *Enterprise*.

2. Yesteryear

Following a trip into the past to research Orion's history, Kirk and Spock emerge from the time portal known as the Guardian of Forever (see p. 30) and discover that the crew no longer recognizes Spock. Realizing that the flow of time has somehow been altered, Spock uses the Guardian to travel back in time to the Vulcan of his childhood, where he hopes to reestablish his own existence.

3. One of Our Planets Is Missing

The *Enterprise* crew discovers that an enormous cloud creature has entered Federation space and begun to dine on planets. With the cloud on course for the inhabited world of Mantilles, Kirk decides that the only way to stop it is to take the *Enterprise* into the creature and order the starship to self-destruct. But Spock has an unorthodox alternative: a Vulcan/cloud mind-meld.

4. The Lorelei Signal

Responding to the sirenlike call from an uncharted region of space, Kirk, Spock, and McCoy beam down to the surface of a planet inhabited by a race of incredibly beautiful women. It seems like paradise, until they're captured and hooked up to devices that drain their life forces, causing them to age rapidly.

5. More Tribbles, More Troubles

The crew has an unhappy reunion with Cyrano Jones, who claims to have invented "safe tribbles." After bringing Jones on board, Kirk discovers that the tribbles aren't safe, and the trader is being sought by the Klingons for environmental sabotage. When Kirk refuses to hand Jones over, the Klingons turn a powerful new weapon on the *Enterprise*.

6. The Survivor

Near the border of the Romulan Neutral Zone, the crew finds a damaged vessel. Aboard the ship is Carter Winston, a human philanthropist who's been missing for several years. His old fiancée, an *Enterprise* security officer, realizes that Winston's not the man she once knew. In fact, he's not a man at all. He's a Vendorian shape-shifter who's working for the Romulan Empire.

7. The Infinite Vulcan

Keniclius, the gigantic cloned duplicate of a Eugenics Wars survivor, works to create an equally large clone of Spock. Keniclius intends to enlist the Spock clone as an ally and force peace upon the galaxy. Despite Kirk's protest that the Federation has already accomplished that goal, Keniclius insists on proceeding.

8. The Magicks of Megas-Tu

While investigating the creation of matter at the center of the universe, the *Enterprise* is swept into a dimension where magic is real and technology doesn't function. Most of the inhabitants of the planet Megas-Tu are extremely unhappy to see Kirk's crew; they fear that the humans are planning to attack them, just as the humans' ancestors did long ago on Earth, in colonial Salem, Massachusetts.

9. Once Upon a Planet

The *Enterprise* returns to the "shore leave" planet, where weary space crews can enjoy a unique form of rest and relaxation, courtesy of the realistic creations generated by the amusement park's master computer (see p. 27). But the crew is unaware that the Keeper, the park's sole human occupant, has died. The master computer is no longer interested in fulfilling visitors' fantasies; instead, it wants to "turn the humans off."

10. Mudd's Passion

Captain Kirk once again takes con man Harry Mudd (see p. 32) into custody, this time for attempting to sell fake love potions. Mudd escapes from the *Enterprise*'s brig after he convinces Nurse Chapel that his potion will make Spock fall in love with her.

11. The Terratin Incident

The *Enterprise* intercepts a mysterious transmission originating from a world of crystalline structure. When the starship nears the planet, it is struck by a strange ray, and all organic matter on board, including the crew, begins to shrink at an alarming rate. As the crew tries to figure out a way to reverse the effects of the ray, Kirk pays a visit to the inhabitants of the crystalline planet, which is undergoing life-threatening volcanic activity.

12. The Time Trap

The *Enterprise* explores a region of space known as the Delta Triangle where, like the Bermuda Triangle on Earth, ships have vanished over the years. Suddenly attacked by Klingon vessels, the *Enterprise* passes through a space-time warp, closely followed by a Klingon ship. They wind up in a strange ship graveyard that resides in another dimension. The inhabitants of the ships that are already there have made the best of their fate by forming a council that enforces peace in the small society, which they call Elysia. Since neither Kirk nor his Klingon counterpart, Captain Kor (see p. 29), is interested in staying, they agree to work together to escape.

13. The Ambergris Element

The crew travels to Argo, an unstable world almost completely covered by water. As Kirk and Spock explore the planet, a giant sea creature attacks their aquashuttle, and the *Enterprise* loses contact with them. Days later, a landing party finds the two men alive but somehow transformed into water breathers who can't survive on land. The planet's inhabitants, known as the Aquans, have a deep distrust of air breathers, even former air breathers, and they refuse to help Kirk and Spock. Who turned them into water breathers in the first place?

14. The Slaver Weapon

Spock, Sulu, and Uhura, aboard the *Shuttlecraft Copernicus*, have retrieved a stasis box and are transporting it to Starbase 25, when they're taken prisoner by a group of hostile Kzinti. The Kzinti are hoping that the stasis box—an exceedingly rare artifact of the long-extinct Slaver species that once controlled most of the galaxy—contains a powerful weapon that will allow them to crush their enemies.

15. The Eye of the Beholder

The *Enterprise* finds the *Starship Ariel*, without crew, orbiting the planet Lactra VII. Transporting to the planet below, Kirk, Spock, and McCoy meet the sentient residents of Lactra: a group of twenty-foot-long slugs whose intellect is so far above that of humans that they ignore the

The animated series brought back familiar faces—including Cyrano Jones and tribbles.

possibility of communication. The Lactrans place the trio into a zoolike environment where the *Ariel*'s crew also is being held.

16. The Jihad

Someone has stolen the Alar, a centuries-old religious artifact that helped to transform the warlike Skorr into a peaceful people. If the Alar is not recovered, a galaxy-wide holy war could erupt. A member of the Vedala—the oldest spacegoing race known—puts together a disparate group with unique skills to find the Alar. The members of the formidable group, which includes Kirk and Spock, are told that they must work together if they are to survive their quest. Unfortunately, one of their number is plotting against the others.

17. The Pirates of Orion

Spock is stricken by choriocytosis, a disease that is fatal to Vulcans. Strobolin is the only cure, but the nearest supply is located on a planet four days away—and Spock has only three days to live. Kirk arranges for a cargo vessel to quickly bring the precious drug to the *Enterprise*, but en route that ship is attacked by Orions, who steal its supply of dilithium crystals *and* its strobolin.

18. Bem

Starfleet is eager to open diplomatic relations with the Pandronians, so they order Kirk to host Commander Ari bn Bem of planet Pandros as an independent observer. Bem, an arrogant pacifist, accompanies a landing party to Delta Theta III, where the locals—primitive aboriginal reptiles—promptly take Bem hostage after he wanders off against Kirk's orders. In attempting to rescue Bem, Kirk and Spock are themselves captured and confronted by a noncorporeal entity who wants to know why they are interfering with the lives of her "children," the planet's simple lizard people.

19. The Practical Joker

The *Enterprise* avoids a dangerous confrontation with Romulans by hiding in a strange energy field. The crew members then find themselves plagued by a practical joker whose pranks grow increasingly harmful. The revelation of the culprit's identity only confirms how much trouble they're in. The ship's computer—corrupted by the encounter with the energy field—has developed a deadly sense of humor and it's not about to let anyone shut it down for repairs.

20. Albatross

While the *Enterprise* is delivering medical supplies to the planet Dramia I, Dramian authorities arrive to arrest McCoy. The physician is charged with spreading a plague that resulted in the decimation of the inhabitants of Dramia II. McCoy swears that the inoculation program he oversaw was meant to stave off a virus, but the doctor can't help wondering if he inadvertently caused the deaths. Kirk and Spock head for Dramia II to conduct an investigation. But even as they find what they hope will lead to the dismissal of the charges against McCoy, the deadly plague resurfaces, threatening the lives of everyone aboard the *Enterprise*.

21. How Sharper Than a Serpent's Tooth

The *Enterprise* encounters a highly advanced spaceship, home to Kulkukan, a huge feathered serpent who visited Earth centuries earlier, inspiring the mythos of a powerful serpent god in many ancient cultures. Kulkukan is angry; he left Earth thinking that the planet's inhabitants would signal him to return, but they never did. Now they've forgotten him, an unforgivable sin. As Spock works to free the *Enterprise* from a seemingly impenetrable force globe that Kulkukan has placed around the ship, Kirk tries to convince the alien that humans no longer need a godlike entity to keep their more aggressive instincts in check.

22. The Counter-Clock Incident

Kirk is honored to be transporting Commodore Robert April, the first captain of the NCC-1701, and his wife, Sarah, to Babel for the commodore's retirement ceremony. En route, sensors detect a vessel traveling at the incredible speed of warp 36, heading directly for the Beta Niobe nova. Hoping to save the pilot from certain death, Kirk orders Sulu to latch onto the ship with a tractor beam. Unfortunately, the tractor beam barely slows the ship down, and when Sulu is unable to switch it off, the *Enterprise* is dragged into the nova. Suddenly, the crew finds itself in a reverse universe, where space is white and stars are black, and humans are born old and grow younger.

Picard listens skeptically to Q.

THREE

STAR TREK:
THE NEXT GENERATION

"Not your father's *Enterprise*"

178 hour-long episodes, 1987–1994

SERIES PREMISE

IN THE TWENTY-FOURTH CENTURY, NEARLY ONE HUNDRED YEARS AFTER

the *Starship Enterprise* NCC-1701 patrolled the galaxy, a heroic captain and his crew

explore space in a new incarnation of that vessel, the *Starship Enterprise* NCC-1701-D.

The crew's standing orders from Starfleet are much the same as those that motivated

Kirk and company:

> Space, the final frontier. These are the voyages of the *Starship Enterprise*. Its
> continuing mission: to explore strange new worlds, to seek out new life and
> new civilizations, to boldly go where no one has gone before.

THE SHIP

The *Enterprise*-D is a *Galaxy*-class spacecraft with a crew complement of 1,012 men, women . . . and children! Somewhere along the way, Starfleet decided that it would be easier to get people to sign up for long-term exploratory missions if they thought of their ship as home, with plenty of creature comforts. You can see that right away when you look at the bridge. Kirk's bridge was colorful but bare boned. It looked like a place to work. The new bridge looks like the lobby of a hotel. The chairs are cushy, the color palette soft and subdued.

The *Enterprise*-D has everything Kirk's ship had, and more. It's bigger, faster, better armed—and the food service is better, allowing crew members to gratify their desires for everything from "Tea, Earl Grey, hot" to Thalian chocolate mousse by stepping up to one of the ship's replicators (more on that later). Entertainment values have jumped as well, with three-dimensional holodeck scenarios beating out Spock's three-dimensional chess as an off-duty pastime.

THE MAIN CHARACTERS

JEAN-LUC PICARD (Patrick Stewart), captain

> **Let's see what's out there.**
>
> —"ENCOUNTER AT FARPOINT"

Picard is a legendary Starfleet captain and a man to be reckoned with on the battlefield. He is equally comfortable in the role of diplomat—something Kirk never was—and he takes greater pleasure in analyzing the intricacies of each new civilization that he encounters.

Despite his British accent, Picard was born in France, where his family owned a vineyard. His father and brother were annoyed when young Jean-Luc chose Starfleet over the Chateau Picard winery.

He may be the very model of a proper Starfleet captain today, but at the Academy Jean-Luc was a bit of a hellion. He developed a more mature point of view after he made the mistake of picking a fight with several aliens. One of them stabbed him through the heart, and Picard received an artificial one.

Picard was captured by a species known as the Borg, who "assimilated" him into their hive-like society and forced him to lead a battle against the Federation. He never completely lost the psychological scars from the experience.

His career has kept him from taking full advantage of the generous benefits package offered by Starfleet: family (just as well since he's not fond of children). He's had a few flings with members of the opposite sex and a long-term unconsummated crush on the *Enterprise*'s chief medical officer, Beverly Crusher.

Key Picard Episodes
- "The Best of Both Worlds"
- "The Inner Light"
- "Tapestry"
- "All Good Things . . ."

"Let's make sure history never forgets the name Enterprise."—Picard, "Yesterday's *Enterprise*"

WILLIAM THOMAS RIKER (Jonathan Frakes), first officer

> Fate protects fools, little children, and ships named *Enterprise*.
>
> —"CONTAGION"

Riker is quintessential first officer material, and he excels at just about everything. The worst thing on his Starfleet record is the fact that he turned down command of his own starship three times. Considering that two of the three vessels offered were destroyed shortly after Riker turned down the commissions, it's probably all for the best.

Riker was born in Valdez, Alaska. His mother died when he was two years old, and his father, a civilian strategist who works for Starfleet, left Will on his own at age fifteen. Will considers Captain Picard his mentor.

Strong and athletic, Riker has a healthy interest in the female sex. His ex-girlfriend, Deanna Troi, is the *Enterprise*'s counselor, but although the two were once involved, they are now "just good friends."

Key Riker Episodes

- "A Matter of Honor"
- "Chain of Command"
- "Second Chances"
- "The *Pegasus*"

DATA (Brent Spiner), operations officer

I am superior, sir, in many ways. But I would gladly give it up to be human.
—"ENCOUNTER AT FARPOINT"

Technically, Data is an android—an artificial life-form—who looks like a human being. He's smarter, faster, and stronger than anyone else on the ship.

Data holds the position of operations manager, overseeing the ship's assorted technical functions from the operations (ops) console in front of him. It's the perfect job for someone who has a computer for a brain.

Despite his obvious advantages, Data has a "Pinocchio" complex. More than anything, he wants to be "a real live boy"—a human.

Data was constructed by brilliant robotics scientist Noonien Soong, who built several faulty prototypes before he got it right. One of those mechanical lemons was Data's "evil twin," Lore, who got all of Data's looks but none of his benevolent personality. Soong abandoned his research and left the deactivated Data on a deserted planet, where Starfleet discovered him years later. The android chose to emulate his rescuers and attend Starfleet Academy.

Key Data Episodes

- "The Measure of a Man"
- "Brothers"
- "Data's Day"
- "Descent"

"If being human is not simply a matter of being born flesh and blood, if it is instead a way of thinking, acting, and feeling, then I am hopeful that one day I will discover my own humanity."—Data, "Data's Day"

GEORDI LA FORGE (LeVar Burton),
chief engineer

> There's theory . . . and then there's application.
> They don't always jibe.
>
> —"GALAXY'S CHILD"

Blind from birth, La Forge was assigned to the position of flight controller (see Who's "Conning" Who?, p. 75). In other words, a sightless man was placed in charge of piloting the ship. Apparently he was good at his job, for he was soon promoted to chief engineer.

Although Geordi can't see in the traditional sense, his VISOR (an acronym for Visual Instrument and Sensory Organ Replacement) allows him to visualize the stuff around him.

Geordi is an "army brat." Both of his parents served in Starfleet, and he spent much of his childhood tagging along on their assignments. The experience gave him the ability to fit in just about anywhere, and he's well liked by the crew—although he does have problems lining up a date. Perhaps because of Geordi's affinity for machinery, Data is his best friend.

Key La Forge Episodes

- "Booby Trap"
- "The Enemy"
- "Interface"

DEANNA TROI (Marina Sirtis), ship's counselor

Would you like to talk about what's bothering you, or would you like to break some more furniture?
—"BIRTHRIGHT"

Deanna Troi is a highly specialized psychologist who monitors and attends to the crew's emotional condition. She's the Doctor Phil of the *Enterprise*, dealing with all manner of personal personnel issues.

Troi is the daughter of a human Starfleet officer and a Betazoid ambassador. Full-blooded Betazoids like Troi's mother, Lwaxana, are powerful telepaths. As a hybrid, Troi can't read minds, but she *can* read the emotions of most species. Troi can tell at once whether the alien of the week is on the level or lying through its teeth/fangs/mouthparts. That's why she rates her very own chair on the bridge—the better to whisper into Picard's ear: "He's hiding something, Captain—I sense great fear."

Years ago, Troi was Riker's lover—his beloved, or *imzadi*, as they say on Betazed. Today they share a deep but platonic friendship—which may explain why she has shifted much of her passion into her relationship with chocolate.

Key Troi Episodes
- **"The Child"**
- **"The Loss"**
- **"Thine Own Self"**

"I never met a chocolate I didn't like."
—Troi, "The Game"

WORF (Michael Dorn), chief of security

I am *not* a merry man!

—"QPid"

Worf is a full-blooded Klingon, and he tries very hard to live up to his warrior heritage—but several things about him make other Klingons talk behind his back.

For one thing, he's renowned as the first Klingon to join Starfleet. While Starfleet is a worthy vocation for most, Klingons think of it as a pantywaist employment opportunity.

For another, Worf was raised by *humans* following the slaughter of his Klingon parents by Romulans. To add insult to injury, those humans brought him up in a farming colony. Farming is *not* a warrior pursuit.

There was also a vicious rumor about his blood father being a Romulan collaborator. It was a lie, but that didn't stop the Klingon High Council from subjecting Worf to "discommen-dation"—Klingon ritual shaming.

Worf's personal life is as melodramatic. His passionate affair with strong-willed K'Ehleyr was cut short by her murder. Worf then took it upon himself to raise Alexander, his son by K'Ehleyr, on the *Enterprise*. Deanna Troi's efforts to help the two Klingons bond have made Worf and the counselor a bit more than "just good friends."

Key Worf Episodes

- "Sins of the Father"
- "Reunion"
- "Redemption"

"I am a Klingon. . . . If you doubt it, a demonstration can be arranged."

—Worf, "Sins of the Father"

BEVERLY CRUSHER (Gates McFadden), chief medical officer

Where are the calluses that we doctors are supposed to grow over our feelings?
—"CODE OF HONOR"

Beverly Crusher already knew Picard when she first reported to the *Enterprise*. Her husband, Jack, had been a good friend of Picard's and served under him on the *Stargazer*. The three had spent a lot of time together . . . and, well, you know how it goes. Boy meets girl. Boy falls for girl. Girl marries boy's best friend. Boy sends best friend to his death on away mission. Okay, Picard didn't *deliberately* send Jack Crusher to his death, but he felt guilty about it. He kept his feelings for Beverly to himself.

Crusher, as the chief medical officer, often clashes with the captain over what she should do, leave a dying Borg or save him. Nevertheless, Beverly is one of Picard's closest confidantes aboard the *Enterprise*, and they regularly have cozy breakfasts together in the captain's quarters. In other words, they have most of the attributes of a marriage . . . except for the fun stuff.

In her spare time, Beverly writes and directs plays on board the ship, and reportedly cuts a mean tango.

Key Beverly Crusher Episodes
- "Remember Me"
- "Attached"
- "Sub Rosa"

"Who needs rational when your toes curl up?"—Beverly Crusher, "The Price"

WESLEY CRUSHER (Wil Wheaton),
conn officer

> So just tell me to "Shut up, Wesley," and I will.
> —"DATALORE"

Wesley's father is a dead Starfleet officer. His mother is the *Enterprise*'s renowned "dancing doctor." Both were friends with Picard before Wesley was born, but that didn't win any points with the captain when he first arrived on the ship. Picard disliked children—particularly on the bridge—and Wesley's propensity for winding up there didn't sit well. The captain came to appreciate Wesley's precocious skills after they saved the crew on a particularly harrowing mis-

sion. Picard rewarded Wes by appointing him an "acting ensign" and making him the flight controller (the person responsible for steering and navigation) on the bridge—all before the kid reached legal drinking age.

Wesley was accepted at Starfleet Academy, but he eventually dropped out, opting to further his education instead by accompanying a friendly transdimensional entity on a road trip through a nonhuman plane of existence. Well, wouldn't you?

Key Wesley Crusher Episodes
- "Final Mission"
- "The First Duty"

TASHA YAR (Denise Crosby), chief of security

> You *are* fully functional, aren't you?
> —"THE NAKED NOW"

Alas, poor Tasha. She served but a year on the *Enterprise*-D, but she made a big impression on her coworkers, particularly Data, with whom she explored human-android interpersonal relations (in other words, they got it on). A gutsy security officer, Yar lost her life to a sentient oil slick. However, thanks to the wonders of alternate timelines and temporal rifts, this was not the last viewers would see of Tasha Yar (see Who Is Sela?, p. 91).

Key Yar Episode
- "Skin of Evil"

KATHERINE PULASKI (Diana Muldaur), chief medical officer

> It's a time-honored way to practice medicine—
> with your head and your heart and your hands.
> —"CONTAGION"

Pulaski was Doctor Crusher's replacement on the *Enterprise*-D for the year that Crusher headed up Starfleet Medical. She was a throwback to doctors of an earlier era. Like Leonard McCoy, she hated transporters and distrusted coworkers who she felt had more in common with computers than with human beings.

Key Pulaski Episode
- "Unnatural Selection"

GUINAN (Whoopi Goldberg), bartender

> I tend bar. And I listen.
> —"ENSIGN RO"

Guinan is the female bartender in Ten-Forward (see Ten-Forward, p. 75). Her people describe themselves as "listeners." Guinan and Picard share a mysterious unspoken bond. That may be why he trusts her instincts implicitly, despite her somewhat offbeat taste in hats.

Key Guinan Episode
- "Yesterday's *Enterprise*"

REGINALD BARCLAY (Dwight Schultz), diagnostic engineer

> I am the guy who writes down things to remember
> to say when there's a party.
> —"HOLLOW PURSUITS"

On a professional level, Barclay is competent, but on a social level, he's a washout—a nerd. He's prone to paranoia, hypochondria, and any number of neurotic tendencies, but his friends find his many quirks endearing.

Key Barclay Episode
- "Hollow Pursuits"

MILES O'BRIEN (Colm Meaney), transporter operator

> I had a choice: Do I walk away and let the emitter
> blow itself to hell . . . or do I crawl into a Jefferies
> tube with twenty hook spiders?
> —"REALM OF FEAR"

O'Brien possesses myriad engineering skills. On the *Enterprise*, however, his talents were generally confined to the transporter room—which may explain why he eventually transferred to space station Deep Space 9. Data introduced O'Brien to his future wife, Keiko, and Worf delivered O'Brien's daughter, Molly.

Key O'Brien Episode
- "The Wounded"

MAJOR ALIENS

Borg

The Borg collective is an amalgamated group of many subjugated races: human, Klingon, Vulcan—you name it. The Collective assimilates every sentient being it encounters, improving the individual by removing "imperfect" organic body parts and replacing them with technologically superior artificial ones—such as eyes that emit laser beams and hands that double as buzz saws.

What the Collective lacks in free will, it makes up for in wholehearted dedication. All members dress the same (basic black, with complementary circuitry and tubing), act the same (zombie-like), and spout the same party line: "You will be assimilated" and "Resistance is futile."

Their most common form of transportation is the gigantic and deadly Borg cube, armed with powerful energy weapons and capable of self-repairing major damage almost immediately.

HAVE YOU EVER WONDERED why so many of the alien species in *Star Trek* look human? One answer is that over four million years ago, an ancient race known as the Preservers seeded primitive humanoid DNA samples across the galaxy ("The Chase"). Another answer is that it's really hard to cast nonhumans who can memorize their lines, let alone act.

LOCUTUS (Patrick Stewart), spokesman for the Borg collective

The Borg kidnapped Jean-Luc Picard from the *Enterprise*, made him into a Borg, and dubbed him Locutus ("The Best of Both Worlds"). He served as the voice of the Borg during the Collective's attack on humanity.

HUGH (Jonathan Del Arco), Borg drone

"Third of Five," as he was known by the Collective, opted for the human nickname "Hugh" when the *Enterprise* crew rescued him from the wreckage of a Borg vessel ("I, Borg"). Hugh's reawakened sense of self eventually infected other Borg in his group, causing the hive to break out in individuality.

Betazoids

People from Betazed look just like people from Earth except for their extremely dark eyes. Adult Betazoids are powerful mind readers. Although an advanced civilization, Betazoids have a few bohemian habits, like expecting wedding parties—bride, groom, and guests—to attend the ceremonies completely naked.

LWAXANA TROI (Majel Barrett), Betazed ambassador to the Federation

Lwaxana is the Auntie Mame of the twenty-fourth century. Alternately haughty, horny, and happy-go-lucky, she's generally a pain in the neck to her daughter, Deanna, and to the crew of the *Enterprise*.

Q

The Q, a species of all-powerful, godlike entities, reside in an "extradimensional domain" known as the Continuum. Like most godlike beings, the Q seem to have nothing better to do than tinker with and/or test humanity. They are so self-confident that they can't be bothered with names; *they* know who they are, after all, and they rarely have one-on-one conversations with other species.

Q (John de Lancie), omnipotent being

Q has been responsible for lots of mischief within our dimension and is considered something of a rebel by the rest of the Q. Although he's omnipotent, Q is inordinately fascinated by Picard and his crew.

Cardassians

Cardassians are an aggressive humanoid species with gray lizardlike skin and a coldly reptilian mind-set. The Cardassians adopted a policy of brutal conquest to compensate for poverty and disease on their homeworld: think Germany during the period the Nazis gained control. The residents of the planet Bajor were enslaved when the "Cardies" occupied their world and stripped it of its resources.

KLINGON FOOD. Klingons prefer to eat food that's still alive. A favorite dish is *gagh*—slimy, squirmy serpent worms. And there's nothing better to wash them down with than a big mug of bloodwine, which, as any oenophile ("lover of wine," okay?) knows, is best served warm.

Bajorans

Except for some curious wrinkles at the bridge of the nose, Bajorans look a lot like humans. A deeply spiritual race with high-minded pursuits, the Bajoran people were easy prey for the Cardassians. Millions were thrown into "resettlement camps," tortured, and murdered. Eventually the populace resorted to terrorist-style tactics to deal with their oppressors.

IMPORTANT BAJORAN

RO LAREN (Michelle Forbes), *Enterprise* conn officer

Ro Laren spent much of her childhood in Cardassian resettlement camps. She grew up with an understandable chip on her shoulder, and after joining Starfleet she continued to find it difficult to play well with others. Picard trusted her enough to make her a bridge officer.

> **DID YOU KNOW** that Ro Laren is Ensign Ro to the crew but Laren to her friends? Like some Asian and Middle Eastern cultures, Bajorans refer to themselves with their family name first and their given name last.

Vulcans

With two notable exceptions, viewers won't see many of this highly logical race. As a species, they're unchanged from the beings first encountered in *Star Trek*.

IMPORTANT VULCANS

SAREK (Mark Lenard), Vulcan ambassador

Spock's father. As a senior citizen, Sarek struggles with Bendii Syndrome, the Vulcan equivalent of Alzheimer's disease ("Sarek"), which eventually kills him ("Unification").

SPOCK (Leonard Nimoy), Vulcan ambassador

Spock emulates the kind of "cowboy diplomacy" that his friend Kirk was famous for when he takes it upon himself to heal the schism between Vulcans and Romulans ("Unification").

Klingons

The Klingons are very much a presence; however, these are new, improved Klingons. They *look* different—with craggy domes and long, wild manes—and they *act* differently, in that they are now allies rather than sworn enemies of the Federation. Things that haven't changed are the size of their egos (jumbo) and their lust for combat (unquenchable). And they still have that Asian warrior thing going for them, although they now have more in common with the Japanese samurai than with the Mongol hordes. Honor is a really big deal to them. Klingons are the most political species in the galaxy. At any given time there are more shenanigans going on in the Klingon High Council than there were at the Watergate hotel.

IMPORTANT KLINGONS

GOWRON (Robert O'Reilly), leader of the Klingon Empire

A political outsider, Gowron won the position of chancellor on the High Council when Worf killed Gowron's opponent. After Worf backed him during the Klingon Civil War, Gowron used his clout to restore the honor of Worf's family. So does that make them lifelong buddies? Nah.

KURN (Tony Todd), Worf's kid brother

Worf was unaware that he had a brother until Kurn sought his help clearing their father's name ("Sins of the Father").

K'EHLEYR (Suzie Plakson), Federation ambassador to the Klingon Empire

With a sardonic sense of humor inherited from her human mother and a fierce temper derived from her Klingon father, K'Ehleyr had all the requisite ingredients to drive Worf crazy. Worf got custody of their child, Alexander, following K'Ehleyr's murder.

KAHLESS (Kevin Conway), ceremonial emperor of the Klingon people

Ostensibly the same mythical warrior mentioned in the *Star Trek* episode "The Savage Curtain," except this one is a clone created by a group of Klingon clerics who hope to use him to restore the empire's ancient values.

DURAS FAMILY (Patrick Massett, Barbara March, Gwynyth Walsh, and J. D. Cullum), politically ambitious Klingon clan

In a bid for political power, patriarch Duras accused Worf's father of a treasonous act that his own father had committed, and later murdered the leader of the Klingon Council. As if that wasn't bad enough, he also killed Worf's mate to prevent her from revealing the truth. Worf, understandably annoyed, killed Duras ("Reunion").

Duras's sisters Lursa and B'Etor continued the clan's quest for power through Duras's illegitimate son, Toral ("Redemption").

Romulans

In 2364, the Romulans emerged from self-imposed isolation and informed Picard, "We're back!" During their absence, the Romulans apparently abducted the costume designer who had created Joan Crawford's oversized shoulder pads during the golden age of Hollywood. They also obtained new brow ridges, courtesy of a beefed-up makeup budget.

> **ROMULAN WARBIRD** is big and bad: nearly twice the length of Picard's *Enterprise*. It has a cloaking device, destructive energy weapons, and a prow that looks like a big bird head. Not only that, but this baby is powered by an "artificial quantum singularity"—a black hole—and it's a lot more powerful than a hemi.

> **THE GRATEFUL DEAD.** Klingons believe in embracing death, rather than avoiding it. The idea of dying in bed at a ripe old age is repugnant to them. Dying in battle is a more noble aspiration, which is why they say things like, "It is a good day to die." When a Klingon gets his or her wish and expires honorably, the survivors gather around the body and let loose with a deafening howl to alert the dead that a warrior is on the way to *Sto-Vo-Kor*, the Klingon afterlife.

> *"Part of being human is learning how to deal with the unexpected . . . to risk new experiences even when they don't fit into your preconceptions."*—La Forge, "Inheritance"

A young Picard has not learned that Nausicaans are quick-tempered.

THE MENAGERIE

Ferengi

Have orange skin, huge ears, and an insatiable appetite for attaining wealth (see "The Last Outpost," p. 77). The males are extremely sexist: they don't believe in allowing their females to work, go out in public, or wear clothing. Next to getting rich, their favorite activity is *oo-mox* (having their ears fondled by females of any species).

Pakleds

Act dumb and look dumpy. But beware. Their "dumb" act is a trick to take advantage of sympathetic folk who offer a helping hand (see "Samaritan Snare," p. 83).

They really are dumpy, though.

Trill

Are humanoids that have a symbiotic relationship with sentient slugs they keep in their abdominal pouches—kind of like kangaroos, if kangaroos carried slimy worms instead of cuddly joeys (see "The Host," p. 91).

KLINGON OPERA is loud and dissonant, causing many a non-Klingon to rush from the bar on Klingon karaoke night.

"Five card stud, nothing wild. And the sky's the limit."—Picard, "All Good Things . . ."

Bolians

Blue-skinned aliens with a vertical ridge running down the center of the face. Neither the males nor the females have any hair, yet strangely, Picard's barber on the *Enterprise* is a Bolian. Think about it.

Nausicaans

Really unattractive by human standards, Nausicaans are tall and gangly, with boarlike fangs and tangled, knotted manes. On top of that, they're surly, uncouth, and exceedingly violent—which Picard learned firsthand when he found himself impaled on the business end of a Nausicaan blade (see "Samaritan Snare," p. 83).

A KLINGON'S BEST FRIEND IS HIS *BAT'LETH.* Klingons can handle an energy pistol with the best of them, but they really prefer hand-to-hand combat. The best weapon for such down-and-dirty fighting is a *bat'leth*, a meter-long curved blade with deadly points on either end.

KLINGON BIRD-OF-PREY. Despite the similar name—which apparently was too cool for the producers to discard—the Klingon bird-of-prey has nothing in common with the Romulan bird-of-prey of Kirk's era. It's a bigger, more powerful vessel, capable of warp-speed travel or atmospheric entry. Still, like the old Romulan ship, it's equipped with a cloaking device and bears some resemblance to a large predatory bird.

TEN ESSENTIAL EPISODES

1. **"Encounter at Farpoint" Written by D. C. Fontana and Gene Roddenberry.**

On the *Enterprise*-D's maiden voyage, Picard and his crew face Q, an omnipotent being who threatens to destroy them unless they prove that humanity has earned the right to expand its exploration of space.

Eighteen years after the first series ended, this two-hour premiere marked the return of Star Trek *to the airwaves. While not the best episode on which to judge the quality of the series, it does serve to introduce the characters and provides a cameo from the actor who played* Star Trek's *Doctor McCoy.*

2. **"The Measure of a Man" Written by Melinda M. Snodgrass.**

Is Data a piece of Starfleet equipment or a sentient being? Picard defends the android's rights after a Starfleet scientist demands to disassemble Data in order to study him.

This futuristic homage to such classic courtroom dramas as Inherit the Wind *sets the bar for all future episodes that explore Data's "humanity."*

3. **"Q Who?" Written by Maurice Hurley.**

Q sends the *Enterprise* to a distant part of the galaxy where the crew encounters the Borg, a race that is half-machine, half-human, and wholly relentless. Once Picard realizes that he can neither reason with nor defeat the emotionless beings, he's forced to admit to Q that perhaps humanity *isn't* ready for every challenge the universe has to offer.

This marks the first time viewers meet the show's toughest and most popular foe, the Borg.

4. **"Yesterday's *Enterprise*" Teleplay by Ira Steven Behr & Richard Manning & Hans Beimler & Ronald D. Moore. From a story by Trent Christopher Ganino & Eric Stillwell.**

The *Enterprise*-C, a ship presumed destroyed twenty-two years earlier, emerges from a temporal rift in front of Picard's ship, but only Guinan notices that the flow of time has been altered. To restore the timeline and prevent a bloody war with the Klingons, she tells Picard he must convince the crew of the *Enterprise*-C to return to the past to fulfill its date with destiny.

A taut, action-packed episode. Guinan's presence serves as a "Greek chorus"; she's there to point out the differences between the real and the alternate timelines to Picard.

5. **"Sins of the Father" Teleplay by Ronald D. Moore & W. Reed Moran; based on a teleplay by Drew Deighan.**

Hearing that his dead father has been branded a Romulan collaborator, Worf travels to the Klingon homeworld to clear his family name, but he ultimately keeps the truth to himself in order to prevent a Klingon civil war.

This first look at the Klingon homeworld, which introduces Worf's brother, Kurn, is a favorite among Klingon fans.

6. **"The Best of Both Worlds, Parts I & II" Written by Michael Piller.**

Assimilated by the Borg, Picard leads an attack against Earth. Starfleet forces are decimated in the subsequent battle, but the crew of the *Enterprise* manages to retrieve the "Borgified" Picard and use him to turn the tables on his former captors.

A horrific future of war, for the lack of a starship called *Enterprise*.

Generally acknowledged as the show's most popular episodes. Part I served as the finale for the third season, leaving viewers anxious about Picard's fate until September.

7. "The Inner Light" Teleplay by Morgan Gendel and Peter Allan Fields. Story by Morgan Gendel.

An alien space probe instills Picard with the living history of its builders, a long-dead race of people who wished to be remembered.

This sentimental story is capable of bringing the most jaded viewer to the edge of tears.

8. "Relics" Written by Ronald D. Moore.

The *Enterprise* discovers the wreckage of a crashed ship . . . and one survivor kept alive for the past seventy-five years within the ship's still-functioning transporter: Montgomery Scott, former chief engineer of Captain Kirk's *Enterprise*.

Highlights of the episode include James Doohan reprising his role as Scotty and the lovingly re-created bridge set of the NCC-1701.

9. "Tapestry" Written by Ronald D. Moore.

Given the opportunity to relive his life and change a few details along the way, Picard learns that those very details are what made him the man most suited to command the *Enterprise*.

It's a Wonderful Life Star Trek–style and a fascinating glimpse into Picard at the Academy.

10. "All Good Things . . ." Written by Ronald D. Moore & Brannon Braga.

Q sends Picard on a disorienting journey between past, present, and future in order to unravel a mystery posed by the Q Continuum. At stake: the existence of humankind itself.

Like a bookend, this two-hour finale neatly matches the series premiere, with Q once again presiding over mankind's fate.

"The search for knowledge is always our primary mission." —Picard, "Lonely Among Us"

THE "SPOCK'S BRAIN" AWARD. "Genesis" is the most . . . ahem . . . curious episode of *The Next Generation*. When the *Enterprise* crew gets the flu, the cure proves worse than the illness, causing them to "devolve" into a variety of primeval creatures. The lovely Deanna, for instance, turns into a gilled amphibian, while Riker becomes an unfriendly ape-man. The cure for the cure has something to do with a litter of kittens. Seriously.

SHIP SEPARATION. The *Enterprise* is made up of two sections: a saucer module on the top, and the engineering section on the bottom. The saucer houses the living quarters and can, in emergencies, be separated from the lower section, making it an honest-to-goodness flying saucer. What constitutes an emergency? A major attack. The captain heads for the engineering section and orders nonstrategic personnel and families to the saucer, which is sent off into safer territory while he fights the bad guys. Nice concept, but it doesn't happen very often, because in order for the visual effects experts to separate the ship, they must separate a lot of money from their budget. The effect was done only three times on the show.

WHAT IT IS . . .

REPLICATOR

Uses transporter technology to dematerialize matter at a molecular level and rematerialize it as just about anything—a triple chocolate banana split, an engineering tool, you name it. Just lean toward the terminal and say, "One arch-top, f-hole, six-string guitar." What it can't replicate is living tissue, so don't bother saying, "Halle Berry, please." For that, or at least a facsimile of that, you'll have to visit the holodeck.

HOLODECK

Humans have long searched for the ultimate in entertainment venues. Along the way they've developed CinemaScope, surround sound, 3-D glasses, Smell-O-Vision, stadium seating, and "butterlike flavoring." But all of these advances combined do not come close to the ultimate in synthesized recreational systems, the holodeck—the twenty-fourth century's answer to the multiplex. The *Enterprise* has four of them.

A holodeck combines three-dimensional holographic projections and transporter-based replications to create the best in interactive entertainment: entire worlds for you to touch, taste, hear, smell, feel, and even *wear*. Want to be a hard-boiled detective out to save a beautiful broad in distress? Play poker with Albert Einstein? Fulfill a personal fantasy with that ensign who doesn't know you're alive? Load your program!

> **SIZE MATTERS.** At 641 meters, the *Enterprise*-D is more than twice the length of Kirk's ship. That's as big as the Paramount Studios lot in Hollywood.

TEN-FORWARD

The rec room on Kirk's *Enterprise* resembled a school lunchroom. But the *Enterprise*-D's rec room, known as Ten-Forward, actually has a bar in it.

SYNTHEHOL

The only "official" intoxicant served in Ten-Forward is an artificial booze that loses its inebriating effects the minute you leave the bar—which is why starship navigators don't get ticketed for DUI. And the other great benefit? No hangover!

STARFLEET ACADEMY

Where there's a quasi-Navy, there's a quasi-Annapolis. Most of the Starfleet officers are graduates of Starfleet Academy. This four-year institution is located in San Francisco.

PADD

An acronym for personal access display device. It's the handheld information storage unit that Starfleet personnel carry. You probably have one too, but you call it a PDA or a Palm Pilot. *Star Trek* got there first. Again.

WHO'S "CONNING" WHO?

On Kirk's *Enterprise*, two guys sat in front of the captain: one controlling the helm (steering) and one navigating (plotting a course). On Picard's *Enterprise*, those two functions have been combined into one station, known as the conn (or flight controller) position.

You may have seen episodes where the captain leaves the bridge and says to Riker, "You have the conn." Yet, rather than going over to sit at Wesley's station, Riker sits down in the captain's chair. What's up with that?

Conn is a naval term that refers to control of a ship's movements; to pilot a ship is referred to as "conning." When Picard tells Riker to take the conn, he's informing him that he is in charge of all personnel and activities related to piloting the ship. In short, he's the boss—which is why he gets to sit in the big chair.

"MAKE IT SO"

You'll hear this concise command only from Picard. He says it to his crew when he wants them to carry out the last bit of business that was discussed. Depending on the urgency of the situation, it could mean anything from "Good idea" to "Get your ass in gear."

PHASER

Same old ray gun as before, and works pretty much the same—but now it looks more like a very small DustBuster-type hand vac than a pistol.

STARDATE

Time marches on, so twenty-fourth-century Starfleet uses a five-digit numerical system for its stardates rather than the four-digit system that Kirk employed a century earlier.

COMMUNICATOR

You may recall that a communicator once looked like a cell phone. No longer. Now it looks like a pin that doubles as a uniform insignia. The eye-catching design—a silver arrowhead on a horizontal gold oval—is the official Starfleet emblem. You wear it right where Starfleet insignias always go—over the heart. To activate, tap it with a finger, say something like, "Riker to engineering," and suddenly you're talking to Geordi La Forge. Cool. Convenient. More high tech than a cell phone.

AWAY TEAM

Kirk referred to that group of people sent down to explore a planet's surface as a "landing party." Picard calls it an "away team." Hey, it's his ship.

PRIMARY COLORS

Remember when wearing a gold shirt meant you were the guy giving orders, and wearing a red shirt meant you were going to die a horrible death on a planet's surface? That was then, this is now: red signifies the command track and gold means support services (engineering and security). Blue still means the wearer is in the sciences.

The color distinctions are less pronounced than they were in *Star Trek*. Command red is a muted burgundy, gold is a mustard tone, blue is actually teal. The uniforms are primarily black; the contrasting color serves as an accent.

We don't know if there's any truth to the rumor that the color changes were instigated by the guys who previously wore red shirts.

WHO IS SPOT? The *Enterprise* now allows children on board, so why not pets? Spot was Data's cat. Spot initially was a long-haired male but somewhere along the way became a short-haired female. Neither Data nor Spot seemed to notice.

EPISODE SYNOPSES

Season One

1./2. Encounter at Farpoint

Starfleet's new flagship, the *U.S.S. Enterprise* NCC-1701-D, embarks on its maiden voyage, traveling to Farpoint Station, where Captain Jean-Luc Picard and his newly assembled crew attempt to determine how the low-tech inhabitants of Deneb IV have managed to construct such an impressive high-tech facility. Picard's efforts to solve the mystery are hampered by Q, the arrogant representative of an all-powerful species that considers humanity too barbaric for space exploration.

3. The Naked Now

After encountering the *Tsiolkovsky*, a research vessel where all aboard have died under peculiar circumstances, members of the *Enterprise* crew begin acting strangely. The good news is that the bizarre virus that's affected both the *Tsiolkovsky* and the *Enterprise* is in the medical database—it's the same one that affected Kirk's crew decades ago (see p. 25). The bad news is that the virus has mutated and the old antidote doesn't work.

4. Code of Honor

The *Enterprise*'s mission to obtain a lifesaving vaccine on Ligon II is complicated when the planetary leader abducts Security Chief Tasha Yar to make her his wife. The crew must abide by Ligon's strict code of honor; therefore, Picard knows that he can't just beam Yar home. But when he learns that Yar and the leader's current wife are expected to engage in a battle to the death, Picard realizes that he'd better come up with a plan.

5. The Last Outpost

The *Enterprise* becomes the first Federation ship—on record—to encounter the Ferengi, after they steal a piece of equipment from a Federation outpost. When both the *Enterprise* and the Ferengi vessel lose power above a planet that once belonged to the extinct Tkon Empire, teams from both ships join forces to investigate an abandoned Tkon outpost. Since the Ferengi don't share the Federation's values, is it any surprise that they double-cross Riker's away team soon after beaming down?

6. Where No One Has Gone Before

While testing an alleged advance in starship propulsion systems, the *Enterprise* is thrown into a region of space where thought becomes reality and dangers abound. Kosinski, the arrogant Starfleet engineer who claims to be responsible for the advance, doesn't seem to know how to get the ship back home. It's Kosinski's mysterious assistant, "the Traveler," who's really behind the ship's astounding journey through time and space. Unfortunately, the excursion has brought the Traveler to the brink of death. Picard discovers that he will need to rely on young Wesley Crusher to help the crew find its way back.

7. Lonely Among Us

A diplomatic mission to ferry two adversarial ambassadors to a Federation conference is disrupted when the *Enterprise* passes through a strange energy cloud and inadvertently picks up a noncorporeal life-form. After inhabiting the bodies of several crew members, the entity opts to hijack Picard's in order to return to its cloud. Unfortunately, neither the crew nor Picard has any say in the decision.

A life that never was, a family that never existed, an entire civilization gone,
reach out to Picard to have their world, their lives, remembered.

8. Justice

The planet Rubicon III seems to be the perfect place for rest and recreation, a pastoral paradise populated by scantily clad inhabitants who believe in living life to its sensual heights. But if the rules governing the attainment of pleasure on Rubicon are simple, so are the rules for breaking the law. Death is the sentence for every infraction, even tromping on some flowers, which is Wesley Crusher's crime—leaving Picard with a choice between upholding the Prime Directive or saving Wesley's life.

9. The Battle

Picard receives a strangely generous gift from a Ferengi: the derelict *Stargazer*, the ship that was the captain's previous command. Years earlier, Picard and the *Stargazer* crew had abandoned the vessel after it was badly damaged in an attack by an unidentified enemy. Although DaiMon Bok, the Ferengi commander, claims that he's merely returning an abandoned ship to its rightful owner, the handover is actually part of a scheme to discredit and destroy Picard, whom Bok holds responsible for his son's death.

10. Hide and Q

As part of a wager he's made with others of his species, Q (see p. 67) returns to test the *Enterprise* crew by offering Riker the powers of the Q. With those powers, Q explains, Riker will be able to do anything, even bring the dead back to life. But is any reward actually worth making a deal with the devil . . . or rather, the Q?

11. Haven

Deanna Troi's outlandish mother, Lwaxana, arrives on the *Enterprise* to make her daughter fulfill a prearranged vow to wed a friend of the Troi family. Although Deanna isn't interested in getting married, her mother reminds her that it's a traditional Betazoid obligation, and Deanna reluctantly agrees. But an encounter with a ship full of plague-ridden aliens soon changes everyone's options.

12. The Big Goodbye

En route to a delicate diplomatic mission with an extremely irritable alien species, Picard attempts to relax by inviting a few of his friends to participate in his favorite holodeck program: the fictional life of a hard-boiled Earth detective named Dixon Hill. Unfortunately, a glitch in the system makes the once-amusing program lethal—and there's no way to shut it down.

13. Datalore

The *Enterprise* travels to Omicron Theta, once home to a group of colonists who mysteriously disappeared twenty-six years ago. Omicron Theta is also the planet where Starfleet discovered Data, unactivated. In the lab that belonged to Data's creator, Noonien Soong, the *Enterprise* away team finds the disassembled parts of a second android: a twin to Data named Lore. When Lore is reactivated, he claims that he was disassembled because the colonists found him "too perfect," but it soon becomes obvious that this isn't the truth.

14. Angel One

Riker leads an away team to the surface of Angel One to search for the crew of a lost freighter. However, he receives a chilly reception from the female leader of the planet, who is accustomed to dealing with submissive males. Riker learns that the survivors from the freighter—all males—have become fugitives because they refuse to accept the social status quo of this matriarchal society

15. 11001001

The *Enterprise* stops at Starbase 74 for an upgrade to its computer system, a task that is to be performed by Bynars, a diminutive species so dependent on computers that they speak to each other in binary language. However, the Bynars program the computer to fake an emergency that will trick the crew into evacuating the *Enterprise*. Once the ship is empty, they plan on taking it to their homeworld—but Picard and Riker would rather destroy the ship than let it fall into an alien's hands.

16. Too Short a Season

Elderly Admiral Jameson, renowned for his diplomatic skills, is aboard the *Enterprise* en route to Mordan IV to resolve a hostage situation. What few know is that Jameson once resolved a similar crisis on Mordan by supplying each side with weapons. As a result, the planet has suffered through four decades of bloody civil war. Karnas, the planetary governor, has engineered this new hostage situation as a ploy to lure Jameson back so he can execute him.

17. When the Bough Breaks

The peaceful people of Aldea have long hidden their world from outsiders through the use of a powerful cloaking device. When they decide to reveal their presence to the crew of the *Enterprise*, no one suspects an ulterior motive— at least not until the Aldeans, who have become sterile over the years, kidnap a group of children from the starship, including Wesley Crusher, to perpetuate their race.

18. Home Soil

When an engineer is mysteriously killed at a remote terraforming station on Velara III, the crew of the *Enterprise* discovers that the man's death wasn't an accident. The planet, thought to be uninhabited, is actually populated by microscopic inorganic life-forms that are extremely displeased with the Federation's plans to change their world.

19. Coming of Age

While Wesley Crusher beams down to Relva VII to compete for the sole opening at Starfleet Academy, Picard and his senior officers are grilled by Lieutenant Commander Remmick. Although Remmick is conducting his inquisition on behalf of Picard's old friend Admiral Quinn, the admiral refuses to explain the rationale behind the hostile interrogations.

20. Heart of Glory

Worf finds himself torn between his Klingon heritage and his loyalty to Starfleet when he befriends a pair of renegade Klingons. They wish to end the alliance between the Federation and the Klingon Empire, which they claim is destroying their people's warrior spirit.

21. The Arsenal of Freedom

After discovering that the planet Minos, home to a civilization renowned for its devotion to the manufacture of weaponry, is now devoid of life, members of an *Enterprise* away team are targeted by automated attack drones. As Picard and Crusher attempt to flee, they tumble into a cavern, leaving the doctor badly hurt and both of them trapped. It's up to Picard to figure out what happened on Minos to turn the place into such a deadly nightmare.

22. Symbiosis

The *Enterprise* comes to the aid of a disabled freighter that was transporting valuable cargo. For two centuries the Brekkians—owners of the freighter—have been supplying the Ornarans with a drug to treat a terrible plague. In exchange, the Ornarans have been supporting the Brekkians' lifestyle. Now, as they fight over payment of the undelivered shipment, Doctor Crusher discovers that the Ornarans are cured, and the drug only acts as a narcotic.

23. Skin of Evil

Counselor Troi's shuttlecraft crash-lands on Vagra II, home of Armus, a malevolent being created from the cast-off negative emotions of the civilization that once lived there. As an away team from the *Enterprise* mounts a rescue effort, Armus, who derives pleasure from the suffering of others, tortures and taunts the counselor's closest friends—and ultimately kills one of them, simply because it can.

24. We'll Always Have Paris

A distress signal leads the *Enterprise* to a science outpost on Vandor IV, where Doctor Paul Manheim has been performing experiments in nonlinear time. Manheim's wife, Jenice, is an old flame of the captain's, but it's her husband's work that soon has Picard's undivided attention. Manheim's most recent experiment seems to have created an opening between dimensions that could destroy the fabric of space.

25. Conspiracy

Following the death of an old friend who was concerned that there was a conspiracy within the upper ranks of Starfleet, Picard takes the *Enterprise* to Earth, where he quickly discovers that his friend may have been right. When Admiral Quinn pays a visit to the ship while Picard is occupied at Starfleet Headquarters, the captain warns Riker to keep an eye on him. But Riker is hardly prepared when the admiral attacks him with a display of inhuman strength. Nor is Picard prepared when he's invited to dine with a group of senior Starfleet officers—and the main course turns out to be bowls of wriggling maggots!

26. The Neutral Zone

While three human survivors of cryogenic preservation from the twentieth century reacclimate aboard the *Enterprise*, Captain Picard receives the disquieting news that Federation outposts along the edge of the Romulan Neutral Zone are disappearing. Starfleet has not had any contact with the Romulans in fifty-three years. Picard feels that the recent activity near the Neutral Zone means the hostile species has decided to make their presence felt again.

Season Two

27. The Child

The *Enterprise*'s mission to transport samples of a deadly plague to a science station is disrupted by the revelation that Troi is pregnant. She's been impregnated by a noncorporeal alien entity whose intentions, Troi believes, are not malevolent. Troi gives birth in just thirty-six hours, and the child, Ian, grows from an infant to an eight-year-old child within a day. However, Ian appears to be a normal boy. Meanwhile, an unknown source of radiation is causing the plague samples to grow so rapidly that they will soon pose a threat to the entire crew.

28. Where Silence Has Lease

The ship and its crew are trapped within a featureless void by an alien named Nagilum. The alien tells Picard that it is curious about human life—particularly the species's mortality. After Nagilum explains that it plans to kill up to half of the crew just to see the different ways humans can die, Picard sets the *Enterprise* to self-destruct.

29. Elementary, Dear Data

La Forge programs the holodeck to create a Sherlock Holmes adventure for Data. But because Data has memorized every published Holmes story, the adventure isn't a challenge. Doctor Katherine Pulaski, the ship's new chief medical officer, challenges La Forge to have the holodeck come up with a new adventure and an opponent who could actually beat the android. The holodeck simulator responds by creating Doctor Moriarty, the villain in the Holmes books, who promptly kidnaps Pulaski and threatens to take over the ship.

30. The Outrageous Okona

Picard's decision to help Okona, a trader, to repair his ship draws the crew into an unpleasant situation between two worlds. Each planet demands that Picard turn over Okona, Straleb because the trader stole a sacred jewel, and Atlec because Okona impregnated the daughter of the planetary ruler.

31. Loud as a Whisper

Hoping to put an end to a civil war, the *Enterprise* transports Riva, a renowned mediator, to Solais V. Riva was born deaf, and he travels with three telepathic assistants who communicate for him. But as Riva attempts to begin negotiations, a terrorist opens fire and kills Riva's aides.

32. The Schizoid Man

Responding to a distress call, the *Enterprise* travels to the research facility of Doctor Ira Graves, the brilliant scientist who mentored Data's creator. Graves's young assistant, Kareen, has summoned the ship, hoping someone can help the brilliant scientist, but his illness is terminal. Graves strikes up a rapport with Data and shares his last breakthrough with the android: a device capable of transferring a human personality into a computer. When Graves dies, Data begins displaying uncharacteristically human tendencies, including a profound yen for Kareen.

"Shut up, Wesley."—Picard, "Datalore"

33. Unnatural Selection

Upon discovering that the entire crew of the *Lantree* has died of old age, the *Enterprise* travels to that ship's last port of call, the Darwin Genetic Research Station. Darwin's lab personnel also have been afflicted with a virus that causes rapid aging. However, the staff is more concerned about the status of the genetically bred children in isolation.

34. A Matter of Honor

An exchange program gives Riker the opportunity to become the first Starfleet officer to serve on a Klingon ship. After receiving some vital tips from Worf, Riker proves that he can hold his own with the warrior race—or so it seems until he faces a real challenge. A nasty strain of bacteria is eating away the hull of the vessel, and the Klingons believe that the *Enterprise* is responsible.

35. The Measure of a Man

Noted robotics specialist Commander Bruce Maddox has long wanted to know what makes Data "tick." Starfleet has approved his request to disassemble the android. When Data learns that Maddox may not be able to put him back together again, he refuses to submit to the experiment and resigns his commission. Unfortunately, Starfleet proclaims that Data is their property.

36. The Dauphin

The *Enterprise* is called upon to ferry Salia, a sixteen-year-old girl, and Anya, her overprotective guardian, to the troubled planet she will rule. Although Salia and Wesley Crusher immediately hit it off, her guardian is determined to keep them apart. Troi senses that there is something odd about the two women.

37. Contagion

In response to a distress call, the *Enterprise* crosses into the Romulan Neutral Zone. It arrives just in time to witness the *Yamato*'s destruction, apparently triggered by computer malfunctions. Retracing the *Yamato*'s course, the crew finds itself at the planet of Iconia, a long-dead civilization of advanced beings who traveled via gateways through time and space. Now, *Enterprise* has been infected with the same computer virus that destroyed the *Yamato*—and the Romulans are displeased that the *Enterprise* is on their side of the Neutral Zone.

38. The Royale

Beaming down to an uninhabited planet after recovering a bit of space refuse that appears to have come from a twenty-first-century Earth spacecraft, Riker, Worf, and Data find themselves within an artificial environment that resembles a resort casino. Inside one of the hotel rooms, they find the remains of an astronaut, a novel called *The Hotel Royale*, and the astronaut's diary. According to the diary, he was unable to leave the resort—leading the away team to wonder if its members' fate will be any different.

39. Time Squared

The *Enterprise* crew comes upon a disabled shuttlepod that apparently is from their ship. Stranger still: inside the shuttlepod is a disoriented double of Picard. An examination reveals that the Picard from the pod is the real thing—but he's from six hours in the future. Apparently, the *Enterprise* will encounter a gigantic energy whirlpool and will be destroyed, leaving the captain as its only survivor.

40. The Icarus Factor

Riker ponders accepting command of his own ship and leaving the crew he's come to think of as family. Complicating the decision is an un-anticipated reunion with his father, Kyle. At the same time, members of the crew learn that Worf's uncharacteristically hostile behavior toward them has to do with his feelings of cultural isolation.

41. Pen Pals

Given responsibility for a survey mission investigating the dangerous geological events on the planet Drema IV, Wesley Crusher learns that managing his team is as important as conducting the scientific research. The increasing instability of the planet threatens the lives of its inhabitants, including a young girl Data has been communicating with.

42. Q Who?

After Picard refuses to allow the omnipotent entity known as Q to become a member of the *Enterprise* crew, Q hurls the ship into a distant region of the galaxy, toward an encounter that Q predicts the crew is not prepared for. The crew spots a gigantic cube-shaped vessel manned by the Borg—cybernetic beings that are part organic and part machine, and linked via a group mind. The Borg call for the ship's surrender. Instead, Picard engages the massive ship in battle. Both ships sustain damage, but the Borg ship and its crew quickly adapt to the *Enterprise*'s tactics. As casualties mount, Picard has no choice but to ask for Q's help.

43. Samaritan Snare

Picard accompanies Wesley Crusher on a shuttle trip to Starbase 515, where Wesley will take the admission test for Starfleet Academy and Picard will undergo an artificial heart replacement. Back on the *Enterprise*, Riker underestimates a slow-witted crew of Pakleds who ask for help repairing their vessel. After La Forge completes the repairs, the Pakleds take the engineer hostage and demand all of the data in the *Enterprise*'s computer.

44. Up the Long Ladder

The *Enterprise* rescues two groups of Earth colonists. The Bringloidis are a simple people who favor a nontechnological lifestyle. The Mariposans are so devoted to technology that their entire populace is made up of clones derived from the five colonists who left Bringloid. Unfortunately, the Mariposans are facing extinction; they need fresh DNA to clone new citizens. They find the idea of natural reproduction repugnant; however, the theft of DNA samples from kidnapped *Enterprise* crew members is quite appealing.

45. Manhunt

As the *Enterprise* takes delegates to a Federation conference, the crew finds that one of their passengers is Counselor Troi's mother, Lwaxana. Upon learning that Lwaxana is in the throes of "the phase"—a time of life that quadruples a Betazoid woman's sex drive—Picard flees to the holodeck to escape her advances, passing time as his favorite gumshoe, Dixon Hill.

46. The Emissary

K'Ehleyr, a special envoy from the Klingon Empire, arrives to assist the crew of the *Enterprise* in intercepting the *T'Ong*, a Klingon sleeper ship launched during a period when the Federation was at war with the Empire. If the *T'Ong*'s crew awakens before the *Enterprise* reaches the ship, it is likely to begin attacking key Federation outposts. Half-Klingon, half-human, K'Ehleyr is an untraditional member of the warrior race—which is one of the reasons the passionate relationship between her and Worf soured years earlier.

47. Peak Performance

Realizing that the Borg represent a threat to the entire Federation, Picard asks Starfleet to send an expert to oversee a battle simulation. But in the midst of the war games, an attacking Ferengi ship renders the *Enterprise* helpless and demands that Picard surrender a ship that the Ferengi believe is equipped with a secret weapon.

48. Shades of Gray

While on an away team mission, Riker is injured by a thorn that introduces a deadly alien microorganism into his nervous system. His condition rapidly deteriorates, and when traditional treatments fail, Doctor Pulaski begins stimulating areas of Riker's brain in hopes that the induced primitive emotions will eradicate the lethal organism.

Season Three

49. Evolution

Following Beverly Crusher's return to the *Enterprise*, her son, Wesley, discovers that his science project involving nanites—robots so tiny they can enter living cells—has gotten out of hand. The rapidly multiplying minuscule machines have entered the starship's computer core, causing system malfunctions throughout the ship. There's evidence they've evolved to the point of sentience. When an impatient visiting scientist attempts to destroy the nanites, they strike back, endangering the entire crew of the *Enterprise*.

50. The Ensigns of Command

The *Enterprise* heads for Tau Cygna V, a world ceded by Federation treaty to the Sheliak—a very reclusive species. The Sheliak want Federation colonists evacuated from the planet within three days. Unfortunately, there are far more of them than Picard was expecting. There's no way he can remove fifteen thousand settlers in three days.

51. The Survivors

The crew discovers that all but two of the eleven thousand inhabitants of Delta Rana IV have been destroyed by a warlike race known as the Husnock. The surviving pair—Kevin and Rishon Uxbridge—claim to have no idea why their lives were spared, but they refuse to evacuate, even when the Husnock ship returns to the area. The heavily armed vessel fires on the *Enterprise*, damaging its weapons systems, and later obliterates the Uxbridges' home. Picard suspects that the Uxbridges are responsible for the Husnocks' actions.

52. Who Watches the Watchers?

When natives of Mintaka III discover Federation anthropologists, it starts a chain of events that threatens to push the Mintakans' culture back to more primitive beliefs. During an attempt to retrieve the anthropologists, a Mintakan, Liko, is injured, and Doctor Crusher brings him to the ship for treatment. Crusher fails to erase Liko's short-term memory, and he spreads tales of the "gods" he has encountered. The Mintakans capture Troi and threaten to sacrifice her to "the Picard," whom they believe is the overseer of the gods. The captain is forced to step in and demonstrate that neither he nor his crew is divine.

53. The Bonding

After the ship's archaeologist is killed on an away mission, Picard and Troi convey the sad news to her young son, Jeremy, who is surprisingly stoic. Not long after, the crew discovers that an energy being from the planet has come aboard the ship and is masquerading as Jeremy's mother so the boy will not suffer her loss—a situation that Picard fears will harm the boy.

54. Booby Trap

Picard is excited when the *Enterprise* comes across an ancient relic: a Promellian battle cruiser that has been in space, untouched, for one thousand years. However, the crew soon discovers that the Promellians aboard fell victim to a booby trap set by their enemies—and it's still active. La Forge consults with an interactive facsimile of Leah Brahms, designer of the *Enterprise*'s engines, to find a way to escape the trap.

55. The Enemy

After finding the remains of a small Romulan vessel on a world plagued by fierce magnetic storms, La Forge is separated from the rest of the away team and captured by an injured Romulan. The engineer tries to convince the Romulan that they must work together if they hope to survive. Picard engages in brinksmanship with Romulan Commander Tomalak in the hopes of avoiding a war.

56. The Price

The *Enterprise* plays host to a group of dignitaries who have gathered to negotiate for the rights to a stable wormhole discovered near the planet Barzan II. The wormhole could provide a valuable shortcut to a distant part of the galaxy. But as an underhanded empath attempts to manipulate the bidders, and some conniving Ferengis threaten to destroy the wormhole, La Forge and Data discover that the passage isn't what everyone thinks.

57. The Vengeance Factor

Picard attempts to reconcile the inhabitants of Acamar III with the Gatherers, a group of renegades that broke off from Acamarian society a century earlier. Both sides express tentative interest in reuniting. The peace talks are complicated when Riker discovers that the Acamarian woman he's fallen in love with is an assassin who lives only for revenge against the Gatherers.

58. The Defector

A Romulan defector attempts to convince Picard that an invasion by the Romulan Empire is imminent. Unfortunately, the only way to prove the claim is to take the *Enterprise* across the Romulan Neutral Zone, an act that could trigger a war. Despite warnings from the Klingons, Picard opts to cross into Romulan territory—only to run into his old nemesis, Commander Tomalak.

59. The Hunted

After emerging from a lengthy period of war, the planet Angosia III applies for membership to the Federation. During a visit from the *Enterprise*, a prisoner escapes from Angosia's lunar penal colony, and Picard's crew helps to capture the man. The captain learns that the colony's prisoners are actually former war veterans who are now too violent to live among Angosia's civilians.

60. The High Ground

While delivering aid to victims of a civil war, Doctor Crusher is taken hostage by one side, who have the ability to transport via the dangerous technology of "dimensional-shifting." Although sympathetic to the rebels' cause, Picard begins to realize that this is a planet where the Federation cannot take a stand, not even to save Crusher's life.

61. Déjà Q

The normally omnipotent Q seeks refuge aboard the *Enterprise* after the Q Continuum evicts Q from their realm and strips him of his powers. His presence complicates Picard's mission to prevent the Bre'elian moon from crashing into the inhabited planet and ultimately threatens the safety of the entire crew when an enemy of Q's decides that this would be the perfect time to take revenge.

62. A Matter of Perspective

During a stopover at a Starfleet research station, Riker is accused of murdering Doctor Apgar, a scientist who was developing a new source of energy. Two witnesses claim Riker's actions support the accusation, and scientific evidence points to the same conclusion. Picard attempts to defend his first officer by using the *Enterprise*'s holodeck to re-create the events leading up to the scientist's death.

63. Yesterday's *Enterprise*

The *Enterprise*-D encounters the *Enterprise*-C, a vessel that was lost some twenty-two years ago. As soon as the *Enterprise*-C passes through a temporal rift into the time frame of the *Enterprise*-D, Guinan notes that the ship has changed from a vessel of exploration to a battleship, and that Worf is conspicuously absent, replaced by Tasha Yar. Apparently the C's actions allowed the Federation to establish a peaceful alliance with the Klingon Empire two decades earlier. If the *Enterprise*-C returns to the past, its crew will die, but if the ship stays in Picard's time, the Federation will suffer a long and brutal war.

64. The Offspring

Data's creation of an android "daughter" named Lal sparks a fierce debate with Starfleet over whether the female android should be studied in a lab or allowed to remain with Data on the *Enterprise*. When Admiral Haftel insists on coming to the starship to observe Lal's behavior and determine her fate, the visit triggers an unanticipated response in Lal.

"What the hell—nobody said life was safe."

—Riker, "Peak Performance"

65. Sins of the Father

Kurn, a Klingon exchange officer serving on *Enterprise*, turns out to be Worf's long-lost brother. Kurn brings bad news: their long-dead father, Mogh, has been branded a traitor, apparently responsible for the deaths of four thousand Klingons at the hands of the Romulans, with whom he allegedly collaborated. For Worf, there's only one choice: he must go to the Klingon homeworld and face the High Council in order to challenge the accusations.

66. Allegiance

Picard is kidnapped and imprisoned by beings who want to study his behavior and his crew—who are unknowingly serving under a double planted by the aliens. As the real Picard and his cell mates plan an escape, the captain begins to suspect that one of them may actually be their captor.

67. Captain's Holiday

While reluctantly vacationing on the pleasure planet Risa, Picard finds romance and adventure with Vash, an attractive female archaeologist. She will do just about anything to beat a Ferengi and several time-traveling Vorgons at finding the *Tox Uthat*, a dangerous superweapon from the twenty-seventh century. The Vorgons tell Picard that he's destined to find the weapon and give it to them so that they can return it to its appropriate place in time.

68. Tin Man

The *Enterprise* risks Romulan warbirds and an impending supernova to help a Federation emissary establish relations with Tin Man, a sentient life-form that resembles an organic spaceship. The emissary, Tam Elbrun, has a fragile psyche. After Picard learns that Elbrun has developed an empathic bond with Tin Man, he begins to question the unstable emissary's loyalties.

69. Hollow Pursuits

Nervous, insecure Reg Barclay, one of La Forge's engineers, compensates for his inability to cope with real life by living out elaborate fantasies in the ship's holodeck. But when a runaway acceleration problem threatens to destroy the *Enterprise*, La Forge is forced to seek a solution from Barclay.

70. The Most Toys

Data is captured by Kivas Fajo, an unethical collector of one-of-a-kind artifacts who thinks that Data will be the jewel of his collection. Initially unwilling to "perform" for his captor, Data succumbs to Fajo's demands when he threatens to harm his assistant if the android refuses. The assistant attempts to help Data escape, and Fajo kills her, pushing Data to the brink of murder.

71. Sarek

The success of diplomatic negotiations between the Federation and the Legarans is thrown into doubt after Picard learns that Sarek, the Vulcan ambassador conducting the negotiations, is suffering from Bendii Syndrome. The Legarans will speak only to Sarek, who is unfit to deal with them.

72. Ménage à Troi

Riker, Troi, and Troi's mother, Lwaxana, are kidnapped by a Ferengi who is bent on making Lwaxana his mate and exploiting her telepathic skills for profit. Riker attempts to signal the *Enterprise* for assistance, but Wesley Crusher, the one person aboard who might be able to understand the strange transmission, is about to leave the ship to take his Starfleet Academy oral exams.

73. Transfigurations

After the *Enterprise* rescues an injured amnesiac with strange healing powers, the crew discovers that he is being pursued by the Zalkonian government. The Zalkonians claim that the alien "John Doe" is an escaped prisoner sentenced to death for his heinous behavior. Beverly Crusher, who's grown fond of "John," suspects that something far stranger is behind their desire to see "John" exterminated.

74. The Best of Both Worlds, Part I

After a Federation colony disappears, Starfleet suspects that the Borg have finally arrived. Lieutenant Commander Shelby, a Borg specialist, is assigned to assist in the investigation. Her strategies clash with those of Riker, but the pair must find a way to work together after the Borg captures and assimilates Picard. When an attempt to retrieve Picard ends in failure, they realize that they may have to kill the captain in order to save Earth.

Season Four

75. The Best of Both Worlds, Part II

Failing to destroy the Borg vessel, Riker struggles to find a way to stop the invaders from assimilating the people of Earth. Realizing that the Collective is using Picard's knowledge to defeat the humans, Riker sends an away team to the Borg ship to recapture the captain.

76. Family

With the *Enterprise* in drydock for repairs following its encounter with the Borg, Picard beams down to Earth to visit the family he hasn't seen in twenty years. The reunion is not pleasant for the captain, who is still coming to grips with his brutalization by the Borg. Picard considers abandoning Starfleet for a safer life on Earth, but he must also deal with the hostilities of his older brother, who resents Picard for abandoning his family responsibilities.

77. Brothers

A malfunction in Data's programming causes him to alter the course of the *Enterprise*, endangering the life of a desperately ill boy. Data beams down to a laboratory on a mysterious planet, where he finds Doctor Soong, his creator. Soong explains that Data's behavior was triggered by a homing signal he sent out. Soong has summoned his creation because he's perfected a chip that will allow Data to experience human emotions.

78. Suddenly Human

Picard must decide whether to return a human boy—whose parents were killed by Talarians when he was an infant—to his human relatives or allow him to remain with his adoptive father, a tough Talarian captain. The boy's grandmother is a Starfleet admiral who wants Picard to bring the boy home. His Talarian father threatens war if Picard doesn't turn him over.

79. Remember Me

After a warp field experiment conducted by her son, Wesley, is aborted, Crusher finds that her universe has been radically altered. One by one, her friends and colleagues vanish, while the crew that remains insists that the missing people never existed at all!

80. Legacy

The *Enterprise* crew is caught in the midst of a civil war on Turkana IV as they try to rescue Federation engineers. Although Picard doesn't trust either side, he reluctantly accepts assistance from a faction in order to retrieve the engineers. The representative is Tasha Yar's younger sister, Ishara.

81. Reunion

Worf's former lover K'Ehleyr travels to the *Enterprise* to inform him of two vital facts: the Klingon leader K'mpec has been poisoned by one of the two contenders for leadership of the Klingon Council, and Worf is the father of Alexander, the young boy who accompanied her. K'mpec asks Picard to arbitrate the power struggle between Gowron and Duras, the two Klingons vying to become his successor. K'Ehleyr learns that one of the two men has a duplicitous connection to the Romulans.

82. Future Imperfect

During an away mission on Alpha Onias II, Riker falls unconscious and awakens to discover that sixteen years have passed. Doctor Crusher explains that a long-dormant virus in his system recently activated and destroyed his memories of everything that transpired during the past decade and a half. As Riker tries to come to grips with this shocking revelation, he becomes convinced that he is the victim of a Romulan charade.

83. Final Mission

After learning that he finally has been accepted into Starfleet Academy, Wesley Crusher accepts Picard's invitation to accompany him on an away mission that could resolve a mining dispute. A shuttle crash and a disastrous search for water leave the captain near death.

84. The Loss

Following an encounter with a cluster of two-dimensional life-forms, the crew discovers that the ship is unable to resume course, and Deanna Troi finds that she has lost her empathic powers. The ship is dragged toward a spatial phenomenon that will destroy the *Enterprise*. Unable to sense the emotions around her, Troi feels compelled to resign as the ship's counselor.

85. Data's Day

As Data contemplates the impending marriage of his friend Keiko Ishikawa to Transporter Chief Miles O'Brien, he also learns about the rituals that surround human nuptials. At the same time, Data investigates the death of a Vulcan ambassador *Enterprise* was transporting to treaty negotiations with the Romulans.

86. The Wounded

Picard is shocked when a highly respected starship captain turns renegade and begins destroying Cardassian vessels. Captain Maxwell claims that the Cardassians, who recently signed a treaty, are secretly rearming for war. Unfortunately, he has no proof. Picard demands that Maxwell surrender his ship, but the other captain refuses.

87. Devil's Due

Picard arrives at Ventax II to find its inhabitants panicked. According to legend, the Ventaxians made a pact with Ardra, the devil, who would grant them a millennium of peace and prosperity in return for their eventual enslavement. Picard doesn't believe in the devil, but he offers to arbitrate for the Ventaxians against Ardra's claim.

88. Clues

En route to investigate a mysterious planet, the entire crew—with the exception of Data—is rendered unconscious by a wormhole. After they revive, Data explains that the crew was unconscious for only thirty seconds. The android's attempts to prevent them from investigating the planet raises the crew's suspicions.

89. First Contact

During an away mission to observe a prewarp civilization, Riker is injured and brought to a hospital, where the locals quickly realize he is not from their world. Picard and Troi's efforts to retrieve the first officer are stymied by the government's concern about the social crisis that widespread revelation of Riker's presence could trigger.

90. Galaxy's Child

La Forge is thrilled when Doctor Leah Brahms comes aboard the *Enterprise*. Unfortunately, Brahms is nothing like her holographic version; she's cold and humorless. After she inadvertently discovers La Forge's holodeck program, he's the *last* person she wants to associate with. When the *Enterprise* becomes the reluctant nursemaid to a newborn life-form that's draining the ship of its energy, Brahms and La Forge find they must work together in order to save both the baby and the ship.

91. Night Terrors

The *Enterprise* finds the *Starship Brattain* drifting in space, all but one of its crew dead. The survivor, a catatonic Betazoid, offers no clues as to what occurred. Whatever happened to the *Brattain*'s crew is beginning to happen to Picard's crew. Most of them have lost the ability to dream and are becoming mentally unstable, while Troi is suffering from bizarre nightmares that seem to match those of the injured Betazoid.

92. Identity Crisis

La Forge and former shipmate Susanna Leitjen investigate the recent disappearance of colleagues who accompanied them to Tarchannen III five years ago. Leitjen begins to act peculiarly. Doctor Crusher determines that she has been infested by a parasite that is rewriting her DNA and turning her into an alien. Crusher speculates that the same thing may have happened to their former crewmates, whose abandoned shuttles have been found in orbit around Tarchannen III.

93. The Nth Degree

The crew of the *Enterprise* discovers an alien probe hovering near the malfunctioning Argus Array telescope, which they've been sent to repair. As Lieutenant Reginald Barclay approaches the probe in a shuttle, the device emits an energy surge that knocks him unconscious. He recovers quickly but is a changed man, a supergenius who knows how to fix the Array in a fraction of the time it would normally take. As the crew struggles to adjust to Barclay's new abilities, he surprises them all by connecting his brain to the ship's computer and putting the *Enterprise* on course for an unknown destination 30,000 light-years away!

94. QPid

Picard and Vash are reunited when the *Enterprise* hosts an archaeology symposium, but their disparate personalities soon have them sparring. Q, the near-omnipotent entity from the Q Continuum, wants to do Picard a favor by getting him and Vash together. When Picard rejects the notion, Q transforms the captain into Robin Hood and sends him, Vash, and several members of Picard's senior staff to Sherwood Forest.

95. The Drumhead

An explosion aboard the *Enterprise* leads to an inquest headed by Admiral Norah Satie, a retired officer renowned for her investigative skills. Satie quickly determines that a visiting Klingon officer was attempting to smuggle diagrams, but the Klingon denies any involvement in the explosion. Satie refuses to give up on her investigation, even after the explosion is proved to be an accident.

"Engage."—Picard, "Encounter at Farpoint"

96. Half a Life

During a visit to see Deanna, Lwaxana Troi falls in love with Timicin, a scientist who is participating in an experiment to test his theories of stellar ignition. Timicin hopes to save his own world's dying star, but the experiment fails. Although Lwaxana encourages Timicin to continue his research, the scientist reveals that he can't. It's time for him to go home for "resolution"—a ritual suicide invoked at the age of sixty to save children from the burden of a parent's aging.

97. The Host

After Doctor Crusher's lover, Odan—a Trill mediator assigned to settle a bitter dispute—is mortally injured, the doctor discovers that "Odan" is actually a symbiotic worm that lives inside a host body. He will survive only if he's quickly transplanted into the body of another Trill, but that world is a long way from the *Enterprise*. With the dispute reaching a crisis and Odan weakening, Crusher transfers the symbiont into a human volunteer: Riker.

98. The Mind's Eye

La Forge sets out for a vacation on Risa, but never makes it. His shuttle is apprehended by Romulans who hope to use the engineer in a plot to drive a wedge between the Federation and the Klingons. A few days later, La Forge returns with no memory of the encounter—or of the fact that he's just been exposed to days of mind-control techniques that have turned him into the perfect assassin.

99. In Theory

In his quest to learn about the nature of humanity, Data accepts the romantic advances of Jenna D'Sora. However, Jenna soon comprehends the ups and downs of a relationship that is literally programmed. As the couple attempts to work out its problems, the *Enterprise* moves into an area of space that is deadly because a nebula is creating small gaps in the fabric of space.

100. Redemption, Part I

Picard heads for the Klingon homeworld to oversee Gowron's installation as leader of the High Council. The *Enterprise* is intercepted by Gowron's ship. Gowron reveals that he has discovered that the surviving members of the Duras family are plotting to incite civil war within the Empire. Gowron's installation ceremony is interrupted by the arrival of the Duras sisters, Lursa and B'Etor, who announce that Toral, son of their dead brother Duras, will challenge Gowron for leadership. Worf, taking a leave of absence from Starfleet, meets with Gowron and offers him the support of an alliance of Klingon warships led by his brother, Kurn, *if* Gowron will restore his family's honor.

Season Five

101. Redemption, Part II

Captain Picard decides that Starfleet must help expose the fact that the Romulans are supporting the disruptive Klingon faction led by the

> **WHO IS SELA?** Tasha Yar died childless in 2364. So how was it possible for Picard to meet her full-grown daughter, Sela, three years later (see "Redemption," above)? In 2366, after the *Enterprise*-C popped out of a temporal rift, an alternate version of Tasha appeared on the *Enterprise*-D (see "Yesterday's *Enterprise*" p. 86). The alternate Tasha accompanied the *Enterprise*-C back twenty-two years into the past, where she was captured by the Romulans and eventually had a half-Romulan daughter who looked just like Tasha—except for the pointed ears. Got it?

conniving Duras sisters. Meanwhile, Worf is kidnapped and delivered to Lursa and B'Etor, who want him to join them. And Picard is unnerved when he's approached by Sela, a mysterious Romulan officer who bears an uncanny resemblance to Tasha Yar, the *Enterprise*'s dead security chief.

102. Darmok

Picard's attempts to communicate with aliens known as the Children of Tama are interrupted when Dathon, the captain of the Tamarian ship, kidnaps Picard and beams him to a nearby planet. Eventually, Picard realizes that the alien is well-intentioned and determined to bridge the communications gap.

103. Ensign Ro

The crew is unsettled by the arrival of Ensign Ro, a disgraced Bajoran Starfleet officer. Ro was previously court-martialed for disobeying orders that led to eight deaths. Admiral Kennelly has pardoned her and assigned her to the *Enterprise*. Her mission is to persuade Bajoran rebels to stop attacking and raiding Federation colonies.

104. Silicon Avatar

The deadly Crystalline Entity—which years earlier killed the colonists of Omicron Theta—attacks another colony. Picard joins forces with a scientist, Kila Marr, to hunt it down. Marr has been searching for the entity for years, ever since it destroyed her son. But Picard's determination to find a peaceful way to stop the creature's onslaught on humanity is at odds with Marr's obsession for revenge.

105. Disaster

A catastrophe leaves the *Enterprise* severely damaged, with Troi in charge on the bridge, an injured Picard trapped in a turbolift with three frightened children, and a pregnant Keiko

O'Brien about to give birth. With an explosion of the ship's antimatter pods likely at any moment, Troi must decide whether to separate the saucer section from the stardrive section, a decision that would doom anyone in engineering.

106. The Game

Riker returns from a vacation on Risa with a game he's eager to share. The game is psychologically addictive, and it quickly turns virtually every member of the *Enterprise*'s crew into a mind-controlled pawn of the Ktarians. After Data—who is unaffected by the game—is "incapacitated," only visiting Starfleet Academy cadet Wesley Crusher and Ensign Robin Lefler stand in the way.

107. Unification, Part I

Hearing that the legendary Spock may have defected to the Romulan Empire, Picard travels to Vulcan to talk to Spock's father, former ambassador Sarek, who is near death. In a rare lucid moment, Sarek discloses that Spock has long harbored hopes of peacefully reuniting Vulcans and Romulans, who once were part of the same civilization. Spock actually may be initiating steps to achieve that goal. Determined to find the truth, Picard and Data, disguised as Romulans, set out for the Romulan homeworld.

108. Unification, Part II

Upon finding Spock, Picard learns that the Vulcan is indeed on an unauthorized mission to reunify his people with the Romulans. Spock counts among his allies a Romulan senator named Pardek and the Romulan Proconsul Neral. But why is Neral secretly meeting with Commander Sela, the Romulan who helped to incite the Klingon civil war? And why have the Romulans recently stolen Vulcan ships from a space salvage yard?

109. A Matter of Time

The crew's attempts to save the inhabitants of Penthara IV from a devastating massive asteroid strike are interrupted by the arrival of Berlinghoff Rasmussen, a purported historian from the twenty-sixth century who claims to be studying their era. The curious nature of Rasmussen's questions about the twenty-fourth century, and his interest in gathering—and stealing—technological "artifacts," make the crew suspicious.

110. New Ground

Worf is less than thrilled when his foster mother, Helena, arrives with Alexander, his son. Helena and Worf's foster father had agreed to raise the boy after his mother's death. But the boy is having a difficult time adjusting to his new life; he needs to be raised by his father on the *Enterprise*.

111. Hero Worship

The *Enterprise* comes upon the wreckage of a research vessel that was investigating the interior of a Black Cluster, a region of intense gravitational waves. The only survivor of the ship is Timothy, a traumatized young boy who won't reveal what damaged the ship and killed his parents. Timothy forms an attachment to Data, who rescued him, and begins emulating the android.

112. Violations

A delegation of Ullians, telepathic historians who conduct research by probing subjects' long-forgotten memories, comes aboard the *Enterprise*. Soon after, Troi experiences a peculiar twist on a pleasant memory and then lapses into a coma. Riker and Crusher attempt to figure out if there is a connection between the presence of the Ullians and Troi's condition.

113. The Masterpiece Society

Picard is frustrated when Aaron, the leader of a colony on Moab IV, resists the *Enterprise*'s efforts to save his world from a fragment of a stellar core. The inhabitants of the colony have been genetically engineered to constitute a "perfect" society. Aaron is unhappy about the "corruption" factor of Picard's crew mixing with his society as they work together to prevent the disaster.

114. Conundrum

The entire crew of the *Enterprise* suffers complete memory loss after an alien ship scans the starship. Unable to recall their names or duties, the crew realizes that somehow everyone still knows how to operate the ship. In all the confusion, no one notices that Kieran MacDuff, the man who the ship's computer indicates is the *Enterprise*'s executive officer, is someone they've never seen before. The computer also provides evidence that they are on a mission to cross into Lysian space and destroy their central computer, as well as any Lysian vessel that attempts to stop them.

115. Power Play

While investigating a distress call from what they believe to be an uninhabited moon, Troi, Data, and O'Brien are possessed by alien entities who hijack their bodies and use them to take hostages aboard the *Enterprise*. Their ultimate goal: to help the noncorporeal spirits of condemned criminals from the moon's penal colony to escape and take command of Picard's ship.

116. Ethics

Paralyzed after an accident, Worf would prefer to commit ritual suicide than live. When he realizes that Klingon customs dictate that his young son must assist in the ceremony, Worf changes his mind. He will instead accept the dangerous surgical option offered by a neuro-specialist whom Doctor Crusher considers to be unethical.

117. The Outcast

The J'naii, an androgynous species, asks for the *Enterprise*'s help in locating a missing shuttle, and Riker finds himself working with Soren, a J'naii pilot. The pair pass the time by comparing their cultures. Soren explains that the J'naii are forbidden to engage in gender-specific relationships and never publicly identify themselves as either male or female. Those J'naii that do express sexual preference are brainwashed into "healthy" attitudes. Soren admits that "she" has always felt female and is attracted to Riker.

118. Cause and Effect

A mission to chart a region known as the Typhon Expanse leads the *Enterprise* to repeat a disaster again, and again, and again. The ship's propulsion system fails and the crew is on a collision course with a ship that seems to appear out of nowhere. The *Enterprise* strikes the other vessel and explodes—and then pops back into existence a short time later as the crew repeats the routine.

119. The First Duty

A member of Wesley Crusher's flight squadron at Starfleet Academy has been killed during a complicated maneuver. Wesley and the other members of the team say that the cadet panicked, inadvertently triggering the accident. But as Starfleet conducts an investigation, Picard begins to suspect that the four survivors are hiding something, and he pressures Wesley to come forward with the truth.

120. Cost of Living

Lwaxana Troi arrives with the startling news that she plans to marry a man she has never met. Then the *Enterprise* begins to experience a bizarre number of system malfunctions that gradually increase in severity. La Forge and Data trace the problem to metallic parasites that infested the ship when it passed through an asteroid field. With life support failing and the oxygen supply low, time is running out.

121. The Perfect Mate

The *Enterprise* is sent to transport a beautiful woman—Kamala—to Valt Minor, a world that has been at war with her own planet, Krios, for many years. An empathic metamorph—a being who can sense her mate's desires and become exactly what he wishes—Kamala is overwhelmingly attractive to all men. She has been prepared since birth to bond with Alric, Valt Minor's ruler, in the hopes of bringing peace to their two planets. After a Ferengi injures the Kriosian ambassador, Picard must step in and take his place, forcing him to spend considerable time in Kamala's tantalizing presence.

122. Imaginary Friend

Picard attempts to figure out how and why the *Enterprise* is being drained of power. Troi tries to figure out why Clara Sutter has recently become such an unruly little girl. Clara keeps blaming an imaginary friend, Isabella. No one believes her, until Isabella attacks Troi and tells Clara that her people are going to kill everyone aboard the *Enterprise*.

123. I, Borg

Tracking a distress signal to a distant world, the crew of the *Enterprise* finds the wreckage of a Borg ship and one surviving drone. Picard wants no part in assisting the injured Borg, but Crusher convinces him to allow her to treat it. Separated from the Borg collective, the drone begins to gain a sense of individuality. Members of the crew who were skeptical about its presence begin to feel empathy for the drone, who takes the name "Hugh."

124. The Next Phase

Picard responds to a distress signal from a Romulan vessel, assigning Ro and La Forge to assist its crew. But when the pair attempts to return to the *Enterprise*, something goes wrong and they never arrive. Reluctantly, Picard declares them dead. However, Ro and La Forge are alive and well but "out of phase" with everyone else, thanks to the ill-fated—and illicit—test of a new cloaking field that the Romulans were conducting.

125. The Inner Light

After being struck by a beam from an ancient probe floating in space, Picard finds himself on the drought-stricken world of Kataan. Although the captain retains all of his memories of life aboard the *Enterprise*, the Kataan insist that he has always lived on their world. He is Kamin, the husband of Eline. It's a reality that Picard rejects for as long as he can, but with no sign of the *Enterprise*, he chooses to make the best of his new life.

126. Time's Arrow, Part I

The discovery of an unusual five-hundred-year-old artifact—Data's head—at a site beneath San Francisco leads scientists to summon the *Enterprise*. The excavation was initiated following the discovery of triolic wave traces in a cavern. No one on Earth could have produced those waves during the nineteenth century, a finding that suggests alien visitors in Earth's past. The *Enterprise* travels to Devidia II and discovers both a time rift and traces of beings that the crew can't see because they are slightly out of phase. Picard is hesitant to send Data into a situation that could lead to his eventual decapitation, but the android is the only one capable of manipulating the equipment that

will render the aliens visible. Data succeeds; however, another time rift opens, sending the android back to the nineteenth century.

Season Six

127. Time's Arrow, Part II

Picard, Riker, Crusher, Troi, and La Forge travel to Earth's nineteenth century in the hopes of finding Data before the android loses his head, and also to determine why the Devidians are interested in that era. They learn that the aliens have assumed human form to sap the energy from dying cholera victims. That energy then is taken to the twenty-fourth century and eaten by their waiting brethren. After Crusher steals a crucial piece of their technology and flees, the away team runs into Data. The entire group heads for the cavern where Data's head will be discovered in five centuries. As they realize that the cavern is the focal point for the Devidians' time travel, the aliens open a time portal, triggering an explosion that blows off Data's head.

128. Realm of Fear

Perennially nervous Reginald Barclay earns the respect of his peers by coming up with a plan to reach a crew that's trapped in a plasma stream. However, when he's invited to join the rescue team, Barclay's lifelong fear of transporters won't allow him to accept.

129. Man of the People

The *Enterprise* transports Alkar, a Lumerian ambassador, and his aged mother, Sev, to Rekag-Seronia. Alkar hopes to mediate a cease-fire between two warring local factions. When Sev unexpectedly dies during the journey, Alkar asks Troi to help him perform a funeral meditation. Not long after, Troi begins to age rapidly as she experiences a tsunami of irrational emotions. The captain orders Crusher to conduct an autopsy on Alkar's mother—without the ambassador's permission—in order to determine what's wrong with the counselor.

130. Relics

The crew chances upon three historic finds in the same day: an immense artificial habitat known as a Dyson Sphere; the wreckage of the *Jenolen*, a Starfleet vessel that crashed on the sphere's surface seventy-five years ago; and the *Jenolen*'s captain, Montgomery Scott. He's still alive after spending three-quarters of a century suspended in the *Jenolen*'s transporter system. Scotty was once the chief engineer of James Kirk's *Enterprise* and is considered a Starfleet legend. It doesn't take long for him to get on La Forge's nerves as the younger engineer tries to do his job without input from the legend.

131. Schisms

La Forge's experiment channeling warp energy through the main deflection grid appears to work perfectly until an explosion occurs in the cargo bay. While the damage appears to be minimal, it's just the first of a series of inexplicable events. Although they have no memory of it, crew members, including Riker, La Forge, Worf, and Data, disappear from the ship at different times. After they're returned to the *Enterprise*, the hijacked officers are changed in minute ways, some the victims of exhaustion, others suffering from mysterious pains—and worse.

132. True Q

Amanda Rogers, the newest intern to serve on the *Enterprise*, is smart, pretty, and tremendously enthusiastic. Although she appears normal, Amanda has some unusual powers that she's kept to herself. She's forced to reveal them in order to prevent an explosion in engineering. Amanda then receives a surprise visitor: Q, the nigh omnipotent being from the Q Continuum. Q reveals that her parents, who were killed by a freak tornado, weren't human. They were Q—and so is she.

133. Rascals

A transporter accident transforms Picard, Ro, Keiko O'Brien, and Guinan into twelve-year-old children who retain the minds of their adult selves. After La Forge researches the situation, he determines that the transporter can be used to bring the group safely back to normal. Before they can make the attempt, the *Enterprise* is attacked by renegade Ferengi, who disable the vessel and announce that they're claiming the starship for salvage.

134. A Fistful of Datas

With some spare time to kill, La Forge conducts an experiment to see if Data could be used as a backup to the ship's computer. Meanwhile, Alexander gets Troi and Worf to participate in his "Wild West" holodeck program. It's soon apparent that La Forge's experiment isn't succeeding. System glitches are appearing all over the ship, most dramatically in Alexander's holodeck program, where all of the bad guys resemble Data—and the program refuses to shut down.

135. The Quality of Life

Doctor Farallon, the director of an orbital mining station, has created a marvelous machine, a computer tool that she calls the exocomp. The small mobile device can solve problems and replicate parts on its own as it deals with dangerous situations that might harm humans. After working with the exocomps, Data realizes that the little machines actually are sentient.

136. Chain of Command, Part I

Starfleet orders Picard, Crusher, and Worf to leave the *Enterprise* and participate in a top-secret mission to investigate a facility where the Cardassians are thought to be creating biological weapons. Picard's replacement is Captain Edward Jellico, a tough martinet who immediately butts heads with members of the command crew, particularly Riker and La Forge. On Celtris III, Picard, Crusher, and Worf survive the rigors of their search for the hidden Cardassian facility, only to discover that they've walked into a trap.

137. Chain of Command, Part II

Picard's Cardassian captor, Gul Madred, quickly learns the nature of Picard's mission to Celtris III. He tells the captain that the rumor about biological weapons was spread in order to lure someone like Picard to the site. Madred wants to know what strategy the Federation will use if Cardassia actually does attack, and he plans to torture Picard until he finds out. On the *Enterprise*, Jellico relieves Riker of duty when he voices strenuous objections to the captain's plan to mount a first strike against the Cardassians.

138. Ship in a Bottle

After Barclay inadvertently activates the stored data file containing the sentient Professor Moriarty holoprogram, Moriarty informs the crew that he has become a living being who can exist in the real world—and he proves it by walking out of the holodeck. Becoming flesh and blood isn't enough; Moriarty wants the crew to create a living version of his love, Countess Regina Barthalomew, to share his life. And he won't release control of the ship's computer until the crew complies with his wishes.

"It's difficult to work in a group when you're omnipotent."—Q, "Déjà Q"

139. Aquiel

The *Enterprise* investigates an abandoned relay station and finds the remains of one of the station's missing residents. The crew initially believes that the remains belong to Starfleet officer Aquiel Uhnari, until Aquiel reappears. The remains belong to Rocha, Aquiel's superior. La Forge forms an attachment to Aquiel, but evidence begins to mount that she may be responsible for the murder.

140. Face of the Enemy

Deanna Troi awakens to find that she has been kidnapped, taken to a Romulan warbird, and disguised to look like a Romulan officer. As Troi tries to figure out how she got there, N'Vek, a Romulan subcommander, arrives at her quarters. N'Vek explains that it is imperative for her to pretend to be a Romulan intelligence officer and order the captain to take the ship to a specified sector of space. On the *Enterprise*, a former Starfleet officer who defected to Romulus years earlier tells Picard to head for the same sector of space. At stake are the lives of several Romulan defectors—and the life of Picard's counselor.

141. Tapestry

An injury to his artificial heart leaves Picard on the verge of death. The captain finds himself face-to-face with Q, who attempts to convince Picard that he is God. Picard is skeptical. Q offers to prove it by allowing the captain to go back and change his life, specifically the exploits that led to his needing an artificial heart. Recalling the foolhardy young man that he once was—a man so rash that he entered into a brawl with three huge Nausicaans, only to be stabbed through the heart—Picard agrees.

142. Birthright, Part I

While the *Enterprise* is docked at space station Deep Space 9, Data discovers that his creator, the late Doctor Soong, programmed him with the ability to dream. Worf learns that his father, Mogh, may still be alive in a Romulan prison camp. While Data welcomes the input from his "father," Worf is disturbed by the news about his own father; a Klingon who is willing to live as a prisoner has no honor. Unable to ignore the possibility that his father lives, Worf travels to the alleged Romulan prison.

143. Birthright, Part II

At the Romulan prison camp, Worf discovers that the rumor about his father's survival was untrue. However, there are Klingons on the planet, living in harmony with the Romulans who imprisoned them there years ago. Disgusted by the warriors' relationship with their former enemies, Worf tries to leave. The camp's residents aren't about to allow Worf to reveal their existence to the outside world and dishonor their families.

144. Starship Mine

The *Enterprise* docks at the Remmler Array for a baryon sweep, a routine maintenance procedure. Because the procedure is deadly, the crew is required to leave the ship. Picard returns to retrieve something before the sweep begins. The captain discovers a group of terrorists intent on stealing the ship's trilithium resin, which they plan to use to create a deadly weapon.

145. Lessons

Picard enters into a romantic relationship with the ship's new chief of stellar sciences, Lieutenant Commander Nella Daren. Riker is concerned about the relationship; he questions whether the captain will be able to separate his responsibility to the ship from the dictates of his heart. Picard vows he will, but when the time comes to send Daren on a deadly mission, he realizes that duty and love do not mix.

146. The Chase

Picard is pleased to receive a surprise visit from Professor Galen, his archaeology professor, but he's puzzled by the old man's request. Galen asks Picard to accompany him on a lengthy archaeological hunt. Picard regretfully declines, but a short time later he learns that Galen has been mortally injured. Galen's secret work dies with him, leaving Picard determined to find out what his friend was searching for. Soon the captain and his crew find themselves vying against the Cardassians, Klingons, and Romulans.

147. Frame of Mind

On the eve of an undercover mission to rescue Federation hostages, Riker experiences reality shifts, bouncing between life on the *Enterprise* and life in an alien mental asylum. As if that weren't confusing enough, his time on the *Enterprise* is spent practicing for an amateur theatrical production in which he plays a mental patient trapped in an asylum. Riker begins to believe the alien therapist who tells him that he is a patient—and that he's been locked up because he's a murderer!

148. Suspicions

Crusher invites scientists to the *Enterprise* to hear the theories of Doctor Reyga, a brilliant Ferengi who claims to have invented a shield that will protect a ship from the deadly effects of a star's corona. After Jo'Bril, one of the scientists, is killed testing Reyga's theory, the Ferengi vows to prove that his shields didn't fail; something else must have killed Jo'Bril. Reyga is found dead, ostensibly a suicide. Crusher risks both her career and her life in order to clear the Ferengi scientist's name.

149. Rightful Heir

A disillusioned Worf takes leave from his duties and travels to a Klingon monastery where he hopes to find Kahless—metaphorically—via meditation. But although the Klingon Empire's legendary leader has been dead for many centuries, Worf discovers what appears to be a real flesh-and-blood Kahless, who wishes to rally the Klingons under his leadership. While Worf finds merit in the plan, Gowron, the head of the Klingon Council, sees it as a threat to his leadership.

150. Second Chances

Riker returns to Nervala IV, intending to recover data from an away mission he was forced to abandon. The planet's peculiar atmospheric conditions allow use of a transporter only during a brief period every eight years. When Riker arrives, he's shocked to discover an exact duplicate of himself. Because of the planet's unique distortion field, the duplicate was created when the original beamed off the planet. This Riker has spent the last eight years alone and is eager to pick up his life where he left off, particularly his relationship with Deanna Troi.

151. Timescape

Picard, Troi, Data, and La Forge return from a Federation conference to find the *Enterprise* and its crew frozen in time with a warp core breach in progress, and a Romulan warbird firing on the starship. This strange scenario seems to be caused by the presence of an alien whose young have taken up residence in the warbird's engine core. The four realize that the minute time "unfreezes," the *Enterprise* will be destroyed!

152. Descent, Part I

The crew discovers that inhabitants of an outpost have been killed by a group of Borg drones that are impulsive and vicious. As an *Enterprise* away team fights them off, Data experiences a surge of rage and kills one of the Borg. Startled, Data takes himself off duty

while the crew tracks down the Borg ship. When they find the ship, a pair of drones materializes on the bridge, where one is destroyed and the other captured. The drone's presence has a strange effect on Data, who releases it and accompanies it aboard a shuttle. Following the shuttle to an unexplored planet, Picard leads a search party—only to find himself surrounded by the Borg, led by Data's unstable android sibling, Lore.

Season Seven

153. Descent, Part II

Following their capture, Picard, Troi, and La Forge learn that it was their release of the Borg drone Hugh a year earlier that led to the evolution of the twisted Borg group that Lore leads. When Hugh returned to the Borg cube, his awakened individuality destroyed the hive's sense of shared identity, leading to chaos. Lore's encounter with the group gave them a much-needed sense of purpose. Lore sets out to bring Data into the fold by covertly instilling him with negative feelings.

154. Liaisons

The presence of Iyaaran ambassadors creates confusion among members of the *Enterprise*'s staff who are assigned to facilitate a cultural exchange. Troi finds that her ambassador is interested in nothing but the gluttonous intake of food and drink, while Worf is goaded to violence by his charge. Meantime, Picard—who was to meet with dignitaries on the Iyaaran homeworld—finds himself trapped on a desolate planet with a love-starved woman who would do anything to keep Picard there with her.

155. Interface

La Forge prepares to test a new technology that will allow him to use his VISOR as an interface between his mind and a probe, when he learns that his mother's ship, the *Hera*, has been lost with all hands aboard. Despite his feelings about the tragedy, La Forge refuses to postpone his assignment because it could save the lives of seven men and women aboard the *Raman*, a science vessel caught in the atmosphere of a gas giant. The probe establishes that the *Raman*'s crew is dead, and it also provides some less reliable information: La Forge's mother is aboard the *Raman*. She wants him to use the probe to send the vessel deeper into the atmosphere where she claims the *Hera* is trapped.

156. Gambit, Part I

The crew receives word that Picard has been killed by mercenaries while on an archaeological trip, but Riker refuses to accept the report. Traveling to Barradas III, Riker finds evidence of Picard's attackers—right before he is taken captive. On board the mercenaries' ship, Riker discovers that Picard is part of the crew. Following Picard's lead, Riker too takes on a false identity—corrupt Starfleet officer—in order to gain the trust of the cutthroat group.

157. Gambit, Part II

Picard and Riker continue to deceive the mercenary crew they have joined while trying to determine the reason behind the group's series of archaeological lootings. Tallera, a member of the crew, reveals that they are seeking fragments of the Stone of Gol, an ancient weapon that is powered by thought. Tallera claims she's a Vulcan agent assigned to keep the weapon out of the hands of a Vulcan isolationist.

158. Phantasms

Data's dream program begins to generate disturbing nightmares. Even after Data deactivates the program, the strange images won't go away, and one of them drives him to stab Troi. After Troi is taken to sickbay and examined, Crusher

realizes that there may be a reason for Data's visions. The ship is infested with invisible leech-like creatures that are extracting amino acids from the crew. When Data attacked Troi, he was trying to destroy one of the creatures.

159. Dark Page

Troi's mother, Lwaxana, returns to the *Enterprise* when the ship hosts a delegation of the Cairn. The telepathic species is new to the spoken word, and Lwaxana, a powerful telepath, serves as both escort and tutor to the group. Troi notices that her boisterous mother seems despondent, and she is shocked when Lwaxana falls into a coma. One of the Cairn suggests that Lwaxana's close contact with a young girl in their group seems to have triggered repressed memories.

160. Attached

Two unaffiliated societies reside on the planet Kesprytt: the Kes, who wish to join the Federation, and the isolationist Prytt, who are extremely suspicious. Picard and Crusher respond to a request to meet with the Kes, only to find themselves in a Prytt prison. The Prytt hope to prevent the alliance with the Federation. They implant electronic devices in Picard and Crusher that they say will reveal the truth. After the Starfleet officers escape, Picard and Crusher discover that the devices allow them to hear each other's thoughts.

161. Force of Nature

En route to recover a missing medical ship, the *Enterprise* is forcibly boarded by a pair of scientists who demand that the Federation halt the use of warp drive near their world. Warp fields, they say, are destroying the very fabric of space and eventually will render their planet uninhabitable. Although the claim seems outlandish, Data feels the theory has merit and could represent a threat to the entire galaxy. Data suggests the matter be referred to the Federation Science Council, but one of the frustrated scientists opts for quicker action. She takes off in her ship and triggers a warp breach, sacrificing her life to create a dangerous rift in space that proves her theory.

162. Inheritance

Data discovers that one of the scientists working to reignite the core of a planet is Juliana Tainer, former wife of Data's inventor, Noonien Soong. Tainer claims to think of herself as Data's "mother," but she admits that she was against his creation; she was afraid he'd turn out badly, like Lore. For that reason, she and Soong left him behind when they abandoned Omicron Theta.

163. Parallels

Worf inexplicably finds himself slipping from one alternate universe to the next. After experiencing realities where Deanna Troi is his wife, La Forge is dead, and Picard was never rescued from the Borg, Data concludes that Worf's shuttle inadvertently passed through a quantum fissure in the space-time continuum. Worf must take the shuttle back through it and return to *his Enterprise.*

164. The *Pegasus*

Riker's first captain, Erik Pressman—now an admiral—leads the *Enterprise* on a mission to retrieve the *Pegasus*, lost a dozen years ago with most of its crew. Time is of the essence; the ship has been spotted by the Romulans, who also hope to salvage it. Only Riker and Pressman know there's a secret on board that could destroy the Federation's tenuous truce with the Romulans: a Starfleet cloaking device. Riker fears his former commander will begin conducting further experiments if he gets his hands on the device. But if he reveals the device's existence to Picard, he will violate a direct command from Pressman. With the Romulans moving in to force the situation,

Riker must decide which man deserves his loyalty.

165. Homeward

Worf is dismayed to learn that his adoptive brother, Nikolai Rozhenko, has violated the Prime Directive while stationed as a cultural observer on Boraal II. Although the planet is doomed, Rozhenko has fallen in love with the inhabitants of a small village, including a local woman who's carrying his child. He has kept them alive long enough to summon the *Enterprise*, and now he wants Picard to relocate the villagers to a different world.

166. Sub Rosa

While attending her grandmother's funeral, Beverly Crusher is seduced by Ronin, a ghost-like alien that has romanced the women of her family for hundreds of years. The *Enterprise*'s chief medical officer abruptly resigns her post and announces her intention to live out her days on Caldos. Picard decides that he must find out the truth about Crusher's phantom lover.

167. Lower Decks

Picard, Riker, and Worf consider four young ensigns for possible promotion aboard the *Enterprise*. One of them, a Bajoran named Sito Jaxa, is an unlikely candidate. She was involved in a Starfleet Academy cover-up, and Picard seems to dislike her for her actions at the Academy. Her mentor, Worf, encourages Sito to stand up for herself.

168. Thine Own Self

As Troi struggles to earn a promotion to command status, Data travels to a preindustrial world to retrieve radioactive debris from a Federation probe. A power surge from the probe causes Data to lose his memory, leading the android inadvertently to endanger a village by bringing the radioactive substance into their midst. With the townspeople getting sick, Data searches for a way to help them.

169. Masks

The *Enterprise* crew accidentally activates and downloads an alien society's archive of information about its iconic characters. Immediately, the program begins to transform portions of the ship into a facsimile of the civilization's temple, and Data becomes the repository for the personalities of the assorted gods and goddesses. Realizing that he will need to learn more about the mythology in order to halt the archive's efforts to re-create the ancient culture, Picard attempts to communicate with Data's many personae.

170. Eye of the Beholder

The suicide of the seemingly well-adjusted Lieutenant Kwan surprises the crew. When Troi investigates the scene of the death, she experiences an overwhelming sensation of panic and fear. Crusher notes that Kwan was a partial empath—like Troi—and wonders if the counselor was picking up an "empathic echo" of his feelings before he died. Troi experiences visions that suggest Kwan's suicide may be related to a crime of passion that took place on the *Enterprise* during the starship's construction.

171. Genesis

During a brief lull in the *Enterprise*'s schedule, Picard and Data depart in a shuttle to recover a torpedo, and Crusher gives Barclay a synthetic immunizing agent to help him fight a flu bug. By the time Picard and Data return, things have changed radically. The *Enterprise* is drifting unpowered in space, and every member of the crew has de-evolved into a bizarre lower lifeform. Data deduces that something has triggered the crew's long-dormant genes to cause the transformation.

172. Journey's End

Picard's orders to remove a colony of Native Americans from a planet ceded to Cardassia—the result of a Federation-Cardassian peace treaty—are challenged by the colonists and a surprisingly sullen Wesley Crusher, who is visiting the ship. As Picard battles with an intractable Starfleet admiral, a stubborn Cardassian commander, and his own troubled conscience, Wesley has a vision of his dead father that leads him to make a radical decision.

173. Firstborn

Hoping to increase his son's interest in his Klingon training, Worf takes Alexander to a festival at a Klingon outpost. The pair fall prey to three assailants who attempt to kill Alexander. The attack is thwarted by the sudden appearance of a stranger named K'mtar, who claims to be a close friend of Worf's family, sent to protect him and his son. A knife left behind suggests that the Duras sisters sent the assassins.

174. Bloodlines

Released from prison, a vengeful Ferengi DaiMon Bok sends a disturbing message to Picard stating that he will avenge the death of his son by killing Picard's son, Jason Vigo. Picard recalls having a relationship with the now-deceased Miranda Vigo, but he is unaware of the existence of a son. The captain tracks down Jason, and Crusher establishes that Jason is Picard's child. The captain decides to protect Jason by keeping him on board until Bok is captured.

175. Emergence

A string of bizarre and unexplained malfunctions lead Data to postulate that the *Enterprise* may somehow be on the verge of achieving sentience. The holodeck seems to provide all the clues. There, the holographic passengers aboard an antique train seem to represent different aspects of the ship. As Troi attempts to find out what the passengers are looking for, the *Enterprise* takes itself into warp and heads for a white dwarf star.

176. Preemptive Strike

After graduating from Starfleet's advanced tactical training program, Ro Laren is sent to infiltrate the Maquis, a group of self-professed freedom fighters who refuse to accept the changes enacted following the Federation's treaty with the Cardassians. Victims of Cardassian violence, the Maquis colonists have begun attacking Cardassian vessels near the Demilitarized Zone established by the treaty. Ro's mission is to gain the trust of a Maquis cell and lure it into a Starfleet snare.

177./178. All Good Things . . .

Picard begins slipping back and forth among three distinct periods: his mission to Farpoint Station seven years in the past; his retirement years in France twenty-five years in the future; and the present. He discovers that his time shifting is being caused by Q, and that humanity is *still* on trial. According to Q, Picard is responsible for the impending doom of humanity, not Q.

Q takes Picard to the dawn of time—the exact moment when life sprang into being on Earth—except now the events that triggered the creation of life never happen. Q admits to the captain that the presence of a spatial anomaly that Picard spotted in the present day is somehow involved in the end of all things. Since the anomaly is even larger in the past—and not apparent in the future—Picard can't understand the relevance. If he doesn't solve the conundrum, the captain will prevent the evolution of humankind.

HOW COME IT'S THE *ENTERPRISE*-D? Just as "there'll always be an England," there'll always be an *Enterprise*. It is Starfleet's legendary flagship, after all.

Star Trek: The Next Generation is set on the *Starship Enterprise* NCC-1701-D. *Star Trek* was set on the NCC-1701. Obviously, there were other *Enterprises* in between, each designated by a sequential letter of the alphabet. What happened to them? You'll find details on those vessels in other chapters of this book, but here, for your convenience, is a capsule summary of their onscreen performances:

- NCC-1701: Appeared in seventy-nine episodes of *Star Trek*. Retrofitted (think face-lift) for its big-screen debut in *Star Trek: The Motion Picture*. Also appeared in *Star Trek II: The Wrath of Khan*. Destroyed in *Star Trek III: The Search for Spock*.
- NCC-1701-A: Appeared in *Star Trek IV: The Voyage Home*, *Star Trek V: The Final Frontier*, and *Star Trek VI: The Undiscovered Country*.
- NCC-1701-B: Appeared only in *Star Trek Generations*.
- NCC-1701-C: Appeared only in "Yesterday's *Enterprise*." Presumed destroyed in battle.

There's also an *Enterprise* that preceded Kirk's and another one after the *Enterprise*-D—but you'll find out about them later on.

Benjamin Sisko learned that compromising his principles by striking a deal with "the devil" was something he could live with.

FOUR

STAR TREK: DEEP SPACE NINE

"At the Edge of the Final Frontier"

176 hour-long episodes, 1993–1999

SERIES PREMISE

DURING THE SAME TIME PERIOD THAT CAPTAIN PICARD PATROLS THE galaxy, a heroic Starfleet commander and his crew hold down the fort at a distant outpost called Deep Space 9 (DS9). Think of a frontier town in space. Unlike their compatriots aboard the *Enterprise*-D, these folks don't seek out new life and new civilizations; they boldly wait for travelers from strange new worlds to come to them.

THE STATION

Deep Space 9 is a space station located near the planet Bajor. It originally belonged to the Cardassians, who had conquered Bajor in 2328. The Cardassians enslaved the populace, exploited the planet's resources, and built the station as an ore-refining facility. After Bajoran freedom fighters forced the Cardassians to withdraw in 2369, the Bajorans took control of the station and asked Starfleet to manage it while they sorted things out on their newly liberated world. Of the station's three hundred permanent residents, approximately fifty are Starfleet personnel. There's also a contingent of Bajoran militia and a gaggle of civilians, most of whom work in the station's Promenade (think shopping mall).

DS9 is old and dilapidated. The life support systems are out of warranty, the replicators aren't attuned to human taste buds, and the architecture is uncomfortably angular. You might wonder why Starfleet cares about maintaining a presence there. The answer is, "Location, location, location!" DS9 may be situated in the boonies, but it's strategically positioned at the entrance to a wormhole (see What Wormholes?, p. 126) that serves as a shortcut to a distant, unexplored section of space called the Gamma Quadrant (see Which Way Is Up?, p. 126). This makes the crew of DS9 the de facto gatekeepers to the passage and, perhaps more important, the Federation's first line of defense against unfriendlies from the other side.

> "I don't care if the odds are against us. If we're going to lose, then we're going to go down fighting." —Sisko, "Statistical Probabilities"

BENJAMIN LAFAYETTE SISKO (Avery Brooks), station commander

> I'm not Picard.
> —"Q-LESS"

Sisko is a clever strategist and a courageous warrior who faces adversaries head-on. He's also a family man, a compassionate widower who puts the welfare of his son, Jake, above all else. And he's considered a major religious figure on Bajor.

Sisko grew up in New Orleans, the son of Joseph, a gourmet Creole chef, and the mysterious Sarah (see Wormhole Aliens, p. 123). At Starfleet Academy, Sisko met and married Jennifer, future mother of Jake. Jennifer was killed during a Borg attack on the Federation in 2367 (see Why Does Sisko Hate Picard?, p. 122).

Two years later, Starfleet assigned Sisko to Deep Space 9. His first few days on the job were eventful: he discovered a nearby wormhole and met its mystical inhabitants, an event that prompted the deeply religious Bajoran people to proclaim him their "Emissary," a prophesized savior.

Sisko played a leading role in defending the Federation against forces from the Gamma Quadrant (see The Dominion, p. 118). He planned to spend his post-Starfleet years on Bajor with his second wife, freighter pilot Kasidy Yates.

Unfortunately, his pals in the wormhole had other ideas . . .

Key Sisko Episodes
- "Emissary"
- "Far Beyond the Stars"
- "In the Pale Moonlight"
- "Shadows and Symbols"

KIRA NERYS (Nana Visitor), first officer

I have the bad habit of telling the truth, even when people don't want to hear it.
—"EMISSARY"

Kira is a Bajoran militia officer. She functions as second in command aboard DS9. Her background in the resistance movement against the Cardassians often prompts her to act first and ask permission later.

Kira initially resented the Federation's presence in the Bajoran system, but she later came to think of the Starfleet team on DS9 as family.

Having grown up in a refugee camp, Kira has a tendency to feel that the only good "Cardie" is a dead one. She is very spiritual and worships the Prophets. Kira often experiences conflicted feelings about Sisko; she respects him as a commanding officer but finds it "hard to work for someone who's a religious icon."

Key Kira Episodes

- "Duet"
- "Crossover"
- "Ties of Blood and Water"
- "Wrongs Darker Than Death or Night"

"That's the thing about faith . . . if you don't have it, you can't understand it. And if you do, no explanation is necessary." —Kira, "Accession"

NOW HEAR THIS! Starship crews encounter a situation, take action, and move on. The crew members on *Deep Space 9* don't have that option; they stick around to deal with the consequences of their actions. That's why DS9's story lines often continue for many weeks before wrapping up (kind of like a Russian novel). As Captain Sisko explains to Worf, "Let's just say that DS9 has more . . . shades of gray."

ODO (Rene Auberjonois), chief of security

*I'm the outsider. I'm on no one's side. All
I'm interested in is justice.*

—"NECESSARY EVIL"

Odo is the law in this "frontier town." He's good
at it because he judges everyone on the station
impartially (except, perhaps, Quark); he doesn't
identify with anyone there because he *isn't* like
anyone there. He's a shape-shifter, a being who
can turn himself into a physical replica of just
about anything, although he's not very good at
replicating humanoid faces. In his natural state,
Odo is a big puddle of orange-colored goo. He
sleeps in a bucket.

Odo was found as an "infant" drifting in
space near Bajor. A Bajoran scientist studied
the goo and learned of its sentience and
morphing abilities. Eventually Odo left Bajor
for the nearby Cardassian space station, where
he was put in charge of security. When
Starfleet took over the station, he kept the job.
Odo's best friend on DS9 is Kira Nerys, for
whom he harbors a deep, unspoken love.

For a long time, Odo wondered about his
origins. Were there others of his kind? Did he
have gooey parents? Eventually Odo discovered
that his brethren were known as the Founders,
and they hung out together—literally—in a big
orange ocean of goo known as the Great Link.
Odo thought that finding his relatives would put
an end to his lifelong feelings of loneliness and
alienation.

He was wrong.

Key Odo Episodes

- "Necessary Evil"
- "The Search"
- "The Begotten"
- "His Way"

JULIAN BASHIR (Siddig El Fadil, later Alexander Siddig), chief medical officer

> When you make someone well, it's like you're chasing death off, making him wait for another day.
>
> —"THE QUICKENING"

Having graduated second in his class at Starfleet Medical, Julian Bashir could have requested an assignment just about anywhere. He chose DS9 because he wanted to experience "the excitement of the frontier."

Bashir was born with severe learning disabilities. To compensate, his parents put him through dangerous—and highly illegal— genetic enhancement therapy, which made him really, really, really smart. For years, Julian kept this part of his past a secret, lest he be thrown out of Starfleet. When the truth finally was revealed, his father did time, but the doctor was granted special dispensation to stay in Starfleet (see "Doctor Bashir, I Presume?", p. 147).

Julian's associates found his somewhat naïve enthusiasm about "frontier medicine" a little hard to take when he first arrived at the station. Eventually he won them over, even Chief O'Brien, who initially thought the doctor a pompous ass but later became his friend. Bashir also befriended the station's sole Cardassian resident, Garak.

Key Bashir Episodes

- "Our Man Bashir"
- "The Quickening"
- "Doctor Bashir, I Presume?"

MILES EDWARD O'BRIEN (Colm Meaney), chief of operations

Have you any idea how bored I used to get sitting in the transporter room waiting for something to break down?

—"THE BAR ASSOCIATION"

Miles O'Brien may like to complain about the jury-rigged systems on DS9, but he loves his work. Transferring over from the *Enterprise*-D, where he served for nearly six years, seemed like a great opportunity.

Since his transfer, O'Brien has been falsely accused, incarcerated, and tortured by several alien governments; kidnapped and cloned; killed by exposure to radiation, then replaced by a future version of himself; and . . . well, the list goes on. He may be the Job of DS9, but at least he has Keiko, his beautiful wife (who once was possessed by an evil alien entity), lovely daughter Molly, and adorable son Kirayoshi.

Other than that, he likes to play darts.

Key O'Brien Episodes

- "Visionary"
- "Hard Time"
- "Honor Among Thieves"

JADZIA DAX (Terry Farrell), science officer

Don't mistake a new face for a new soul.

—"BLOOD OATH"

Jadzia is a joined Trill, one of an exclusive segment of the Trill populace that, just like Cracker Jack, holds a nifty surprise inside. Dax isn't her last name; it's the name of the "prize"—an intelligent sluglike creature known as a symbiont.

When Jadzia was joined to Dax, she retained all of the memories the symbiont had acquired while in its previous hosts. Jadzia is the eighth host to the Dax symbiont; the sev- enth was Curzon, a male diplomat and mentor to Ben Sisko—which explains why Sisko often calls the beautiful young Jadzia "old man." She's a bit of a party girl and enjoys playing *tongo* with Quark, drinking Black Holes, and wrestling with burly men.

Jadzia inherited Curzon's fondness for all things Klingon; eventually she married one: Worf.

Key Jadzia Episodes
- **"Blood Oath"**
- **"Facets"**
- **"You Are Cordially Invited"**

QUARK (Armin Shimerman), entrepreneur

I'm a Ferengi businessman. . . . I'm not exploiting and cheating people at random. I'm doing it according to a specific set of rules.
—"BODY PARTS"

Quark is the owner/operator of DS9's bar, an intergalactic version of Rick's Place from the classic Bogart film *Casablanca* (see Quark's Bar, p. 126). Like Rick, he's a mercenary and a cutthroat businessman . . . and a bit of a soft touch when it comes to females. He's a romantic trapped in the body of a money-grubbing troll.

Despite his bad habit of breaking the law whenever it gets in his way (making him the number one suspect whenever Odo investigates a reprehensible crime), Quark occasionally rises to levels of nigh heroic bravery. He's faced down a room full of Klingons to settle a financial dispute, organized a motley band of Ferengi to rescue his mother from the clutches of the Dominion, and confronted Jem'Hadar guards to prevent his brother's execution.

It's hard to despise a guy like that. Just keep an eye on your wallet.

Key Quark Episodes
- "The Nagus"
- "The House of Quark"
- "Little Green Men"

"Dignity and an empty sack is worth the sack."
—Quark, "Rivals"

"I think an honorable victory is better than an honorable defeat." —Jadzia Dax, "Blood Oath"

JAKE SISKO (Cirroc Lofton), aspiring writer

My father has never let me down. And right now he needs me . . . I don't want to let him down.
—"IN THE CARDS"

The only child of Ben and Jennifer Sisko, Jake is the quintessential good son. Aside from a few run-ins with Odo for loitering on the Promenade, Jake's reputation is spotless.

Even when given the opportunity to drift into mischief, he's always gone in the other direction. Jake dated a sexy older woman who worked as a hostess in Quark's bar—and encouraged her to put on some clothes and go back to school. His best friend, Nog, is a Ferengi who had shown some criminal tendencies. But Jake took it upon himself to teach Nog to read and to treat women with respect.

Jake did make one questionable decision in his life. He shunned his father's chosen line of work in favor of a much shadier profession: writer.

Key Jake Episodes

- "The Visitor"
- "Nor the Battle to the Strong"
- "In the Cards"

"I lied. I cheated. I bribed men to cover the crimes of other men. I am an accessory to murder. But the most damning thing of all . . . I think I can live with it. And if I had to do it all over again . . . I would."
—Sisko, "In the Pale Moonlight"

WORF (Michael Dorn), strategic operations officer

It is not what I owe them that matters—it is what I owe myself. Worf, son of Mogh, does not break his word.

—"THE WAY OF THE WARRIOR"

Worf, the Klingon who served as the *Enterprise*-D's chief of security, has spent most of his life living among humans. Following the destruction of the *Enterprise*, Worf had to decide whether to remain in Starfleet or live among his Klingon brethren.

Fortunately, Starfleet had an assignment that allowed him to do both: go to Deep Space 9 and find out why the Klingons in that region had gone bonkers. The entire warrior race seemed stricken with unprecedented paranoia—they imagined shape-shifters everywhere and were preparing for battle. Starfleet figured that a Klingon might be able to talk sense into them.

Starfleet was wrong.

Key Worf Episodes

- "The Way of the Warrior"
- "The Sword of Kahless"
- "Sons of Mogh"

EZRI DAX (Nicole deBoer), counselor

I'm Dax.

—"IMAGE IN THE SAND"

Ezri is the ninth host of the Dax symbiont. Prior to joining with Dax, she was Ezri Tigan, assistant counselor on the *U.S.S. Destiny*. Ezri's personal destiny took an unexpected turn while her starship was transporting the Dax symbiont to Trill. En route, the symbiont grew weak, requiring relocation to a new host. As the only Trill on the *Destiny*, Ezri won the jackpot in the slug lottery, despite being unprepared for the experience.

In addition to inheriting all of Jadzia's emotional baggage, Ezri has a few skeletons in her own closet, including a domineering mom and a brother who's a murderer.

Key Ezri Episodes

- **"Afterimage"**
- **"Field of Fire"**

ELIM GARAK (Andrew Robinson)

> The truth is usually just an excuse for a lack
> of imagination.
> —"IMPROBABLE CAUSE"

Garak is a Cardassian exile who lives on DS9. He calls himself a "plain, simple tailor," but no one believes that. Doctor Bashir finds Garak fascinating, and he loves to fish for information about the Cardassian's past. There are plenty of rumors: one has it that Garak was once a spy; another suggests that he has a very special relationship with the retired director of Cardassia's Obsidian Order (think Mafia, but not as nice). Are any of the stories true? According to Garak, they're all true—especially the lies.

Key Garak Episode
- "The Wire"

ROM (Max Grodénchik), bartender's assistant, engineer

> I've always been smart, brother. I've just lacked
> self-confidence.
> —"LITTLE GREEN MEN"

Rom is Quark's brother and Nog's father; he's bad with money and good with tools. For a long time, Rom was Quark's chief flunky; he helped Quark in the bar, even though his brother made it clear that Rom would never be managerial material. Eventually, Rom's exposure to human ideals altered the course of his life. He organized a labor union in the bar, earning the respect of friends and coworkers. Not long after, he left Quark's employ to work as one of the station's technicians, a job he truly enjoyed.

Key Rom Episode
- "The Bar Association"

NOG (Aron Eisenberg), aspiring engineer

> I know I've got something to offer; I just need
> the chance to prove it.
> —"HEART OF STONE"

Nog is Quark's nephew, Rom's son, and Jake's best friend. He's the first Ferengi to attend Starfleet Academy, no doubt due to Jake's "bad" influence. While he was still a cadet, Nog earned a field commission to ensign. He lost a leg in battle and later was promoted to lieutenant for his courageous service. Pretty impressive for a kid who, to the best of our knowledge, still hasn't graduated from the Academy.

Key Nog Episode
- "It's Only a Paper Moon"

DUKAT (Marc Alaimo), Cardassian military officer

> I should've killed every last one of them, I
> should've turned their planet into a graveyard
> the likes of which the galaxy had never seen!
> —"WALTZ"

Gul Dukat—gul is his rank, not his first name—is a Cardassian military officer who was once in charge of his government's occupation of Bajor. Think Heinrich Himmler but more self-deluded. Dukat believes his reign of brutality was in the best interests of his victims. Sisko describes him as "truly evil."

Dukat has a weakness for Bajoran women and harbors a yen for Kira, but the feeling is far from mutual.

Key Dukat Episode
- "Waltz"

"It's easy to be a saint in Paradise."
—Sisko, "The Maquis"

MAJOR ALIENS

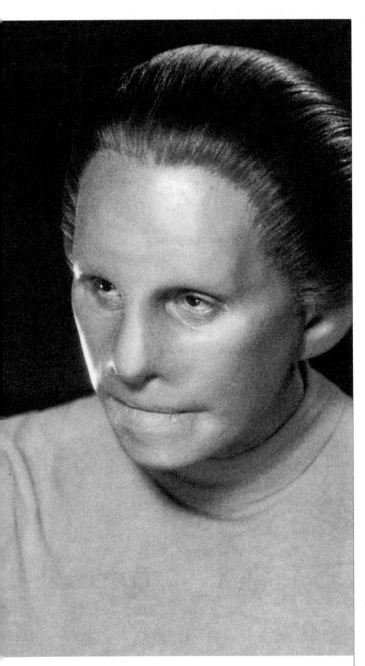

The Dominion

A coalition of three species from the Gamma Quadrant: Founders, Vorta, and Jem'Hadar. The Founders—shape-shifters like Odo—run the show and use the other two species as support staff. The Founders are xenophobic because they've had some bad experiences among "solids" (that's what they call people who don't look like a plate of melted Jell-O). They conquer other worlds and expand their domain by employing a carrot-and-stick approach. First they send an ambassador, a member of the Vorta race (a used car salesman with "wraparound" ears), who offers an opportunity to "peacefully" join the Dominion as subjects. If the offer is not accepted, the Founders send in the muscle: an invasion force of Jem'Hadar, a genetically engineered species of warriors who look like two-legged rhinoceroses. The Jem'Hadar are so fierce that even the Vorta are afraid of them, but their obedience is ensured by their dependence on ketracel-white, a powerful drug that only their superiors can provide.

Relations between the Federation and the Dominion got off to a bad start. The result: the Dominion War, a cataclysmic conflict that also drew in the Cardassians, the Romulans, the Klingons, and the Breen.

DIVORCE, KLINGON STYLE. Tired of your mate? Just slap your spouse, recite the words *"N'Gos tlhogh cha!"* and spit in his or her face. That's it. You're free. You don't even need a lawyer.

FEMALE SHAPE-SHIFTER (Salome Jens), leader of the Dominion

This shape-shifter generally makes herself look like a female version of Odo, maybe because imitation is the sincerest form of flattery. She wants to persuade him to return to the Great Link. During the Dominion War against the Federation, she called all the shots.

WEYOUN (Jeffrey Combs), a Vorta

Weyoun, the Female Shape-shifter's personal flunky, interacts with the crew of DS9 more than any other Vorta. Weyoun is slick and smarmy—the perfect obnoxious bureaucrat. He's also a clone, which means the Founders can order a new one from the copy center whenever someone, Worf—for instance—is provoked into killing him.

The reprehensible behavior of the Cardassians made it almost palatable to hear the heroes refer to them as "spoonheads."

Bajorans

Following the ouster of the Cardassians from Bajor, you might think that life there was all sunshine, lollipops, and roses. But *nooo*. Petty bickering broke out among various religious and political factions. The arrival of the Emissary (Benjamin Sisko)—whose role as the person destined to unify Bajor had been foretold by the Prophets—raised the spirits of the general populace but unnerved the politicians and religious leaders, who saw him as competition.

IMPORTANT BAJORANS

WINN (Louise Fletcher), kai (think: pope)

She's probably the most power-hungry person on all of Bajor. Winn's campaign to become kai included an assassination attempt and an arsenal of dirty tricks that rivaled Richard Nixon's. You'd think that being a planet's religious leader would be enough, but Winn also wanted to be Bajor's political leader. Failing in that attempt, Winn turned her attention to usurping Sisko's role as the voice of the Prophets. The Prophets declined to take her up on the offer, but the Pah-wraiths (evil Prophets) proved more accommodating.

Cardassians

The Cardassian military's exit from Bajor didn't do a lot for their reputation as the bullyboys of the quadrant. Soon everyone was kicking sand in their faces. When the Klingons invaded their homeworld, the Cardassians were forced to accept help from the Federation. That was so demeaning that Gul Dukat, hoping to restore his world to its former position of power, formed an alliance with the Dominion—a move that ultimately brought about the deaths of more than eight hundred million Cardassians.

DAMAR (Casey Biggs), military officer

Damar served as Gul Dukat's first officer at the beginning of the Dominion War. When Dukat lost his marbles, Damar took Dukat's place leading Cardassia in the war against the Federation. But after he realized that the Dominion was using the Cardassians as cannon fodder, he switched sides and rallied his people to fight against the Founders.

ENABRAN TAIN (Paul Dooley), intelligence official

Tain, the "retired" head of the Obsidian Order and father of Elim Garak, joined forces with the Romulans in an attempt to destroy the Founders' homeworld. It failed.

Ferengi

Greed isn't just a way of life for the Ferengi—it's their whole reason for being. They even have a holy book that lays it all out for them: The Rules of Acquisition. This collection of 285 guiding principles forms the foundation of Ferengi society. It's kind of a cross between the Bible and the regulations of the Federal Trade Commission. Pearls of wisdom range from "Once you have their money, you never give it back" to "No good deed ever goes unpunished."

If humans think of freedom as the cornerstone of civilization, Ferengi regard business contracts with the exact same reverence. In fact, breaking a contract is just about the worst thing a Ferengi can do. His business license will be revoked and all his assets seized—a fate considered worse than death.

ZEK (Wallace Shawn), grand nagus of Ferenginar

A master of commerce known as the Grand Nagus rules the Ferengi homeworld. That position is held by Zek, an elderly, utterly brilliant profiteer. Think Donald Trump, Alan Greenspan, and Scrooge McDuck all rolled into one diminutive wrinkled body.

ISHKA (Andrea Martin and Cecily Adams), mother ("Moogie") to Quark and Rom

Quark's lobes for business didn't come from his dad. They came from his mom, Ishka, the Susan B. Anthony of Ferenginar. This headstrong female offended the menfolk by wearing clothes and secretly conducting business. Nevertheless, Ishka's financial acumen—along with her bald, saggy beauty—won the heart of Grand Nagus Zek and changed Ferengi society, much to Quark's dismay.

Klingons

They're pretty much what we've come to expect. Twenty-fourth-century Klingons are big, craggy-domed, and boisterous—and they like to fight a lot. Prior to the outbreak of the Dominion War, the Klingons decided that Cardassia was rife with shape-shifters and put that entire species on their hit list. When Starfleet intervened, Chancellor Gowron canceled the accords that united the Federation and the Klingon Empire. Sisko and Worf eventually proved that Gowron's own top general had been replaced by a shape-shifter, and the Klingons got back to being our friends just in time to become the Federation's staunchest ally in the fight against Dominion forces.

MARTOK (J. G. Hertzler), general

Martok commanded the Empire's defense forces during the Dominion War; his efforts helped turn the tide for the Federation. Although he had no political aspirations, best buddy Worf convinced Martok to step into Gowron's shoes after the chancellor's untimely demise.

GOWRON (Robert O'Reilly), leader of the Klingon Empire

Gowron became jealous when Martok's heroic victories in the Dominion War drew too much adulation from the Klingon populace. So he began to push Martok out of the limelight and into increasingly dangerous situations, risking the welfare of Klingon warriors just to salvage his own ego. Gowron's on-again, off-again ally Worf told the chancellor that his behavior wasn't honorable. Them's fightin' words to a Klingon, so of course the two had to fight to the death.

Worf won.

"I have a sense of humor. On the Enterprise, I was considered to be quite amusing."

—Worf, "Change of Heart"

> DID YOU KNOW that Klingons, like humans, have a creation myth explaining how their gods made the first male and female? But instead of being kicked out of paradise, the Klingon version of Adam and Eve immediately destroyed their gods and "turned the heavens to ashes." That's gratitude for ya.

KANG (Michael Ansara), KOLOTH (William Campbell), and KOR (John Colicos), warriors

Although these three Klingons once were nemeses of Captain Kirk's, it's a different era, and they're back, a little (okay, a lot) older but feisty as ever. They come to DS9 to invite Jadzia Dax (whom they'd previously known as Curzon Dax) to join forces with them in "a glorious battle" against their sworn enemy, the Albino. Kang and Koloth don't survive the battle. Kor lives on to mingle with the DS9 crew a few more times before going out in a noble blaze of glory.

Trill

Although the stuff on the inside (the worm in the belly pouch) is still the same, Trills look a little different from the ones we first met on *The Next Generation*. Instead of bumps on their forehead, they have spots—very pretty spots that run the length of their body, all the way down to their toes. Trills take "joining" (the assignment of a host to a symbiont) very seriously. They even have a powerful government body—the Trill Symbiosis Commission—that oversees the process.

> WHY DOES SISKO HATE PICARD? It all started back in *The Next Generation* episode "The Best of Both Worlds," when the "Borgified" Picard attacked all those Starfleet ships (see p. 88). One of the ships was the *Saratoga*. Jennifer Sisko died in the attack, and Sisko held a grudge against Picard for a long time. A cathartic session with the wormhole aliens eventually helped Benjamin let bygones be bygones (see "Emissary," p. 129).

THE MENAGERIE

Wormhole Aliens (the Prophets)

Someone once said that time was invented so that everything wouldn't happen all at once. For the aliens that live in the wormhole, the past, present, and future *do* take place at the same time. The Bajorans worship the wormhole aliens as their gods, calling them the Prophets, and their home in the wormhole, the Celestial Temple. The wormhole aliens, in turn, refer to those of us who take one thing at a time as "linear."

The Prophets are good gods, but there are evil gods too: the Pah-wraiths. Did you ever read Milton's *Paradise Lost*, where Satan and his minions get tossed out of heaven? The Pah-wraiths would identify.

IMPORTANT WORMHOLE ALIEN

SARAH (Deborah Lacey), Benjamin Sisko's mom . . . sort of

Knowing that they'd need someone like Ben Sisko to help them out at some point in the future, the wormhole aliens arranged for his arrival. One of them inhabited the body of a human female long enough for her to conceive a child with a human male (Ben's dad, Joseph). Which makes Ben a demigod. Think Hercules.

"It has been my observation that one of the prices of giving people freedom of choice . . . is that sometimes they make the wrong choice." —Odo, "Shakaar"

Breen

The Federation knows very little about the Breen. We've never been to their place, and whenever they show up at ours, they're wearing hermetically sealed suits. Breen weapons can instantly neutralize every major system on a starship—which was bad for Federation forces when the species sided with the Dominion. There's an old Romulan saying: "Never turn your back on a Breen." Good advice.

Romulans

Although we don't see a lot of them on DS9, the Romulans do figure in some significant interactions with the Dominion. They join up with the Cardassians to make an ill-fated preemptive strike on the Founders' homeworld. And a few years later, as the war between the Dominion and the Federation rages, Ben Sisko manipulates them into joining the Federation's coalition against the Gamma Quadrant invaders.

BAJORAN ORBS. The Bajoran religion's most sacred artifacts are the Tears of the Prophets, or the Orbs. The Bajorans believe that the Prophets sent nine hourglass-shaped relics to teach and guide them. Gazing into the light emitted by an Orb evokes a vision in accordance to the Orb's nature: the Orb of Prophesy, the Orb of Time, the Orb of Wisdom, etc.

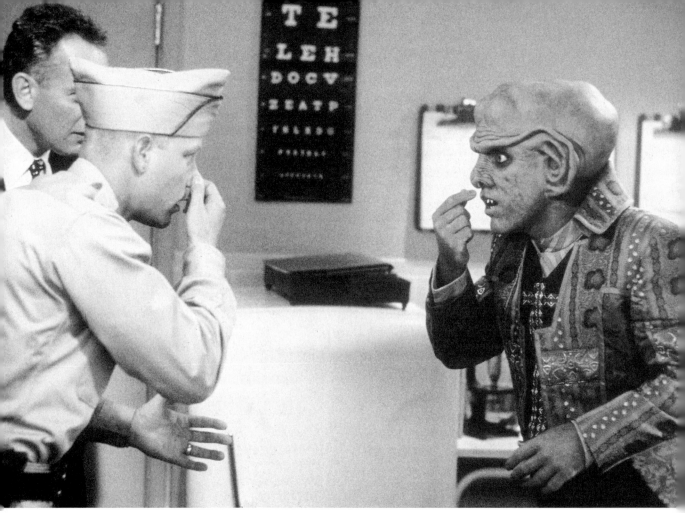

An army officer tries to decipher Quark's "sign language."

TEN ESSENTIAL EPISODES

1. "Emissary" Teleplay by Michael Piller. Story by Rick Berman & Michael Piller.

Starfleet Commander Benjamin Sisko, newly assigned to space station Deep Space 9, discovers a mysterious wormhole that becomes the focal point for hostilities between the Bajorans and the Cardassians.

The two-hour pilot introduces the show's main characters and themes, which include religion, pol-itics, and racism, all conveyed in the unique blend of science fiction and modern-day allegory that Star Trek *does so well.*

2. "Duet" Teleplay by Peter Allan Fields. Story by Lisa Rich & Jeanne Carrigan-Fauci.

Kira's inquisition of an alleged Cardassian war criminal reveals disturbing truths about both his identity and her personal prejudices.

This engrossing episode, essentially a fiery debate between two conflicted characters, examines Kira's ability to transcend the harsh lessons of her youth.

3. **"Necessary Evil" Written by Peter Allan Fields.**
Odo's investigation into an assassination attempt uncovers a connection to a five-year-old murder case in which Kira was a suspect.

An homage to hard-boiled detective stories that discloses Odo's history aboard the station and the roots of his relationship with former terrorist Kira.

4. **"Crossover" Teleplay by Peter Allan Fields and Michael Piller. Story by Peter Allan Fields.**
Kira and Bashir are trapped in an alternate universe, where a brutish alliance between Klingons and Cardassians has taken the place of the Federation, and humans serve as slave labor for tyrannical Bajorans.

Nearly twenty years after Star Trek's "Mirror, Mirror" episode, DS9's *writers take viewers back to that fascinating, slightly kinky universe. (Watch for the lascivious Mirror Kira in a steamy milk bath.)*

5. **"The Way of the Warrior" Written by Ira Steven Behr & Robert Hewitt Wolfe.**
The Klingon Empire's paranoia about the threat posed by the Dominion leads to their invasion of Cardassia. When the DS9 crew—joined by Commander Worf—defends the Cardassians, the Klingons mount a vicious attack on the station.

This action-packed episode introduces The Next Generation's *Worf as a permanent cast member and a war that will resonate throughout the next four seasons.*

6. **"Little Green Men" Teleplay by Ira Steven Behr & Robert Hewitt Wolfe. Story by Toni Marberry & Jack Treviño.**
When Quark, Rom, and Nog accidentally crash-land near Roswell, New Mexico, circa 1947, military officials assume the Ferengi are invaders from Mars.

Arguably DS9's *funniest hour, this story spoofs the popular speculation that the military covered up the crash and recovery of an alien spaceship just after World War II.*

7. **"Far Beyond the Stars" Teleplay by Ira Steven Behr & Hans Beimler. Story by Marc Scott Zicree.**
Sisko experiences a vision in which he is a struggling pulp science fiction writer during the 1950s, an era when racism is the order of the day.

Perhaps DS9's *most thought-provoking episode, Sisko's head trip provides a jarring contrast to the idealistically color-blind nature of Starfleet that viewers have come to expect. And seeing the entire cast out of alien makeup and in twentieth-century clothes is a real treat.*

8. **"In the Pale Moonlight" Teleplay by Michael Taylor. Story by Peter Allan Fields.**
Sisko compromises his personal ethics when he seeks Garak's aid in order to trick the Romulans into joining the Federation's battle against the Dominion.

Taut, well written, and surprisingly controversial among viewers. Sisko's "deal with the devil" makes him complicit in several murders and has him lying to both his friends and to Starfleet—a first for a Star Trek *captain, even if it was for a good cause.*

9. **"The Siege of AR-558" Written by Ira Steven Behr & Hans Beimler.**
Sisko and company try to hold on to a critical outpost that the Jem'Hadar are determined to recover at all costs.

This uncompromising episode demonstrates that war isn't just about exploding ships and special effects; the combat is up close and personal—and light-years away from Star Trek's *traditional philosophy of a peaceful future.*

10. **"What You Leave Behind" Written by Ira Steven Behr & Hans Beimler.**

The battle between good and evil comes to a head as the Federation and its allies finally face off with the combined Dominion forces, and Sisko fights a demonic Pah-wraith.

There's a lot of stuff to fit into two hours, but somehow the writers manage to address just about every major ongoing plotline from the series. Lots of fighting, lots of tears, and a song from Vic Fontaine serve as counterpoint to one character's transcendence to another realm.

WHAT IT IS . . .

WHICH WAY IS UP?

Start with a map of the Milky Way, the galaxy that we all live in. Fold the map once down the middle, and then fold it again. Now open it back up. You'll see that the fold lines split the map into four equal sections, or quadrants. Starting with the quadrant in the lower left, and moving in a counterclockwise direction, label each of the quadrants with a letter from the Greek alphabet—Alpha, Beta, Delta, Gamma.

Most Federation planets, including Earth, are in the Alpha Quadrant. So is Bajor. The wormhole leads from there to the Gamma Quadrant, home of the Dominion. The Klingon and Romulan empires are primarily located in the Beta Quadrant.

OPS

Short for Operations Center. The *Enterprise* has the bridge; DS9 has Ops. But instead of a captain's chair, Sisko supervises activities from a strategically placed office just up the stairs, in what once was the Cardassian overseer's office.

THE *DEFIANT*

A small, sporty ship that holds a fighting complement of fifty people. It's fast—warp 9.8—and it's armed to the max. The interior is spare and functional, with state-of-the-art weapon and tactical systems. The ship is one of a kind, a prototype that Sisko helped to design back when Starfleet's biggest enemy was the Borg. Sisko asked Starfleet to assign the *Defiant* to DS9 after he discovered a potential enemy—the Dominion—on the other side of the wormhole. It came equipped with a cloaking device, on loan from some helpful Romulans.

WHAT WORMHOLES?

Wormholes are shortcuts through space. Physicists call such phenomena quantum fluctuations; it was Doctor Stephen Hawking who gave them the nickname wormholes. While natural wormholes are thought to be temporary, existing for only a moment, the Bajoran wormhole was artificially created by the aliens that dwell within (see Wormhole Aliens, p. 123), and is stable, permanent, and a cool visual effect.

QUARK'S BAR

A drinking and gambling establishment located on the DS9 Promenade. It's the first stop for every soldier, sailor, scoundrel, or spy stepping off a ship.

Quark's drinks menu offers exotic concoctions like the aptly named Black Hole, while the

gambling tables include *tongo* (played with a combination of cards and a roulette-type wheel), and *dabo* (played on a wheel operated by lovely, scantily clad *dabo* girls). Quark rakes in still more loot from the two upstairs holosuites, where your wildest fantasies can be programmed and enjoyed. While you're at Quark's, look for a guy who resembles a tuskless walrus sitting at the bar. That's Morn, Quark's most faithful customer. Think Norm from *Cheers* without dialogue. Or Cliff.

RUNABOUT

Just because they're stuck on a space station doesn't mean the crew never gets out. They generally use runabouts: small, short-range Federation starships with warp drive, seating for four people, a tiny living area, and a transporter. DS9 goes through them like potato chips. When in doubt, take the *Rio Grande*; it's the only one that never blows up.

THE THREE-LETTER AGENCY

Just as Washington has the CIA, Starfleet has a covert intelligence unit: Section 31. Section 31 operates quietly, and sometimes questionably, to protect and serve the Federation. An operative named Sloan once attempted to recruit Doctor Bashir to assist in extralegal activities. Bashir refused, but that didn't discourage Sloan.

Starfleet isn't the only organization that conducts covert activities through a secret agency. There's also the Romulans' Tal Shiar and Cardassia's Obsidian Order.

WHEN IS A HOLOGRAM MORE THAN A HOLOGRAM?

When it's one named Vic Fontaine. Vic (James Darren) is an element in one of Julian Bashir's holosuite programs—a re-creation of a 1960s Las Vegas lounge. Vic, a singer in the Frank Sinatra vein, is "self-aware"—a hologram that *knows* he's a hologram. He has an uncanny ability to solve people's emotional problems; among his successes: helping Odo to tell Kira he loves her and convincing Nog that he's still a man despite having lost a leg in battle.

LATINUM

As *Star Trek* would have it, life is so rosy in the future that folks don't have any need for money. (Don't ask us how they get stuff—it's one of *Star Trek*'s fuzzier areas.) The Ferengi, on the other hand, *love* money—or rather, latinum, a highly precious liquid metal. It's generally referred to as gold-pressed latinum, because it comes inside gold ingots, in denominations of slips, strips, bars, and bricks.

"You can't change a writer's words without his permission. That's sacrilege."
—Jake Sisko, "The Ascent"

"There is something attractive about a lost cause." —Sisko, "Blaze of Glory"

THE RETURN OF THE TRIBBLE. "Trials and Tribble-ations" is so special that we didn't want to hide it in the Top 10 list. *DS9*'s producers updated *Star Trek*'s perennial favorite "The Trouble With Tribbles," using the latest visual effects technology. When a vengeful Klingon tampers with the Orb of Time, the crew of DS9 is thrown into the past, where it encounters Kirk, Spock, and those 1,771,561 tribbles at Space Station K-7. Their task: find the tribble with the bomb inside. Seeing Sisko's crew interacting with Kirk's is irresistible to two generations of viewers. Just watch the scene where Sisko is tossing fur balls onto Kirk's head, and you'll see what we mean.

THE "SPOCK'S BRAIN" AWARD. "Profit and Lace" generated the most heat from viewers (and we're not talking ardent affection). Why? Quark gives his mother a heart attack and then he has a sex change. 'Nuff said.

EPISODE SYNOPSES

Season One

1./2. Emissary

Commander Benjamin Sisko accepts an assignment to oversee space station Deep Space 9, a former Cardassian outpost orbiting Bajor. The Cardassians have withdrawn, leaving the Bajorans free after decades of oppression. Starfleet intends to use Deep Space 9 to serve as headquarters for a Federation presence in the war-torn region. The station is to be staffed by a mixed contingent of Starfleet officers and Bajoran militia, the latter headed by Major Kira Nerys. Odo, a shape-shifting being whose origins are unknown, oversees security. An old friend of Sisko's holds the position of science officer: Jadzia Dax, a joined entity—humanoid and a wormlike symbiont—from the planet Trill.

Bajor's spiritual leader, Kai Opaka, tells Sisko that ancient prophecies have predicted his arrival. He is the Emissary, the person who will unite the Bajoran people by finding the Celestial Temple where their gods dwell. Opaka presents him with a mystical relic, an orb, which Sisko carries with him when he takes a ship to investigate the region where the relic originated. After the ship is drawn into an oddly stable wormhole, Sisko is approached by a group of aliens who seem to have been expecting him.

Kira, aware of the wormhole's potential importance to her people, prepares for a confrontation with Cardassian warships. With Sisko temporarily out of the picture, Kira orders the space station moved to the mouth of the wormhole where she can better defend it.

3. Past Prologue

Kira Nerys is surprised to learn that the pilot of a ship arriving at the station is Tahna Los, an old acquaintance of hers from the Bajoran underground. The captain of a pursuing Cardassian ship says that Tahna is a terrorist, but Sisko grants the Bajoran asylum. Soon, the Duras sisters, a pair of treacherous Klingons well-known to Starfleet, arrive for a clandestine meeting with Tahna. After the meeting, Tahna asks Kira to join his terrorist group. When she learns that he plans to obtain a bomb from the Klingons in order to blow up the wormhole, the major must choose between her loyalty to the past and her responsibilities to the people on Deep Space 9.

4. A Man Alone

Security Chief Odo orders Ibudan, a Bajoran he once arrested for murder, to get off the space station. Not long after, Ibudan is found murdered. With all the evidence pointing to Odo and an angry crowd demanding justice, Sisko reluctantly relieves the shape-shifter of his duties. It seems that only Doctor Bashir's experiment—using DNA found near the crime scene—will establish Odo's guilt or innocence.

5. Babel

Chief Miles O'Brien begins speaking in unintelligible gibberish after repairing the station's faulty food replicators. Doctor Bashir is puzzled, and soon other residents become afflicted, leading Sisko to quarantine the station. Apparently, O'Brien triggered a dormant terrorist device, releasing an unknown virus. Kira's investigation establishes that Bajorans implanted the device during the occupation.

Deep Space Nine dared to push the envelope and show that not everything in the *Star Trek* universe was paradise.

The creator of the virus is long dead and his former assistant is reluctant to discuss it, so an antidote seems impossible.

6. Captive Pursuit

A reptilian traveler who calls himself Tosk stops at Deep Space 9 while being pursued as the prey in a ritual hunt sanctioned by his culture. A team of hunters arrives soon after and demands their prey be turned over. Although Sisko and O'Brien are disgusted, Starfleet's Prime Directive dictates that they cannot interfere in another culture's rituals. However, O'Brien takes it upon himself to reinterpret the rules of the hunt and give Tosk a chance to escape.

7. Q-Less

O'Brien is surprised when a human rescued in the Gamma Quadrant turns out to be Vash, an archaeologist that the chief had previously met on the *Enterprise*. He's even more surprised when a second visitor arrives: Q, a mischievous, omnipotent being. As Vash strikes up a friendship with Quark over a stash of potentially valuable artifacts she has brought through the wormhole, the station is struck by a series of power outages. Sisko suspects that Q is responsible, but Q suggests that the real threat to the station is Vash.

8. Dax

Jadzia Dax is arrested for a murder that was committed thirty years earlier, at a time when Curzon was host to the Dax symbiont. Sisko insists that Jadzia cannot be held responsible for the acts of previous hosts. He demands that Jadzia be given a hearing. Jadzia admits to having Curzon's memories of the incident, but she refuses to testify in her own defense.

9. The Passenger

An injured criminal named Vantika pleads for Doctor Bashir to "make him live," but his injuries are too severe and he dies. Ty Kajada, a security officer who had been pursuing Vantika, insists that the criminal only *appears* to be dead and is about to hijack a shipment of deuridium, a rare drug. When Kajada is injured falling from a balcony, she insists that Vantika threw her off. Dax surmises that before Vantika's body died, the criminal transferred his consciousness into someone else.

10. Move Along Home

Sisko hopes to make a good impression on the Wadi, the first alien delegation to arrive from the other side of the wormhole. He's disappointed when the aliens are interested only in playing games. Quark, on the other hand, is delighted, and he welcomes them to his establishment to play *dabo*. After catching Quark cheating, the Wadi demand that he play *their* game, chula. Shortly after Quark starts to play the Wadi game, Sisko and other crew members disappear from the station, only to find that they have become game pieces in a gigantic labyrinth.

11. The Nagus

When Zek, the grand nagus of the Ferengi business community, arrives at the station, Quark worries that Zek will make him an offer he can't refuse and take over his bar. Instead, Zek announces that Quark is to become his successor as nagus. The bartender is thrilled until he learns that the job comes with death threats, and is horrified when several attempts are made on his life.

12. Vortex

Croden, a quiet man who recently arrived from the Gamma Quadrant, kills a suspected thief during a scuffle. While in custody, Croden gets Odo's attention by claiming to know the location of a colony of shape-shifters. The pris-

oner's words rekindle Odo's curiosity about his own origins, so while delivering Croden to his home planet for punishment, he veers off course to check his story.

13. Battle Lines

During Kai Opaka's first trip through the wormhole, Sisko, Kira, and Bashir pick up a signal from a distant moon. Crash-landing on the moon, they find themselves in the midst of a bloody war. Opaka is killed. However, the trio is shocked when only moments later she returns from the dead. Bashir deduces that the soldiers fighting on the moon have died many times, and that an unknown metabolic transformation revives them to continue fighting in an eternal war.

14. The Storyteller

O'Brien accompanies Doctor Bashir to Bajor, where, they've been told, an entire village is in medical peril. When they arrive, they learn that only one man—a spiritual leader known as the Sirah—is dying . . . of old age. But his death will endanger the entire village since only the Sirah can protect them from the Dal'Rok, a terrible creature expected to attack this very evening. As the old man dies, he tells O'Brien the words that will repel the Dal'Rok. That evening as the creature attacks, O'Brien repeats the words, prompting the people to proclaim him the new Sirah.

15. Progress

Kira discovers a trio of farmers living in a cottage on a small Bajoran moon that soon will be made uninhabitable. Knowing that the Bajoran government plans to tap into the energy available at the moon's molten core, Kira informs the farmers that they must evacuate. But their spokesman, an elderly man named Mullibok, insists that they're refugees who fled to the moon many years earlier to escape the Cardassian occupation of Bajor; they'd rather die than leave their home. Kira attempts to mediate a compromise, but with the Bajoran energy project proceeding on schedule, she is forced to make a decision that she knows she will regret.

16. If Wishes Were Horses

The station's sensors detect unusual emissions coming from a nearby plasma field, but other than that, it's a quiet day on Deep Space 9. This is the perfect time for O'Brien to read the story of Rumpelstiltskin to his daughter, Molly. Things take a turn for the strange, when the fairy tale character comes to life. As Jake Sisko leaves the holosuite, he's followed by long-dead baseball player Buck Bokai. At the same time, Bashir is awakened in his quarters by a flirtatious duplicate of Jadzia Dax.

17. The Forsaken

A visit from Betazoid ambassador Lwaxana Troi disrupts Odo's day when the ambassador becomes enamored with the shape-shifter. After O'Brien downloads the data from an alien space probe, the station's systems begin to malfunction—including the turbolifts. Unfortunately, Odo and Lwaxana are in one at the time. O'Brien realizes that he may have downloaded a nonbiological life-form that is endangering the station.

18. Dramatis Personae

A Klingon ship blasts through the wormhole and explodes, but one Klingon manages to beam to the station before dying. A short time later, Odo realizes that all of the officers have gone through drastic personality changes. Kira begins recruiting others to mutiny against Sisko, who doesn't seem to care. Even the normally placid Bashir has uncharacteristic political aspirations. Odo theorizes that the dying Klingon may have inadvertently brought aboard a strange energy matrix that is causing the aggressive behavior.

19. Duet

Kira's interest is piqued when she learns that a freighter's passenger is suffering from a syndrome that exists only among survivors of Gallitep, a Bajoran forced-labor camp. Years ago, Kira helped to liberate Gallitep. This survivor is not Bajoran but Cardassian. He wasn't a prisoner at the camp; he was one of the oppressors—a war criminal. The Cardassian, who goes by the name Marritza, initially denies having served at the camp. Finally he swears that he is the camp's commander, Gul Darhe'el.

20. In the Hands of the Prophets

Vedek Winn, a Bajoran spiritual leader who hopes to become the new kai, protests when Keiko O'Brien teaches Bajoran children the scientific principles behind the wormhole. Winn tells Sisko that only the religious aspects of the Celestial Temple, as she calls the wormhole, should be taught. Keiko insists that her secular teaching does not dishonor their religion. Winn then instructs the Bajorans of Deep Space 9 to boycott the school. Sisko speaks with Vedek Bareil, Winn's competitor for kai, but soon discovers that Winn may have motives for stirring up the controversy on the station.

Season Two

21. The Homecoming

An earring bearing the insignia of Li Nalas, hero of the Bajoran resistance, is delivered to Kira. Li may not be dead but imprisoned in a Cardassian labor camp. Sisko grants Kira permission to search for Li. Meanwhile, an extremist group, the Circle, dedicated to ridding the region of all non-Bajorans, is gaining support among the station's residents.

22. The Circle

Kira experiences an odd orb-induced vision of a future after being reassigned to a new post by Minister Jaro. A short time later, she is kidnapped. On the station, Odo discovers that the Circle is acquiring weapons from Cardassia. Sisko urges reluctant hero Li Nalas to speak with Bajor's Council of Ministers. The Circle, influenced by the Cardassians, has succeeded in starting a revolution among the Bajorans.

23. The Siege

With hostile Bajoran military troops nearing DS9, Sisko evacuates everyone but essential crew. Meanwhile, Kira and Dax steal a vessel in hopes of warning the Council of Ministers about the Cardassian scheme to retake Bajor. As Bajoran troops reach the seemingly deserted station, Sisko speaks to a Bajoran officer, Colonel Day, but Day refuses to believe that Cardassians are behind the uprising.

24. Invasive Procedures

Prior to the arrival of a plasma storm, Sisko orders the station evacuated, leaving behind only a small critical staff. Not long after, the crew of a damaged ship takes the staff hostage. The intruders intend to steal the Dax symbiont from Jadzia and join it with their leader, Verad, a Trill man who was judged unsuitable for joining. Bashir points out that removing the symbiont spells certain death for Jadzia. Verad and his female companion, Mareel, threaten to kill the entire crew if Bashir doesn't perform the transfer.

25. Cardassians

Rugal, a young Cardassian boy, attacks Garak, the station's tailor. Hearing of the incident, Gul Dukat contacts Sisko to say that the boy, an

orphan who was abandoned after the occupation, should be returned to Cardassia. Sisko deliberates whether or not to allow the boy to stay with his adoptive Bajoran father. Garak and Bashir discover that Dukat's interest in Rugal is politically motivated.

26. Melora

Starfleet's first Elaysian recruit, Melora Pazlar, accustomed to the low-gravity of her homeworld, needs a wheelchair to move around in DS9's gravity. Fallit Kot, an old business acquaintance of Quark's, arrives and makes no secret of his intention to kill the Ferengi bartender. As Melora prepares for a mission, she suffers a fall, requiring treatment. Smitten with the pretty alien, Bashir researches a neuromuscular therapy technique that may allow Melora to walk in heavy gravity without her chair.

27. Rules of Acquisition

Quark is pleased when Grand Nagus Zek appoints him chief negotiator with the Dosi, a species living in the Gamma Quadrant. Quark chooses Pel, a young employee at the bar, as his assistant. However, Quark is unaware that Pel is a female Ferengi masquerading as a male because Ferengi law forbids females to wear clothes or acquire profit. Pel is a great help with Quark's negotiations until the Dosi admit they don't have the merchandise Zek wants. However, they're willing to put the Ferengi in touch with a more powerful group called the Dominion.

28. Necessary Evil

Pallra, a beautiful Bajoran woman, hires Quark to retrieve a box she'd hidden. Before turning the box over, Quark looks inside and finds a list of names. As he reads the list, Pallra's partner shoots the Ferengi. Odo investigates and finds connections to an unsolved crime from during the Cardassian occupation. Back then, his prime suspect was Kira Nerys. Realizing that Quark's injury is connected to that unsolved murder, Odo is forced to wonder if Kira did the crime.

29. Second Sight

Sisko meets a beautiful alien woman who says her name is Fenna. Then she disappears. The next day the commander and Jadzia Dax welcome Gideon Seyetik, who has come to re-ignite a dead star. That evening, Sisko runs into Fenna, who disappears again. The senior staff is invited to dine with Seyetik on his ship and discovers that Fenna is Seyetik's wife, Nidell. Confused, Sisko returns to his quarters and finds Fenna waiting there. She denies being Nidell, and after she kisses Sisko, she disappears—literally—right before his eyes.

30. Sanctuary

Sisko assigns Kira to look after four refugees who have come through the wormhole. The spokeswoman, Haneek, tells Kira that three million Skrreeas are about to arrive. A legend told them that the wormhole would lead to their ancestral home, Kentanna, which they believe is Bajor. Soon the Promenade is bursting with Skrreeas, but Bajor's provisional government rejects their plea for immigration.

31. Rivals

Martus Mazur is a scam artist—which is why Odo throws him in jail. There, Martus's cell mate shows him a gambling device that changes a player's luck, then he dies. When released, Martus takes the device to Quark's and beats him at a game of chance, inspiring him to open a bar that competes with Quark's. After Martus puts additional gaming devices in his place, luck begins changing all over the station.

32. The Alternate

Doctor Mora, the Bajoran scientist who first studied Odo, claims to have evidence that DNA similar to Odo's exists on a Gamma Quadrant world. Odo and Dax accompany Mora to the planet, where they find a tiny shape-shifting life-form—and a cloud of gas that incapacitates Dax and Mora. Odo seems unaffected by the gas, and he carries the others to safety. Back on the station, something or someone threatens the residents, leading Mora to offer himself as bait to trap whatever it is.

33. Armageddon Game

On T'Lani III, Bashir and O'Brien help destroy a stockpile of the deadly chemical weapons known as harvesters. But before the last cylinder of harvesters can be neutralized, Kellerun soldiers begin firing on them. Bashir and O'Brien manage to kill the attackers, but a small amount of the deadly chemical splashes on the engineer. As the two hide, ambassadors from the T'Lani and the Kellerun arrive on Deep Space 9, claiming that the humans were killed in an accident.

34. Whispers

Returning from the Parada system, O'Brien finds that everyone on DS9 is behaving weirdly. Sisko assigns him to nonessential tasks while the rest of his engineering team conducts crucial work for an upcoming peace conference. O'Brien's friends seem strangely aloof, and he is denied access to all computer logs. Even his wife, Keiko, doesn't seem to be herself. O'Brien suspects they all are part of some sort of conspiracy. Stealing a runabout, the engineer heads back to the Parada system to look for answers where his troubles began.

35. Paradise

While surveying an unexplored area of space, Sisko and O'Brien come upon a human colony stranded for ten years because none of their technology will function. The colony's leader, Alixus, believes that this is a good thing—her group has made great progress despite their lack of technology. The planet, she says, is paradise. Sisko discovers that "paradise" has a dark side.

36. Shadowplay

The residents of Yadera II in the Gamma Quadrant are inexplicably disappearing. Rurigan, the elderly man who helped to found the colony, has no explanation. When Odo and Dax come upon the colony, they promise to help. A mysterious phenomenon at the edge of Yadera's peaceful valley leads them to the truth.

37. Playing God

While Jadzia Dax and Arjin—a young, insecure Trill male she is tutoring—travel through the Gamma Quadrant, their ship snags a bit of protoplasm. Back on the station, the crew learns that the protoplasm is expanding and eventually may displace their own universe. The substance contains life—possibly an entire civilization of unknown beings—so they cannot simply destroy it. It must be returned to its original location, but doing so will be hazardous.

38. Profit and Loss

A damaged Cardassian vessel arrives at DS9 and Quark is ecstatic to learn that one of the passengers is Professor Natima Lang, a Cardassian woman who once was the love of his life. A Cardassian official claims that Natima and her students are terrorists wanted by their government and demands that Sisko turn them over. Quark attempts to rekindle Natima's affections while Garak, the station's exiled Cardassian, sees this as an opportunity to make amends with the Cardassian Central Command.

39. Blood Oath

Three aged Klingon warriors come to the station to find Curzon Dax. They are surprised that their old male friend is now the beautiful young female, Jadzia. The three—Kor, Koloth, and Kang—have discovered the whereabouts of their enemy, the Albino. The time has come to fulfill the blood oath they made years ago to kill the man who had destroyed each of the Klingons' firstborn. Knowing that a Klingon blood oath can never be broken, Jadzia has to decide between violating her duty to Starfleet and the Federation's laws and her desire to honor her former host's oath.

40. The Maquis, Part I

A Federation device destroys a Cardassian freighter near Deep Space 9. Sisko wonders if Cardassian fears about Federation terrorism are true. Sisko and Gul Dukat discuss the treaty violations with Starfleet's attaché to the Federation colonies—Sisko's old friend Cal Hudson—and his Cardassian counterpart, Gul Evek. Unfortunately, Evek has proof that Federation colonists blew up the freighter. Then an unknown group calling itself the Maquis kidnaps Dukat and Sisko.

41. The Maquis, Part II

While holding Sisko captive, Cal Hudson states that he'll never turn his back on the colonists in the Demilitarized Zone; thus he's joined the Maquis. Hudson lets Sisko and his team go free, and disappears. The commander discovers that Cardassian officers are smuggling weapons into the zone. Sisko rescues Gul Dukat from the Maquis group that had him, and although they make very unlikely allies, the two join forces.

42. The Wire

After Garak, the station's Cardassian tailor, collapses in pain, Bashir finds an odd implant in his brain. The implant—from Garak's days as an Obsidian Order spy—had been designed to help him resist interrogations by stimulating the pleasure centers of his brain. Garak has been using the implant to cope with the psychological pain of his exile. The device is breaking down—and killing the tailor as it fails. In order to save his friend's life, Bashir must travel into Cardassian territory.

43. Crossover

Returning from the Gamma Quadrant, Kira and Bashir find themselves in a disorienting and brutal parallel universe (see "Mirror, Mirror," p. 31). Everything from their own universe is duplicated, but with a dark twist. This space station is controlled by a cruel mirror image of Kira who goes by the title of Intendant. After Bashir is imprisoned in Bajor's ore mines, Kira is approached by Garak, who promises to spare them if she helps him to overthrow the Intendant.

44. The Collaborator

Only days before Bajor's election of a new spiritual leader, Vedek Bareil and Vedek Winn are the two leading candidates. Kubus, a known Cardassian collaborator, is spotted conferring with Winn. Still wondering about Winn's part in a recent attempt on Bareil's life, Kira grows suspicious. After Winn reveals that Kubus plans to implicate Bareil in the massacre of Bajorans, Kira confronts Bareil, demanding the truth.

45. Tribunal

While on vacation with his wife, O'Brien is arrested and taken to Cardassia Prime to stand trial. His accusers refuse to state the engineer's crime, saying only that the trial will reveal how his guilt was established. Both the verdict and the punishment—execution—already have been determined. With Sisko looking for clues, and Odo arguing for the chief in the courtroom, O'Brien has a chance to beat Cardassia's draconian justice system.

46. The Jem'Hadar

While camping with Jake and Quark's nephew Nog on an uninhabited planet, Sisko and Quark are taken captive and imprisoned, along with a woman named Eris. The trio's captors are the Jem'Hadar, the most feared soldiers in the Dominion. On Deep Space 9, the crew is startled when a Jem'Hadar ship emerges from the wormhole. A soldier tells Kira that Alpha Quadrant vessels are violating the Dominion's territory by coming through the wormhole.

Season Three

47. The Search, Part I

In response to recent threats from the Dominion, Starfleet gives Sisko a powerful new ship—the *U.S.S. Defiant.* As Sisko and his crew fly into the Gamma Quadrant to look for the Founders—a group they've heard is in charge of the Dominion—they're attacked by Jem'Hadar vessels. Odo and Kira manage to escape in a shuttlecraft. While Kira worries about the fate of her crewmates, Odo is interested in only one thing—finding a region he has spotted on a star chart—the unexplored Omarion Nebula.

48. The Search, Part II

Odo discovers that a planet in the Omarion Nebula is his homeworld, and the shape-shifting Founders are his people. Odo begins to learn things about himself. Odo's people don't trust Kira because she—unlike them—is a "solid." Back on Deep Space 9, Sisko learns that the Federation is negotiating a peace treaty with the Dominion. The price of peace: Bajor.

49. The House of Quark

When Kozak, a Klingon warrior, falls on his own knife and dies in Quark's bar, the Ferengi brags about being a "slayer of Klingons." Curious customers accumulate, leaving large profits in their wake. Unfortunately, Klingons also appear, starting with the dead warrior's vengeful brother, D'Ghor, followed by the victim's wife, Grilka.

50. Equilibrium

When Jadzia Dax starts hallucinating and hearing an unfamiliar melody in her head, Bashir realizes that she is seriously ill and must be treated on the Trill homeworld. Jadzia learns that the hallucinations are memories from one of the Dax symbiont's previous hosts and that the melody was written eighty-six years ago by an unstable Trill named Joran. But the head of the Trill Symbiosis Commission would rather let Jadzia die than reveal the long-hidden truth that could save her life.

51. Second Skin

Kira is kidnapped by Cardassians, who tell her that she isn't Bajoran—she's Cardassian. Her real name is Iliana Ghemor. She doesn't remember because she's been a field operative on a deep-cover assignment for the past decade. Kira looks in a mirror and is horrified to see that she now looks Cardassian. Lovingly greeted by Tekeny Ghemor, who claims to be her father, Kira begins to doubt herself.

52. The Abandoned

One of the items that Quark acquires in a deal turns out to be a newborn alien. The Ferengi hands it over to Bashir, who eventually realizes it is a young Jem'Hadar. The baby grows rapidly, becoming a teenaged warrior in just two weeks, and is too violent to handle. Starfleet orders Sisko to turn the young Jem'Hadar over to them. Odo, who feels a connection with the boy, asks that he be allowed to work with him. As the boy's bloodlust intensifies, Odo worries that no one on the station is safe.

53. Civil Defense

Everyone on DS9 is trapped when O'Brien and Jake accidentally activate an old Cardassian security program. When Dax tries to shut down the program, she inadvertently activates the program's second level; a deadly gas will be released in five minutes. Garak suggests that destroying the station's life-support system may prevent the gas release, so Kira blasts the machinery. It works, but the blast activates a third security level; the station now will self-destruct in two hours. Only Gul Dukat, the Cardassian who installed the program, can stop it. Dukat arrives but refuses to deactivate the program unless Kira makes some unacceptable concessions.

54. Meridian

On a mission in the Gamma Quadrant, the *Defiant* is surprised to witness a planet appear out of nowhere. The crew learns that the planet—Meridian—periodically shifts between two separate dimensions. The populace is concerned because the time between shifts is decreasing, which may destroy their world. As *Defiant*'s crew volunteers to help find a way to stabilize the shifts, Jadzia and a Meridian man, Doral, fall in love. An imbalance in the core of Meridian's sun triggers the shifts, but it can't be equalized in the time Meridian has left in this dimension.

55. Defiant

No one on Deep Space 9 was expecting a visit from Commander William Riker, first officer of the *U.S.S. Enterprise*. Kira is happy to accommodate his request for a tour of the *Defiant*. Once they're on board, Riker stuns Kira and steals the ship. Sisko quickly figures out that the thief isn't Will Riker; it's Thomas Riker, a transporter duplicate of Will who now is a member of the Maquis. Fearing that the Cardassian government will misinterpret the theft as support for the Maquis, Sisko joins Gul Dukat on a hunt to destroy the *Defiant*. But Tom surprises everyone when he heads for the Orias System.

56. Fascination

The yearly Bajoran Gratitude Festival is a happy celebration. As the event progresses, Vedek Bareil falls in love with Jadzia Dax, while Dax falls for Sisko. Quark makes a pass at Keiko O'Brien, and both Bashir and Jake Sisko declare their love for Kira. All of these spontaneous couplings were triggered after Lwaxana Troi arrived at the station hoping to have a romantic visit with Odo, which makes Sisko think Bashir should examine the Betazoid.

57. Past Tense, Part I

A transporter accident sends Sisko, Bashir, and Jadzia Dax into the past, to San Francisco in the year 2024. Dax is befriended by a wealthy businessman, but Sisko and the doctor are apprehended and taken to the Sanctuary District, where the poor, the homeless, and the mentally ill are segregated. Sisko becomes concerned when he learns the date. It is only days before the Bell Riots—the most violent civil actions in American history—are due to ignite in San Francisco. When Gabriel Bell, the man the riots are named for, gets killed, Sisko realizes that someone will have to assume Bell's identity or history will be irrevocably altered.

58. Past Tense, Part II

Posing as Gabriel Bell in the year 2024, Sisko takes charge of a hostage situation, as rioting begins in the downtrodden Sanctuary District. In the twenty-fourth century, Kira and O'Brien search through different time periods, hoping to find their friends. Meanwhile, Sisko and other Sanctuary residents meet with Detective Preston. They demand that all of the segregated districts be closed and an employment act be reinstated.

59. Life Support

Vedek Bareil is seriously injured as he and Kai Winn attempt to initiate peace talks between Bajor and Cardassia. Bashir is able to save the Vedek's life but warns that it is crucial for him to rest. Bareil was the driving force in the talks, and Winn insists that Bareil must be allowed to help her. When Bareil suffers a setback, Bashir uses experimental medical procedures that keep the man functioning. Bareil's organs continue to deteriorate, but Bashir manages to keep him alive with implants. When his brain begins to fail, however, it's up to Kira to decide whether the peace talks are really worth turning her lover into a machine.

60. Heart of Stone

Searching for a Maquis fugitive on a seismically unstable moon, Odo and Kira split up to cover more ground. Odo receives a distress call from Kira; she's been immobilized by a crystalline formation that is growing around her foot. Unable to free her or send for help—atmospheric interference is blocking his signal—Odo attempts to keep Kira calm as the crystal encases her body. As increasingly dangerous tremors shake the moon, Kira orders Odo to leave her behind and save himself.

61. Destiny

Sisko and a team of Cardassian scientists prepare to deploy a communication relay that will provide communication through the wormhole. Vedek Yorka comes to Sisko with a warning: details of this project are similar to a Bajoran prophecy that predicts the destruction of the wormhole. As the Emissary, Sisko should stop the project. However, Sisko sees himself as a Starfleet officer, not a religious figure, and he rejects Yorka's plea.

62. Prophet Motive

Grand Nagus Zek announces that he's rewritten the Ferengi Rules of Acquisition, the guiding words that all Ferengi live by. Rather than extolling the traditional virtues of profit and greed, Zek's new rules suggest kindness and generosity—qualities abhorrent to every self-respecting Ferengi. Learning that Zek had this disastrous change of heart after an encounter with the Bajoran Prophets, Quark decides to confront the wormhole aliens and make them see the error they've made.

63. Visionary

A mild case of radiation poisoning has a bizarre effect on O'Brien; he suddenly finds himself leaping back and forth in time. At first the temporal shifts are a minor annoyance, but it's unsettling when O'Brien sees himself being killed in the near future by a phaser blast. Knowing about that deadly event may help him to avoid it—but how is he going to prevent the destruction of DS9 and the wormhole?

64. Distant Voices

While gloomily pondering his thirtieth birthday, Bashir is blasted unconscious by an angry Lethean trying to steal from the Infirmary. When Bashir revives, he finds that he is aging rapidly and the station is damaged and deserted. He finally stumbles upon the other officers, but they seem unwilling or unable to discuss what has happened on the station. Left alone and growing weaker, the doctor can't be sure which will kill him first, the violent Lethean or his accelerated aging.

65. Through the Looking Glass

Sisko is caught off guard when the man he thinks is O'Brien turns out to be O'Brien's double from the mirror universe. This O'Brien transports the surprised commander to the alternate universe because that universe's Sisko has been killed. The commander isn't interested in replacing his dead double until he learns that the mirror Sisko was attempting to halt the work of a scientist who happens to be the mirror version of his deceased wife, Jennifer.

66. Improbable Cause

An explosion in Garak's shop appears to be a failed attempt on the tailor's life. Odo soon learns that similar incidents have killed five of Garak's former associates. When Odo confronts him, Garak admits that he and the deceased were all associates of Enabran Tain, the retired leader of Cardassia's secret intelligence agency. Garak and Odo head to Cardassia to find Tain but are captured en route by a Romulan warbird commanded by Tain.

67. The Die Is Cast

The crew of DS9 is shocked to see a huge fleet of Romulan and Cardassian vessels enter the wormhole. Garak has joined with the attack force's leader, Enabran Tain, while Odo is in a holding cell. When Tain orders Garak to find out what Odo knows about the Dominion, he tortures the shape-shifter mercilessly. Sisko and the *Defiant* pursue the fleet in hopes of rescuing Odo.

68. Explorers

Enthralled with a legend that the ancient Bajorans had explored their star system in delicate solar sailing ships, Sisko re-creates one. He invites his son, Jake, to join him on a voyage to test the vessel and the legend. Jake sees the trip as an opportunity to reveal to his father that he's been offered a writing fellowship back on Earth.

69. Family Business

Ishka, Quark's and Rom's mother, has been charged with an illegal activity for Ferengi females: earning profit. The brothers return home and are shocked when Ishka confirms the accusation. As her eldest son, Quark must repay the amount of her profit to the Ferengi Commerce Authority. However, even if he sells everything he owns, Quark won't have enough to pay back what she earned.

70. Shakaar

With Kai Winn running for the position of Bajor's first minister, Kira is worried that the unscrupulous woman may soon control both Bajor's spiritual and political future. Winn asks Kira to convince Shakaar, a former resistance leader, to return some government-owned farming equipment. Kira reluctantly complies, but security officers arrive to arrest Shakaar. Infuriated that Winn has used her as a pawn, Kira helps Shakaar to escape.

71. Facets

Jadzia Dax prepares for the Rite of Closure, a Trill ritual that requires the participation of several close acquaintances. All they have to do is let the personalities of her symbiont's previous hosts be telepathically transferred into their bodies so that Jadzia can meet them "face-to-face." All goes well as Kira, O'Brien, and Quark are transformed into people from Dax's memories. Sisko has a harder time hosting the murderer Joran. Dax's real challenge comes when she faces her most recent host, the charming and manipulative Curzon.

72. The Adversary

The celebration surrounding Sisko's promotion to captain is cut short when the station's senior officers are ordered to investigate an apparent coup on the Tzenkethi homeworld. Traveling in the *Defiant*, the crew discovers that the ship's communication system has been sabotaged. As Dax scans the crew for evidence that could link the culprit to the deed, she discovers that a visiting Federation ambassador is a changeling— a spy from the Dominion.

Season Four

73./74. The Way of the Warrior

With the fear of Dominion forces slipping unnoticed into the Alpha Quadrant, the Federation and Cardassia prepare for war. Hoping to learn why the Klingons seem more paranoid than the other allies about the potential threat, Captain Sisko sends for Lieutenant Commander Worf, formerly of the *U.S.S. Enterprise*. Worf learns that his people believe the Dominion's changelings already have infiltrated the Cardassian government and that Klingon Chancellor Gowron is about to attack Cardassia's homeworld. The Federation officially condemns the Klingon's actions. Gowron then dissolves the peace treaty between his people and the Federation, and also severs Worf's ties to the empire. Bashir offers proof that the Cardassian leaders aren't shape-shifters. When Sisko provides a refuge to Cardassia's ruling council, the Klingon leader turns his attack against DS9.

75. The Visitor

On a stormy night in New Orleans, an elderly Jake Sisko receives a visitor. It's a young woman, a fan of Jake's novels, asking why he quit writing. It all began, he tells her, when he was eighteen years old and his father, Ben, was the captain of a space station known as Deep Space 9. They were traveling near a wormhole, and a bolt of energy shot out from their ship's warp core, striking his father. Jake watched in horror as his father dematerialized, apparently dropping into subspace. From time to time his father reappeared, but for moments only. Jake abandoned his writing to study subspace mechanics in hopes of rescuing his father.

76. Hippocratic Oath

After crash-landing on a remote planet, Bashir and O'Brien are taken prisoner by Jem'Hadar soldiers. The humans expect to be killed, but when the leader, Goran'Agar, learns that Bashir is a doctor, he has the pair taken to a makeshift lab where he orders Bashir to conduct scientific research. Goran'Agar explains that he has overcome his addiction to the drug ketracel-white, even though the need for the drug is genetically engineered into his species. Goran'Agar wants Bashir to find out how he has been cured and then to cure the rest of his soldiers.

77. Indiscretion

Kira reluctantly agrees to let a Cardassian accompany her as she searches for the *Ravinok*, a Cardassian ship that went missing six years ago with its Bajoran prisoners. But she regrets her decision when she finds out that the Cardassian representative is her longtime nemesis, Gul Dukat. Remarkably, the two manage to find the *Ravinok*'s wreckage, and the nearby graves suggest there may be survivors from the crash. Dukat grieves when he discovers that one grave contains the remains of the Bajoran woman who was his mistress and with whom he says he had a daughter, Tora Ziyal. If Ziyal is one of the survivors, Dukat plans to kill her, since her existence would threaten both his marriage and his government position.

78. Rejoined

Jadzia Dax faces a personal dilemma when a group of Trill scientists comes to the station to conduct tests related to the creation of an artificial wormhole. One member of the group is Doctor Lenara Kahn, a joined Trill whose symbiont once was joined with Nilani Kahn, wife of Torias, one of Dax's former hosts. Their relationship ended tragically when Torias died in a shuttle crash. Trill society forbids relationships between lovers from past lives, but despite the care that Dax and Lenara take in their dealings with one another, an attraction begins to develop between them.

79. Starship Down

The *Defiant* is crippled after a Jem'Hadar warship lures the ship into a remote planet's gaseous atmosphere. As the poisonous gas fills the *Defiant*'s corridors, the crew members are forced to take refuge in various parts of the ship while the Jem'Hadar vessel launches torpedoes at them. With Sisko incapacitated, Bashir and Dax trapped in a turbolift, and Worf and O'Brien stuck in engineering, only Quark and Karemma Commerce Minister Hanok can defuse the armed Jem'Hadar torpedo lodged in the ship.

80. Little Green Men

As Nog prepares to depart for his first year at Starfleet Academy, his uncle Quark announces that he'll give both Nog and his father, Rom, a ride to Earth in the shuttle he's just received from his cousin Gaila in payment for an old debt. Quark plans to sell a little contraband on the trip as well. When the shuttle enters Earth's star system, the trio realizes that Cousin Gaila has sabotaged the ship's warp drive. Although they manage to make a soft landing, the three travelers discover that their emergency maneuvering has thrown them into the past—they're now prisoners at a military base at Roswell, New Mexico, site of a long-rumored alien invasion in the year 1947.

81. The Sword of Kahless

Worf, Jadzia Dax, and legendary Klingon warrior Kor travel to the Gamma Quadrant on a mission to recover the long-missing Sword of Kahless, the weapon of the Klingon Empire's first leader. Despite being threatened by a group of Klingons led by Worf's sworn enemy

Toral, the trio soon discovers that the greatest danger they face in reclaiming the sword may be from the feelings the weapon inspires in each of them.

82. Our Man Bashir

While Bashir plays the role of a 1960s secret agent in his favorite holosuite program, Sisko, Kira, Dax, Worf, and O'Brien manage to beam out of a runabout just before it explodes. The force of the blast damages the transporter. Luckily, Security Officer Eddington stores their physical patterns with an emergency computer override, but he doesn't know where they've been stored. Bashir quickly finds out, as each of the officers appears in his program. Unfortunately, the reconstituted officers are unaware of their true identities. They believe themselves to be the characters in Bashir's spy fantasy.

83. Homefront

Concerned that changelings are responsible for an explosion at a diplomatic conference on Earth, Starfleet Admiral Leyton summons Captain Sisko and Odo to San Francisco, where the captain is put in charge of security on the planet. Their worst fears are confirmed when Odo proves that a man who appears to be Leyton actually is a changeling. Federation President Jaresh-Inyo and others—including Sisko's father, Joseph—balk at Starfleet's seemingly paranoid plan to conduct blood screenings to search for changelings, but when Earth's entire power-relay system goes down, Starfleet feels a state of emergency must be declared.

84. Paradise Lost

With Starfleet personnel stationed all over Earth, Sisko begins to suspect that a group of cadets may be responsible for a planetwide power outage, and that Starfleet Admiral Leyton is planning to replace the Federation government with military rule. When Sisko refuses to join Leyton, the admiral has the captain thrown into a cell.

85. Crossfire

Shortly after First Minister Shakaar arrives at Deep Space 9, Odo learns that a Cardassian extremist group is planning to assassinate the Bajoran leader. Odo shadows Shakaar and learns that the minister has a romantic interest in Kira. Odo's own secret feelings for the major distract him, interfering with his ability to do his job.

86. Return to Grace

Kira travels to a Cardassian outpost in a run-down freighter manned by Gul Dukat, who has brought along his daughter, Tora Ziyal. Dukat's decision to take his half-Bajoran offspring to Cardassia has led to a change in circumstances. He's lost his position and his Cardassian family. Arriving at the outpost, the group learns that the crew of a Klingon bird-of-prey has slaughtered its inhabitants. Adapting the outpost's weapons for use on his freighter, Dukat pursues the bigger ship and manages to capture the bird-of-prey.

87. Sons of Mogh

Worf's brother, Kurn, has lost everything and become an outcast because Worf sided with the Federation against the Klingon Empire. Kurn asks Worf to restore his honor by performing a Klingon ritual that will end his life. Worf reluctantly carries out his brother's wish and plunges a knife into Kurn's chest, but Odo and Dax save Kurn.

88. The Bar Association

After Quark cuts his employees' salaries at his bar, his brother, Rom, encourages his fellow employees to form a union. Rom's suggestion gets them all in trouble with the Ferengi

Commerce Authority (FCA). The workers go on strike and picket outside the bar, driving away Quark's clientele. FCA Liquidator Brunt announces that the most effective way to threaten the union leader, Rom, is by hurting someone he cares about. Someone like Quark.

89. Accession

A ship emerges from the wormhole carrying Akorem Laan, a legendary poet who's been missing for two hundred years. Akorem reveals that he had an accident and was saved by the Prophets so that he could complete his role as the Bajoran Emissary—a position already ordained upon Sisko. The captain steps aside but begins to have qualms when Akorem decrees that the Bajoran people give up their modern ways and revert to ancient caste-based rules of society.

90. Rules of Engagement

Worf is put on trial for ordering the *Defiant* crew to fire on a vessel that is determined to have been a Klingon transport carrying noncombatants. Ch'Pok, the Klingon advocate, accuses Worf of negligence brought on by his inherent bloodlust. Sisko, acting as Worf's defense counsel, counters that it was a tragic accident. But as Worf's fellow officers are called to the stand in his defense, Ch'Pok discredits each of their testimonies. Although Worf's fate seems sealed, Sisko refuses to concede defeat.

91. Hard Time

O'Brien returns to Deep Space 9 after having been convicted of espionage. As punishment, the Argrathan authorities implanted manufactured memories representing twenty years of brutal incarceration into his mind. Although the engineer understands that the memories are false, he finds it impossible to forget them, particularly the ones regarding his cell mate,

Ee'Char. O'Brien has a difficult time readjusting. The memories become all-pervasive, causing dangerous behavior that threatens him and those around him.

92. Shattered Mirror

Jake Sisko is thrilled when his father introduces him to a woman who looks exactly like his dead mother, Jennifer. It's his mother's double from the mirror universe. "Jennifer" convinces the boy to visit her universe, knowing that Sisko will follow. In the mirror universe, Sisko learns that the rebel group has built its own version of the *Defiant*. They need Sisko to make the ship operational before they are attacked.

93. The Muse

Jake Sisko is flattered when an exotic female who's visiting the station takes an interest in his writing. Onaya offers to show him techniques to strengthen his skills, and Jake accepts. He fails to notice that he's growing weaker and Onaya is growing stronger. Meanwhile, Betazoid Ambassador Lwaxana Troi has a surprise for Odo—she's pregnant, and she needs his help.

94. For the Cause

Concerned that the Maquis may attempt to hijack a shipment, Odo and Security Officer Eddington keep a tight watch. Soon they suspect that a Maquis smuggler may be on the station—and all the evidence points to Sisko's lover, Kasidy Yates. When Kasidy seems overly insistent that she make a cargo run at a specific time, Sisko suspects she may be planning to rendezvous with the Maquis.

95. To the Death

After a Jem'Hadar warship attacks Deep Space 9, Sisko learns from Weyoun—a Vorta who oversees Jem'Hadar troops for the Dominion—that the attackers have rebelled. The renegades are trying to restore a recently discovered "gateway" that would allow them to move great distances without the use of a ship. Sisko reluctantly agrees to help Weyoun and his team of loyal Jem'Hadar to destroy the gateway.

96. The Quickening

Responding to a distress call, Bashir, Dax, and Kira come upon a planet whose entire populace is inflicted with a deadly plague. Trevean, a healer, doesn't even attempt to cure people; he eases their suffering by poisoning them when they reach the "quickening"—the final stage of the disease. Trevean assures Bashir that the blight is incurable. The Dominion contaminated them with it as a punishment more than two hundred years ago.

97. Body Parts

A near tragedy is averted when Bashir transports the embryo that expectant mother Keiko O'Brien has been carrying into Kira's womb after Keiko is injured. Kira will have to carry the baby to term. Quark returns from a visit to Ferenginar with bad news: he has Dorek syndrome. With less than a week to live and pay off his debts, Quark lists his remains on the Ferengi Futures Exchange and is shocked when a huge anonymous bid is made. Quark accepts and then learns that he does *not* have Dorek syndrome. Ferengi Liquidator Brunt was the purchaser, and he intends to collect, no matter what.

98. Broken Link

Odo suddenly collapses, and Bashir determines that the shape-shifter is losing his ability to hold a solid form. There is only one place for him to find help—with his people, the Founders. Soon after arriving in the Gamma Quadrant, a squadron of Jem'Hadar warships intercepts the *Defiant*, and the Female Shape-shifter—who confronted Odo previously—materializes on the bridge. She states that only by returning Odo to his homeworld's Great Link can he be helped.

Season Five

99. Apocalypse Rising

With animosity between the Klingon Empire and the Federation heating up, Sisko prepares to take a team into Klingon territory to confirm the information that Odo received in the Great Link—that a changeling has replaced Klingon Chancellor Gowron. Starfleet provides Sisko with four small polaron emitters that will cause a changeling to revert to its natural gelatinous state. Sisko and his team—Worf, O'Brien, and Odo—have to get past the large enemy fleet surrounding Klingon military headquarters, avoid detection, set up the emitters, and get Gowron to walk into the field.

100. The Ship

Sisko, Dax, Worf, O'Brien, and an engineer, Muniz, observe a Jem'Hadar warship crashing into a planet's surface, killing all of its crew. Starfleet would love to analyze the vessel, so Sisko takes a runabout down. Before O'Brien and Muniz can get the ship's systems online, another Jem'Hadar warship appears. Inside the crashed ship, the crew prepares for battle—but no one comes. Finally, a Vorta, Kilana, offers to allow Sisko to keep the ship in exchange for an item hidden aboard.

101. Looking for *par'Mach* in All the Wrong Places

Worf is shocked to learn that the new arrival on the station, a Klingon woman named Grilka, once was married to Quark. The idea of a Ferengi-Klingon match disgusts Worf, and when the bartender asks him for advice on how to win back Grilka's heart, Worf can't resist getting involved. Worf's instructions to Quark in the ways of Klingon love could get Quark killed.

102. Nor the Battle to the Strong

En route to the station, Bashir and Jake Sisko receive a distress call from a Federation colony under attack by Klingons. Detouring to the scene, Jake is shaken by the number of casualties. For a time, Jake helps Bashir tend to the patients as he attempts to master his fear of death and suffering—and an impending Klingon invasion. But when explosions rip into the ground around him, Jake panics and runs away.

103. The Assignment

Keiko O'Brien isn't herself. She looks and sounds like O'Brien's wife, but her body has been possessed by an entity that threatens to kill Keiko unless the chief reconfigures some sensor arrays on the station. With only hours to complete his task, O'Brien gratefully accepts Rom's help. Rom points out that once finished, the changes will destroy the inhabitants of the nearby wormhole.

104. Trials and Tribble-ations

Returning from Cardassia with the long-lost Bajoran Orb of Time, Captain Sisko and the *Defiant* crew suddenly find that the ship has been thrown more than a century into the past. A hitchhiker named Barry Waddle is to blame. Waddle actually is a Klingon named Arne Darvin, who's been surgically altered to look human—the same Arne Darvin who long ago was caught by Captain Kirk after he'd poisoned a shipment of grain (see "The Trouble with Tribbles," p. 33). Darvin intends to change history by killing Kirk. Sisko and his officers don historical Starfleet uniforms, intent on stopping Darvin.

105. Let He Who Is Without Sin . . .

When Worf and Jadzia's burgeoning romance hits a rough spot, Jadzia talks him into taking a vacation on Risa. After they arrive, things go downhill. Worf grows jealous of Jadzia's friendship with the resort's social director—a woman who once had been Curzon Dax's lover before the Dax symbiont was joined with Jadzia. Then the Klingon is approached by a group bent on "restoring morality" to the Federation by shutting down Risa.

106. Things Past

No matter what he does, Bashir cannot awaken Sisko, Odo, Dax, and Garak as they lie unconscious in the Infirmary. But from their perspectives, they are awake and living in the Bajoran ghetto of Deep Space 9 during the Cardassian occupation. Although they recognize each other, everyone else on the station sees them as Bajorans, and Odo soon realizes exactly *which* Bajorans. They are in the bodies of three men who once were accused of trying to assassinate Dukat. Despite the fact that the accusations turned out to be false, the three were executed.

107. The Ascent

Odo is escorting Quark to a Federation grand jury hearing, when an explosion in their runabout forces them to crash-land on a cold and desolate planet. With the communications system down, and most of their rations destroyed, they are left with a horrifying choice—starve or freeze to death. But Quark has an idea: if they haul the runabout's heavy subspace transmitter to the top of a mountain, they may be able to signal for help.

108. Rapture

Starfleet isn't pleased that Sisko is more obsessed with finding the legendary Bajoran lost city of B'hala than with preparing for a ceremony celebrating Bajor's admission into the Federation. Not even Kasidy Yates's return can distract him from his search. Sisko does locate the ancient ruins of B'hala, but Bashir worries that the visions and psychic insights may kill the captain.

109. The Darkness and the Light

A very pregnant Kira is saddened when a member of a resistance cell she once belonged to is murdered. Kira's sorrow turns to fear when she realizes that it's only the first in a series of assassinations. She's relieved when her friends Furel and Lupaza come to the station looking for information that will help them hunt down the assassin, but they, too, are murdered. It seems that whoever is bent on wiping out the resistance cell is saving Kira for last.

110. The Begotten

Odo acquires a vial of goo that he recognizes to be a baby changeling. The security officer is ecstatic at being a "father" and looks forward to teaching the infant. But his joy is tempered by the arrival of Doctor Mora, the scientist who once studied Odo and who wants to conduct similar studies on this new "child."

111. For the Uniform

As Sisko pursues Michael Eddington, the security chief who betrayed Starfleet and joined the Maquis, the fugitive triggers a computer virus that cripples the *Defiant*. While Sisko waits for his ship to be repaired, Starfleet informs him that Captain Sanders of the *Malinche* is being assigned to apprehend Eddington, since Sisko doesn't seem able to do it.

112. In Purgatory's Shadow

After Sisko asks Garak to interpret a coded message from the Gamma Quadrant, the tailor reveals that it's a distress call sent by his mentor, Enabran Tain. Sisko allows Garak to take

a runabout to investigate, but he sends Worf along as a "chaperone." After entering Dominion territory, the pair discover that a fleet of ships is about to invade the Alpha Quadrant. Worf manages to notify the station just before they're taken and placed in an internment camp, where they join an elite group: Tain, Klingon General Martok, and Doctor Bashir. Obviously, the Bashir back at the station has been replaced by a changeling.

113. By Inferno's Light

As a fleet of Dominion ships pour through the wormhole, Gul Dukat shocks everyone by announcing that the Cardassians have formed a pact with the Dominion. In the Gamma Quadrant, Bashir, Worf, and Garak are held prisoner in a Dominion internment camp, where Worf is forced to fight in an unending series of brutal matches with Jem'Hadar warriors. Unaware that the changeling posing as Bashir is planning to blow up the Bajoran sun, Sisko attempts to get Chancellor Gowron to reinstate the treaty between the Federation and the Klingon Empire.

114. Doctor Bashir, I Presume?

Bashir is flattered to be chosen as the human prototype for Starfleet's new holographic doctor program. But he's alarmed when the scientist in charge of the program, Doctor Lewis Zimmerman, explains that he'll need to interview Bashir's family, friends, and coworkers. Bashir asks Zimmerman to refrain from contacting his parents, but the scientist immediately invites Richard and Amsha Bashir to Deep Space 9. Bashir wonders if either of them will inadvertently reveal the "little secret" that could destroy Bashir's career and send them all to prison.

115. A Simple Investigation

Odo finds himself attracted to a mysterious woman named Arissa who claims to be waiting for someone to join her on DS9. After Odo discovers that the man has been killed, he catches Arissa retrieving a data crystal that belonged to the dead man. Arissa claims the crystal contains information that would help her break her ties with a powerful criminal organization known as the Orion Syndicate. As he investigates her story, Odo realizes that he doesn't know the truth about Arissa's identity—and neither does she.

116. Business as Usual

Although Quark needs the business, he's not thrilled when his cousin Gaila comes to him with a proposition. Gaila wants Quark to handle customer relations for an arms dealer by showing prospective buyers a good time and allowing them to test replicas of weapons in the holosuites. Since the activity would be both legal and profitable, Quark agrees. But he has second thoughts when he meets Hagath, who warns Quark never to cross him. Quark learns that one of Hagath's customers plans to kill twenty-eight million people. If Quark lets his conscience get the better of him, he'll forfeit not only all that profit but also his life.

117. Ties of Blood and Water

Hoping to find someone to lead Cardassian opposition against Gul Dukat, Kira meets with Tekeny Ghemor, the elderly Cardassian dissident who came to think of her as a surrogate daughter. Ghemor reveals that he hasn't long to live but still may be able to help. He tells Kira of a Cardassian tradition in which the dying tell all of their secrets to a family member. Since Kira is the closest thing he has to family, Ghemor will tell his secrets to her.

118. Ferengi Love Songs

Quark is depressed. First he was blacklisted by the Ferengi Commerce Authority, and now his bar has been shuttered due to a vermin infestation. What he needs is a trip home for some love and sympathy from his mother, Ishka. Ishka seems oddly uneasy over having her son stay with her. Quark soon learns the reason: Grand Nagus Zek, the Ferengi leader, is hiding in a closet, and Zek and Ishka are in love. As Quark ponders this, Liquidator Brunt confronts him with a proposition: if Quark wants his business license reinstated, all he has to do is break up Zek and Ishka.

119. Soldiers of the Empire

Worf and Dax join General Martok on the *Rotarran*, only to discover that the crew's morale has been destroyed by recent losses against the Jem'Hadar. Worf suggests to Martok that scoring a decisive victory would turn things around, but when they come across a Jem'Hadar patrol ship, Martok chooses to cloak the *Rotarran* rather than fight. The crew begins taking its frustrations out on one another, and Worf realizes he must challenge the general for control of the ship, even if that means he must kill Martok.

120. Children of Time

Kira is injured as the *Defiant* crew investigates a strange energy barrier surrounding a planet. The crew is hailed by the planet's inhabitants and invited to visit their settlement, Gaia. They're greeted by representatives from a colony of eight thousand people who claim that Gaia actually was founded by the *Defiant* crew two centuries ago. The barrier will prevent the *Defiant*'s departure from orbit and throw it into the past. Dax's scans prove that the leaders, Miranda O'Brien and Yedrin Dax, are telling the truth. Yedrin also reveals that Kira's injuries are severe; she's destined to die, just as she did two hundred years ago, if they don't get Kira to Deep Space 9. If they attempt to leave, they likely will repeat history and be thrown into the past again. And if they do find a way to leave unscathed, the lives of their eight thousand descendants will abruptly cease.

121. Blaze of Glory

An intercepted message alerts Sisko that the Maquis have launched a missile attack against Cardassia. Fearing the attack will prompt the Dominion to retaliate against the Federation, Sisko turns to the only man who might be able to stop it: jailed Starfleet turncoat Michael Eddington. When he reveals that the missiles can be aborted only from the launch site, Sisko forces Eddington to help him find the base. When they finally arrive at Athos IV, the captain learns too late that Eddington has been manipulating him all along.

122. Empok Nor

O'Brien leads Garak, Nog, and a small engineering team on a salvage mission to Empok Nor, an abandoned Cardassian space station. They find that two stasis units in the Infirmary have been activated—and moments later their runabout explodes. Obviously, the occupants of the stasis units—Cardassian soldiers—are on the loose. Garak discovers the Cardassians are under the influence of a drug designed to make them aggressive. Although he dispatches both soldiers, Garak gets exposed to the drug and kills a member of the DS9 salvage team.

123. In the Cards

Noticing that his father has become depressed, Jake Sisko plans to raise the captain's spirits with a gift. With help from Nog, Jake bids on a vintage baseball card, but Doctor Giger outbids him. Giger agrees to trade the card for various pieces of equipment that he needs to build an immortality machine. As Jake and Nog conduct a series of barters to meet Giger's requirements, the scientist disappears. It seems that Kai Winn may be responsible, but when they accuse her, they set off a series of events that ultimately land them in the clutches of the Vorta Weyoun.

124. Call to Arms

When Starfleet Command orders Sisko to prevent further Dominion reinforcements from reaching Cardassia, the captain orders mines to be placed at the entrance to the wormhole. Weyoun goes to Sisko with an ultimatum: remove the mines or the Dominion will take DS9. Refusing to back down, Sisko alerts the crew to the Dominion's impending attack; all civilians are sent away, and Sisko suggests that Bajor sign a nonaggression pact with the Dominion. As the battle with Jem'Hadar warriors begins, Martok and his troops protect the *Defiant*, allowing Dax and O'Brien time to finish laying the minefield.

Season Six

125. A Time to Stand

The Federation's war against the Dominion/Cardassian alliance is not going well. Having abandoned Deep Space 9, Sisko and his senior staff now operate from the *Defiant*. Back at the station, Kira is forced to work alongside her nemesis, Gul Dukat, who makes no secret of his desire to have a closer relationship with her. Hoping to eliminate the main source of ketracel-white—the drug the Jem'Hadar are addicted to—Admiral Ross orders Sisko to take the Jem'Hadar vessel he captured a year earlier into enemy territory and destroy the storage facility.

126. Rocks and Shoals

Traveling in a crippled Jem'Hadar warship, Dax is seriously wounded when Sisko and his crew crash on a desolate planet. Bashir stabilizes her condition, but soon Jem'Hadar soldiers—who also are stranded—capture Garak and Nog. Keevan, a badly wounded Vorta and leader of these Jem'Hadar, learns there is a doctor with the Starfleet group. He offers a deal: he'll trade Garak and Nog for Sisko and the doctor. Sisko agrees and Bashir attempts to save Keevan's life. The Jem'Hadar are suffering from ketracel-white withdrawal, and once the drug is completely gone, they will go insane and kill everyone.

127. Sons and Daughters

When Klingon General Martok docks his ship, the *Rotarran*, at Federation Starbase 375 to take on reinforcements, Worf is shocked to see that one of the new recruits is his estranged son, Alexander. After Alexander gets involved in a fight with another Klingon, Worf intervenes, humiliating his son in the process. Feeling that the *Rotarran*'s crew is content to accept his son as the ship's fool rather than a true warrior, Worf sets out to make the boy into something he isn't.

128. Behind the Lines

At Starbase 375, Starfleet learns that a Dominion sensor array has been monitoring all activity across their area of space, thus detecting Starfleet's plans in advance. Sisko comes up with a way to put the array out of commission. Back on the station, Kira forms a resistance cell—Jake, Rom, and Odo. But Odo's loyalties become suspect when he starts consorting with the Female Shape-shifter that heads the Dominion. Then Kira learns that the Cardassians are about to deactivate the minefield that's been preventing Dominion troops from coming through the wormhole.

129. Favor the Bold

With morale sinking fast, the Federation needs a major victory against the Dominion. Sisko formulates a Starfleet-Klingon strike to retake Deep Space 9. On the station, Rom is sentenced to death for attempted sabotage, and Odo struggles between feelings for the Female Shape-shifter and loyalty to his friends. Meantime, Quark learns that the minefield is about to be destroyed, allowing Jem'Hadar troops to flood the area—and making Sisko's attack a suicide mission.

130. Sacrifice of Angels

With Sisko in command of the *Defiant*, the fleet faces a much larger Dominion force standing between them and Deep Space 9. Sisko orders his troops to target only the Cardassian vessels, hoping to provoke them into breaking formation. Gul Dukat sees through his strategy and orders resistance cell members Kira, Jake, and Leeta be taken into custody so they can't prevent destruction of the minefield. Quark and Dukat's daughter, Ziyal, mount a bold prison break. As the battle in space rages, Sisko realizes he has only one choice: take the *Defiant* into the wormhole.

131. You Are Cordially Invited

With Deep Space 9 back in Federation and Bajoran hands, life is returning to normal on the station, so Worf and Dax resume planning their wedding. Worf has become a member of the House of Martok, meaning that Dax must be accepted by General Martok's wife, Sirella, who disapproves of Worf marrying a non-Klingon. Meanwhile, Sisko, O'Brien, Bashir, and Alexander join Worf in *kal'Hyah*, a traditional Klingon bachelor party, but are surprised to learn that the "party" consists of fasting, blood-letting, and other uniquely Klingon rites. Dax also throws a party, but Sirella demands she leave to perform a Klingon ritual.

132. Resurrection

Kira is surprised when a man who looks like Bareil beams aboard the station. But she's even more surprised when he takes her hostage. He is not the man she loved. This man is Bareil's doppelgänger from the mirror universe. When he admits that he wouldn't mind some spiritual guidance in his life, Kira takes the intruder to a Bajoran shrine and lets him experience the powers of the Orb of Change and Prophesy.

133. Statistical Probabilities

Starfleet asks Bashir to work with a group of misfits—genetically modified individuals who are unable to assimilate into society. The four—manic, hyperactive Jack; overly sensual Lauren; timid, childlike Patrick; and mute, withdrawn Sarina—are intelligent, amusing, and exasperating. Bashir doesn't know what to do with them—until they see a speech given by Cardassian Legate Damar. Just by watching Damar's body language and listening to his words, they determine the Dominion/Cardassian alliance's strategy.

134. The Magnificent Ferengi

Quark learns that his mother, Ishka, has been captured by the Dominion. After being promised a huge reward by Ishka's boyfriend, Zek, Quark recruits Rom, Nog, and fellow Ferengi Leck, Gaila, and Brunt for a rescue mission. Quark calls in a favor from Kira to obtain the release of the Vorta Keevan from prison so he can exchange Keevan for Ishka. Before they can make the exchange, the Ferengi get into a fight over the reward money and kill Keevan.

135. Waltz

En route to testify before a war crimes commission, Sisko meets with former Cardassian leader Gul Dukat, now held in a Starfleet cell. The ship transporting them is attacked by Cardassians and Sisko is seriously injured. Dukat rescues Sisko and escapes to a nearby planet. When Sisko regains consciousness, Dukat informs him that they are stranded but claims that he is sending out a distress signal.

136. Who Mourns for Morn?

Quark receives word that his most loyal bar patron, Morn, has died and has left his entire estate to him. Soon, Quark meets a woman claiming to be the Lurian's ex-wife, who insists that she deserves a portion of the large financial holdings Morn has hidden somewhere. Quark agrees to share the assets with her—if only they can find them. They instead find two alien brothers and an apparent security officer from Morn's home planet, all of whom insist they are the true heirs.

137. Far Beyond the Stars

Sisko begins seeing visions of himself as Benny Russell, a writer for a 1950s science fiction magazine. Other staffers resemble O'Brien and Bashir, and human versions of Kira, Dax, Odo, and Quark. The stories that Benny writes are about a space station captain named Benjamin Sisko. When he submits them to his editor, the man refuses to publish them, saying the readers will not accept a black man as the head of a space station. Benny grows more obsessed with his dream. After a young friend is killed and he's fired, Benny's world unravels, leaving him certain of only one thing—that his characters and their stories are real.

138. One Little Ship

Dax, Bashir, and O'Brien take their runabout into a region of space where compression shrinks them to near-microscopic size. The *Defiant* is standing by waiting to pull them back to normal space with its tractor beam. But when a Jem'Hadar vessel attacks the *Defiant*, the tractor beam is disrupted. Now the tiny trio must overpower the towering Jem'Hadar soldiers in order to rescue the *Defiant* and her crew, or spend the rest of their lives on the head of a pin.

139. Honor Among Thieves

O'Brien is recruited by Starfleet Intelligence to infiltrate the Orion Syndicate. A member, Bilby, is impressed by O'Brien's skills at repairing weapons. The two bond as each discusses his love for his wife and children. Finally, Bilby takes O'Brien to a syndicate meeting, where the chief is surprised to see a Vorta in attendance. O'Brien realizes that Bilby is a pawn who will surely be killed in a Dominion plot to assassinate a Klingon ambassador.

140. Change of Heart

Lasaran, a Cardassian double agent, offers to give Starfleet valuable information about the Dominion, but only if they help him to defect. Worf and Dax plan to rendezvous with him on Soukara, behind enemy lines. As they make their way through the planet's jungle, Dax is shot by a Jem'Hadar patrol, and her only hope for survival is immediate surgery. Worf faces the prospect of leaving his wife behind to die.

141. Wrongs Darker Than Death or Night

Nerys doesn't believe Dukat when he claims that her mother, Meru, had been his lover for many years. Consulting the Bajoran Orb of Time, Kira finds herself in the past, at the refugee center where her family once lived. When Kira and Meru are rounded up to become "comfort women" for Cardassian troops, Meru is singled out by Gul Dukat.

142. Inquisition

Bashir becomes the focus of an investigation by Starfleet Intelligence when Deputy Director Sloan interviews him about an alleged security breach. Although his initial questions seem innocuous, Sloan accuses Bashir of having been brainwashed by the Dominion, and he has the doctor placed in a holding cell. Sisko and his fellow officers side with the doctor, but as the internal affairs officer grills Bashir, his friends start believing that Bashir may be a Dominion spy.

143. In the Pale Moonlight

The Federation needs allies in its war against the Dominion; therefore, Sisko recruits Garak to program a data rod with false evidence. Sisko hopes that the forgery will jolt the Romulans into joining the Federation's side. In order to obtain the forgery, Sisko must free a criminal from a Klingon prison and supply the man with a highly illegal medical substance. Unfortunately, Romulan Senator Vreenak determines that the information is false, and he threatens to expose Sisko's deception.

144. His Way

Unable to express his feelings for Kira, Odo turns to the holosuite character Vic Fontaine for advice. Vic is a holographic facsimile of a 1960s Las Vegas lounge singer who is strangely perceptive about affairs of the heart. Vic turns Odo into a tuxedo-clad piano player. He then sends him on a "trial run" with a pair of beautiful holosuite showgirls—so that Odo can get the hang of being romantic. Next Vic introduces him to Lola, a sexy hologram chanteuse who looks exactly like the major. Odo learns to flirt, but he can't bring himself to kiss her because she doesn't *act* like Kira. Finally, Vic lies and tells Odo that he's overhauled the Lola program. The woman Odo will be taking to dinner actually is the object of his dreams.

145. The Reckoning

A stone tablet found on Bajor is inscribed in ancient Bajoran writing that translates to "Welcome, Emissary." A vision from the Prophets prompts Sisko to take the artifact to Deep Space 9 to translate the rest of the inscription. Kai Winn protests that removing the tablet will anger the Prophets. Earthquakes and volcanic eruptions on Bajor lend credence to the kai's words, and Starfleet orders Sisko to return the tablet. Inexplicably, Sisko destroys the tablet. Two strands of energy escape from the broken shards. One inhabits the body of Kira, who announces that the time has come for her to battle Kosst Amojan—an evil Pah-wraith who is the enemy of the Prophets. The other strand chooses to occupy the body of Sisko's son, Jake.

146. Valiant

En route to Ferenginar, Jake Sisko and Nog are saved from an attack by a Jem'Hadar vessel by the *U.S.S. Valiant*. The ship is crewed by a group of young adults that Nog identifies as Red Squad, an elite corps of Starfleet cadets. The "captain," Tim Watters, explains that they were on a training mission when all of the senior officers were killed. The cadets are intent on proving themselves by gathering data on a new Dominion battleship. Jake says that the plan is too risky, but Watters insists that Red Squad is capable of doing anything.

147. Profit and Lace

Following Grand Nagus Zek's decree that Ferengi women should be given equal rights, Ferenginar falls into financial chaos and Zek is deposed by the Ferengi Commerce Authority. Certain that Ishka's amazing business sense will convince the FCA commissioners that gender equality is a good idea, Zek invites them to a meeting. One commissioner, cola magnate Nilva, agrees to attend, but Ishka collapses with coronary distress, leaving Zek without a female to prove his point—unless Quark is willing to allow Bashir to temporarily turn him into a female.

148. Time's Orphan

During a picnic, O'Brien's eight-year-old daughter, Molly, falls into a vortex of swirling energy. The Deep Space 9 crew determines that the girl has slipped through a time portal that sent her back three hundred years. When they transport her out of the portal, Molly materializes as an eighteen-year-old who is so traumatized from having lived alone for a decade that she doesn't recognize her parents and has lost her ability to speak.

149. The Sound of Her Voice

The *Defiant* receives a message from stranded Starfleet Captain Lisa Cusak. The crew plots a course to the remote planet where her ship has crashed. When O'Brien opens communications with Cusak, the relieved captain takes comfort knowing that she will be rescued. But when Bashir learns that Cusak has been giving herself injections to compensate for the carbon dioxide in the atmosphere, he realizes there's not enough to last until the *Defiant* arrives.

150. Tears of the Prophets

As Starfleet Command takes the offensive in the Dominion War, they choose Sisko to lead the invasion of Cardassia. On the eve of the invasion, Sisko experiences a vision from the Prophets, telling him to stay behind. Admiral Ross orders him to decide whether he is the Emissary or a Starfleet captain. Sisko moves ahead with plans to lead the mission. The crazed Gul Dukat comes up with his own plan—to attack the Prophets in the wormhole. Using an ancient Bajoran ritual, Dukat allows a Pah-wraith to take possession of his body. On

Deep Space 9, Jadzia Dax visits the Bajoran shrine just as the Dukat/Pah-wraith enters.

Season Seven

151. Image in the Sand

Following the death of Jadzia Dax and the disappearance of the Bajoran wormhole, Sisko takes a leave of absence from Starfleet and retreats to Earth to contemplate how to "make things right." As he attempts to contact the Prophets, who have been imprisoned by the Pah-wraiths, Sisko has a vision of a woman's face buried beneath the sands of the arid world of Tyree. After finding a photo of the woman in his father's house, he learns that the woman, Sarah, was his biological mother. Joseph shows Sisko Sarah's locket, upon which is inscribed in Bajoran, "The Orb of the Emissary." Sisko decides that he must travel to Tyree to find this orb. As he prepares to leave, an assassin plunges a knife into him.

152. Shadows and Symbols

The late Jadzia's husband, Worf, and her friends on Deep Space 9 embark on a mission to win a great victory in her name. On Earth, the new host of the Dax symbiont, Ezri, arrives at Sisko's door. Ezri is looking for help through her difficult period of adjustment, but Sisko is about to embark on a trek to Tyree. Ezri, Jake, and Joseph opt to accompany Sisko, but the captain's path is blocked by nightmarish visions sent to him by the Pah-wraiths.

153. Afterimage

With the wormhole restored, Counselor Ezri Dax joins Sisko and Jake as they return triumphantly to Deep Space 9. Despite the familiar atmosphere, Dax feels like a stranger amid her old friends, who have difficulty getting used to her new appearance. As she struggles to fit in, Sisko asks her to counsel Garak, who has become increasingly moody and claustrophobic while decoding Cardassian military strategies for Starfleet. But Garak resists her efforts and attempts to throw himself out of an airlock. Meanwhile, she tries to reconnect with Worf, but the Klingon rejects her efforts, saying he does not want to know her.

154. Take Me Out to the Holosuite

When Sisko's longtime rival Solok, a Vulcan Starfleet captain, challenges Sisko to a game of baseball, he readily accepts. The Vulcan team is well practiced at the ancient Earth sport, while no one on Sisko's crew has ever played the game. The practice sessions for the Niners—Sisko's team—are grueling. Sisko is especially hard on Rom, whose attempts at playing are hopeless.

155. Chrysalis

Genetically enhanced geniuses Jack, Lauren, Patrick, and Sarina escape from their medical facility to seek out Bashir. They're hoping that he can develop a cure for the near-catatonic Sarina. Bashir experiments with a surgical procedure, and after a few days the beautiful young Sarina speaks for the first time. As she begins to blossom, Bashir can't help falling in love with her.

156. Treachery, Faith, and the Great River

Odo responds to a coded message directing him to rendezvous with the sender on a deserted moon, but he is surprised to discover that the sender is a clone of the Vorta Weyoun. This Weyoun claims that he wants to exchange valuable information for asylum. As they head back to Deep Space 9, Weyoun tells Odo the history of the Vorta and the Founders, and he makes a startling revelation: the Founders are dying of a mysterious illness that has spread throughout the Great Link.

157. Once More Unto the Breach

Elderly Klingon warrior Kor seeks one last fight so he can die with honor. Worf secures a commission for him as third officer on Martok's flagship. But that appointment angers Martok, who holds a grudge against the old warrior. Martok continually belittles Kor, but when the general and Worf are injured, Kor takes charge of the ship, revealing that he is not up to the task.

158. The Siege of AR-558

Sisko, Ezri, Nog, Bashir, and Quark beam down to an outpost located at the war's front lines on the barren planet AR-558. The shell-shocked troops there have been under attack by the Jem'Hadar for months. While Ezri attempts to find a way to make the Dominion's deadly subspace mines visible, Sisko sends Nog and the base's ranking officer, Chief Larkin, on a scouting patrol to find the enemy's base. The patrol is successful, but Larkin is killed, and Nog is badly injured.

159. Covenant

Kira is thrilled when Vedek Fala, the monk who first instructed her in the Bajoran faith, pays her an unexpected visit. His visit is an excuse to kidnap and transport her to a space station that's peopled by Pah-wraith disciples. Kira's shock at her old friend's behavior turns to horror when she meets the leader of the cult: Dukat, who is determined to prove to her that they're bound together by destiny.

160. It's Only a Paper Moon

Traumatized by the loss of his leg, Nog attempts to hide from reality by retreating into Vic Fontaine's holographic lounge. Ezri's attempts to counsel the Ferengi fail to have an impact, so Vic offers Nog a more unorthodox brand of "therapy."

161. Prodigal Daughter

O'Brien disappears while searching for his friend Bilby's wife, so Sisko sends Ezri Dax to ask her family, which has close ties with authorities in that region, to help find O'Brien. Ezri sees that little has changed at home; her mother, Yanas, still dominates her two brothers, Janel and Norvo. The local authorities discover that the criminal Orion Syndicate is holding O'Brien as their prisoner.

162. Emperor's New Cloak

Quark, who always had a crush on Jadzia Dax, is jealous when Ezri Dax begins spending time with Bashir. He's so obsessed with the Trill that he pays little attention as Rom tells him that the nagus has disappeared. When Ezri shows up at his door, Quark is delighted, although the knife she's brandishing is a bit disconcerting. He learns that this is the Ezri from the mirror universe, and she has brought some news: Grand Nagus Zek is being held prisoner in her universe. All Quark has to do to save his leader is to steal a ship's cloaking device.

163. Field of Fire

Not long after Ezri joins in the celebration for a young pilot's successful turn at the helm of the *Defiant*, she learns that the man has been murdered. The counselor feels a deep need to investigate his death. It appears the murderer used a prototype rifle that only Starfleet officers have access to. When a second murder takes place, and then a third, Ezri decides to consult with her homicidal former host, Joran.

164. Chimera

As Odo and O'Brien return to the station, they encounter a large life-form "swimming" through space. When the creature shape shifts and enters the runabout, Odo realizes that it is one of the hundred changelings—like himself—that were sent out to explore the galaxy by the Founders. The changeling, Laas, admits that he doesn't like humanoids. When Laas invites Odo to join him on his search for the rest of the hundred, Odo must choose between his love for Kira or living as a changeling.

165. Badda-Bing, Badda-Bang

Vic Fontaine's holosuite program suddenly shifts to a new level, and a gangster named Frankie Eyes takes over the lounge and has Vic beat up. O'Brien and Bashir would like to help Vic, but they can't deactivate the program without impairing the holographic character's memories. The program will reset if Frankie Eyes's character is eliminated. Bashir recruits the rest of the Deep Space 9 crew to help him get rid of Frankie in a way that will fit the program's 1960s Las Vegas context.

166. *Inter Arma Enim Silent Leges*

Sloan, the nefarious operative from the covert intelligence agency Section 31, asks Bashir to gather information about the Romulan leadership at a conference the doctor is about to attend, but Bashir refuses. Sisko suggests Bashir change his mind and do as Sloan asks; that way they may be able to learn more about Sloan's organization. At the conference, Bashir meets with Admiral Ross and Romulan Senator Cretak. To the doctor's surprise, Sloan is also in attendance, as a Federation cartographer. Bashir consults with Ross, who advises the doctor to let Sloan play out his hand.

167. Penumbra

Sisko makes plans to build a house on Bajor and asks Kasidy to marry him. The Prophet that he's come to know as "Sarah" appears to Sisko in a vision and warns him that marriage is not a part of his destiny. Kira reports that Worf's ship has been ambushed in Dominion territory, and he isn't listed among the sur-vivors. Ezri disobeys Sisko's orders, steals a runabout, and goes looking for her former host's husband.

168. 'Til Death Do Us Part

At long last, Kai Winn seems to experience a vision from the Prophets, giving her apparent insight into the restoration of Bajor. Meanwhile, Ezri and Worf find themselves prisoners on a Breen ship. On the station, Gul Dukat, surgically altered to resemble a Bajoran farmer, pays Winn a visit. As he echoes the words delivered to her by the Prophets, Winn believes that they wish her to work with this "simple man of the land" who calls himself Anjohl. Winn joins her fate with Anjohl, unaware that she has become her worst enemy's pawn.

169. Strange Bedfellows

After learning that the Breen have formed an alliance with the Dominion, Worf and Ezri are transferred to a Jem'Hadar ship that takes them to Cardassia. On the planet, Legate Damar begins to see that his people's alliance with the Dominion is not going to have a happy ending. After Weyoun allows five hundred thousand Cardassian soldiers to die because it wasn't strategically advantageous to help them, Damar makes a surprising decision about his future. Meanwhile, Kai Winn is dismayed to learn that the visions she's been receiving come from the evil Pah-wraiths.

170. The Changing Face of Evil

The Breen have attacked Earth. Deciding that he must protect Cardassia at all costs, Damar orders attacks on several Dominion outposts and urges all Cardassians to rise up against the Founders. On the station, Kai Winn discovers that Anjohl actually is Gul Dukat, but their mutual involvement with the Pah-wraiths keeps them together in an unholy alliance.

171. When It Rains . . .

Sisko awaits a replacement for the destroyed *Defiant*, and Starfleet decides to help Damar and his resistance fighters by sending a strategic task force of Kira, Odo, and Garak to Cardassia. On Deep Space 9, Gowron shocks everyone by announcing that he personally is replacing Martok as commander of the Klingon forces. Bashir has devastating news: Odo is showing signs of the disease that is killing the Founders.

172. Tacking Into the Wind

Odo grows weaker, but he insists on continuing his mission with Kira and Garak. Bashir has discovered that Section 31 is behind the Founders' disease and works around the clock to find a cure. Gowron refuses to take the blame for his failing strategies, using the critically wounded Martok as a scapegoat. Sisko advises Worf to find a way to prevent the chancellor from leading the Klingon Empire into ruin. Meanwhile, Damar, Kira, Odo, and Garak attempt to steal an energy-dampening weapon from a Jem'Hadar ship.

173. Extreme Measures

Garak and Kira bring Odo back to the station for treatment. Bashir and O'Brien plot to lure someone from Section 31 to the station so they can find out if there's a cure. When Section 31 operative Sloan arrives, Bashir stuns him, but as the doctor prepares to interrogate him, Sloan activates a suicide device.

174. The Dogs of War

Quark believes that Grand Nagus Zek—who has announced his retirement—is going to name him as the new nagus. Meanwhile,

Kira, Garak, and Damar beam down to Cardassia and find that Jem'Hadar forces have destroyed Damar's resistance bases. Trapped in a cellar, the trio hopes that Damar's growing stature can rally the Cardassians to revolution. At the Dominion's Cardassian headquarters, the leader of the Founders learns that the Federation has developed a countermeasure to the Breen weapon. She orders her forces to concentrate in one area of space until they can build more ships and clone more warriors.

175./176. What You Leave Behind

On Deep Space 9, the crew says good-bye to their loved ones—including the newly pregnant Kasidy—as they prepare to depart for their attack on the Dominion defense perimeter. Even the ailing Founder leader knows that this battle will determine the outcome of the war. On Bajor, Kai Winn has discovered how to release the Pah-wraiths from the fire caves the Prophets trapped them in eons ago. Dukat offers Winn his assistance, particularly in dealing with Sisko, the Prophets' Emissary. On Cardassia, Kira, Damar, and Garak mount an assault on Dominion headquarters.

Even as the tide begins to turn in the Federation's favor, Odo makes a personal plea to the Founder leader to surrender. Down in the fire caves of Bajor, a dark ritual has begun, and Sisko knows he's the only one who can stop it.

> *"That's one of the great things about this station. You never know what's going to happen next . . . or who you're going to meet."* —Sisko, "Second Sight"

Kathryn Janeway learned to work with and totally trust Chakotay.

FIVE

STAR TREK: VOYAGER

"Are We There Yet?"

172 hour-long episodes, 1995–2001

SERIES PREMISE

DURING THE SAME TIME PERIOD THAT CAPTAIN SISKO IS DEFENDING DEEP SPACE 9 from threats originating in the Gamma Quadrant, a heroic Starfleet captain and her crew are swept up by powerful alien technology (see "A Three-Hour Tour . . . ," p. 177) and stranded in the distant Delta Quadrant, seventy thousand light-years from home. Even at maximum warp, the trip back to the Alpha Quadrant will take the *Starship Voyager* seventy-five years. What's a captain to do during that lengthy voyage? Pretty much the same thing as her Starfleet predecessors: explore strange new worlds, seek out new life and new civilizations—and make sure there's enough coffee on board for the journey.

THE SHIP

The *U.S.S. Voyager* NCC-74656 is an *Intrepid*-class spacecraft with a combined crew complement of approximately 150. (That number fluctuates, decreasing by unfortunate mishaps and increasing by the captain's propensity for picking up hitchhikers, refugees, and former militants.) Most primary crew members are Starfleet personnel, but the Maquis—a group of militants who oppose certain Federation policies (see Who or What Are the Maquis?, p. 178)—also serve in key positions.

Voyager is a lot smaller than Picard's *Enterprise*, but it's fast and powerful. It has the capacity to land on a planet's surface and take off again—no small accomplishment when it comes to starships. And it's one of the most technologically advanced ships in the fleet, with computer circuitry that actually utilizes synthetic neural tissue (see A Very Brainy Ship!, p. 178). However, because they have a long journey ahead, crew members conserve resources where they can. *Voyager* is equipped with state-of-the-art holodecks, just like those on the *Enterprise*-D, but you'll often find the crew watching low-tech (less energy-consuming) movies. They have replicators, but the crew usually chows down on food prepared by the ship's self-appointed cook, Neelix. Equipped primarily for exploration and research, *Voyager* can operate independently for three years without refueling. Too bad it will be away from Federation service stations for seven and a half decades . . .

> "Part of becoming human is learning to have compassion for those who are suffering . . . even when they're your bitter enemies."
>
> —Janeway, "Prey"

KATHRYN JANEWAY (Kate Mulgrew), captain

> We're alone in an uncharted part of the galaxy . . . but our primary goal is clear: somewhere, along this journey, we'll find a way back.
> —"CARETAKER"

Born in Indiana, Kathryn Janeway is a scientist with a Starfleet pedigree (her dad was an admiral). She's a natural leader who has what it takes to command a ship—that's why she was entrusted with *Voyager*. Unfortunately, one of her earliest command decisions sentenced her crew to what could be a lifetime away from home.

What did Janeway do? After *Voyager* got zapped to the Delta Quadrant, she decided *not* to push the button that would have instantly sent the ship back home. She had a good reason. By *not* pushing the button, she prolonged the lives of a dying species. That's the kind of rationale that motivates a Starfleet captain, particularly one who's worthy of their own television series.

Janeway's crew approves of her decisions most of the time, even the Maquis—who joined her crew after their ship was destroyed.

Janeway left her fiancée and dog back on Earth; it's unclear which one she misses more. Her biggest vice is coffee; the fact that Starbucks has yet to extend its franchise to the Delta Quadrant only intensifies her compulsion to get home as quickly as possible.

Key Janeway Episodes

- "Macrocosm"
- "Year of Hell"
- "Bride of Chaotica!"
- "Endgame"

CHAKOTAY (Robert Beltran), first officer

> No one chooses for me. I choose my own way.
> And if that makes me a Contrary, I'll have to
> live with it.
> —"TATTOO"

Chakotay (just one name, like Cher) might best be described as "conflicted." Born on a colony world inhabited by expatriate Native Americans, Chakotay is deeply proud of his ancestry, although he spent his youth rebelling against that heritage. He defied his father's wishes by leaving their tribe to join Starfleet, yet he wears a tribal tattoo to honor his father. He believes in Starfleet ideals, yet he left that organization to join the Maquis—a group that opposes Starfleet policies. He cast his lot with Janeway—a by-the-book Starfleet captain— and stood against those Maquis who refused to follow her orders.

To Chakotay, all of these U-turns in behavior make perfect sense. His father blamed Chakotay's "contrary" nature on his breech birth (he was delivered feet first)—which is as good an explanation as any.

Key Chakotay Episodes

- "Tattoo"
- "Unity"
- "Nemesis"
- "Shattered"

TOM PARIS (Robert Duncan McNeill), conn officer

I made a mistake . . . and it nearly ruined my life.

—"FAIR TRADE"

Descended from a long, distinguished line of Starfleet career officers, Tom Paris proved a disappointment to everyone, particularly himself. He was drummed out of Starfleet Academy after he lied about his involvement in an accident that killed several students. With nowhere to go, he joined a group of rebel Maquis but was quickly captured by authorities and thrown into a Federation prison. He was released after he agreed to help Kathryn Janeway find his former Maquis colleagues. He found them all right, but then *Voyager* was tossed into the Delta Quadrant, and Paris found himself serving alongside a lot of men and women—both Starfleet and Maquis—who didn't particularly like him.

Fortunately, Tom is a surprisingly likable guy, not to mention a damn good pilot. Eventually, he gained the captain's confidence, mended fences with the Maquis, became best friends with the most straight-arrow person on board, designed a one-of-a-kind shuttlecraft, and successfully wooed the ship's lovely half-Klingon engineer.

Key Paris Episodes

- "Threshold"
- "Thirty Days"
- "Bride of Chaotica!"
- "Alice"

TUVOK (Tim Russ), chief tactical officer

My logic was not in error—but I was.

—"PRIME FACTORS"

He may not look it, but Tuvok is probably the oldest person on the ship. He's over one hundred—middle-aged by Vulcan standards—and he's been in Starfleet a long time. Granted, he did take a fifty-one-year leave at one point (during which time he got married and raised a family), but he's still a senior officer, no matter how you look at it.

Like most Vulcans, Tuvok is dedicated to the proposition that logic is the cornerstone of civilization. Unlike most Vulcans, he has an illogical ornery streak that dates back to his adolescent years. Back then, Tuvok could have given James Dean a run for his money as a rebel without a cause—questioning adult authority, balking at emotional constraints, falling in love with the wrong girl. He eventually shaped up, but even as an adult he has an occasional tendency to err on the side of the not quite logical. Of course, none of those errors in judgment stop him from espousing all of the traditional platitudes about how disciplined the Vulcan mind is. Right.

Key Tuvok Episodes

- **"Meld"**
- **"Flashback"**
- **"Gravity"**

HARRY KIM (Garrett Wang), operations/communications officer

> I'm like some kind of Borg drone, programmed, except I was designed to be the perfect Starfleet officer.
>
> —"THE DISEASE"

Harry is the newbie, the earnest guy on his first posting, still wet behind the ears. His lack of experience is balanced by his fervent desire to live up to the captain's expectations, which makes him a bit of a Boy Scout. Ironically, his best friend is *Voyager*'s resident black sheep, Tom Paris.

Harry is the only son of warm, loving parents. He was the perfect child—bright, ambitious, and talented. Wholesome Harry has a sweetheart back in San Francisco to whom he's pledged his love. However, under Paris's tutelage, Harry has come to realize that San Francisco is far, far away, while coworkers like the Delaney sisters are right down the corridor.

Key Kim Episodes

- "Non Sequitur"
- "The Disease"
- "Nightingale"

B'ELANNA TORRES (Roxann Dawson), chief engineer

When I was a child, I did everything I could to hide my forehead.
—"FACES"

Voyager's chief engineer is half-Klingon, half-human. Torres has always been deeply ashamed of her nonhuman lineage and blames her lifelong inability to play well with others on her Klingon temperament and appearance. During her brief stint at Starfleet Academy, she excelled in the sciences but found herself at odds with her instructors and colleagues over almost every aspect of Starfleet life. She left during her second year. Like fellow dropout Tom Paris, she followed her stint at Starfleet by joining the Maquis resistance, where she met Chakotay and found her true calling as an engineer. After the Maquis were stranded in the Delta Quadrant, Torres accompanied Chakotay to *Voyager*, where Janeway recognized her skills and rewarded her with the top slot in engineering.

B'Elanna dislikes her Klingon side, and she still finds it hard to deal with interpersonal relationships, particularly intimate ones. But if anyone is more hardheaded than Torres, it's Tom Paris, who's determined to make theirs a coupling that lasts.

Key Torres Episodes
- "Parallax"
- "Faces"
- "Lineage"

"Get the cheese to sickbay."
—Torres, "Learning Curve"

THE DOCTOR (Robert Picardo), Emergency Medical Hologram

> **Please state the nature of the medical emergency.**
> —**"CARETAKER"**

Although he looks and sounds just like a human being, the Doctor actually is an extremely sophisticated interactive program. You may not be able to find the software at your local Best Buy, but you can on most new Federation starships. He's officially referred to as the Emergency Medical Hologram (EMH), designed to assist flesh-and-blood medical personnel in dire situations. But after all of *Voyager*'s medical personnel were killed en route to the Delta Quadrant, the EMH was put into service full-time.

The Doctor resents being viewed as just another piece of equipment. Since he is, for all intents and purposes, a permanent member of *Voyager*'s crew, he feels he should be treated as one. His acquisition of an autonomous holo-emitter (see Mobile Emitter, p. 178) helped his cause, allowing him to leave sickbay and to share more experiences with his biological colleagues.

Although an excellent physician, programmed with more than five million medical treatments, the Doctor is a bit of a pill: condescending, arrogant, and often downright insulting. He got his personality (and his looks) from Doctor Lewis Zimmerman, the crusty fellow who designed him.

Key Doctor Episodes

- "Real Life"
- "Someone to Watch Over Me"
- "Author, Author"

NEELIX (Ethan Phillips), trader/cook/guide/morale officer

Whatever you need is what I have to offer. . . . And I anticipate your first need will be me.
—"CARETAKER"

Neelix is a Talaxian. For a guy whose homeworld was ravaged by a war that destroyed his entire family, he is annoyingly chipper.

He was a trader of junk and debris when *Voyager* came upon him. Janeway enlisted his aid to help her find missing members of her crew on the Ocampa world. She subsequently allowed Neelix and his Ocampan beloved, Kes, to accompany them on *Voyager*'s long journey.

Although Neelix's relationship with Kes didn't last, he's been able to develop an alliance with the crew, despite the fact that he isn't terribly good at any of his responsibilities aboard the ship.

Neelix is brave when it counts, and a loving father figure to little Naomi Wildman. When push comes to shove, most of the crew would prefer to keep him around than vote him off the starship.

Key Neelix Episodes

- "Tuvix"
- "Mortal Coil"
- "Homestead"

"Well, whatever happens, I try to keep in mind that things could be worse."
—Neelix, "Scientific Method"

KES (Jennifer Lien), amateur botanist/medical assistant

If I were captain, I'd open every crack in the universe and peek inside.

—"THE CLOUD"

Kes is a native of Ocampa, a barren rock ball of a world that she chose to abandon in order to hitch a ride on *Voyager*. She was nearly two years old then, and since the Ocampan life span is only nine years, two is theoretically old enough to vote, drink, *and* run away from home. Kes's sweetheart at the time was a Talaxian named Neelix, but she eventually outgrew him (at three).

During her journey, Kes sought ways to expand her range of knowledge. She learned about hydroponics and grew veggies for the crew. She became a promising medical assistant. And Tuvok taught her how to expand her latent telepathic abilities. Eventually, however, those abilities intensified to a point where she could no longer control them.

Realizing that she was becoming a danger to her shipmates, Kes left *Voyager* and struck out on her own. Her parting gift to her friends was to teleport the ship nine thousand five hundred light-years closer to the Alpha Quadrant.

Key Kes Episodes

- "Elogium"
- "Warlord"
- "The Gift"

"There are things that I'm not satisfied with. I want . . . complication in my life."

—Kes, "Darkling"

SEVEN OF NINE (Jeri Ryan), Borg drone

> I am no longer Borg . . . but the prospect of
> becoming human is . . . unsettling. I don't know
> where I belong.
>
> —"HOPE AND FEAR"

Born Annika Hansen, she was captured and
assimilated by the cybernetic species known as
the Borg when she was very young. The Borg
renamed her Seven of Nine, Tertiary Adjunct
of Unimatrix Zero One. That's a real mouthful,
so her new friends on *Voyager* just call her
Seven.

Seven was assigned as the Borg liaison to
Voyager when the Collective formed a temporary alliance with Janeway to defeat their
mutual enemy, Species 8472. But you just can't

trust a Borg; after they got rid of Species 8472,
Seven tried to hand *Voyager* over to the
Collective. Janeway responded by destroying
Seven's link to the Borg and removing most of
her high-tech hardware (she was allowed to
keep a fetching piece of facial jewelry and a
punk-looking glove).

Seven initially resisted Janeway's attempts
to restore her humanity, but eventually she
came to accept her new life—even the
Doctor's occasionally overbearing attempts to
play Professor Higgins to her Eliza Doolittle.

Key Seven Episodes
- "Scorpion"
- "Drone"
- "Dark Frontier"

MAJOR ALIENS

Ocampa

A short-lived—nine years, on average—species of humanoids native to the Delta Quadrant. A thousand years ago, Nacene exploring the planet Ocampa accidentally caused an ecological disaster that destroyed the atmosphere's ability to generate rain. They felt kind of bad about this, so they left behind two of their people to look after the Ocampa. One, who became known as the Caretaker, created an underground city for the Ocampa to live in and provided power for the city from the Array, his nearby space station. The other one, Suspiria, left after a while, taking two thousand Ocampa with her to settle on a second Array in a different part of the Quadrant.

Talaxians

A humanoid species from the planet Talax, in the Delta Quadrant. Their recent history is rather sad: thirty thousand Talaxians were killed in a war with a species known as the Haakonians. For the most part, Talaxians are a sociable bunch that enjoy many homespun traditions—like recounting the history of a meal before eating it (which, in Neelix's case, helps to distract from the unpredictable quality of his cuisine).

Kazon

A violent race that was once culturally and technologically advanced (probably friendlier too)—until it was conquered by another species. These days, all that remains of Kazon society is a bunch of tribal sects that live primarily aboard their spaceships and never stop warring with each other (see You Can't Tell the Kazon Without a Scorecard, p. 173). The Kazon are fond of stealing other species's ships and technology, making *Voyager* a natural target.

Vidiians

Contracted a horrific disease known as the phage (think the black plague but a lot worse) that decimated their population. The phage literally consumed the Vidiians' bodies, leaving them terribly scarred and destroying their internal organs. To prolong their lives, they became experts at organ transplantation. When they ran out of healthy Vidiian organs, they looked to other species for donors, voluntary or involuntary. Mostly the latter.

Species 8472

We don't know the actual name of this highly advanced, telepathic life-form from fluidic space (a dimension where all matter is made up of organic fluid). They were designated Species 8472 by the Borg (who number every species they come upon). The Borg decided to assimilate them into the Collective, but 8472's powerful immune systems rejected all intrusion by Borg nanoprobes (see Little Things Mean a Lot, p. 179). Species 8472's technology is biologically based—they fly organic spacecraft and use biogenetically engineered weapons that are more powerful than anything the Borg have.

Hirogen

Humanoid with slightly reptilian features, the Hirogen are relentless hunters. Their sole occupation is to hunt down and kill prey—pretty much anyone they encounter. A Hirogen's social status is determined by the prizes—mostly body parts of their prey—gathered in the hunts. The Hirogen once created an extremely powerful communications network; some of their relay stations were still operational, so *Voyager*'s crew used one to send a message to the Alpha Quadrant.

Borg

The Delta Quadrant is the Borg's home turf. They're essentially the same Borg we met in *The Next Generation*, obsessed with assimilation of every worthwhile culture and technology. In the Delta Quadrant, however, we learn that resistance isn't always futile; Borg drones who are cut off from the Collective have a good chance of regaining their individuality, as evidenced by Seven of Nine and a number of others. We also learn how the sneaky Borg can pop up just about anywhere at any time—via a system of "transwarp hubs" that connect with thousands of intragalactic conduits to every part of space.

BORG QUEEN (Susanna Thompson and Alice Krige), Borg leader

Although Captain Picard and the crew of the *Enterprise* eliminated the first Borg queen that humanity ever encountered (see p. 236), the Collective apparently can create a new queen whenever it needs to. Bad luck for Janeway.

Vulcans

Only two Vulcans were aboard *Voyager* when the ship entered the Delta Quadrant, both of them male. Since Vulcans experience the *Pon farr* mating urge every seven years, this was bound to cause certain . . . uh . . . problems sooner or later. Tuvok dealt with his problem by spending some private time with a holographic re-creation of his wife. Vorik chose a more direct approach by attempting to convince B'Elanna Torres to be his one and only. Torres rejected his advances and engaged the Vulcan in a ritual battle. Although Vorik lost the match, the battle purged him of the *Pon farr.*

Ktarians

A humanoid species native to the Alpha Quadrant. Ktarians have a row of sharp exocranial ridges that run down the center of the forehead.

NAOMI WILDMAN (Brooke Stephens and Scarlett Pomer), precocious young girl

Naomi was the first baby to be born on the *Starship Voyager.* She didn't stay a baby for long; although her mother is human crew member Samantha Wildman, Naomi inherited her forehead ridges and her rapid development from her Ktarian father. By the time Naomi reached her second year, she had the size and smarts of a child several years older. With Dad back in the Alpha Quadrant, Neelix fills in as a quasi father figure. Naomi also is fond of Seven of Nine.

"I'm willing to explore my humanity. Take off your clothes." —Seven of Nine, "Revulsion"

YOU CAN'T TELL THE KAZON WITHOUT A SCORECARD. The Kazon Collective is made up of a loose alliance of various sects that hate each other's guts: the Kazon-Hobii, the Kazon-Mostral, the Kazon-Nistrim, the Kazon-Ogla, the Kazon-Oglamar, the Kazon-Pommar, and the Kazon-Relora. Janeway once tried to bring all of the players together for a peace conference, but since it was rather like trying to get the CIA and the FBI to play together, the conference didn't go well.

THE MENAGERIE

Q

What's up with the Q? They're the same extradimensional species we first met in *The Next Generation*. However, after spending billions of years doing the same old, same old, the Q Continuum as a whole goes through some radical (for a set-in-its-ways species) changes during this period. Immortal for as far back as they can recall, one Q breaks ranks and commits suicide. The resulting chaos in the Continuum triggers a civil war between those who want to preserve the status quo and those who wish to experience individualism.

IMPORTANT Q

Q (John de Lancie), omnipotent being

Yeah, it's that pushy guy who used to bug Picard, but he has a friendlier, more flirtatious relationship with Janeway. Ultimately, he hooks up with a female Q whom he's been dating for about four billion years, and they conceive a child. Janeway is young Q's godmother.

> **NOW HEAR THIS!** *Voyager* takes place on a starship and is about exploration, just like *Star Trek* and *The Next Generation*. Unlike those shows, however, the crew of the *Starship Voyager* isn't exploring to increase humankind's knowledge of space; it's exploring to find a shortcut home.

Cardassians

Voyager's crew doesn't like this species any better than the folks in the Alpha Quadrant do. Fortunately, there's only one of them to contend with in the Delta Quadrant.

IMPORTANT CARDASSIAN

SESKA (Martha Hackett), undercover agent

Seska is a Cardassian whose appearance was surgically altered so she could infiltrate the Maquis. She was aboard Chakotay's Maquis ship when it got pulled into the Delta Quadrant, and she subsequently became a member of Janeway's crew. The captain discovered her duplicity only after Seska started dealing with the Kazon behind her back. At that point, Seska jumped ship and linked her fate to the Kazon, with whom she managed to capture *Voyager*. The crew took it back, and Seska was killed in the ensuing battle.

> *"There's coffee in that nebula."*
> —Janeway, "The Cloud'

> **DID YOU KNOW** that when an Ocampan female becomes fertile, she gets insatiably hungry and starts eating everything, including any flowers her suitor may send her—and the dirt in which they're planted. Maybe the Delta Quadrant FTD franchise should promote a bouquet of hamburgers with extra pickles.

TEN ESSENTIAL EPISODES

1. **"Caretaker" Teleplay by Michael Piller & Jeri Taylor. Story by Rick Berman & Michael Piller, and Jeri Taylor.**

While searching for a missing officer, Janeway and the crew of the *Starship Voyager* are swept seventy thousand light-years from home.

Voyager's two-hour premiere introduces us to most of the series's main characters and to the predicament that will occupy them for the next seven years.

2. **"Flashback" Written by Brannon Braga.**

Tuvok experiences a repressed memory that's linked to his first Starfleet assignment under command of the renowned Sulu.

This tribute episode produced for the thirtieth anniversary of Star Trek *plays upon an incident from the motion picture* Star Trek VI: The Undiscovered Country, *and brings back* Star Trek *favorites Sulu, Janice Rand, and Klingon warrior Kang.*

3. **"Scorpion, Parts I and II" Written by Brannon Braga & Joe Menosky.**

Faced with a more dangerous enemy than the Borg, Janeway makes a deal with the Borg—and adds a new shipmate to *Voyager's* roster: a Borg drone.

She's one of Voyager's *most fascinating characters—and, yes, she's also the sexiest woman in the Delta Quadrant. This suspenseful two-parter introduces ex-Borg Seven of Nine.*

4. **"Year of Hell, Parts I and II" Written by Brannon Braga & Joe Menosky.**

After an alien scientist deploys a temporal weapon of mass destruction, Janeway and the crew spend a horrific year dodging his attacks and trying to restore the altered timeline.

This intellectually stimulating two-parter, which had enough plot to fill an entire year's worth of episodes, succeeds in putting every character through . . . well, hell, before its explosive conclusion.

5. **"Timeless" Teleplay by Brannon Braga & Joe Menosky. Story by Rick Berman & Brannon Braga and Joe Menosky.**

An older and wiser Kim attempts to revise history after his mistake causes *Voyager's* destruction.

One of the highlights of this episode— Voyager's *one hundredth episode—is an appearance by Geordi La Forge (of* The Next Generation) *and* Voyager's *sensational crash landing on an ice planet.*

6. **"Bride of Chaotica!" Teleplay by Bryan Fuller & Michael Taylor. Story by Bryan Fuller.**

A holodeck installment of "The Adventures of Captain Proton" (see Captain Proton, p. 178) becomes serious business for the crew when confused aliens wage war against the perceived threat of the fictional Doctor Chaotica.

Watching the main cast of Voyager *play out a Flash Gordon scenario is a treat—particularly Kate Mulgrew's turn as the seductive Arachnia, Queen of the Spider People.*

7. **"Dark Frontier, Parts I and II" Written by Brannon Braga & Joe Menosky.**

When Seven of Nine is lured back to the Borg collective, Janeway launches an all-out mission to rescue her.

The film Star Trek: First Contact's *deliciously*

Voyager becomes a pawn in an alien's obsession to restore his family.

evil Borg queen returns to the Star Trek *universe, in this, the first of several appearances the character makes in the series.*

8. **"Relativity" Teleplay by Bryan Fuller & Nick Sagan & Michael Taylor. Story by Nick Sagan.**

Voyager's future depends on Seven's success in preventing an explosion in the past.

An enjoyably convoluted tale that introduces the notion that Starfleet of the twenty-ninth century will be able to travel through time as routinely as twenty-fourth-century starships travel through space.

9. **"Blink of an Eye" Teleplay by Joe Menosky. Story by Michael Taylor.**

Trapped in orbit above a prewarp planet, *Voyager* must wait until the planet's technology advances to the point where it can help free the ship.

Each second on Voyager *is equivalent to a day on the planet below—which sets up the intriguing plot for this episode.*

10. **"Endgame" Teleplay by Kenneth Biller & Robert Doherty. Story by Rick Berman & Kenneth Biller & Brannon Braga.**

An aging Janeway travels into the past to help her younger self bring *Voyager* home sooner than later.

The writers combine two of Voyager*'s most successful plot devices—time travel and the Borg— to generate a satisfying conclusion to the series.*

"Captain . . . I think I should tell you I've never actually landed a starship before."
—Paris, "The 37's"

WHERE'D THEY GET ALL THOSE SHUTTLECRAFTS? Standard equipment on a vessel like *Voyager* includes an allotment of two, count 'em, two shuttlecrafts. But over the course of seven years, they went through what seems like dozens of them. Blame it on some sort of inventory malfunction.

THE "SPOCK'S BRAIN" AWARD. "Threshold" is the *Voyager* episode most likely to give Darwin a migraine. Here we learn that one unfortunate result of a human achieving warp 10 (*Star Trek*'s starships typically can't reach this tantalizing threshold) is that the human mutates into a big salamander thingy.

WHAT IT IS . . .

WHO OR WHAT ARE THE MAQUIS?

The Federation's treaty with the Cardassians put an end to years of hostilities between the two powers. It also established new territorial boundaries in space, ceding certain regions to Federation worlds and others to the Cardassians. Many Federation colonists who lived in those regions were ordered to evacuate their homes. Those who refused to relinquish their turf opted to fight against the Cardassians *and* the Federation. They called themselves the Maquis, after members of the French underground who fought against the Nazis in World War II. While the Maquis clearly see themselves as noble, both the Federation and the Cardassians consider them outlaws.

DELTA QUADRANT

No, it's not fraternity row. The Delta Quadrant is the section of the Milky Way galaxy farthest from Federation space. Prior to the *U.S.S. Voyager*'s journey there, little was known about the Delta Quadrant other than that it was home to the Borg.

CAPTAIN PROTON

Leave it to Tom Paris to devise an old-fashioned, black-and-white 1930s-style serial to entertain himself and the crew on *Voyager*'s holodeck (think the adventures of Buck Rogers or Flash Gordon). Tom, of course, cast himself as Captain Proton, Spaceman First Class, Protector of Earth and Scourge of Intergalactic Evil. Captain Proton's archnemesis is the villainous Doctor Chaotica, who, thanks to

Tom's vivid imagination, never runs short of dastardly schemes.

DELTA FLYER

A small and sporty shuttlecraft designed primarily by Tom Paris and built by the *Voyager* crew. The *Flyer* has an "ultra-aerodynamic" shape, a very retro-looking control panel, extremely high-tech hull plating, and superior shielding, not to mention some Borg-style weapons systems, courtesy of Seven of Nine. It's a handy little ship to have around when you're in a tight spot.

MOBILE EMITTER (autonomous holo-emitter)

A miniature holographic imaging projector built with twenty-ninth-century technology. It allows *Voyager*'s Emergency Medical Hologram to leave sickbay and function where holographic equipment has not been installed. The Doctor generally wears the mobile emitter on the sleeve of his uniform.

A VERY BRAINY SHIP!

Voyager's computer system uses bioneural circuitry, or gel packs, that utilize synthetic brain cells. Yup, brain cells that supplement the ship's data-processing capabilities, making them faster and more efficient. It's the first Federation starship to use the new technology—which means *Voyager*'s crew was the first to realize that the gel packs can fall prey to some of the same viruses as organic beings.

Captain Proton and Buster Kincaid, or Tom Paris and Harry Kim.

LITTLE THINGS MEAN A LOT

Nanites are tiny machines that are already in common use—inside your laptop computer, for instance. In *Star Trek*'s bright future, of course, such machines have become much more sophisticated and have many more uses. They're pretty much the Swiss Army knives of the twenty-fourth century. On *Voyager*, you'll also hear a lot about nanoprobes, the end product of the dark side of nanotechnology. The Borg use these submicroscopic robots to assimilate other beings. They inject some nanoprobes into their victims, then sit back and wait for them to turn pasty faced and compliant as the busy little probes attach themselves to blood cells and take over their functions, spreading Borg technology throughout the body. At that point, resistance is . . . Well, you know the rest.

WHAT IS SUBSPACE?

Here's the official definition: "a spatial continuum with significantly different properties from our own." *Oh,* you say, eyes glazing over. Okay, how about this: a region of space that coexists with our own universe but is disconnected in some way. A lot of *Star Trek* gizmos work only when accessing subspace. Warp-drive spaceships, for example, travel through subspace at the speed of light. Messages are transmitted via subspace. Lots of stuff in subspace is different from our stuff. Never read about subspace in science class? That's because *Star Trek*'s writers made it up.

Seven of Nine slowly regains her humanity under Janeway's tutelage.

EPISODE SYNOPSES

SEASON ONE

1./2. Caretaker

Janeway leads the *Starship Voyager* on a mission to find Tuvok, her Vulcan tactical officer. He has been on an undercover assignment to infiltrate a Maquis group led by former Starfleet officer Chakotay. Their ship has been reported missing in the Badlands. Janeway has enlisted the aid of Tom Paris—a Starfleet prisoner and former Maquis—to guide *Voyager* through the Badlands. However, the starship suffers the same fate as Chakotay's ship—it is struck by an unknown energy beam that sends it traveling deep into the Delta Quadrant. Far from home, both Janeway's and Chakotay's crews are subjected to experimentation by a non-humanoid life-form known as "the Caretaker," who is searching for a way to help the devastated Ocampa world.

The trip to the Delta Quadrant kills a number of both ships' crews, making it natural for the crews to combine. Janeway must decide between using the Caretaker's failing equipment to send them all home or protecting the Ocampa from their enemies. She takes the moral high road: Janeway, Chakotay, and their united crew begin taking the slow route back to the Alpha Quadrant.

3. Parallax

Meshing the disparate Starfleet and Maquis crews together proves to be a challenge. The hot-tempered Maquis B'Elanna Torres chooses to end a dispute by breaking a Starfleet officer's nose. Janeway understandably is reluctant to follow Chakotay's suggestion and appoint Torres the ship's chief engineer. But Torres's creative approach to dealing with a trapped vessel leads the captain to reconsider.

4. Time and Again

Voyager's crew comes upon a planet where a cataclysmic explosion has destroyed all life. Janeway and Paris beam down to investigate the cause of the destruction, only to be transported back in time to the day before the explosion. Perceived as spies and taken prisoner, the two can only watch as a group of environmentalists attempts to sabotage a power station— an act that Janeway believes will cause the devastating explosion.

5. Phage

An unidentified alien attacks Neelix and steals his lungs. The Doctor keeps the Talaxian alive by temporarily fitting him with a set of holographic lungs. Meanwhile, Janeway and her team search for the thief. They discover a medical lab filled with harvested organs that have been gathered by the Vidiians and are horrified to learn that Neelix's lungs already have been recycled.

6. The Cloud

Entering a cloudlike nebula, *Voyager* encounters an energy barrier and is bombarded by globules that attach themselves to the ship's hull. Janeway orders the crew to take the ship out of the nebula by firing a photon torpedo. Torres discovers that the globules are organic elements of a larger life-form. The captain worries that they inadvertently may have wounded a living entity. She proposes returning to repair any harm they've done to the nebula—in spite of the entity's natural defense system.

7. Eye of the Needle

Janeway and her crew discover a wormhole that may serve as a shortcut back to the Alpha Quadrant. Although it's too small for *Voyager* to enter, the crew can send a probe—which they discover is being scanned by someone on the other side of the wormhole. When communication finally is established, they realize they've reached a suspicious Romulan scientist.

8. Ex Post Facto

On Banean, Paris is declared guilty of murder. His punishment is to relive the victim's death over and over again, from the victim's point of view. As Janeway works to prove her pilot's innocence, *Voyager* is attacked by the Numiri. With Paris's life in danger, Tuvok launches his own investigation and soon comes up with his own theory.

9. Emanations

After stumbling upon an ancient burial site on an uncharted asteroid, Kim is caught up in a dimensional distortion and trapped in a ceremonial burial pod. Next stop: the planet Vhnori, in another dimension. The body that had been destined for the burial pod is taken to the *Starship Voyager*. As Kim tries to find a way to get home, the *Voyager* crew tries to find a way to get rid of the bodies that are suddenly appearing throughout the ship.

10. Prime Factors

Knowing that shore leave would be good for her crew, Janeway orders *Voyager* to follow hospitable Gath Labin to his planet, Sikaris. Eudana, a Sikarian smitten with Kim, reveals that her planet has the technology to whisk them forty thousand light-years away. *Voyager's* crew realizes the technology could knock decades off their trip home. But when Labin refuses to share the technology, Tuvok and other crew members plot to steal it, over Janeway's objections.

11. State of Flux

Detecting a Kazon vessel nearby, Janeway orders an away team back to *Voyager*, but one crew member, the Bajoran engineer Seska, is missing, apparently trapped by the Kazon. Chakotay rescues her but is injured. Shortly afterward, a Kazon ship is damaged in an explosion that seems to have been caused by Federation technology. Tuvok investigates whether someone on board *Voyager* may have provided technology to the Kazon.

12. Heroes and Demons

After the crew beams aboard samples of photonic matter from a protostar, Kim disappears from a holodeck. Chakotay and Tuvok investigate the program Kim had been running—a holonovel based on *Beowulf*—and meet the character Freya. She reveals that her hero, Kim, acting as Beowulf, has been killed by the monster Grendel. When they encounter Grendel, Chakotay and Tuvok also disappear. Rather than lose more of her crew, Janeway transfers the ship's holographic doctor to the holodeck.

13. Cathexis

Tuvok and Chakotay return from an away mission with Tuvok injured and the first officer apparently brain-dead. Tuvok explains that a strange vessel emerged from a nebula and attacked their shuttlecraft. Janeway orders *Voyager* to the nebula to investigate, but when the ship inexplicably changes course and the warp core shuts down, the captain realizes that the tampering is being caused by an unseen force that is taking over the minds of her crew.

14. Faces

While on an away mission, Paris and Torres fall into the clutches of Sulan, a Vidiian scientist who hopes to use Torres to show that Klingon genes are resistant to the deadly phage disease. Sulan extracts Torres's Klingon genetic material, creating two versions of the engineer: one all-Klingon and one all-human.

15. Jetrel

Neelix is aghast when Jetrel, the Haakonian scientist responsible for the deaths of three hundred thousand of his people, beams aboard *Voyager*. Jetrel claims that he has come to save Neelix from a fatal blood disease many of the Talaxians still carry. Janeway agrees to detour the ship to Talax. When they arrive, Neelix learns that Jetrel's intentions are not what he had told the captain.

16. Learning Curve

Realizing that several of her Maquis crew members can't be expected to follow Starfleet protocols without training, Janeway gives Tuvok the task of training them. One of the students, Dalby, complains to Torres that the sessions are a waste of time. Then some of *Voyager*'s partially biological components begin to malfunction. As an infection spreads throughout the ship's bioneural gel packs, Tuvok and his charges struggle to work together as a team.

Season Two

17. The 37's

Voyager's scanners detect a 1930s pickup truck floating in space. Stranger yet, the truck's AM radio is picking up an old-fashioned SOS signal that leads them to a remote planet—and an airplane from the same era. An away team searching the planet finds a chamber with eight humans held in stasis—including Amelia Earhart. Awakening the humans, Janeway explains who—and when—they are. As the group leaves the chamber, snipers fire at them from the surrounding hills.

18. Initiations

Chakotay takes a shuttlecraft to perform a solitary ritual commemorating his father's death. When the vessel drifts into Kazon territory, a youth named Kar attempts to earn his warrior name by killing the intruder. Chakotay destroys Kar's ship and beams the boy aboard, inadvertently condemning the youth to contempt for failing to win the honor he sought. When Chakotay returns Kar to his people, he is taken prisoner by the Kazon and given a choice: kill Kar or die.

19. Projections

The ship's holographic Doctor is activated in what appears to be the midst of a shipwide emergency. The computer informs him that the crew has been forced to abandon ship, but Torres appears and reports that she and Janeway stayed aboard to repair damage from a Kazon attack. Using new holo-emitters that allow him to move about the ship, the Doctor first assists the unconscious Janeway, then Neelix, who is battling a Kazon soldier. The Doctor finds he is bleeding from an injury—which is impossible for a hologram. Reg Barclay appears, stating that the Doctor isn't a hologram, he's Doctor Lewis Zimmerman, the human who invented the EMH. Barclay claims that Zimmerman is on a simulation of *Voyager* and he must stop a deadly radiation surge by destroying the ship. Chakotay then appears and says Barclay is lying.

20. Elogium

Kes is strangely affected by the unusual energy patterns emitted by a swarm of space-dwelling life-forms encompassing *Voyager*. Their influence pushes Kes to prematurely enter the phase in which Ocampan women become fertile. Since she can give birth only once in her life, Kes realizes that if she ever wants to have a child, she must do so now. When Kes asks

Neelix to father her child, he hesitates, causing Kes to question whether he really wants to have a child.

21. Non Sequitur

Kim is surprised when he awakens on Earth and learns that neither he nor Paris were ever posted to *Voyager*. The starship did make its ill-fated journey to the Badlands and is now listed as missing. Realizing that his last memory was of being in a shuttlecraft with Paris, Kim tracks down his friend. Paris doesn't recognize him, or have any interest in Kim's attempts to befriend him. The dejected Kim might have chalked up the whole experience as a bad dream if not for the surprising revelation that the guy who owns the local coffee shop has a lot to do with his fate.

22. Twisted

A spatial distortion wave surrounds *Voyager*, disabling communications and warp drive—and even changing the vessel's structural layout. Paris and Torres team up to find engineering. Chakotay, Neelix, Janeway, and Kim team up to locate the bridge. Chakotay manages to locate Tuvok, but he loses Neelix, while Janeway is nearly dragged into another distortion. With Janeway losing consciousness, Chakotay takes command, but the spatial distortion continues to squeeze the ship, and Tuvok estimates that the unstoppable wave will crush the vessel in an hour.

23. Parturition

With competitive romantic feelings for Kes causing friction between Neelix and Paris, Janeway sends the pair on an away mission, hoping they will work out their differences. Their shuttlecraft loses power and they make an emergency landing. Sealing themselves in a cave in order to keep out the planet's toxic atmosphere, Paris and Neelix come upon a

clutch of reptilian eggs and a newly born hatchling that needs the nutrients in the toxic atmosphere to survive. They must choose between their safety and the needs of the baby creature.

24. Persistence of Vision

Janeway makes first contact with the Botha in hopes of being allowed to pass through their space, but the Bothan representative gives her a chilly reception. Afterward, Janeway imagines that she sees a character from a holonovel in the ship's corridor. While the captain undergoes medical testing, Chakotay meets with the Bothan representative. This time the alien initiates an attack, leaving *Voyager* damaged and other crew members seeing friends and family members who can't possibly be in the Delta Quadrant.

25. Tattoo

Symbols found on an alien moon are strikingly similar to ones Chakotay saw as a teenager while accompanying his father on a journey to discover the descendants of his tribe's ances-tors. Intrigued, the crew follows a warp signa-ture to an uninhabited planet, which triggers more of Chakotay's youthful memories. Suddenly, a violent storm kicks up and sepa-rates Chakotay from the away team. Left alone on the planet, the Native American officer encounters its inhabitants and is surprised to learn that they have more in common with his father's people than he could have expected.

26. Cold Fire

Evidence that another Caretaker may be in the vicinity gives Janeway hope that the entity can provide her crew with a quick means to get back home. *Voyager* follows an energy trail to a space station inhabited by Ocampa—who fire on the ship. Kes, *Voyager*'s resident Ocampan, approaches the station's leader, Tanis, and assures him they have come in peace. Tanis confirms that their Caretaker, a female named Suspiria, is nearby. Tanis tutors Kes in powerful psychokinetic skills that Suspiria has helped him to refine. Kes doesn't realize that the benevolent-seeming Ocampan may be using her to lead the *Voyager* crew into a trap.

27. Maneuvers

Surprised when sensors pick up a Federation signal, *Voyager*'s crew responds, only to be attacked by the Kazon, who penetrate their shields and steal a transporter module. When Janeway informs the Kazon leader, Culluh, that the module is useless without Federation know-how, he tells her that he has joined forces with former Maquis and *Voyager* crewman Seska. Fearing that Seska could provide the Kazon with enough technical information to conquer *Voyager*, Chakotay leaves the ship and goes after her.

28. Resistance

While searching for material to power the ship, Tuvok and Torres are imprisoned in a city that is under siege by enemy forces. While Janeway attempts to free them, Caylem—an elderly, eccentric man who thinks she is his daughter—befriends her. The captain approaches a member of the city's resistance movement who promises to help her. But after he leads her into a trap, it is Caylem who proves most helpful.

29. Prototype

Torres is delighted when she is able to reactivate a robot that the crew has beamed aboard, especially after she learns that it is sentient. Introducing itself as Automated Personnel Unit 3947, a worker created by an extinct species of humanoids known as the Pralor, the robot asks Torres to help it build other robotic units. Janeway states that this would be a violation of the Prime Directive, so 3947 kidnaps Torres and takes her to an alien ship that threatens to destroy *Voyager* if the engineer doesn't comply. Another vessel, this one populated by sentient robots built by the Pralors' enemy, the Cravics, attacks. Janeway realizes she must rescue her engineer while the warring robots battle each other.

30. Alliances

Hoping to reduce Kazon assaults, Janeway attempts to form an alliance between opposing Kazon sects. Neelix approaches one sect; Janeway meets with Seska and Culluh, who lead another. Neelix is imprisoned, but a fellow prisoner—a Trabe named Mabus—helps Neelix escape. Although the Trabe and the Kazon are enemies, Janeway agrees to Mabus's suggestion to call a conference of all the Kazon sect leaders.

31. Threshold

Believing the crew may have found a way to surpass warp 10, Paris prepares to test the technology in a shuttlecraft. The pilot manages to break the warp barrier, but the trip has a dramatic effect on his biochemistry. Despite the Doctor's efforts, Paris dies—then spontaneously recovers. Now suffering from paranoia, the still-deteriorating pilot kidnaps Janeway and launches another transwarp journey.

32. Meld

Tuvok's investigation into the death of a crewman suggests murder, a theory that proves true when Suder, a Maquis, confesses. Uncertain how to punish Suder, Janeway confines him to quarters. Tuvok, hoping to establish a motive, performs a Vulcan mind-meld on the killer. Following the meld, the previously violent Suder seems to act calmer, while the pacifistic Vulcan becomes increasingly agitated. As Suder's comments about the seductive lure of violence affect him more and more, Tuvok seals himself in his own quarters.

33. Dreadnought

The crew of *Voyager* is surprised to discover a Cardassian-designed weapon in the Delta Quadrant—and even more surprised that it is the same weapon that Torres had reprogrammed to blow up a Cardassian installation in the Alpha Quadrant. The weapon is approaching a highly populated planet. Torres beams aboard to disable it, but the missile's computer believes her to be a Cardassian saboteur and rejects being reprogrammed, turning off life support.

34. Death Wish

Voyager inadvertently beams aboard a member of the Q Continuum and is shocked when the omnipotent entity announces that he wants to commit suicide. Suddenly another Q shows up — this time the entity that often has disrupted events on the *Enterprise*. The second Q tells Janeway that the first Q is an escaped prisoner. The Continuum has kept him locked up because of his suicidal tendencies. Rather than turn the former prisoner over to the Continuum, Janeway agrees to consider his request for asylum.

35. Lifesigns

In an effort to save the life of Doctor Danara Pel, a Vidiian female suffering from phage, *Voyager*'s holographic Doctor puts her into stasis and transfers her synaptic patterns into a holographic body. After convincing the reluctant Torres to donate some Klingon brain cells to Pel, the Doctor finds that he is developing feelings for Danara.

36. Investigations

Neelix is surprised to hear that Paris is leaving *Voyager* to join a Talaxian convoy. As Janeway ponders Paris's replacement, an accident in engineering injures three crew members, including Jonas, and the warp engines shut

---

GUESS WHO'S COMING TO DINNER? *Voyager* may be lost on the far side of the universe, but that doesn't mean the crew can't visit with old friends every now and then. *The Next Generation*'s Will Riker and Q stopped by in person (p. 186), *Star Trek*'s Sulu and Janice Rand popped in via a persistent memory of Tuvok's (p. 188), and Deanna Troi and Barclay were able to chat with the Doctor when he made a special trip to Earth to help his creator, Lewis Zimmerman (p. 205). One wonders why these guys feel so homesick.

---

down. Then the Talaxian vessel reports that the Kazon have kidnapped Paris. Meanwhile, on board a Kazon ship, Paris is greeted by Seska. Back on *Voyager*, Neelix attempts to find out how the Kazon could have known Paris was with the Talaxians.

37. Deadlock

As *Voyager* passes through a plasma cloud in order to evade Vidiian ships, Ensign Wildman gives birth to a baby girl. When the ship emerges from the cloud, its engines stall. Ensign Kim is sucked into space as he attempts to repair a hull breach, Kes literally disappears into a void, and Wildman's newborn baby dies. As Janeway struggles to save her ship and crew, she sees something astonishing: an image of herself on an *un*damaged bridge. Surmising that the cloud caused the ship to duplicate itself, Janeway crosses over to the other ship and meets with her doppelgänger. With the Vidiians attacking the damaged version of *Voyager*, one of the ships must self-destruct in order to save the other.

38. Innocence

Tuvok's shuttle crashes on a moon, and he meets three young children who tell him that

---

their shuttle crashed also. On *Voyager*, Janeway welcomes Alcia, prelate of Drayan II, who brusquely tells the captain to leave the area. When a Drayan search party lands, the three frightened children tell Tuvok that the Drayans sent them here to die. The Vulcan hides them from the searchers, but the children begin to disappear.

39. The Thaw

Passing a supposedly deserted planet, *Voyager* picks up an automated hail that leads the crew to a group of humanoids in stasis, their life functions controlled by a computer program. The Doctor surmises that several have died of heart failure brought on by extreme fear. Hoping to learn how to revive the others, Kim and Torres enter two stasis units. They find themselves in a bizarre carnival run by a malevolent Clown who threatens to kill Kim but lets Torres return to consciousness in order to warn others not to interfere. Realizing that the Clown's survival depends on keeping his victims prisoners of fear, Torres attempts to disable his program. The Clown retaliates by frightening one of the humanoids to death. Janeway orders Torres to stop and instead offers herself in a trade for the other hostages.

40. Tuvix

On an away mission, Tuvok and Neelix come upon an alien orchid with unique properties that affect the transporter, causing it to fuse the pair into a single biological entity who ultimately names himself Tuvix. Paris and Torres gather more of the orchids and are able to use the transporter to make other odd combinations, but they are unable to reverse the process. After several weeks, the Doctor announces that he has devised a way to restore the individuals who were Tuvok and Neelix to normal. Tuvix does not want to be separated,

because the unique entity that he has become will cease to exist.

41. Resolutions

During an away mission, Janeway and Chakotay are infected by a virus and forced to remain on an uninhabited planet because the planet's unique environment will stop the illness. The captain orders Tuvok to go on without them. Unwilling to desert their friends, the crew attempts to contact the Vidiians, hoping their advanced medical knowledge will have a cure.

42. Basics, Part I

While Tuvok works to rehabilitate the unstable crewman Suder, Chakotay receives a desperate message from Seska, who says she has given birth to his child but Culluh is going to take it away from her. An injured Kazon, Teirna, rescued by *Voyager* claims that Culluh has killed Seska. Then several small Kazon vessels attack *Voyager*—and suddenly eight larger ships block her way. Teirna blows himself up aboard *Voyager*, badly damaging the ship. Paris departs, seeking help, but is fired upon as Kazon intruders board the crippled starship.

SEASON THREE

43. Basics, Part II

Stranded on a desolate and dangerous planet, the crew of *Voyager* struggles to survive. Paris solicits help from the Talaxians, while the Doctor tells Seska that her newborn baby isn't Chakotay's—he's Culluh's. Then the Doctor discovers that he's not the only crew member left on the ship; Ensign Suder is still aboard. The Doctor and Suder join forces, and a changed Suder hopes he won't have to kill anyone.

44. Flashback

As *Voyager* approaches a nebula, Tuvok suffers from flashbacks of a girl falling from a cliff. The Doctor suspects the flashbacks are a repressed memory, which can be dangerous to Vulcans. Tuvok asks Janeway to mind-meld with him. The meld takes them back eighty years to the Vulcan's first assignment on the *Excelsior*, commanded by Sulu (see p. 230), who disobeys Starfleet in order to help James Kirk, who is being held for murder. The *Excelsior* passes through a nebula that is similar to the one *Voyager* spotted prior to Tuvok's first flashback. Once again, Tuvok experiences the flashback, but this time he goes into convulsions.

45. The Chute

Falsely accused of a terrorist bombing that killed forty-seven people, Paris and Kim are thrown into an alien prison and forced to wear clamps that affect their nervous systems. While Janeway searches for the real bombers, the pair plans an escape via a long metal chute. Before they can act, another prisoner stabs Paris. With their nerves agitated to the point of emotional instability, the two cannot even trust one another.

46. The Swarm

Voyager enters an area of space populated by a species known for attacking outsiders, and Paris and Torres are badly injured. Navigating around the area would take months, so Janeway stays on course. The Doctor's memory circuits begin to degrade, and the only way to help him is to reset his program at the risk of losing his memories and personality. Kes and Torres transfer his program to the holodeck, where they meet a re-creation of Doctor Lewis Zimmerman, the creator of the EMH program, but even he is unable to come up with a solution. Meanwhile, thousands of small alien vessels attach themselves to *Voyager*'s hull and begin to drain the starship's energy.

47. False Profits

Detecting an unstable wormhole, the *Voyager* crew learns that a replicator from the Alpha Quadrant is in use on a nearby planet. Chakotay and Paris find that two Ferengi are being worshipped as gods. Trapped in the Delta Quadrant after entering the unstable wormhole, they took advantage of the population's religious myths. Janeway comes up with a plan to outdo the Ferengi at their own cunning scheme.

48. Remember

As *Voyager* transports a group of telepathic Enarans, Torres begins having dreams in which she envisions herself as an Enaran woman, Korenna. In the dreams, Korenna loved Dalthan, whose people had fallen out of political favor. But why have these dreams been stirred within Torres?

49. Sacred Ground

When Kes enters the sacred section of a Nechani shrine, an energy field renders her comatose. Janeway receives permission to visit the shrine, hoping to find a way to save Kes. The Doctor implants a monitoring probe and a homing device in the captain. At the shrine, a guide leads Janeway in a ritual of long, grueling tests, including putting her hand into a basket where it is bitten by an unseen creature. The Doctor tracks toxins from the bite and theorizes that this may be the key in treating Kes. But when he applies the cure to Kes, her condition grows worse.

50. Future's End, Part I

Captain Braxton, a time traveler, attacks *Voyager* because he believes the ship will be responsible for a temporal explosion that will destroy Earth.

Voyager manages to deflect Braxton's attack, but both ships are sucked into a rift that sends them to Earth in the year 1996. A startled astronomer, Rain Robinson, detects the ship. Against the instructions of her boss, computer mogul Henry Starling, she transmits a message to the ship. Janeway and Chakotay hunt for Braxton—only to learn that Henry Starling already has found the starship and is cannibalizing its technology for his own purposes.

51. Future's End, Part II

Trapped on Earth in the twentieth century, the crew of *Voyager* attempts to stop Henry Starling from using the twenty-ninth-century technology he has stolen in order to travel to the future. Chakotay and Torres's efforts to beam Starling to their shuttle damage the shuttle's controls, and the pair wind up in the Arizona desert. Tuvok and the Doctor search for the shuttle in Arizona, and Paris looks for the missing starship in Los Angeles.

52. Warlord

After *Voyager*'s crew rescues three Ilarians from their damaged ship, one dies. Kes visits with the survivors, then suddenly tells Neelix that she wants to spend time away from him. On Ilari, Kes kills the leader's representative and flees with the pair of Ilarian survivors. Arriving at a military encampment, she assumes command of waiting troops. Demmas, son of the local leader, explains that Tieran has inhabited Kes's body. Janeway vows to help stop Kes/Tieran, but the tyrant kills Demmas's father and assumes control of the planet.

53. The Q and the Grey

A series of supernova explosions sends out shock waves that threaten to damage *Voyager*. Q appears and announces that he wants Janeway to bear his child. The captain refuses, much to the relief of a jealous female Q who also shows up. Q explains that the supernova explosions are a result of a civil war taking place in the Q Continuum, and he transports Janeway there to see for herself. The conflict was triggered by the death of Quinn, the Q who committed suicide a year earlier. The whole Continuum is on the verge of tearing itself apart over the question of whether or not individualism should be permitted or stopped.

54. Macrocosm

Returning from a trade mission with the Tak Tak, Janeway and Neelix find that *Voyager* is infested with flying, stinging life-forms. One of the creatures sprays Neelix, and he falls ill. Janeway heads for the bridge, but when a creature stings her, she flees to sickbay. The Doctor tells her that the creatures, a kind of oversized virus that migrated from a nearby planet, have spread throughout the ship's systems and infected the entire crew. Although he has developed an antigen, he hasn't tested it. Now infected, Janeway takes the antigen and distributes it to the crew. The Tak Tak, who have decided to eradicate the virus, fire on what they think is the source—*Voyager*.

55. Fair Trade

As *Voyager* enters the Nekrit Expanse, Neelix worries about his usefulness to the crew. When the crew stops at a space station for supplies, Neelix is determined to acquire a map of the region. He borrows one of *Voyager*'s shuttles to help an old friend, Wix, complete a negotiation that will get him that map. When they arrive, Wix kills his contact with a Starfleet phaser. That's when Neelix realizes that Wix was using him in an illicit narcotics deal. The station manager tells Janeway that a Federation weapon was involved in the slaying. Wix insists that Neelix steal warp plasma from the ship in order to pay off the drug smugglers. At the same time, Paris and Chakotay are arrested for the murder. Could there be a way for Neelix to trap the real culprit, free his friends, *and* stay in Janeway's good graces?

56. Alter Ego

Kim tells Tuvok that he's fallen in love with a woman, Marayna; the only problem is that she's a holodeck character. After meeting with the character, Tuvok admits that he also finds her compelling. When *Voyager* attempts to leave a nebula it has been studying, the engines go off-line. A jealous Kim finds Tuvok visiting Marayna and accuses the Vulcan of betraying his trust. Tuvok tries to delete Marayna's program but later finds her in his quarters. It seems that Marayna may be real—and very dangerous.

57. Coda

Forced to make a sudden landing in their shuttlecraft, Chakotay and Janeway are attacked—and killed—by Vidiians. Then suddenly the pair is alive and back on the shuttle. The shuttle explodes, killing them, then seconds later they again are alive in the shuttle. Believing themselves to be trapped in a time loop, they contact *Voyager* and escape. However, the Doctor diagnoses Janeway with the Vidiian phage and euthanizes her. Again Janeway finds herself on the shuttle with Chakotay. Again the shuttle explodes, and the captain finds herself on the planet watching as Chakotay grieves over her body. Janeway doesn't believe she's dead—but how's she going to prove it?

58. Blood Fever

Vulcan crewman Vorik asks Torres to mate with him, but she declines. When Vorik tries to get physical, she dislocates his jaw. The Doctor reveals that Vorik is experiencing the Vulcan mating drive, *Pon farr* (see p. 12). On an away mission, Torres becomes aggressive and Tuvok realizes that Torres is also experiencing *Pon*

farr. Then the away team is attacked by aliens that live underground, hiding from a formidable foe.

59. Unity

Chakotay lands his shuttle on a planet to answer a distress call and is attacked. He is rescued by Riley, a human woman. Riley explains that she is part of a cooperative of various species that were kidnapped and left on the planet to fend for themselves. The two groups have been fighting over the inadequate food supply. The *Voyager* comes upon an inactive Borg cube. The vessel ceased operation five years earlier—the same time that Riley and the rest of the cooperative arrived on their desolate planet.

60. Darkling

Hoping to enhance his performance, the Doctor incorporates personality routines of famous historical figures such as Gandhi and Lord Byron into his program. Meanwhile, Kes grows fond of a space explorer, Zahir, and contemplates leaving *Voyager* to travel with him—until a mysterious figure pushes Zahir off a cliff. Torres finds the problem with the Doctor's new blend of subroutines. Later, Torres is found unconscious, and Kes is kidnapped by the now-unstable medical hologram. Can anyone on board undo the Doctor's ill-advised tinkering?

61. Rise

Voyager attempts to destroy asteroids threatening a Nezu planet. A scientist named Vatm claims he has important information about the fragments plummeting from space. Tuvok, Neelix, and a Nezu, Sklar, take a shuttle and find Vatm, but they crash with no way to contact the ship. Using a mag-lev carriage—essentially an elevator between the planet and a space station—the trio takes Vatm and rises above the atmosphere, where they hope to communicate with the ship. But one of the passengers is poisoned and Tuvok is nearly murdered.

62. Favorite Son

During an encounter with a Nasari ship, Ensign Harry Kim inexplicably fires on the ship, explaining only that he "knew" the Nasari posed a threat. That evening, Kim awakens from a dream and finds alien markings on his face. Following another Nasari attack, the crew seeks refuge on Taresia, a planet populated only by women. Surprisingly, the inhabitants welcome Kim "home," explaining that he was conceived on their planet. His embryo was implanted in an Earth woman so he would bring an infusion of new genetic material back to their race.

63. Before and After

Kes awakens in sickbay on the verge of death and hears the Doctor say that he is activating a biotemporal chamber. Then she experiences a shift of perception and finds herself with a boy, apparently her grandson, and the Doctor. He tells her that he is about to put her in a biotemporal chamber that he hopes will prolong the final phase of her short Ocampan life span. Experiencing another shift, Kes finds herself in her quarters with a younger version of the boy and her apparent husband, Tom Paris. Again Kes shifts to another timeline, and another, each making her younger and ultimately threatening to take her back to the moment of conception, at which point she will cease to exist—unless she can find a way to halt the process.

64. Real Life

In an effort to expand his horizons, the Doctor creates a holofamily consisting of a wife, Charlene, a teenaged son, Jeffrey, and a young daughter, Belle. Kes and Torres tell the Doctor that the family is too perfect, so he agrees to let Torres rewrite their programs to make them more realistic. Meanwhile, Paris takes advantage of a "subspace tornado" in order to capture some valuable plasma particles, but the crew is shocked when the pilot is sucked into subspace. Trapped between subspace and space, Paris's only chance to survive is to enter yet another tornado, hoping it will return him. On the holodeck, the Doctor is not pleased with the changes in his family: his wife works too much, his son's Klingon friends lead Jeffrey into trouble, and his daughter is badly injured in an accident. When the Doctor realizes the young girl may die, he must decide if he wants to experience everything—including the agonizing heartaches—that real life brings to organic beings.

65. Distant Origin

Professor Gegen, a Voth scientist who believes his reptilian species originated in a distant part of the galaxy, boards *Voyager* and uses cloaking technology to observe the crew. When sensors detect Gegen, the professor tranquilizes Chakotay and transports him back to his own ship. Gegen and Chakotay conclude that the Voth evolved from Earth's own dinosaurs, but they are charged with heresy by the Voth Ministry of Elders, which holds the belief that their race was the first to evolve in the Delta Quadrant.

66. Displaced

A Nyrian suddenly appears on the ship at the exact moment that Kes disappears, and another Nyrian appears as Kim disappears. As the exchanges continue, Janeway deduces that her crew is being replaced at nine-minute intervals. Torres works with one of the Nyrians to find a cause. She soon realizes the Nyrians are responsible—it's their method of stealing ships. Torres is transported to a prison colony, where she finds her abducted friends being kept in an Earth-like habitat, as well as the crews of many other ships in corresponding habitats. This is a prison from which no one has ever escaped.

67. Worst Case Scenario

After Torres discovers a holoprogram in the database, Paris becomes fascinated by the subject matter: a mutiny by *Voyager*'s crew. Paris plays the holo to the end, only to find that the story was never completed. Tuvok admits that he wrote the program as a training exercise that ultimately proved unnecessary. Paris volunteers to collaborate with Tuvok to complete the story, but when they do, a holographic version of Seska appears, stating that she discovered the program and gave it the ending that *she* thought was appropriate.

68. Scorpion, Part I

Entering Borg space, *Voyager* encounters Borg cubes racing past the ship. The crew discovers that something has destroyed a Borg armada. Investigating one of the ruined cubes, a life-form attacks Kim and infests his body. The Doctor tries to devise a procedure to reprogram Borg nanoprobes to save Kim. Torres discovers that the life-form—known to the Borg as Species 8472—is blocking their passage home. With no other options, Janeway decides to form an alliance with the Borg.

Season Four

69. Scorpion, Part II

Janeway works out an agreement with the Borg that will help both of them fight Species 8472. At her insistence, the Borg assign a liaison, Seven of Nine. Aware that Species 8472's organic ships are vulnerable to the nanoprobes that the Doctor reprogrammed, the crew plans an attack. However, Species 8472 attacks first, injuring Janeway. Now in command, Chakotay argues with Seven of Nine over the best strategy to defeat their mutual enemy, as *Voyager*'s crew prepares to engage Species 8472 in its own territory—fluidic space.

70. The Gift

Although her link to the Borg collective has been severed, Seven of Nine demands to be returned. Janeway refuses, even when the drone's immune system begins to reject her Borg implants. The Doctor starts to remove the implants, and the captain researches Seven's human life before assimilation. Meanwhile, Kes's telepathic abilities suddenly begin to escalate at an alarming rate. When Kes stops Seven from contacting the Collective, she inadvertently destroys a section of the ship. Tuvok and Janeway worry that Kes is becoming a threat to the crew's safety.

71. Day of Honor

Torres isn't in the mood to celebrate the Day of Honor, an annual Klingon ritual of self-examination. A crew of Caatati refugees—whose civilization was destroyed by the Borg—asks *Voyager* for assistance. Janeway gives them supplies, yet the Caatati are outraged when they see former Borg Seven of Nine on the ship. An engineering accident forces Torres to eject the warp core, and when she and Paris go to retrieve it, the Caatati fire at their shuttle. Before *Voyager* can respond to their distress signal, the Caatati, who have salvaged *Voyager*'s warp core, make Janeway an offer—turn over Seven or they will destroy the ship.

72. Nemesis

Chakotay's shuttle is shot down in the middle of a war zone. He's rescued by the Vori, who are fighting the vicious Kradin. A Vori soldier helps him hunt for his shuttle, but when the man is killed, Chakotay is left on his own. Chakotay finds other Vori, but his allies are continually attacked, and even Chakotay is wounded. The crew learns about the first officer's plight and Janeway meets with a Kradin official. Unaware that Tuvok has joined the Kradin commando unit searching for him, Chakotay prepares to attack them.

73. Revulsion

The Doctor and Torres track a distress signal from a disabled ship and find an alien hologram that says the crew aboard his ship has died and he needs help. The hologram, Dejaren, claims the crew died of a virus and that the lower decks are filled with deadly radiation. When Dejaren lashes out at Torres and criticizes her organic body, she warns the Doctor that the hologram may not be trustworthy. As Torres investigates the vessel, the Doctor keeps Dejaren occupied. He soon realizes that Torres is right: the hologram isn't just pathologically bitter against organics, he's homicidally bitter.

74. The Raven

When Seven of Nine begins hallucinating about being pursued by the Borg and a large black bird, the Doctor believes she is suffering post-traumatic stress disorder. The former Borg drone steals a shuttlecraft and leaves *Voyager*. Seven's flight disrupts Janeway's negotiations with the distrustful B'omar for passage through their space. Tuvok and Paris track Seven through B'omar territory. Eventually, Tuvok beams into her shuttle, where Seven explains that she is responding to a Borg homing beacon. Aware that there are no Borg ships in the area, Tuvok asks to accompany her, despite the threat of the B'omar ships protecting their territory.

75. Scientific Method

The crew begins to experience serious medical problems, from Janeway's extreme headaches to Chakotay's rapid aging. The Doctor diagnoses that their DNA is being altered, but before they can investigate, his program is deactivated. The Doctor manages to communicate with Seven of Nine by tapping into her Borg implants. He tells her that he suspects they are being watched. Adjusting her sensory nodes, Seven sees invisible aliens prodding crew members with instruments. The aliens refuse to stop their medical experiments. Janeway decides she has no choice but to destroy the ship.

76. Year of Hell, Part I

Traveling through an area of space occupied by the Zahl and the Krenim, *Voyager* is hit by a space-time shock wave, and suddenly everything related to the Zahl disappears—even the crew's memory of them. A Krenim captain, Annorax, plans his next step—to restore his culture to the exact status it held years earlier, before its disastrous war with the Zahl. As the months go by, repeated attacks against time damage *Voyager* and the surrounding region. When an active warhead lodges in the ship's hull, Seven of Nine studies how it works just before it blows up and blinds Tuvok. Using Seven's information, the ship survives Annorax's next attack, which causes his weapon-ship to lose strength. An angry Annorax abducts Chakotay and Paris for study, and concentrates the power of his weaponry on erasing *Voyager* from history.

77. Year of Hell, Part II

Following *Voyager*'s encounters with the Krenim temporal weapon-ship, most of the crew has abandoned ship. The senior officers attempt to repair *Voyager*. Prisoners on the weapon-ship, Chakotay and Paris negotiate with Annorax, who promises to restore *Voyager*'s timeline for information about the ship's journey. Annorax relates that the death of his family is his reason for altering time, but even Chakotay's friendship can't halt the Krenim captain's behavior. When Annorax again turns to destruction in an attempt to restore his family, Janeway initiates a kamikaze run that could destroy them all.

78. Random Thoughts

On the world of the telepathic Mari race, Torres accidentally collides with a man named Frane, who later attacks another man. Torres admits to Mari authorities that the encounter with Frane angered her, and she is arrested for "violent thoughts" and sentenced to having her mind purged. Janeway and Tuvok discover that Frane has a record, and when Tuvok mind-melds with Torres, he sees that her mind was telepathically probed after the incident by another Mari, Guill. As the authorities start the purging procedure on Torres, the crew finds that her accusers have a dark side.

79. Concerning Flight

The Doctor's mobile emitter and the main computer processor are stolen from *Voyager*. Tuvok and Janeway detect Starfleet technology at a commerce center—as well as the Leonardo da Vinci character from Janeway's holodeck program that had been downloaded into the mobile emitter. Unaware that he isn't real, Leonardo mentions that he has a "patron" named Tau, and the crew learns there is a technology dealer who has the same name. Finding Tau proves to be easy, but retrieving the stolen equipment and escaping from him does not.

80. Mortal Coil

Neelix is killed by an energy discharge, but Seven of Nine contributes a Borg nanoprobe to revive him. This shatters Neelix's belief in the Talaxian afterlife and sends him into a spiral of doubt and despair. Chakotay guides Neelix on a vision quest to find inner peace. But as the visions he experiences seem to reaffirm that the afterlife is a lie, the distraught Talaxian awakens convinced that he has no reason to go on living.

81. Waking Moments

The crew discovers that everyone had the same dream about an unknown alien, and other crew members cannot be awakened. Chakotay engages in lucid dreaming, a technique that will allow him to control the events in his dream. He encounters the alien, who explains that the dream state is his species's reality. They see "waking species" as their enemy. After Chakotay awakens, the Doctor informs him that the entire crew is now asleep. Chakotay attempts to find the sleeping aliens while he is awake, but the closer he gets to them, the harder it is to stay awake.

82. Message in a Bottle

A series of relay stations built by the Hirogen allows *Voyager* to transmit a holographic data stream—the Doctor's program—to the Alpha Quadrant. The Doctor finds himself aboard the *U.S.S. Prometheus;* however, the Romulans have killed the Starfleet crew and taken over the ship. The Doctor activates the *Prometheus*'s holographic doctor, and together they release a gas through the ventilation system, knocking out the Romulans. With no way to pilot the ship— which is headed into Romulan space—the two doctors are relieved when other Starfleet ships approach. Unfortunately, those ships' crews believe the *Prometheus* is still being flown by Romulans.

83. Hunters

Aware of *Voyager*'s presence in the Delta Quadrant, Starfleet sends a transmission to Janeway, but it gets lodged in one of the Hirogen relay stations. Tuvok and Seven of Nine take a shuttle there but are captured and abducted to a Hirogen ship. The Hirogen leader warns Janeway to disconnect her relay link and leave. Refusing to desert Tuvok and Seven, the crew prepares for battle.

84. Prey

An injured Hirogen is brought to sickbay by an away team. He only wants to continue his hunt for the alien that attacked him. Later, Tuvok and Kim discover that an intruder—a member of Species 8472—has entered the ship. Tuvok establishes that the intruder only wants to return to its home. The Hirogen threatens to destroy *Voyager* if Janeway doesn't turn the creature over to him. Complicating matters: Seven of Nine refuses to follow Janeway's command to protect the being.

85. Retrospect

After an argument with an Entharan trader, Kovin, Seven of Nine exhibits anxiety she's never felt before. The Doctor uses a new psychiatric subroutine and leads her through hypnotic regression therapy. Seven recalls that while she and Kovin were testing weapons, he fired a thoron beam at her and extracted some of her nanoprobes. Kovin denies the charge, pleading that even an accusation of wrongdoing would ruin his reputation. When the Doctor finds nanoprobes in Kovin's lab, the trader flees. It isn't until *Voyager* is in full pursuit of the frightened Kovin that the crew realize they may have accused an innocent man.

86. The Killing Game, Part I

The Hirogen have taken over *Voyager* and implanted devices in the crew to make them believe they are characters in a massive holodeck war game. For the aliens, hunting is a way of life, and use of the holodeck offers them endless possibilities. In a World War II simulation, the Hirogen play the Nazis and Janeway plays the leader of a resistance move-

ment. The crew members, each assigned a fictional role, are regularly wounded. The Doctor objects to repairing the injuries only to send them back to unwittingly do battle.

87. The Killing Game, Part II

With World War II being waged all over *Voyager*, Janeway and Seven of Nine pretend to play the roles programmed by the Hirogen's holodeck scenario. Gathering her crew members, who think they are American soldiers or members of the French resistance, the captain devises a plan to blow up sickbay, deactivating the devices controlling them.

88. Vis à Vis

Paris assists Steth, whose ship's propulsion system is destabilizing, while the alien breaks into *Voyager*'s computer and downloads DNA information. Steth switches bodies with Paris, sending him away as Steth on the malfunctioning vessel and settling into the pilot's life. Meanwhile, Paris awakens to find that he is being arrested by Benthan authorities for theft, just as an angry woman, Daelen, arrives, claiming that she is Steth and wants his body back. When they finally catch up with *Voyager*, they find that the DNA-stealing alien has switched bodies yet again.

89. The Omega Directive

Voyager's sensors have detected the Omega molecule, the most powerful—and unstable—substance known to exist. Janeway's orders are to destroy the Omega molecule. But to the Borg, Omega represents perfection; therefore, Seven believes its power should be harnessed. While the captain works on a technology that would stabilize Omega, Seven decides that she doesn't believe in the mission. The researchers, who currently have possession of the molecule, don't intend to give it up.

90. Unforgettable

An injured female, Kellin, is beamed to sickbay, where she claims to have recently been aboard *Voyager* for several weeks. Explaining that no one remembers her because a pheromone prevents memory of her species from being retained in the minds of others, Kellin says she has returned because she fell in love with Chakotay. The first officer believes her story about being a bounty hunter from Ramura, a closed society that tracks down people who leave their world. Arriving on *Voyager* in search of a stowaway, she planted a computer virus that erased all evidence of their presence. Cloaked Ramuran vessels start firing on *Voyager*, and even as Janeway grants her asylum, Kellin senses that it's already too late.

91. Living Witness

Seven hundred years in the future, a representation of *Voyager* and its crew is on holographic display in the Kyrian museum. The lurid, inaccurate depiction paints the crew in a very unflattering light. The Kyrians believe that Janeway triggered and supported a violent civil war in exchange for information to get her crew back home. A curator has come across a data storage device that includes a backup program of *Voyager's* Emergency Medical Hologram. Once activated, the Doctor tries to establish the truth about the events. But before he can offer proof that the Kyrians were at fault, fighting breaks out, and the Doctor wonders whether clearing *Voyager's* name is worth causing yet another war.

92. Demon

As Paris and Kim attempt to gather supplies on a planet with a toxic atmosphere, their environmental suits fail and they collapse into a pool of metallic compound. A puzzled rescue team finds both men alive and well—without their environmental suits. They're brought back to *Voyager*, however, Paris and Kim can't breathe. After erecting a force field around the men and filling it with atmosphere from the planet, the Doctor surmises that the compound has altered their physiology at a cellular level. Unless a way can be found to reverse that effect, Kim and Paris will have to be left on the planet.

93. One

Voyager's path is about to pass through a huge nebula, and everyone—except the Doctor and Seven of Nine—will be affected by its radiation. Janeway orders that the crew be put into stasis units while Seven and the Doctor take care of the ship. The computer malfunctions, and the Doctor's program begins to degrade, leaving Seven alone, except for odd dreams and apparent hallucinations. Has she beamed an alien aboard? Is he stalking her? While she searches for him, Seven's Borg implants start to degrade. As the ship's propulsion system starts to fail, Seven begins to panic.

94. Hope and Fear

A friendly alien named Arturis manages to translate the encoded message that *Voyager* received from Starfleet before the Hirogen relay stations were destroyed. The message reveals a set of coordinates, and when *Voyager* arrives there, the crew finds the *U.S.S. Dauntless*, an unmanned Starfleet vessel, with new "slipstream drive" engines set on autonavigation. Is it really a new ultrafast Starfleet vessel that's been sent to bring them home—or a trap?

Season Five

95. Night

Voyager travels across the void, a desolate region of space so vast that the crew will see no star systems for two years. With nothing to distract them, everyone aboard is going stir-crazy. The ship loses power and intruders invade the ship. Seven manages to stun one of them; the others flee when a ship comes to *Voyager*'s aid and forces the invaders' vessels to retreat. A Malon pilot, Emck, who lent assistance, tells Janeway that he can lead *Voyager* through a spatial vortex that will quickly take her crew to the other side of the void. All she has to do is hand over the intruder. But something tells Janeway that she should have a conversation with the prisoner before she makes a deal with Emck.

96. Drone

Beaming up from an away mission, some of Seven of Nine's nanoprobes infect the Doctor's mobile emitter. The malfunctioning emitter is taken to the science lab, where—unnoticed by the crew—it sprouts Borg implants, attacks a human ensign, and extracts some of his genetic material. The result is a fetal drone, which quickly matures into a humanoid male that is Borg-like but far more advanced, due to the emitter's twenty-ninth-century technology. Seven of Nine fears the drone may seek out the rest of the Collective—or the Collective may try to find him.

97. Extreme Risk

Rather than allow a Malon ship to steal *Voyager*'s new multispatial probe, Janeway sends the probe into the heavy atmosphere of a gas giant. The Malon ship follows and implodes from the atmospheric pressure. Obviously, *Voyager* can't retrieve the probe either, but Paris thinks the *Delta Flyer*, a technologically advanced shuttle that he's designed, can. First he has to get Janeway's permission to *build* it. Then he has to beat the Malons in the race to finish his supershuttle before they build theirs.

98. In the Flesh

The crew is startled to find what appears to be a facsimile of Starfleet Headquarters—complete with buildings and officers—on an otherwise uninhabited alien world in the middle of the Delta Quadrant. They discover that "Starfleet HQ" is run by cleverly disguised members of Species 8472. The simulated Starfleet facility is being used as a training ground for a planned invasion of the Alpha Quadrant.

99. Once Upon a Time

The *Delta Flyer* suffers severe damage, stranding Paris, Tuvok, and a badly injured Ensign Wildman. As *Voyager* searches for the survivors, Neelix distracts Wildman's young daughter, Naomi, with fairy tales so she won't worry about her mother.

100. Timeless

Kim and Chakotay beam down to the frigid ground of an alien world where the wreckage of *Voyager* has been entombed in the ice for fifteen years. The crew had tried to integrate quantum slipstream technology into *Voyager*. Chakotay and Kim were traveling just ahead of *Voyager* in the *Delta Flyer*, mapping the way to the Alpha Quadrant. Something went wrong. The shuttle made it home—and *Voyager* crashed on this ice planet. Now they have returned with a plan to change history.

101. Infinite Regress

After *Voyager* comes across the debris field of a Borg vessel, Seven of Nine begins to hear voices and experience bizarre personality shifts. The crew traces the source to a Borg vinculum: a processing device that interconnects the minds of the drones. However, this vinculum has been infected with a virus by Species 6339, in hopes the vinculum would be picked up by a Borg vessel. Now Species 6339 wants the vinculum back so they can reset their trap for the Borg, but Janeway won't return it until Seven has been cured.

102. Nothing Human

A wounded alien attacks Torres and attaches itself to her body. The Doctor is uncertain how to separate them without harming the engineer. He and Kim generate a holographic representation of the foremost expert on exobiology, a Cardassian, Crell Moset. The Doctor and Moset decide that the alien is using Torres as a kind of personal life-support system. As Moset determines a method to deliver an incapacitating and most likely deadly shock to the creature, the Doctor hears disquieting information about the real Crell Moset's sadistic experiments during Cardassia's occupation of Bajor.

103. Thirty Days

Sensors detect something astounding: an ocean in the shape of a planet. The body of water is inhabited by the Moneans, who live underwater, farming sea vegetation and extracting oxygen for their ships. After Janeway learns that the water world is losing containment, Paris takes the *Delta Flyer* to the center of the ocean to investigate. The ocean will suffer a complete loss of containment in less than five years. Paris discovers the cause: the computer that restrains the ocean is becoming less efficient due to the Moneans' mining activities, which are depleting the oxygen levels in the water. Although Janeway won't interfere in the aliens' internal affairs, Paris feels no such compunction.

104. Counterpoint

Voyager already is running the risk of attack by members of the Devore Imperium by helping to smuggle telepathic Brenari refugees through Devore space. Suddenly a Devore inspector, Kashyk—who seems to have a weakness for Earth's Romantic composers, coffee, and Janeway—shows up, seeking asylum aboard Janeway's ship. Kashyk says he knows about the refugees and that he can help the captain to evade the Devore. Although the captain likes Kashyk—does she dare trust him?

105. Latent Image

The Doctor wonders if someone is playing tricks on his memory after he finds signs of neurosurgery he performed on Kim eighteen months ago—but doesn't recall performing the procedure. The Doctor discovers that someone has deleted part of his short-term memory buffer, and that some holoimages he took during that period were also deleted. Seven of Nine manages to restore the images; one is of a female ensign he doesn't recognize, and the other is of an alien inside a shuttlecraft. Slowly, the Doctor seems to remember that he was on that shuttle with Kim, along with the female ensign . . . and the alien—who shot Kim and the girl.

106. Bride of Chaotica!

Photonic life-forms from another dimension inadvertently enter *Voyager*'s holodeck while Paris's campy sci-fi *Captain Proton* program is running. The life-forms assume that the black-and-white inhabitants of the program are the only living beings on *Voyager* and that Captain Proton's evil nemesis, Doctor Chaotica, is a threat they must address. Since *Voyager* can't move until the photonic aliens leave, Paris reasons that they must play parts in *The Adventures of Captain Proton* and help the photonic aliens defeat Chaotica.

107. Gravity

A gravity well strands Tuvok and Paris on a desolate planet. The planet is populated by a variety of similarly stranded aliens, among them a female pilot, Noss, who befriends the pair and helps them to survive. Janeway eventually gets a fix on her missing crewmen, but rescuing them is another matter. Time is running out for the stalwart trio, who attempt to fend off Noss's increasingly hostile neighbors even as Tuvok tries to ignore the emotions that lonely Noss has awakened in him.

108. Bliss

Seven of Nine returns to the ship from a survey mission to learn that the crew has found a wormhole that will lead them directly to Earth—or so they believe. A probe launched into the wormhole has detected Starfleet signals, and everyone seems ecstatic about going home . . . except for Naomi Wildman, who doesn't know what to think about the unusual level of optimism. Seven notes some odd things about the neutrino levels of the wormhole, but Starfleet seems to view this data as inconsequential. However, Seven finds it hard to ignore a message from an alien vessel that's actually located *inside* the wormhole. The pilot warns Seven that *Voyager* is being deceived, but the message is cut off.

109. Dark Frontier, Part I

If Janeway's plan to steal a damaged Borg ship's transwarp coil is successful, it could shave twenty years off *Voyager*'s journey. Or the venture could get the entire crew assimilated. As Seven and the others rehearse their mission, Seven hears the voice of the Borg queen (see p. 237). The queen tells her that she knows all about their plans, but that she will allow her crewmates to escape if Seven returns to the Collective.

110. Dark Frontier, Part II

On a Borg sphere, the Borg queen tells Seven of Nine that she "allowed" *Voyager* to liberate the drone from the Collective and that she has decided to leave Seven's individuality intact as an aid to assimilate humanity. Using the stolen

Borg transwarp coil to modify the *Delta Flyer*, Janeway leads a rescue mission. But despite the captain's well-thought-out plan, Seven is a prize the queen isn't prepared to relinquish.

111. The Disease

As *Voyager* assists repairing a Varro ship's warp drive, Kim begins an ill-advised affair with a Varro woman, Tal. Kim's unwillingness to obey Janeway's order to stop seeing Tal turns out to be the least of the captain's worries. Many of the Varro feel that they are prisoners on their own ship and want to leave, despite their leader's refusal to let them. As a result, they are planning violent sabotage that could endanger not only the inhabitants of their own ship—but also the crew of *Voyager*.

112. Course: Oblivion

Just after B'Elanna Torres and Tom Paris say their wedding vows, Torres is called to engineering, where she discovers that the molecular structure of one of the ship's Jefferies tubes is breaking down. Torres becomes ill, and several other crew members are similarly afflicted, Chakotay and Tuvok search for a possible cause. They find it in the trip that *Voyager* made to a Class-Y planet with a toxic atmosphere. The crew discovered a native biomimetic compound that somehow gained sentience after the encounter—and then repopulated its world with duplicates of the crew. Acting on a hunch, the Doctor performs a test and establishes something no one is prepared to hear: B'Elanna—and everyone else aboard *Voyager*—is a biomimetic duplicate of the real thing.

113. The Fight

Voyager is pulled into a disorienting region known as chaotic space, where the laws of physics are in flux. Gravimetric forces may destroy the ship unless the crew can modify the ship's deflectors to work within the disturbance.

To make matters worse, Chakotay is hallucinating. He envisions himself in a boxing ring, pitted against Kid Chaos, while hearing strange voices all around. Chakotay wants no part of the visions; his grandfather was prone to bizarre hallucinations. But could the hallucinations actually be a key to the way out?

114. Think Tank

Voyager manages to escape a snare set by Hazari bounty hunters, but Janeway fears they will have reinforcements in the sector that lies ahead. A strange visitor, Kurros, pays the captain a call, claiming he has the answer to her problem. Kurros is part of a "Think Tank"—a small group that excels at problem solving. He says he can peacefully resolve *Voyager*'s interaction with the Hazari. The captain agrees to do business—until Kurros indicates that Seven of Nine is one of the items he wants as payment. After Janeway downloads information from a Hazari ship that reveals Kurros hired the bounty hunters to go after *Voyager*, she formulates a scheme to get even with the Think Tank.

115. Juggernaut

Voyager picks up two survivors of a disabled Malon freighter. They were hauling toxic waste, they explain, when a dangerous leak forced them to evacuate. But the leak will soon cause the storage tanks to explode and destroy everything within three light-years—including *Voyager*. With *Voyager*'s warp drive incapacitated, the only way to deal with the threat is to return to the Malon vessel and stop the explosion or set the ship on course for a nearby star. But someone—or some*thing*—on board doesn't want either to happen.

116. Someone to Watch Over Me

The Doctor decides that it's time to add dating to Seven's socialization skills. He sets about teaching her the finer points of making small talk, dining, and dancing with the opposite sex. The purely educational nature of the assignment begins to change—at least for the Doctor. Meanwhile, the captain departs the ship to attend a diplomatic function aboard a Kadi vessel, leaving Neelix in charge of the Kadi ambassador, who quickly develops an unfortunate fondness for substances his superiors wouldn't approve of.

117. 11:59

Janeway reminisces about one of her favorite ancestors, Shannon O'Donnel, the brave woman she always thought was responsible for building the Millennium Gate, which became the model for the first habitat on Mars. However, as the captain hears bits of contradictory information from the crew and the ship's database, she begins to wonder: aside from marrying Henry Janeway, exactly what did Shannon do on the eve of the millennium in the year 2000?

118. Relativity

Seven is recruited by Captain Braxton of the Federation *Timeship Relativity* from the twenty-ninth century. Braxton explains that *Voyager* will be destroyed after a time-traveling saboteur plants a device on the ship. In fact, the saboteur has done it several times already, in several different eras. Braxton says Seven can help him because her ocular implant will detect the temporal distortions given off by the device, thus allowing them to remove it before it detonates. Seven has to find and stop the saboteur at all costs, even if that means dying herself—several times.

119. Warhead

A *Voyager* away team beams aboard a device with bioneural circuitry that seems to be suffering from a technical form of amnesia. The team realizes that the unit is a weapon of mass destruction, and when it regains its memory, it quickly commandeers the Doctor's program, demanding that Janeway help it find the target it originally was deployed to hit but never reached. If Janeway *doesn't* comply, the WMD/ Doctor will destroy *Voyager* and its crew.

120. Equinox, Part I

Voyager's crew is surprised to receive a distress call from Captain Ransom of the *Starship Equinox*, a Federation science vessel that, like Janeway's ship, was brought into the Delta Quadrant by the Caretaker. Finding Ransom's ship under attack by life-forms from another dimension, Janeway extends *Voyager*'s shields around it. A rescue party finds that most of the crew is dead. Since *Voyager*'s shields won't hold the aliens back for long, Ransom and the other survivors agree to move to *Voyager*, while secretly planning to steal the ship's field generator for their own vessel. The Doctor discovers the horrific reason that the aliens began attacking the *Equinox*.

Season Six

121. Equinox, Part II

In the midst of battle, Ransom and the *Equinox* crew depart, leaving *Voyager*'s crew to deal with the hostile alien life-forms. Janeway manages to temporarily defeat the nucleogenic creatures and sets out to track down the *Equinox* and recover the abducted Seven of Nine. Ransom has shed his Starfleet ideals and his morality in his quest to get back to the Alpha Quadrant. Now Janeway's crew look on in alarm as they see *their* captain abandoning her own ideals in her obsession to stop Ransom.

122. Survival Instinct

After *Voyager* docks at the Markonian Outpost space station, the crew allows visitors to come on board for an open house. Seven is startled when one visitor brings her a set of relays from her old Borg ship. The equipment and the presence of the visitor trigger memories from the past, which Seven attempts to ignore—until the man and two females show up in the cargo bay. Formerly part of Seven's unimatrix, the trio need the ex-Borg's assistance in breaking their telepathic link so they can become separate individuals.

123. Barge of the Dead

Lying comatose in sickbay following an accident, Torres dreams that she is slaughtered by a marauding band of Klingons and taken on the Barge of the Dead to *Gre'thor*—Klingon hell— where dishonored souls are taken. There, she finds her estranged mother, Miral, and realizes to her horror that her actions in life have caused her mother's fate. When she awakens, Torres pleads for the Doctor to put her back into a coma so that she can restore Miral's honor before the barge reaches the gates of *Gre'thor*.

124. Tinker, Tenor, Doctor, Spy

Disappointed by the treatment he receives from the crew, the Doctor adds daydreams to his program. In those daydreams, he sees himself as a man among men, admired by female crew members and celebrated as the ship's Emergency Command Hologram (ECH)—a newly created position that would fill in for the captain in the event of catastrophic events. An alien surveillance team, looking for targets of conquest, taps into the Doctor's daydream program and interprets it as reality. Suddenly, the Emergency Medical Hologram finds himself playing the role of ECH to protect *Voyager*.

125. Alice

While *Voyager's* crew shops for parts at a junk-yard of old ships, Paris takes an interest in a small junked shuttle. Chakotay gives him per-mission to restore the vessel. Before long, the small ship—which has an interface allowing it to link to its pilot's thoughts—starts occupying *all* of Paris's time. After the shuttle, which Paris has named *Alice*, nearly kills Torres, it takes full control of his body. *Alice* and Paris depart from *Voyager*, disappearing into space.

126. Riddles

Tuvok is badly injured as he attempts to scan a cloaked presence in the shuttle carrying him and Neelix back to *Voyager*. A sympathetic Kesat official suggests that the Vulcan was attacked by a Ba'Neth, a secretive species reputed to cloak itself in order to assess foreigners' technology. The Doctor is unable to reverse all of the dam-age to the Vulcan's brain without a full under-standing of the Ba'Neth weapon, something that isn't attainable from the paranoid aliens.

127. Dragon's Teeth

The crew is caught up in a tunnel of energy as *Voyager* is pulled through a subspace corridor. Suddenly, a Turei vessel hails the ship, accusing the crew of traveling through *their* underspace. Telling the Turei it was an accident, Janeway asks for help getting out. The Turei push them out, and the crew discovers they've traveled two hundred light-years in just two minutes. Janeway asks if she can negotiate passage through their underspace, but the Turei begin firing on them. On a nearby planet, a *Voyager* away team finds stasis pods containing the Vaadwaur. The subspace corridors once be-longed to them, a revived Vaadwaur explains. Janeway offers to help the Vaadwaur regain their corridors—but she soon learns that it doesn't pay to take sides.

128. One Small Step

Janeway allows Chakotay and Paris to take the *Delta Flyer* to investigate a distinctive space anomaly. The same anomaly might have caused the disappearance of Lieutenant John Kelly and the *Ares IV* command module during a historic early Mars mission in 2032. Although the crew finds the story of Kelly and the *Ares* inspirational, Seven of Nine does not.

129. The *Voyager* Conspiracy

Seven installs a powerful cortical-processing subunit in her regeneration alcove that will allow her to assimilate more information in less time. After downloading data regarding a new technology, she tells Chakotay that she is con-vinced Janeway stranded *Voyager* in the Delta Quadrant so the Federation could establish a military presence there. After downloading more data, Seven tells Janeway that Chakotay is part of a Maquis rebellion preparing to attack Federation ships. Janeway and Chakotay decide that Seven may be right. Something def-initely is wrong on *Voyager*. And all indications are that it's Seven.

130. Pathfinder

Lieutenant Reginald Barclay, formerly an offi-cer aboard the *Starship Enterprise*, is assigned—and a little too committed—to the Pathfinder Project, which was established to make con-tact with *Voyager*. Barclay is convinced that directing a tachyon beam at an approaching pulsar will create a small artificial wormhole, allowing communication with the starship. The outlandish theory *might* be more plausible if Barclay weren't spending all of his time in a holographic re-creation of Janeway's ship. It's enough to make his *real* friends, like Deanna Troi, think he's become a bit . . . unhinged.

131. Fair Haven

Paris and Kim create a new holodeck program set in the quaint Irish village of Fair Haven. The program becomes a peaceful respite for the crew when they can't avoid passing through a neutronic wave front, an interstellar hurricane. Stuck in the wave front for three days, Janeway allows everyone twenty-four-hour access to Fair Haven and even takes advantage of the setting herself.

132. Blink of an Eye

Voyager is trapped in orbit around a planet that revolves at an unusually high rate of speed. The space-time differential between the two is extreme; for each second that passes on *Voyager*, a full day passes on the planet. The ship's presence has not gone unnoticed by the inhabitants of the world below. For centuries, the people think of the ship as the "Ground Shaker" or the "Sky Ship." Although Janeway is fearful that *Voyager*'s presence is contaminating the civilization's entire belief system, she eventually realizes that it also is inspiring them to reach for the stars.

133. Virtuoso

The Qomari willingly accept the crew's assistance in repairing their ship, but they are less than impressed by the technology they see aboard *Voyager*, including the ship's Emergency Medical Hologram—until they hear him sing. Janeway arranges a musical concert featuring the Doctor, and the ecstatic Qomari invite him to introduce the concept of music to their world. The reception he receives from the inhabitants turns the Doctor's head, leading him to decide that practicing medicine on a starship isn't the career he was cut out for.

134. Memorial

Returning to *Voyager* following a two-week mission, Chakotay, Paris, Kim, and Neelix begin experiencing anxiety attacks, violent dreams, and auditory hallucinations—all apparent signs of post-traumatic stress syndrome. Unable to diagnose whether these are brought about by delusions or actual memories, or whether the men were forced to take part in an attack on another species, Janeway attempts to trace the mystery back to its surprising source.

135. Tsunkatse

Chakotay and Torres head for a nearby planet to attend a violent Tsunkatse match, while Seven and Tuvok opt to take a shuttle to study a micronebula. Seven and Tuvok are hijacked. An alien, Penk, wants Seven as a combatant for the Tsunkatse ring, where opponents must battle for day-to-day survival. As Seven fights, Chakotay realizes she is a prisoner—but quickly discovers that it won't be easy to get her or Tuvok out of Penk's clutches.

136. Collective

The *Delta Flyer* is intercepted by a Borg cube, and Chakotay, Paris, Neelix, and Kim are taken prisoner. After tracking the shuttle's whereabouts, *Voyager* easily disables the cube's weapons. Seven observes that only five Borg are aboard. When the drones offer to trade the captured crew members for *Voyager*'s navigational deflector, Seven is surprised by this atypical Borg behavior. When she beams over, she understands why. The drones are all children who were forced out of their maturation chambers prematurely when the adult drones died of an unknown virus. Now Seven must convince these dangerous children to release their hostages.

137. Spirit Folk

The Fair Haven holoprogram has been operating nonstop. As a result, the quaint locals are getting suspicious of some of the *Voyager* crew, particularly Paris, whose pranks (such as briefly transforming a Fair Haven girl into a cow) seem like black magic. Still, there doesn't appear to be a problem—until Tom and Harry are trussed up and questioned in the town church while lovelorn pub owner Michael takes the Doctor's mobile emitter to search for his dear Katie.

138. Ashes to Ashes

As Seven adjusts to acting as caretaker to the four Borg children she helped rescue from a disabled cube, a small shuttle approaches *Voyager*. The crew is surprised when the pilot identifies herself as Lyndsay Ballard—a crewmate who died—even though she looks nothing like Ballard. She explains that her body was found by the Kobali, a race that procreates by altering the DNA of dead bodies. Kim, Ballard's former best friend, believes her story, and the Doctor substantiates the biological details. Janeway welcomes her back, but the Kobali also want Ballard to come home to them.

139. Child's Play

The crew believes they have located the home of Icheb, the oldest of the former Borg children. Seven finds that she has mixed feelings about returning the brilliant teenager, who is uneasy about rejoining his family. Ultimately, the boy decides that it would be in his people's best interests for him to stay on their world, but after Seven leaves with *Voyager*, she realizes that decision may not be in *Icheb's* best interests. Icheb's parents have lied about some very important things—and she suspects they may be planning to use their son as a biological weapon against the Borg.

140. Good Shepherd

An efficiency report indicates that three crewmen are functioning far below Starfleet standards. Janeway gives the offenders an opportunity to prove themselves by accompa-nying her on an away mission in the *Delta Flyer*. But when the scientific mission runs into serious problems that threaten the lives of all aboard the shuttle, the captain realizes she may have erred.

141. Live Fast and Prosper

A trio of con artists have been posing as Janeway, Tuvok, and Chakotay, traveling from system to system swindling the locals and leaving the *Voyager* crew to face the blame when promised goods are not delivered. The thieves apparently have managed to download *Voyager*'s database from the *Delta Flyer*. It will take some clever detective work for *Voyager* to locate the stolen items and reestablish the starship's good reputation.

142. Muse

After the *Delta Flyer* crash-lands, Torres becomes the inspiration for Kelis, a local poet who wants to write an epic play that will promote peace between his patron and his enemies. Torres gives Kelis ideas in exchange for his assistance in repairing the shuttle. Ultimately she finds herself taking an active role in the production when Kelis expresses the fear that the play could actually *cause* a war if she doesn't help him.

143. Fury

Gone from the ship for three years, an aged, worn Kes returns to *Voyager* on a mission of vengeance. She blames the crew of *Voyager* for taking her from her planet, making her a prisoner on the ship, and corrupting her with ideas of exploration. Now she wants to return to Ocampa—but not in her present form. Kes plans to turn back time to the first few months she was aboard the ship, at which point she'll make a deal with the Vidiians. She'll give them *Voyager*'s crew, if they'll take her younger self back to Ocampa.

144. Life Line

The first transmitted block of data that *Voyager* receives from Starfleet's Pathfinder Project includes some troubling news: Doctor Lewis Zimmerman, the creator of the Emergency Medical Hologram, is dying. Hoping to help save his father, the Doctor has his program transmitted to the Alpha Quadrant. Instead of being grateful, Zimmerman is annoyed. He considers the older EMH obsolete. He's been examined by much more recent models, as well as the finest *living* doctors in Starfleet. But when the Doctor's own program rapidly begins to deteriorate and only Zimmerman can repair him, it seems that the two may have to work together after all.

145. The Haunting of Deck Twelve

The former Borg children are regenerating in their alcoves for the night, when *Voyager*'s crew powers down the ship. The children awaken to find Neelix waiting nearby with a lantern. The children can tell there's something odd about the fact that Janeway has ordered *all* of the ship's power shut down. They guess that it has something to do with the "ghost" that's said to be sealed in a section of Deck 12. Neelix tells them a story about the nebula that *Voyager* visited right before they came to live on the starship—and the strange life-form that lived in that nebula . . . until *Voyager* unwittingly caused it to lose its home.

146. Unimatrix Zero, Part I

As Seven of Nine regenerates, the ex-Borg dreams that she is in a beautiful forest where she encounters a man who claims to know her. His name is Axum, and the place is a virtual construct known as Unimatrix Zero, accessible only to one in a million Borg drones during their regeneration cycles. In Unimatrix Zero, these unique drones can exist and interact with each other, their individualities intact. The Borg queen has become aware of this place and is beginning to track down and kill those drones with the ability to enter. Axum wants Seven to help him hide their identities from the queen. The captain quickly agrees, and ups the ante, opting to start a Borg civil war that will help the drones regain their independence. And to do so, she's willing to set a trap for the queen—using herself, Tuvok, and Torres as bait.

Season Seven

147. Unimatrix Zero, Part II

The Borg queen believes that she has assimilated Janeway, Torres, and Tuvok. However, they have allowed themselves to be apprehended in order to initiate a plan that will permanently free the Borg of Unimatrix Zero. They were given neural suppressants that prevent their minds from linking to the Collective. Tuvok's suppressant, however, is failing, which allows the queen to gain important information from his mind. The queen can't stop Janeway and Torres from releasing a nanovirus that blocks the hive's perception of thousands of drones' thoughts—but she *can* destroy the ships that carry the newly liberated drones.

148. Imperfection

One of Seven's remaining Borg implants—her cortical node—begins to fail. The implant regulates all of Seven's vital functions; without it, she'll die. Although the crew obtains a replacement node from a deceased drone, it won't help Seven. The node must come from a living drone, and the Doctor says he won't end a life to save Seven—not even a Borg's life. Seven's protégé, Icheb, believes that *his* cortical node could be removed without causing permanent damage, since he was never fully assimilated.

149. Drive

As the romantic relationship between Paris and Torres seems to be reaching a critical turning point, Paris is distracted by the prospect of entering the *Delta Flyer* in the upcoming Antarian Trans-Stellar Rally. Torres offers to become Paris's partner. The race represents the first time four species have ever competed peacefully—and when sabotage begins to affect some of the ships, it's clear that one of the competitors isn't honoring the treaty.

150. Repression

Tuvok launches an investigation after a mysterious assailant attacks several crew members. As a pattern slowly emerges, Tuvok finds himself becoming increasingly uneasy. All of the victims are former members of the Maquis; the attacks began after the most recent transmission of mail from Earth. A transmitted letter from Tuvok's son included a subliminal message from a Bajoran named Teero, who once worked with the Maquis conducting mind-control experiments. Concerned that he is under Teero's control, Tuvok asks Janeway to lock him in the brig. Janeway complies—but it will take more than that to stop the fanatic's plans.

151. Critical Care

The Doctor's program and mobile emitter are stolen from *Voyager* and sold to an overcrowded Dinaali hospital ship. The Doctor resents being trafficked in this manner. He's even more annoyed when he discovers that he's allowed to care only for those people in Dinaali society deemed to have the most important professions, skills, and accomplishments. Meanwhile, the truly sick waste away and die. It's enough to make the Doctor push the boundaries of his ethical subroutines.

152. Inside Man

The crew of *Voyager* receives a surprise in the latest transmission from Starfleet: a hologram of Reg Barclay. Holo-Barclay announces that Starfleet has found a way to bring the crew home. Federation scientists plan to create a geodesic fold that will act as a gateway between a red giant star in the Alpha Quadrant and one in the Delta Quadrant. Janeway questions the plan, noting that *Voyager*'s shields won't protect the crew, but the holo-Barclay insists he's brought modifications that will solve everything. On Earth, the real Barclay wonders why *his* latest transmission to *Voyager* didn't get through.

153. Body and Soul

While Seven, the Doctor, and Harry Kim are on the *Delta Flyer*, they're attacked by a vessel belonging to the Lokirrim, a species with a deep distrust of photonic beings like the Doctor. To protect the EMH, Seven downloads his program into her cybernetic implants, telling Lokirrim Captain Ranek that he has destroyed the EMH. Nevertheless, Ranek decides to confiscate the shuttle and take Kim and Seven into custody. On *Voyager*, Paris discovers that Tuvok's growing neurochemical imbalance actually is the Vulcan mating instinct, *Pon farr* (see p. 12).

154. Nightingale

As *Voyager* conducts a major maintenance overhaul, Kim, Seven, and Neelix depart in the *Delta Flyer* to search for supplies. Suddenly caught in the crossfire between two ships, they receive a distress call from a Kraylor vessel, begging for help against an Annari vessel. Hesitant to get involved, Kim ultimately intercedes and forces the Annari ship to disengage. Kim agrees to help the Kraylor ship deliver its cargo of vaccines to its homeworld.

155. Flesh and Blood, Part I

Responding to a distress signal, a *Voyager* away team beams inside a spacecraft, where it finds an injured Hirogen engineer, Donik, and many dead Hirogen hunters. The Hirogen vessel was a training facility built to take advantage of the holotechnology Janeway gave them in hopes that they would favor stalking holographic prey rather than living beings. But according to Donik, the holograms malfunctioned, deactivated their safety protocols, and attacked the hunters. The renegade holograms then transferred their programs to a ship equipped with holo-emitters and left. Now the Hirogen want to hunt the holobeings down.

156. Flesh and Blood, Part II

Against Janeway's orders, the Doctor willingly helps the renegade holograms with their cause. But he becomes furious when he discovers that their leader, Iden, has kidnapped Torres from *Voyager*. Iden explains that the hologram renegades will need her technical expertise in order to finish building the photonic field generator that will allow them to live in peace on a world of their own, separate from the organics that have tormented them.

157. Shattered

Chakotay's attempt to stabilize *Voyager*'s warp core throws the first officer into a state of temporal flux, with half his body aged, the other half young. Cured by the Doctor, Chakotay soon discovers that he wasn't the only victim. *Voyager* was affected, and crew members in different sections of the ship now inhabit eras that exist in *Voyager*'s past. On the bridge, Janeway looks and acts as she did when *Voyager* first left port, while in engineering, Seska is trying to take control of *Voyager* with a group of Kazon. In the cargo bay, Seven of Nine is still fully Borgified.

158. Lineage

The revelation that B'Elanna Torres and Tom Paris are going to be parents evokes different reactions. Paris is thrilled by the thought of their baby, but Torres is plagued by unhappy memories of her childhood and the troubled marriage of her Klingon mother and human father. B'Elanna grew up feeling that her Klingon nature ultimately caused her father to abandon the family. If she can somehow convince the Doctor to make her unborn child more human, perhaps this time things will turn out better.

159. Repentance

After responding to a distress call from a damaged Nygean vessel, Janeway discovers that she's rescued a group of condemned criminals and their brutal guards. With no alternative, she agrees to keep them aboard until another Nygean ship arrives. Tensions between the warden and his charges result in a prisoner, Iko, being severely beaten by the guards. When the Doctor uses some of Seven of Nine's nanoprobes to heal the damage to Iko's head injuries, the murderer becomes a new man. His criminal behavior was the result of a congenital brain defect. *Voyager*'s crew can't help asking on his behalf: does Iko still deserve to die?

160. Prophecy

Voyager easily fends off an attack by an antiquated Klingon vessel, but it's harder to convince Captain Kohlar and his crew that a peace treaty was signed eighty years ago. Only when Janeway introduces Kohlar to her pregnant Klingon chief engineer Torres does Kohlar believe her. Kohlar sets his ship's warp core to self-destruct so that his crew will be forced to join Janeway's. It seems that Kohlar's ancestors left the Klingon homeworld over a century ago believing that someday they would meet the savior of their people, someone who would lead them to a new empire. And now Kohlar thinks he's found that savior in Torres's unborn child.

161. The Void

Voyager is pulled into an inert layer of subspace with no apparent way out, where two vessels attack the ship, penetrating the shields and managing to steal foodstuffs and supplies. A third vessel approaches and its captain welcomes them to the Void, a region where similarly trapped ships compete for resources—and never escape. Janeway realizes that the alien captain may be right. The crew has a tiny window of time to enact an escape plan—and won't be able to do it alone. The captain will have to convince these space scavengers to work together if any of them expect to do more than simply survive.

162. Workforce, Part I

On the planet Quarra, a severe labor shortage has been assuaged by the arrival of new workers: Janeway, Annika Hansen (Seven of Nine), Paris, Tuvok, and Torres. None of them recall their former lives on *Voyager*. Tuvok has serious reservations about the periodic inoculations the Quarren doctors give all the new workers. Meanwhile, Chakotay, Neelix, and Harry Kim return from an away mission to find *Voyager* disabled and hidden within a nebula, with only the Doctor on board. He explains that the ship hit a subspace mine that filled it with dangerous radiation, and Janeway ordered the crew to evacuate.

163. Workforce, Part II

Chakotay and Neelix go undercover to find *Voyager*'s missing crew. Neelix rescues Torres and brings her back to the ship, while Chakotay evades the security forces. Hiding out in Janeway's apartment, Chakotay attempts to convince the captain that her memories have been altered. While Kim hides *Voyager* from attacking Quarren ships, the Doctor searches for a way to restore Torres's memory. Meanwhile, Annika/Seven has made some disquieting discoveries about the new employees in Quarra's workforce, leading her to open her own line of inquiry.

164. Human Error

Seven decides to explore her feelings by creating holographic simulations of various crew members she can interact with. She has discovered she finds Chakotay particularly appealing on an emotional level. But the encounters have a negative impact, making her late for her shift, causing her to neglect her duties, and possibly affecting her health. After the ship has several close encounters with missiles, Seven realizes that she must reevaluate her experiment in emotional stimulation.

165. Q2

Q's son was conceived just four years earlier, but Q2 is already a teenager, as bored and disobedient as any adolescent—but with the omnipotent powers of the Q. Q delivers his son to Janeway, explaining that the Continuum has given him an ultimatum: teach the boy to become an upstanding citizen of the cosmos or Q2 will spend the rest of eternity as an amoeba. Q admits that *he* can't seem to motivate the boy—so he's hoping Janeway and her crew, with their renowned Starfleet morals, can. To assist their efforts, Q strips the boy of his powers.

166. Author, Author

Voyager now has direct contact with the Alpha Quadrant for eleven minutes a day. This not only allows the crew to reconnect with family but also lets the Doctor contact a publisher. The publisher loves his holonovel, which is a thinly veiled retelling of the Doctor's adventures. All of the characters *except* for the EMH are portrayed in a negative light. When the Doctor's justifiably annoyed compatriots aboard *Voyager* cause him to have second thoughts, he tries to withdraw it but discovers it's too late—the holonovel is already in wide release and he has no rights because he's a hologram.

167. Friendship One

Voyager receives an assignment from Starfleet: locate and retrieve *Friendship One*, a probe launched in 2067 to carry a message of peace. The ship locates the probe on a planet whose skies seem to have been darkened by a radioactive nuclear winter. The away team discovers that the planet's inhabitants have been contaminated by an antimatter containment failure. Because the inhabitants learned about antimatter technology from the probe, the survivors assume that Earth sent the probe as a trick to poison their world.

168. Natural Law

Chakotay and Seven travel to Ledos for a conference, and their shuttle scrapes against an energy barrier and starts to break up. Beaming to the surface, they find themselves stranded in a dense jungle, far from their destination. Seven leaves the injured Chakotay to search for shuttle debris in the hopes of constructing a distress beacon. A tribe of primitive humanoids takes Chakotay to their cave and treats his wounds. When Seven finds him, she's treated with similar kindness, and with the help of a young native girl, she contacts *Voyager* and the more advanced Ledosians. Unfortunately, civilization could now make inroads into this once

protected sanctuary, a development that the energy barrier was meant to prevent.

169. Homestead

Neelix is thrilled when sensors detect Talaxian life signs only a few light-years from *Voyager*. An away team finds that a group of five hundred Talaxians, diaspora from the Haakonians' war against Talax, have formed a mining community. Neelix takes a fancy to Dexa, a pretty widowed Talaxian woman with a young son. Dexa and a number of others have grown weary of the mining life and want to become homesteaders on another planet, but they worry that the other miners will follow and attack them. What they need is someone to act as leader and protect them from attacks—someone like Neelix.

170. Renaissance Man

After the Doctor and Janeway return from a medical symposium, the captain reports they've encountered a hostile species, the R'Kaal, who claim *Voyager* has violated their space. She's agreed to surrender the ship's warp core. When Chakotay confronts her, she knocks him out and hides his unconscious body. The crew notes that the Doctor isn't acting like himself either. Unfortunately, the crew is unaware that the aliens who tapped into the Doctor's daydreams are back. If the Doctor doesn't handle things correctly, the aliens may kill the hostage they're holding: the real Captain Janeway.

171./172. Endgame

On the tenth anniversary of *Voyager*'s successful return from the Delta Quadrant—twenty-three years after it originally was stranded there—Admiral Kathryn Janeway completes her preparations for a highly secret, and highly personal, mission. The admiral takes her advanced, upgraded shuttle to pick up a chrono-deflector, essential for traveling through time. She's forced to steal it when the Klingons renege on the deal. Activating a tachyon pulse, the admiral passes through a temporal rift, emerging directly before the startled crew of the *U.S.S. Voyager* in the Delta Quadrant. She tells the younger version of herself that she's come to take the ship home.

Janeway is a suspicious woman in both eras. The captain can't figure out why her older self would want to tamper with the timeline, since she obviously made it home. The admiral explains they must travel through a Borg transwarp hub, one of only six in the entire galaxy. The younger Janeway wants to destroy it, real-izing that this would represent a serious blow to the deadly species. But the older Janeway disagrees. She came back to show them how they could safely travel through it, because twenty-two people aboard the ship will die if they *don't* take this chance—including Chakotay, Tuvok, and Seven of Nine.

However, the Borg queen seems to be aware of the plan. She enters Seven's mind as the ex-Borg regenerates and warns her not to approach the nebula that hides the transwarp hub—or they all will be destroyed.

"There's one more request . . . something of a personal nature. I would like . . . a name."
—The Doctor, "Eye of the Needle"

"I'm violating about half a dozen regulations just by being in the room—and what we did earlier, I don't know if Starfleet even has a regulation for that." —Kim, "The Disease"

"A THREE-HOUR TOUR . . ." Janeway's assignment to track down the vessel of a known Maquis operative was *supposed* to last about three weeks. But even the best-laid plans often get really screwed up. Janeway's ship—as well as the ship of her Maquis nemesis—was hit by a beam, landing them in the Delta Quadrant. Although the alien responsible didn't have any reason to keep them there, he refused to use his technology to send them home; instead, he wanted Janeway to destroy his powerful gizmo so it wouldn't fall into the hands of the neighborhood bullies, the Kazon. A softy for noble causes, Janeway complied, effectively stranding her group and the Maquis crew far, far from home.

STAR TREK

THE MOTION PICTURE ™

THERE IS NO COMPARISON.

Paramount Pictures Presents A GENE RODDENBERRY Production A ROBERT WISE Film STAR TREK—THE MOTION PICTURE Starring WILLIAM SHATNER LEONARD NIMOY DeFOREST KELLEY Co Starring JAMES DOOHAN GEORGE TAKEI MAJEL BARRETT WALTER KOENIG NICHELLE NICHOLS Presenting PERSIS KHAMBATTA and Starring STEPHEN COLLINS as Decker Music by JERRY GOLDSMITH • Screenplay by HAROLD LIVINGSTON Story by ALAN DEAN FOSTER Produced by GENE RODDENBERRY Directed by ROBERT WISE A Paramount Picture

SIX

THE FEATURE FILMS

"The Flight to the Silver Screen"

Ten feature-length motion pictures, 1979–2002

BEFORE YOU SIT DOWN WITH YOUR POPCORN

THE FIRST SIX *STAR TREK* FILMS FOLLOW THE ADVENTURES OF JAMES KIRK

and his crew in the twenty-third century. So do the first few minutes of the seventh,

Star Trek Generations. The rest of *Generations* and the next three movies focus on

Jean-Luc Picard and company in the twenty-fourth century.

Three of the features—*Star Trek II: The Wrath of Khan, Star Trek III: The Search for

Spock*, and *Star Trek IV: The Voyage Home*—make up a trilogy, a three-act play, if you

will, with a continuous story line. If you have seen *The Wrath of Khan*, you will recognize the characters and understand more of the events in *The Search for Spock*. If you have seen that "middle act," you will understand why the crew is on a Klingon ship and heading for Earth in *The Voyage Home*.

THE TIME FRAME

Star Trek: The Motion Picture—the first *Star Trek* movie—is set in 2271, just a few years after Kirk's five-year mission. *Star Trek II, III,* and *IV* all take place more than a decade later, in the years 2285 and 2286. The events of *Star Trek V: The Final Frontier* occur in 2287. *Star Trek VI: The Undiscovered Country* and the first part of *Star Trek Generations* are set a couple more years down the road, in 2293. Then nearly eighty years pass before the *Generations* story line continues in 2371. The remaining *Next Generation–*based films all follow within the decade after that. (Of course, you really don't need to know any of this unless you want to set your watch.)

"Do you know the Klingon proverb that tells us revenge is a dish that is best served cold?" —Khan

"Are you out of your Vulcan mind?" —McCoy

"The needs of the many outweigh the needs of the few." —Spock

STAR TREK: THE MOTION PICTURE

Screenplay by Harold Livingston. Story by Alan Dean Foster.

Original theatrical release 1979

There's a "thing" out there.

—KIRK

Kirk and his former crew reunite aboard the *U.S.S. Enterprise* NCC-1701 to save Earth from V'Ger, a powerful living machine that's destroying everything in its path as it searches the galaxy for its "creator."

THE SHIP

Following its famous five-year mission, the *Enterprise* has undergone a "refit." Just about every major system has been upgraded. To the casual viewer, the most noticeable changes are the ultra-high-tech engineering section with its pulsating warp core, and the toned-down beige-on-beige color palette employed by the '70s-era (2270s, that is) interior decorators at Starfleet.

THE MAIN CHARACTERS

Pretty much everybody from the *Star Trek* TV series (see p. 1) is here: Kirk, Spock, McCoy, Scott, Sulu, Uhura, Chekov, Chapel, and Rand. Aside from different hairdos and new pajama-like uniforms, they haven't changed much. Except:

James T. Kirk has been promoted to admiral—and he's not particularly thrilled about it. When he hears that Earth is in danger, he leaps at the opportunity to get out from behind his desk and into the captain's chair.

Spock has been living on Vulcan, purging himself of his annoying human emotions. But it's those very emotions that spur him to join his former comrades as they face off against V'Ger.

Doctor Leonard McCoy has retired from active duty and grown a beard. So why does he take part in this mission? Kirk has him drafted.

Pavel Chekov has left his navigation post to head ship's security, Nurse Chapel is now Doctor Chapel, and Janice Rand is now the ship's transporter operator.

"Why is any object we don't understand always called a 'thing'?" —McCoy

"Out there—thataway." —Kirk

"It's life, Captain, but not life as we know it." —Spock

NEW CHARACTERS

WILLARD DECKER (Stephen Collins), captain—oops, make that commander—of the *Enterprise*

Decker got his plum assignment as the *Enterprise*'s captain at Admiral Kirk's recommendation. But after the folks at Starfleet spot a big hostile *thing* headed straight for Earth, they allow Kirk to usurp the ship's coveted center seat. Decker spends the mission trying to make a connection with Ilia, a reconstituted version of the ship's deceased navigator (who was Decker's lost love). Ironically, that connection is exactly what it takes to save the day.

ILIA (Persis Khambatta), navigator—make that "probe"

A native of the planet Delta IV, Ilia serves as navigator of the *Enterprise* until she's killed by V'Ger, which then creates a near-duplicate of her to serve as a probe that can communicate with the *Enterprise* crew. Luckily, the probe retains Ilia's romantic feelings for former boyfriend Will Decker, thus allowing the star-crossed couple to consummate V'Ger's quest to "join" with its creator: someone from Earth.

V'GER, a living machine

V'Ger started out as *Voyager VI*, a twentieth-century space probe launched by NASA to study the cosmos. The probe encountered a planet of living machines on the far side of the galaxy. The alien machines apparently saw *Voyager* as an unsophisticated device in need of improvement, so they modified it, enhancing its ability to gather information and return its knowledge to its creator. Unfortunately, they also gave it the ability to destroy, which complicated matters when the confused probe—no longer clear on its original name, let alone its ultimate purpose—set course for Earth, the home of its creator.

MAJOR ALIENS

Deltans

Members of this humanoid species from Delta IV are known for their bald heads and their highly developed sexuality. Since their pheromones can prove overpowering, Deltans that join Starfleet are required to take an "oath of celibacy" to assure they will not take advantage of "sexually immature" species. Like humans.

Klingons

Klingons now have foreheads as spiny as lobster shells, just like the ones in *Star Trek: The Next Generation* (see p. 68). Although the Klingons Kirk encountered in the *Star Trek* TV series had smooth foreheads, no one in this film seems too concerned about the change.

STAR TREK II: THE WRATH OF KHAN

Screenplay by Jack B. Sowards. Story by Harve Bennett and Jack B. Sowards.

Original theatrical release 1982

KHAAAAAANNNNNNN!

—KIRK

●

Molecular biologist Carol Marcus and her team have invented Genesis, a process that will turn burned-out asteroids into fertile Edens that are capable of supporting humanoid life . . . assuming, of course, that the process actually works. Because Starfleet *wants* Marcus's project to work, they assign the *Starship Reliant* to search for a lifeless world that the scientists can experiment on. Unfortunately, the misbegotten dust ball that *Reliant's* crew investigates turns out to be Ceti Alpha V, the place where the *Enterprise* exiled Khan and his genetically enhanced followers nearly twenty years earlier (see p. 29). Khan steals *Reliant*, appropriates Marcus's Genesis device, and plots suitable revenge on his old nemesis, James T. Kirk.

THE SHIP

Same *Enterprise* as in the first feature, but the old girl has been relegated to use as a training vessel for Starfleet cadets.

THE MAIN CHARACTERS

The original seven senior crew members return: Kirk, Spock, McCoy, Scott, Sulu, Uhura, and Chekov. All now are instructors at Starfleet Academy, except for:

Chekov, who is serving as a commander aboard the ill-fated *Reliant*.

They've got handsome new red uniforms.

James T. Kirk is showing signs of serious ennui. Flying a desk at Starfleet makes him feel old. His birthday gift from McCoy—bifocals—doesn't help, nor does an encounter with his (surprise!) adult son.

Spock, now a captain, has come to terms with that lifelong sense of alienation from his Vulcan brethren; he's quite content with his lot in Starfleet.

KHAN NOONIEN SINGH (Ricardo Montalban), genetic superman

Okay, he's not a member of the crew, but he's certainly a familiar face to the senior staff. Khan has become a bit unhinged during his time on Ceti Alpha V. You can't really blame him: six months after Kirk dropped him off, nearby Ceti Alpha VI exploded, screwing up both the orbit and the ecosystem of Khan's world. Now that he has a ship, he has the means to enact his vengeance.

NEW CHARACTERS

SAAVIK (Kirstie Alley), Starfleet cadet

This attractive Vulcan female, a protégée of Spock's, is among a group of cadets assigned to the *Enterprise* for what begins as a standard training mission.

CAROL MARCUS (Bibi Besch), scientist

Carol once was Kirk's girlfriend; they separated because they were on different career tracks. After the split, Carol asked Kirk to stay away from their son for fear that David would someday choose to follow his dad into Starfleet. David grew up to join his mom in developing Genesis, a device that could transform an uninhabitable planet into one capable of supporting life. Of course, to do it, Genesis would have to blow that planet to smithereens; the planet would then (theoretically) reassemble itself into a new preprogrammed configuration. Now, imagine this wonderfully explosive device in the hands of a madman. Like Khan.

DAVID MARCUS (Merritt Butrick), scientist

Thanks to his mom's down-on-Starfleet attitude, David grew up mistrustful of everyone's favorite galactic protection agency. He's not too keen on James Kirk, either, although he had no idea the renowned officer was his dad until Khan brought the dysfunctional family together.

MAJOR ALIEN

CETI EEL

A foul-tempered mollusklike creature native to Ceti Alpha V—and, in fact, the only remaining indigenous life-form on that world. The eel's parasitic babies like to crawl into the ears of sleeping humans and wrap themselves around the brain's cerebral cortex. This renders the victim extremely susceptible to suggestion—making the eels a useful tool for Khan when he needs Chekov's assistance in capturing the *Reliant*.

NOW HEAR THIS! Call us crazy, but we like to watch movies in numerical order. If you prefer to view them randomly, here are a few additional details from *Star Trek II* that you should know in order to enjoy *Star Trek III*.

In the climax of *Star Trek II*, Khan, mortally wounded in the battle with the *Enterprise*, triggers the Genesis device. Spock sacrifices his life to get the *Enterprise* out of harm's way before the aforementioned device blows up—but before he does, he mind-melds with McCoy. Kirk gives Spock the equivalent of a burial at sea, placing his friend's lifeless body in a photon torpedo tube and launching it toward the newly formed Genesis planet.

STAR TREK III: THE SEARCH FOR SPOCK

Written by Harve Bennett.

Original theatrical release 1984

Jim—Your name is Jim.

—SPOCK

Following the *Enterprise*'s return from the Genesis planet, Spock's father asks Kirk to bring Spock's body and *katra* (his living spirit) home to Vulcan. As it turns out, that's a tough assignment. For one thing, Kirk doesn't have the *katra;* McCoy does. For another, the body's back on Genesis—which Starfleet has declared off-limits. And did we mention that Kirk no longer has a ship? To further complicate matters, a ruthless group of Klingons is determined to learn the secret of Genesis—and will kill anyone who gets in the way.

THE SHIP

Starfleet has decreed that the *Enterprise* be put out to pasture. Surely an inappropriate fate for such a valiant spacecraft. Kirk really needs transportation—*any* transportation—to fulfill his personal mission. So since Starfleet won't be using it anyway, Kirk steals his own ship.

THE MAIN CHARACTERS

Kirk, Scott, Sulu, Uhura, and Chekov are alive and well and back on Earth. However:

Doctor Leonard McCoy isn't quite himself. Ever since Spock mind-melded with him (see p. 218), the doctor's taken to doing wacky impressions of his Vulcan friend. He's also been caught trying to hire a ship to take him to the Genesis planet—which is now considered highly restricted turf. Federation security decides that McCoy would benefit from a trip to the Federation funny farm. Never fear: Kirk breaks him out.

Saavik (Robin Curtis) and David Marcus are on Genesis, conducting Starfleet-sanctioned research on the new planet's development. Violent earthquakes and inclement weather make their work difficult, and their discovery of an unexpected life-form—a rapidly growing toddler with pointed ears—makes them realize that Genesis is more powerful than anyone imagined. In fact, nothing about the planet is normal. Could it have something to do with the fact that David used protomatter, a highly unstable and unpredictable substance, as one of the ingredients in the Genesis device? Well . . . yeah.

Spock was dead . . . but the Genesis effect has regenerated his cellular structure. He's literally been reborn, and he's growing like a weed. Unfortunately, his mind is a void because McCoy has "all his marbles."

"What you had to do. What you always do. Turn death into a fighting chance to live." —McCoy

NEW CHARACTER

KRUGE (Christopher Lloyd), Klingon commander

Kruge is a badass warrior who believes the Federation has developed Genesis as a doomsday weapon. In an attempt to get Kirk to surrender the *Enterprise* and reveal the secrets of Genesis, he takes Saavik, David Marcus, and the young Spock hostage. He has David killed when Kirk is slow to comply. After leading Kruge's crew into a deadly trap, Kirk kills Kruge and captures the Klingon's ship.

MAJOR ALIEN

Klingons

They're back—and they're madder than ever. And they have an impressive new ship for this outing: the Klingon bird-of-prey. Following its introduction in this film, vessels of this type go on to appear in subsequent *Star Trek* features, as well as *The Next Generation* and *Deep Space Nine.*

NOW HEAR THIS! Here are a few more details from *Star Trek III* that you should know in order to enjoy *Star Trek IV.* To escape from his Klingon foes, Kirk sets the controls of the *Enterprise* for a time-delayed self-destruct, then beams out with his crew—just as Kruge's crew beams in. Boom! No more Klingons—but for the first time in *Star Trek* history, no more *Enterprise.* Of course, this leaves Kirk short of transportation, so he and his crew appropriate the Klingon ship in order to take Spock to Vulcan. There, Spock—now miraculously restored to the age he was when he died—gets his marbles back from McCoy.

"My God, Bones. What have I done?" —Kirk

"Don't call me Tiny." —Sulu

"You Klingon bastard! You've killed my son." —Kirk

"Aye, and if my grandmother had wheels, she'd be a wagon." —Scotty

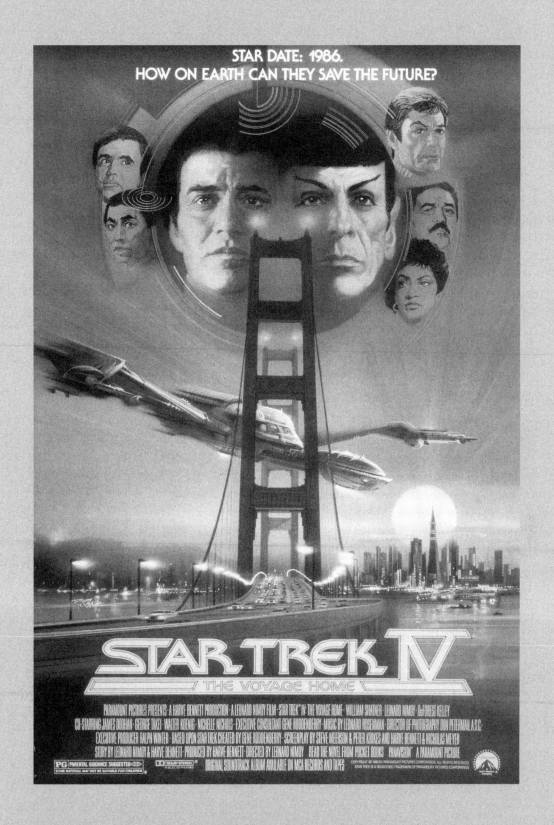

STAR TREK IV: THE VOYAGE HOME

Screenplay by Steve Meerson & Peter Krikes & Harve Bennett & Nicholas Meyer.

Story by Leonard Nimoy & Harve Bennett.

Original theatrical release 1986

I'm from Iowa. I only work in outer space.

—KIRK

Kirk and his crew head toward Earth to face the music for stealing the *Enterprise* and taking it to the forbidden Genesis planet. As they near their destination, however, they receive word that transmissions from an alien probe are wreaking havoc on Earth's biosphere. All starships in the vicinity of the planet have been rendered powerless, so it's up to Kirk and the others to save Earth by traveling into the past to get what the probe wants: whales.

THE SHIP

Yep, it's dead. It blew up real good at the end of *Star Trek III*, so the crew uses a captured Klingon ship to get around. Although this ship isn't particularly comfortable, it does have one advantage over the *Enterprise:* a cloaking device that allows it to remain unnoticed in the middle of San Francisco's Golden Gate Park.

THE MAIN CHARACTERS

The main cast is here, even Spock. However:

Spock isn't the man he once was. As McCoy puts it, "He's not exactly working on all thrusters." The Vulcan's mind is fully restored, but he can't quite grasp the subtleties of life and language. Luckily, his somewhat peculiar behavior (not to mention the bathrobe he wears throughout most of the movie) doesn't seem out of place in San Francisco, where Kirk is able to blame his friend's oddball antics on "too much LDS" during the 1960s.

Pavel Chekov suffers a life-threatening brain injury while stealing high-energy photons from a nuclear reactor to power the ship's return to the twenty-third century. (He gets better.)

"I love Italian. And so do you." —Kirk

NEW CHARACTERS

GILLIAN TAYLOR (Catherine Hicks), marine biologist

Taylor is the assistant director of the Cetacean Institute in San Francisco. Two humpback whales are in her care—so Kirk takes it upon himself to get chummy with the biologist. (It doesn't hurt that she's cute.) Taylor thinks Kirk is rather odd, but she opts to trust him. And, in fact, she tags along on the trip back to the future since no one in the twenty-third century has her experience with whales.

ALIEN SPACE PROBE, communication device for certain cetacean life-forms

This big probe, sent by an unknown alien species, arrives at Earth in the twenty-third century to contact the planet's humpback whales.

(We never find out why.) Seeing as Earth's humpbacks are long extinct by this time, there can be no response—which doesn't seem to sit well with the probe.

GEORGE AND GRACIE, humpback whales from the twentieth century

Humpbacks, already an endangered species in the twentieth century, are extinct in the twenty-third. But the space probe doesn't plan to leave Earth until it "talks" to one. Kirk and his senior officers retrieve the pair from the past so the whales can carry out the conversation. (What they ultimately discuss is known only to George and Gracie.) After the probe leaves, the whales are free to repopulate their species in Earth's oceans.

AND IN THE END . . .

Kirk and his crew face the Federation Council to learn their punishment for their previous actions (conspiracy, assault, theft, sabotage, and a few other odds and ends). Since the group has just saved Earth, the council decides it would be petty to deal with them *too* harshly. It dismisses all the charges but one: Kirk is guilty of disobeying the orders of a superior officer. His punishment: a reduction in rank to captain. He is assigned to the duties for which he has "repeatedly demonstrated unswerving ability: the command of a starship."

And they also give him a new ship: the *U.S.S. Enterprise*-A.

"Well, double dumb ass on you!" —Kirk

"To hunt a species to extinction is not logical." —Spock

"What does it mean, 'exact change'?" —Spock

"The bureaucratic mentality is the only constant in the universe." —McCoy

ON JUNE 9,
ADVENTURE
AND IMAGINATION
WILL MEET
AT THE
FINAL
FRONTIER

STAR TREK V
THE FINAL FRONTIER

STAR TREK V: THE FINAL FRONTIER

Story by William Shatner & Harve Bennett & David Loughery.

Screenplay by David Loughery.

Original theatrical release 1989

What does God need with a starship?

—KIRK

After Starfleet sends the *Enterprise* to Nimbus III to resolve a hostage situation, a renegade Vulcan named Sybok hijacks the ship and forces the crew to accompany him on a quest to find God. As Kirk and company head for the Great Barrier—an energy field surrounding the center of the galaxy—Sybok's influence causes the crew members to realize some disquieting truths about themselves.

THE SHIP

This is a new *Enterprise*, designated NCC-1701-A, an updated version of the ship Kirk destroyed in *Star Trek III*. It looks the same on the outside but has a redesigned interior. The ship is untried, so a few bugs are apparent on her shakedown cruise.

"I need my pain." —Kirk

"I liked him better before he died." —McCoy

THE MAIN CHARACTERS

Kirk, Spock, McCoy, Scott, Sulu, Uhura, and Chekov are happy to be back in space on their own Federation starship. They still have those red uniforms but also have "field duty" outfits for landing party assignments. Other than that, little has changed. Except:

James T. Kirk's demotion to captain has revitalized him. He takes up rock climbing, much to McCoy's distress.

NEW CHARACTERS

SYBOK (Laurence Luckinbill), passionate Vulcan and (surprise!) half brother to Spock

We always thought that Spock was an only child. But now we find out that Sarek had *another* child, a son named Sybok, from his first marriage to a Vulcan princess. Sybok was smart like Spock, but unlike his brother, he became a revolutionary. On Vulcan, that means he chose to reject logic and embrace the animal passions of his ancestors. How revolting! After Sybok was banished from Vulcan, he went on a quest to find the mythical planet of *Sha Ka Ree* (think heaven), reputed to be located at the center of the galaxy. To get there one has to go through an impassable Great Barrier. Sybok decides to steal Kirk's starship to accomplish the allegedly impossible feat.

KLAA (Todd Bryant), hotshot Klingon captain

Klaa is arrogant and ambitious—in short, your average Kingon warrior. He has one burning aspiration: to gain a rep as "the greatest warrior

"Jim, you don't ask the Almighty for his I.D."
—McCoy

in the galaxy." The quickest means to that goal is to defeat a great warrior—so imagine how happy Klaa is when he learns that the legendary James T. Kirk is in the neighborhood.

VIXIS (Spice Williams), female first officer on Klaa's bird-of-prey

She's hot and even more ambitious than Klaa—and she looks like she could beat him at arm wrestling. As Chekov observes, "She has vonderful muscles."

"GOD" (George Murdock), unidentified powerful entity

Okay, he's not really God, but pretending to be the Supreme Being is a great scam when you want to get something from naïve supplicants. Obviously, this fake deity is not a nice guy—which is probably why he's been imprisoned on a planet located beyond the Great Barrier, and why he's so keen to find a way out.

"I know this ship like the back of my hand."
—Scotty

The battle for peace has begun.
STAR TREK
VI
THE UNDISCOVERED COUNTRY
OPENS DECEMBER 6 AT THEATRES EVERYWHERE

STAR TREK VI: THE UNDISCOVERED COUNTRY

Screenplay by Nicholas Meyer & Denny Martin Flinn.

Story by Leonard Nimoy & Lawrence Konner & Mark Rosenthal.

Original theatrical release 1991

This is the final cruise of the *Starship Enterprise* under my command.

—KIRK

An environmental disaster on a Klingon moon forces the warrior race to consider an armistice with the Federation. A reluctant Captain Kirk is assigned to escort Klingon Chancellor Gorkon to an intergalactic peace summit. But the chancellor's ship is attacked, and it appears that the *Enterprise* is the aggressor. McCoy tries to save the mortally injured Gorkon, but since he doesn't know much about Klingon anatomy, Gorkon dies. The Klingons sentence Kirk and McCoy to a lifetime of hard labor at the frigid penal colony, Rura Penthe. Can they survive until Spock finds the real culprit behind the attack?

THE SHIP

Still *Enterprise*-A.

THE MAIN CHARACTERS

Kirk, Spock, McCoy, Scott, Uhura, and Chekov are still on the *Enterprise*, but they're due to "stand down" (retire, that is) in three months. But wait—isn't someone missing?

Sulu is now Captain Sulu. And he's commanding *his* own starship for this voyage: the *U.S.S. Excelsior.*

Janice Rand, once yeoman to Kirk (see p. 10), is now the communications officer on Sulu's *Excelsior*. It's always nice to see old friends gainfully employed.

Spock, as mentioned, is still assigned to the *Enterprise* . . . but it seems he's also been doing a bit of moonlighting, acting as the Federation Special Envoy to the Klingon Empire. Spock has avoided telling Kirk—who's never forgiven the Klingons for killing his son—about this part-time diplomatic position. He's also neglected to mention that he's personally offered up Kirk's services in the peace effort.

"There is an old Vulcan proverb: Only Nixon could go to China." —Spock

NEW CHARACTERS

VALERIS (Kim Cattrall), Vulcan Starfleet officer

Like Saavik, Valeris was mentored by Spock (hmm . . . why no *male* Vulcan protégés, Spock?), and he was very proud when she graduated at the top of her Starfleet Academy class. He isn't so proud when he learns that she played a role in Gorkon's assassination.

GORKON (David Warner), leader of the Klingon High Council

Gorkon is the forward-thinking political head of the Klingon Empire who is assassinated by a coalition of Klingons, humans, Vulcans, and Romulans who, ironically, came together in order to disrupt his efforts to bring them together.

"You have not experienced Shakespeare until you have read him in the original Klingon."
—Gorkon

"In space, all warriors are cold warriors."
—Chang

CHANG (Christopher Plummer), Klingon general

Chang, the chief of staff to Gorkon, cuts a dashing figure in Klingon circles with his prim mustache and riveted eye patch. Although he's crazy for Shakespeare, he can't stand humans—which is why he's part of the coalition to kill Gorkon. Kirk ultimately dispatches him by sending a photon torpedo up his tailpipe.

MARTIA (Iman), chameloid

Depending on Martia's mood, this cigar-smoking shape-shifter appears to be either the most beautiful woman in the world . . . or a big ugly beastie . . . or maybe even a guy who looks like Captain Kirk. Whatever, he/she manages to help Kirk and McCoy escape from the gulag on Rura Penthe. Then she betrays them—and suffers the fate of most double-crossers.

"If I were human, I believe my response would be, 'Go to hell.'" —Spock

"Second star to the right, and straight on 'til morning." —Kirk

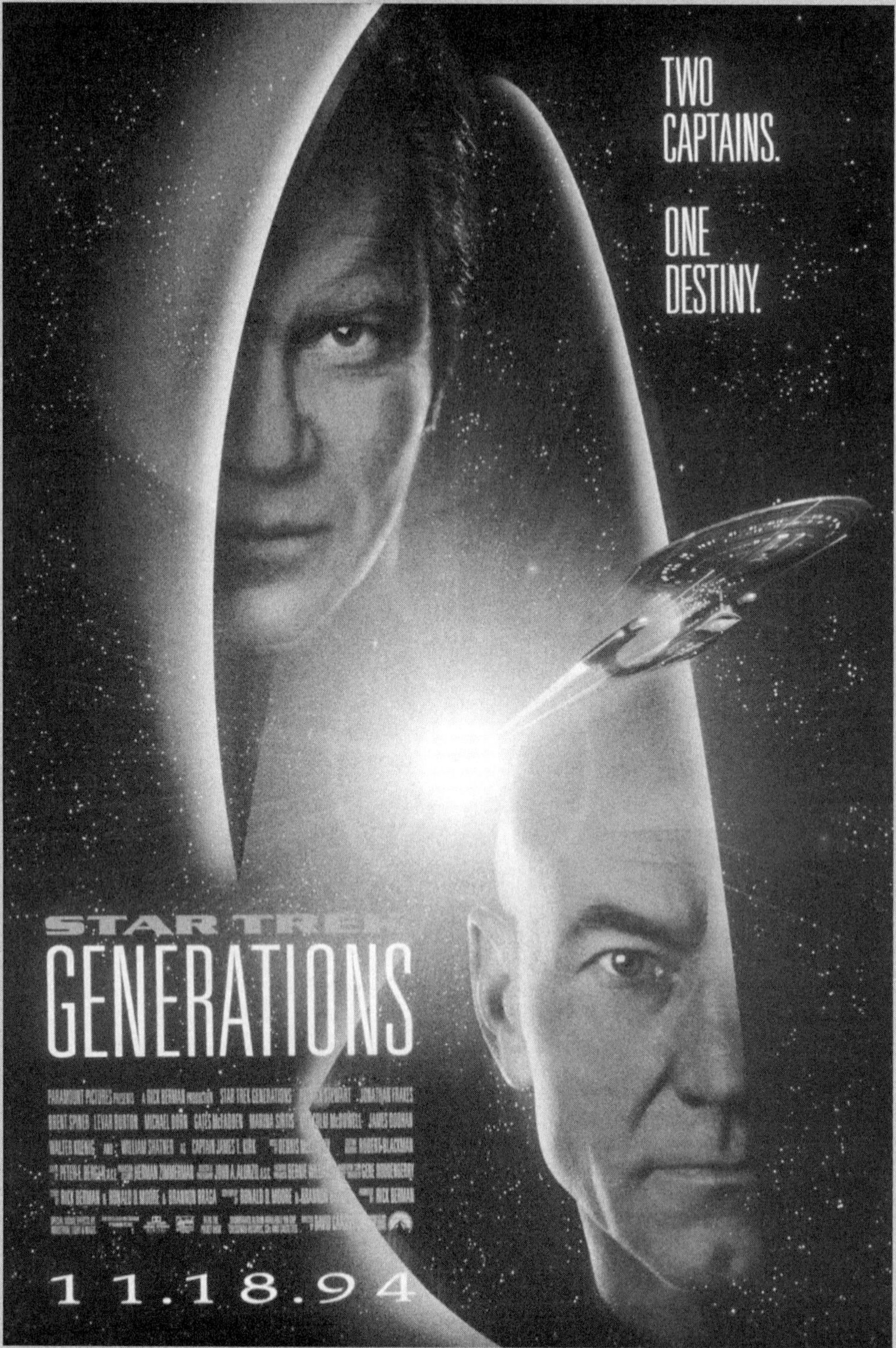
TWO
CAPTAINS.
ONE
DESTINY.
STAR TREK
GENERATIONS
11.18.94

STAR TREK GENERATIONS

Story by Rick Berman & Ronald D. Moore & Brannon Braga.

Screenplay by Ronald D. Moore & Brannon Braga.

Original theatrical release 1994

Captain, this is the first *Starship Enterprise* in thirty years without James T. Kirk in command. How do you feel about that?

—JOURNALIST

In the late twenty-third century, Kirk, Scott, and Chekov are honored guests at a ceremony celebrating the launch of the new *Enterprise*-B, commanded by Captain John Harriman. When the ship receives a distress call from the *Lakul*, a vessel trapped within a bizarre energy ribbon, the three veterans pitch in to help inexperienced Harriman. The *Enterprise* rescues a handful of the *Lakul*'s passengers before being ensnared in the ribbon's wake. Thanks to Kirk's heroic efforts, the *Enterprise* breaks free—but at the apparent loss of Kirk's life.

Seventy-eight years later, Captain Jean-Luc Picard and the crew of the *Enterprise*-D encounter Tolian Soran, an El-Aurian who has invented a deadly device that will draw the previously mentioned energy ribbon to him—but in the process take millions of innocent lives. Why would Soran want to do that? The answer lies within the ribbon, in an intoxicating realm known as the Nexus. Soran had a taste of the Nexus seventy-eight years ago—just before the *Enterprise*-B yanked him from its grasp. His obsession to return to it is overwhelming. No mere Starfleet captain can stop him. But perhaps *two* Starfleet captains . . .

THE SHIPS

There are two, count 'em, two, *Enterprises* in this film. Captain Harriman's *Excelsior*-class *Enterprise*-B is the successor to Kirk's *Constitution*-class *Enterprise*-A. Because the B left port only for a ceremonial outing, it's missing such things as a tractor beam generator, photon torpedoes, and medical staff.

Picard's *Enterprise*-D (see p. 57) is fully equipped. By the end of the film, however, the ship's damaged warp core blows up, destroying the battle section. Fortunately, a ship separation maneuver (see p. 74) saves the saucer section. Most of the crew survives (even Data's cat, Spot), but the ship is unsalvageable.

THE MAIN CHARACTERS

Kirk, Scott, and Chekov from the *Star Trek* TV series make an appearance, as does just about everyone from *The Next Generation*: Picard, Riker, Data, La Forge, Worf, Troi, Crusher, and Guinan. No one has changed much. Except:

James T. Kirk dies . . . twice. The first time he is *presumed* dead, when in fact he's been swept into the Nexus. The second time, a metal ramp crushes him after he helps Picard dispatch the evil Soran. Then—oh, my—he's really most sincerely dead. It's not a flashy death, particularly for a legend like Kirk—but he does get to save the day.

Jean-Luc Picard is devastated when his older brother Robert and his nephew René perish in a fire. The potential end of the Picard line—Jean-Luc has no children of his own—depresses him greatly.

Data, wishing to understand human feelings once and for all, plugs in the emotion chip left to him by his creator, Doctor Soong. Of course, the chip immediately wreaks havoc on his neural net (the android equivalent of a brain). It's enough to make a grown android cry.

Worf is promoted to lieutenant commander. Go, Worf!

Guinan reveals a deep, dark secret: like Soran, she was in the Nexus—and a part of her still is.

The Duras Sisters, those conniving Klingon wenches (see p. 69), show up to aid Soran and once again plague Picard's crew. But it's one time too many. All you characters who survive the movie, take one step forward. Not so fast, Lursa and B'Etor!

NEW CHARACTER

TOLIAN SORAN (Malcolm McDowell), fanatical El-Aurian

He wasn't always a bad guy. He lost his family, then the Nexus affected him like an addictive drug, displacing the emptiness in his life. And like a junkie, he is willing to do anything to get back the feelings the Nexus offers.

"They say time is the fire in which we burn."
—Soran

"Don't let them promote you. Don't let them transfer you. Don't let them do anything that takes you off the bridge of that ship. Because while you're there, you can make a difference." —Kirk

"I take it the odds are against us, and the situation is grim . . . Sounds like fun!" —Kirk

"I was out saving the galaxy when your grandfather was still in diapers." —Kirk

"Somehow I doubt that this will be the last ship to carry the name Enterprise." —Picard

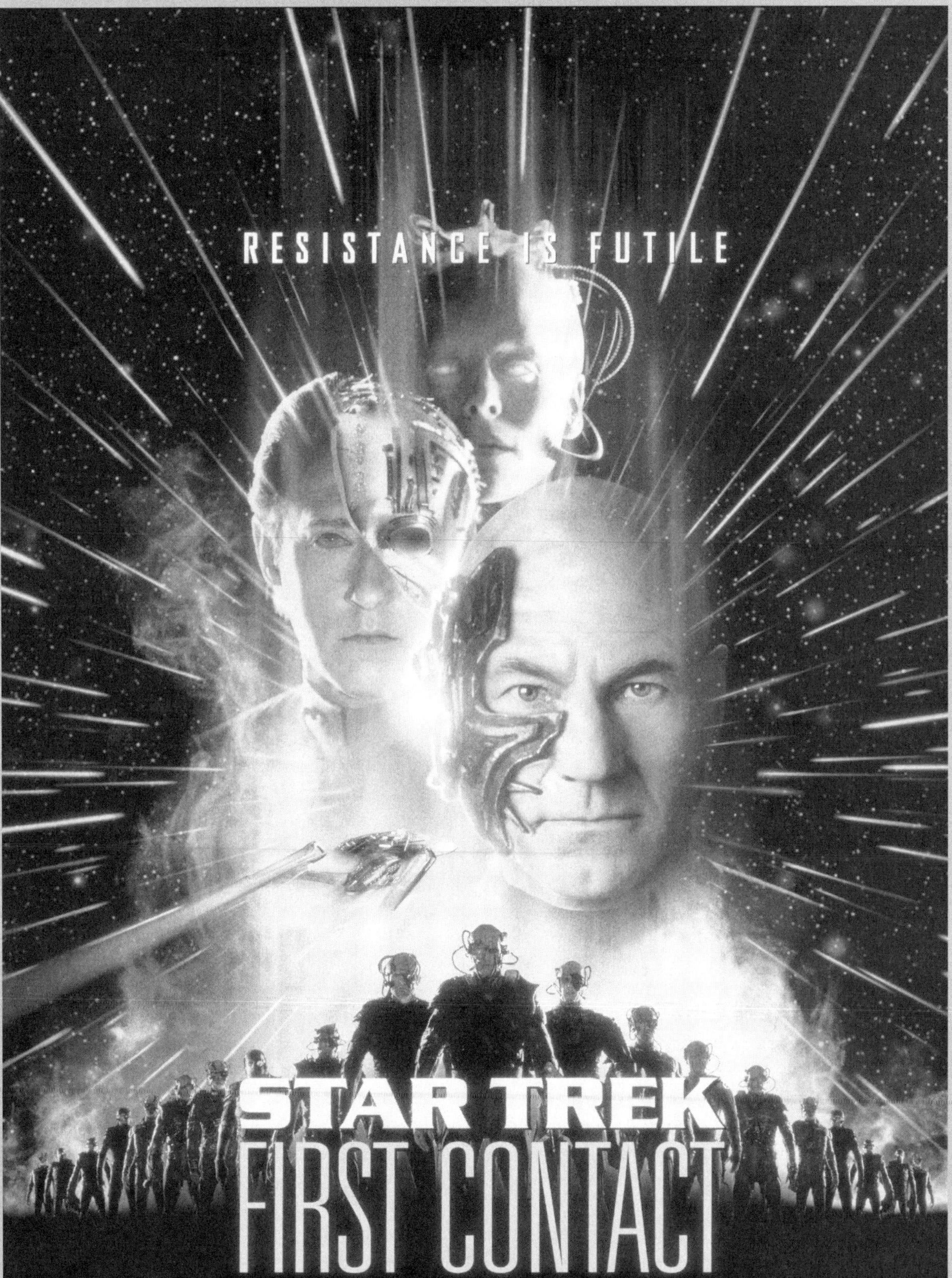
RESISTANCE IS FUTILE
STAR TREK
FIRST CONTACT

STAR TREK: FIRST CONTACT

Story by Rick Berman & Brannon Braga & Ronald D. Moore.

Screenplay by Brannon Braga & Ronald D. Moore.

Original theatrical release 1996

The line must be drawn here! This far, no further!

—PICARD

A coalition of Starfleet vessels intercepts and destroys a gigantic Borg cube (see p. 66) that's en route to Earth, but they fail to catch the small Borg sphere ship that emerges from the cube's debris. Unfortunately, that little ship is the real threat to humanity. The sphere ship creates a temporal passage and leaps into the past, changing history by assimilating Earth's populace at a critical point in time—just before Zefram Cochrane makes Earth's first warp-powered flight. Why is that important? Because it triggers the chance meeting between humans and the aliens that will lead to the founding of the United Federation of Planets. Picard must follow the Borg to the twenty-first century to prevent them from stopping Cochrane's flight.

THE SHIP

The *Enterprise* in this film is the brand-new *Sovereign*-class NCC-1701-E, the successor to Picard's beloved *Enterprise*-D, which bit the dust (literally) in *Star Trek Generations*. The *Enterprise*-E is longer than the D (by about forty meters) and a bit more streamlined, but for all intents and purposes, it's the same reliable standard-bearer as the *Enterprise*s that came before.

THE MAIN CHARACTERS

With the exception of Wesley and Guinan, the entire *The Next Generation* crew is present, even Worf, who, despite having transferred to space station Deep Space 9 (see p. 115), manages to get beamed onto the *Enterprise*-E in time to join the chase after the Borg. Everyone looks pretty sharp; apparently Starfleet thought that it was time to

give the troops some new threads. No jumpsuits this time. The basic uniform—pants paired with a snug-fitting matching jacket—is primarily black. Underneath the jacket is a long-sleeved, high-necked shirt in the telltale what-division-I'm-in colors previously established on *The Next Generation*. There's also a nicely coordinated vest to wear instead of the jacket when you need a little more freedom of movement (say, when you're stalking Borg in the ship's corridors). Nothing else has changed much, except:

Jean-Luc Picard, who once was assimilated by the Borg (see p. 66), has been hearing their voices in his head and having bad dreams, making him very moody.

Geordi La Forge has traded in his sight-enhancing VISOR for a pair of sight-enhancing ocular implants that look a lot less geeky.

NEW CHARACTERS

ZEFRAM COCHRANE (James Cromwell), inventor of warp drive

You might say Cochrane is the guy who made Starfleet possible. His warp drive made faster-than-light travel a reality, which in turn allowed people like Jean-Luc Picard to seek out new life and new civilizations on distant worlds. Cochrane prefers not to be thought of as a hero, however, and truth be told, he'd rather listen to rock 'n' roll and drink than make history. Well, wouldn't we all?

LILY SLOANE (Alfre Woodard), aerospace engineer

Lily helped Zefram Cochrane build the *Phoenix*, Earth's first warp-powered ship. She encountered the crew of the *Enterprise*-E when it traveled back in time to save humanity from assimilation by the Borg. Initially she distrusted Picard but eventually came to be quite fond of him.

BORG QUEEN (Alice Krige), Borg leader

Some viewers may be familiar with the queen from her appearances on *Voyager* (see p. 173), but this adventure marks her memorable debut. No one would ever mistake the Borg leader for a simpleminded drone. She retains an individual personality and seems to experience emotions. She's even sexy, with her Medusa-like cable tresses and leather bustier. The queen's primary goal as top Borg is to stop Cochrane. But she gets sidetracked by her unusual interest in both Data and Picard, and makes the fatal error of underestimating both of them.

"Reports of my assimilation have been greatly exaggerated." —Picard

"Assimilate this!" —Worf

"It's my first ray gun." —Lily

"Borg? Sounds Swedish." —Lily

"Tough little ship." —Riker

"So you're all astronauts on some sort of . . . star trek?" —Cochrane

THE BATTLE FOR PARADISE HAS BEGUN

STAR TREK
INSURRECTION

PARAMOUNT PICTURES PRESENTS A RICK BERMAN PRODUCTION A JONATHAN FRAKES FILM "STAR TREK: INSURRECTION"
PATRICK STEWART JONATHAN FRAKES BRENT SPINER LEVAR BURTON MICHAEL DORN GATES McFADDEN MARINA SIRTIS F. MURRAY ABRAHAM
DONNA MURPHY ANTHONY ZERBE MUSIC BY JERRY GOLDSMITH PRODUCED BY PETER LAURITSON EDITED BY PETER E. BERGER, A.C.E. PRODUCTION DESIGNER HERMAN ZIMMERMAN
DIRECTOR OF PHOTOGRAPHY MATTHEW F. LEONETTI, ASC EXECUTIVE PRODUCER MARTIN HORNSTEIN BASED UPON "STAR TREK" CREATED BY GENE RODDENBERRY PRODUCED BY RICK BERMAN & MICHAEL PILLER
SCREENPLAY BY MICHAEL PILLER PRODUCED BY RICK BERMAN DIRECTED BY JONATHAN FRAKES

www.startrek.com   READ THE NOVEL FROM POCKET BOOKS   SOUNDTRACK ALBUM AVAILABLE ON GNP CRESCENDO RECORDS CD'S AND CASSETTES

1 2 · 1 1 · 9 8

STAR TREK: INSURRECTION

Story by Rick Berman & Michael Piller.

Screenplay by Michael Piller.

Original theatrical release 1998

Who wouldn't be tempted by the promise of perpetual youth?

—ANIJ

The *Enterprise*-E crew uncovers a conspiracy between Starfleet and the Son'a to forcibly relocate the inhabitants of the Ba'ku planet. Something in the planet's atmosphere keeps the inhabitants young. Some of the folks at Starfleet cannot pass up the chance to get their hands on this fountain of youth, despite the fact that interfering with the peaceful Ba'ku is a violation of the Prime Directive. Picard and crew must make a choice: follow an unlawful order and help the Son'a, or protect the Ba'ku and mutiny against Starfleet.

THE SHIP

Still the NCC-1701-E—but with a few surprises, including a really fancy shuttlecraft designated the captain's yacht.

THE MAIN CHARACTERS

Still present and accounted for: Picard, Riker, Data, La Forge, Crusher, Troi, and Worf. Hey, wait a minute . . .

Worf? Is he AWOL from DS9 *again*? Well, no—he just happened to be in the neighborhood when he heard his old friends were in the sector, so he decided to drop by and say hi. Good timing.

NEW CHARACTERS

ANIJ (Donna Murphy), Ba'ku female

She's more than three hundred years old, but she looks great, and it turns out that Picard is attracted to older women. Like most of her people, she has the ability to slow time to experience a perfect moment. Anij and the other residents of the Ba'ku planet aren't indigenous to the region. They immigrated there after fleeing a culture that had grown overly dependent on technology.

RU'AFO (F. Murray Abraham), Son'a leader

You wouldn't know it to look at him, but Ru'afo used to live on the Ba'ku planet. The Ba'ku exiled him and his friends when they tried to take over the peaceful colony. Once they left, however, Ru'afo's group of ex-Ba'ku (renamed the Son'a) began to age, and they didn't do it gracefully. Ru'afo has had his skin stretched and stapled so often there's not much left to work with—which is why he came up with the idea to get Starfleet to help him steal the Ba'ku world's gift of everlasting youth.

MATTHEW DOUGHERTY (Anthony Zerbe), Starfleet admiral

Dougherty conspired to remove the Ba'ku from their planet, thus allowing Starfleet and the Son'a to share in the benefits of the regenerative radiation. He figured it was okay to stretch the parameters of the Prime Directive since the Ba'ku weren't native to the planet anyway. After Picard revealed that the Son'a were related to the Ba'ku, making the whole scheme a blood feud, Dougherty tried to stop it. Too late.

"Saddle up. Lock and load." —Data

"Definitely feeling aggressive tendencies, sir." —Worf

"Does anyone remember when we were explorers?" —Picard

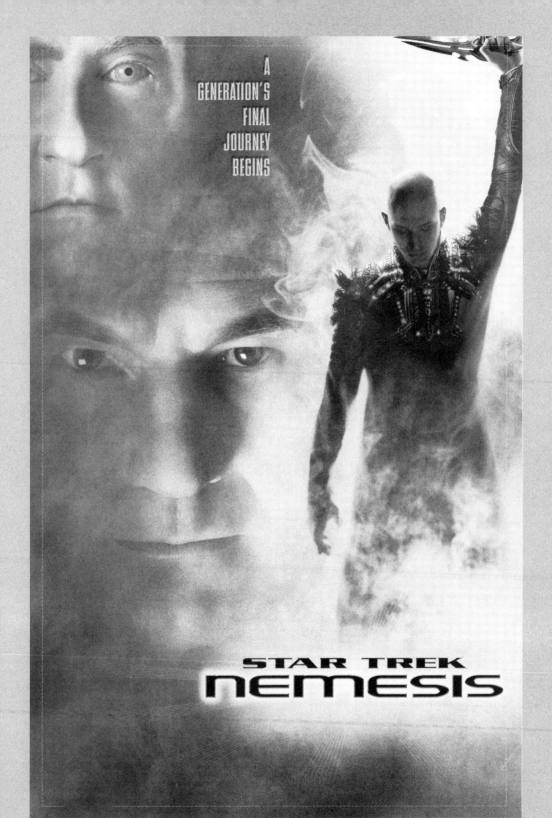

STAR TREK NEMESIS

Story by John Logan & Rick Berman & Brent Spiner.

Screenplay by John Logan.

Original theatrical release 2002

Good-bye.

—DATA

After the *Enterprise*-E picks up an unusual signal from a planet located near the Romulan Neutral Zone, the crew finds the dismantled pieces of an android who looks just like Data. But before the crew has a chance to consider the implications, surprising information arrives from recently promoted Admiral Janeway (see pp. 161, 209–210). There's been an internal political shake-up on Romulus, and Shinzon, the new Praetor (think emperor), has asked that a Federation ship drop by, ostensibly to talk peace. Shinzon is from Remus, Romulus's sister planet, although he's not actually a Reman. He's a human clone of Jean-Luc Picard—the vestige of a failed Romulan plot to infiltrate Starfleet (we'll get to this later). It doesn't take long for the crew to realize that its discovery of the dismantled android wasn't an accident and that it isn't peace Shinzon is looking for. It's revenge—against the Romulans who created him and the humans he resembles.

THE SHIP

Still the *Enterprise*-E.

THE MAIN CHARACTERS

All of *The Next Generation* crew is here—Picard, Riker, Data, La Forge, Troi, Crusher and, once again, Worf . . .

Worf left Deep Space 9 to become a diplomat following the end of the Dominion War (see p. 157), but he soon realized that wasn't his cup of bloodwine. He's back to stay on the *Enterprise*, just in time to celebrate Riker and Troi's wedding.

Will Riker and Deanna Troi have tied the knot. The ceremony takes place in Riker's native Alaska. Marriage is just a small step compared to the bigger commitment Riker just made: he's finally leaving the *Enterprise* to command his own starship, the *Titan*. And he's taking Deanna with him as his counselor. Looks like Picard will have to put in some requests to Starfleet's human resources department.

Data discovers that he has another "brother," or, more accurately, yet another android sibling. This new one, named B-4, is a few bits shy of a byte and is unaware that he's being used as a spy by Shinzon. Nevertheless, Data views his sibling compassionately and even offers to download his own memory into B-4. It doesn't help B-4 much, but it does demonstrate, once again, how "human" Data is—which is why his ultimate sacrifice for his captain shouldn't come as a surprise.

MAJOR ALIENS

ROMULANS AND REMANS

Romulus and Remus are sister planets within the same system. You'd think that would make the "sister" species who inhabit those worlds neighborly . . . but, no. Romulus is your typical alien world, which is to say, habitable. Remus, on the other hand, is a nasty place: unbearably hot on one side of the planet, unbearably cold on the other. It's a hell of a place—literally—to grow up. About the only thing the planet is good for is mining, and for many years the dominant Romulans have forced the Remans to live under brutal conditions and work the mines. Well, what goes around, comes around. The Remans eventually rise up against their Romulan oppressors and kill everyone in the Romulan Senate.

In terms of appearance, Romulans look like their Vulcan ancestors. Remans have gray skin, cadaverous frames, and batlike ears—in fact, the resemblance to Nosferatu is uncanny.

NEW CHARACTERS

SHINZON (Tom Hardy), human leader of the Romulan Empire

Shinzon was created from some of Jean-Luc Picard's DNA, part of a misbegotten Romulan scheme to replace the real Picard with a Romulan agent. When that plan was abandoned, the poor clone was sent to the dilithium mines of Remus, where he labored as a slave. During his years in the mines, he bonded with the Remans and plotted revenge against the Romulans and against all of humanity. He spearheaded the Reman rebellion against their Romulan oppressors and put himself in charge of the empire. Shinzon is hell-bent on fulfilling *all* his vengeance fantasies, including exposing all life on Earth to deadly thalaron radiation (trust us, it's bad stuff). The big question is, can he do it before he dies from a design flaw in his genetic sequencing?

VICEROY (Ron Perlman), Shinzon's number one Reman aide

Shinzon's Viceroy is the first Reman that humans (and *Star Trek* viewers) have laid eyes on. The Viceroy befriended Shinzon when the boy was first sent to Reman's mines. With his spooky psychic powers, the Viceroy helps Shinzon to make lascivious out-of-body visits to Deanna Troi's quarters at night. If that creeps you out, imagine how Troi feels. Can you blame Riker for eliminating the Viceroy when he's presented with the opportunity?

"You have the bridge, Mister Troi." —Picard

"Serving with you has been an honor." —Riker

"The only thing the Romulan guards hated more than the Remans was me." —Shinzon

"I'm afraid you won't survive to witness the victory of the echo over the voice." —Shinzon

Archer was not prepared for the hazards of space, but he would learn.

SEVEN

STAR TREK: ENTERPRISE

"The Beginning of the Story and the End of the Line . . . for Now."

98 hour-long episodes, 2001–2005

SERIES PREMISE

APPROXIMATELY A HUNDRED YEARS BEFORE THE LEGENDARY VOYAGES OF
Captain Kirk, a stalwart captain and his crew set forth from Earth in the very first
starship named *Enterprise*. Their mission: to see what's out there—boldly, of course.
But these space pioneers soon learn that not every species out there is looking for
new friends.

THE SHIP

At a length of 190 meters, the *Enterprise* NX-01 is a bit smaller than Kirk's *Enterprise* and a lot smaller than Picard's. It has a crew complement of just eighty-three men and women, all human except for the Vulcan science officer and the Denobulan doctor. And there's a dog too.

The NX-01 may look like your basic *Star Trek* starship (a big saucer and a big pair of tube-shaped engines), but it's more primitive. The show is set in the early days of interstellar travel (see Now Hear This!, p. 262), and the technology reflects that. This *Enterprise*'s warp engines can reach only warp 5 (as opposed to warp 9 point whatever in the other *Star Trek* incarnations). There are no replicators. There *is* a transporter, but the technology is so new that our heroes have doubts about its ability to reassemble scrambled molecules. And since the ship doesn't have biofilters, crew members who've been exposed to alien microbes must strip down to skivvies and spend some time in *Enterprise*'s decon chamber, smearing neutralizing gel all over one another's bodies. Depending on whom you're "deconning" with, this can be interesting.

THE MAIN CHARACTERS

JONATHAN ARCHER (Scott Bakula), captain

Take her out, straight and steady.

—"BROKEN BOW"

Jonathan Archer is the prototype for all Starfleet captains to come—a strong, honest man who sees the stars as his personal testing ground. He's been itching to get at them since he was a boy building models of starships.

Archer's father, Henry, worked on Starfleet's Warp 5 Project, developing the technology to power starships farther and faster than ever before. It took a while (see Why Does Archer Hate the Vulcans?, p. 264), but Jonathan eventually would pilot the very first warp 5 ship, the *Enterprise* NX-01.

Archer was disappointed by his initial close encounters in deep space. The Klingons were hostile and rude, the Andorians were arrogant and rude, and the Tellarites . . . well, they were just rude. Every week, Archer ran into species who'd just as soon blast the *Enterprise* out of the space lanes as befriend its crew. But he managed to remain positive—until he encountered the Xindi. After that . . . well, how's a guy supposed to remain helpful, friendly, and courteous when millions of Earth's residents are killed? Archer began relating to aliens differently.

Eventually, Archer regained his equilibrium. He went on to play a pivotal role in bringing together the disparate species that would found the United Federation of Planets.

Key Archer Episodes

- "Broken Bow"
- "First Flight"
- "Twilight"
- "Damage"

"Maybe we're not out here to just scan comets and meet new species. Maybe we're out here to prove that humanity is ready to join a much larger community." —Archer, "Cease Fire"

T'POL (Jolene Blalock), Vulcan first officer

"Learning from one's mistakes is hardly exclusive to humans."

—**"SHOCKWAVE"**

The Vulcan High Command wasn't convinced that humans were mature enough to embark on an extended mission of exploration, so when the NX-01 left port, it insisted that Captain Archer take along T'Pol as an "observer" (think chaperone). Archer soon realized that T'Pol had her strong points. And T'Pol discovered that once you got beyond the bad smell, humans demonstrated some highly commendable qualities. In fact, after two years on the *Enterprise*, T'Pol resigned from the High Command and joined Starfleet, ostensibly to accompany the crew on a critical mission into the Delphic Expanse.

She is, to say the least, a bit unusual for a Vulcan. She solicited a one-night stand with a human coworker, ostensibly just for the sake of experimentation, and later dosed herself with a nasty neurotoxin in order to access her emotions. Pretty atypical behavior for a species dedicated to logic. But then, her mother *was* a radical cult member, and her great-grandmother, the "inventor" of Velcro, was pretty odd too. So maybe she's just observing her family heritage.

Key T'Pol Episodes
- **"Fusion"**
- **"Impulse"**
- **"Awakening"**
- **"Terra Prime"**

CHARLES "TRIP" TUCKER III (Conner Trinneer), chief engineer

> My dad's Charles Tucker and so was his dad, and that makes me the third, so . . . triple . . . Trip.
> —"FIRST FLIGHT"

Trip is the third senior officer on the *Enterprise*, after Archer and T'Pol. He's an ace engineer who's always up for the next challenge, whether it's upgrading the ship's weapons systems or extracting a confession of affection from the tight-lipped T'Pol.

He's been friends with the captain since their paths first crossed during the NX test program at Starfleet. Trip's collaboration helped Archer prove to both Starfleet and its Vulcan advisers that the warp engines developed by Henry Archer were capable of taking humankind to the distant stars.

Archer gives Trip plenty of leeway to perform his own personal brand of technological miracles; Trip's impulsive nature occasionally lands him in hot water when he leaves engineering. A seemingly innocent encounter with a Xyrillian female resulted in Trip's discovery that he was pregnant. And his decision to buck Vissian cultural taboos by teaching an unprivileged member of their curiously gendered species to read, write, and think for itself ultimately caused the distraught being to commit suicide.

The death of Trip's sister, Elizabeth, in the Xindi attack on Earth was a huge blow to the engineer. His anger and sorrow left him unable to sleep and darkened his normally upbeat personality. At Phlox's urging, T'Pol offered Trip some unorthodox relaxation therapy, with biologically predictable results. Their brief union resulted in a mental bond that would continue to link them for the rest of Trip's life.

Key Tucker Episodes
- "Cogenitor"
- "First Flight"
- "Similitude"
- "Terra Prime"

MALCOLM REED (Dominic Keating), tactical officer

They're called phase pistols. They have two settings: stun and kill. It would be best not to confuse them.
—"BROKEN BOW"

Descended from a long line of British navy men, Lieutenant Reed is a real straight arrow. He's a to-the-point, by-the-book stickler for discipline. These traits frequently set him at odds with Chief Engineer Trip Tucker, who's more casual about rules and regs. Ironically, Trip is the closest thing Reed has to a best friend on the ship, possibly the result of their surviving a disastrous shuttlepod mission together—and an equally calamitous shore leave on Risa.

As chief of security, Reed's more comfortable deactivating a bomb than revealing details of his inner life, which is why figuring out what flavor to make his birthday cake (pineapple) took Hoshi days of undercover sleuthing. His fondness for secrecy may have been what drew him into serving as an agent for Starfleet's secret intelligence branch—but the spy biz wasn't for him. When push came to shove, he was, like Archer, a Boy Scout and definitely a guy more loyal to his captain than to some shadowy covert ops group.

Key Reed Episodes

- "Shuttlepod One"
- "The Forgotten"
- "Divergence"

"No offense, but when it comes to our weapons frequencies, I wouldn't trust my own mother."
—Reed, "Proving Ground"

PHLOX (John Billingsley), chief medical officer

The opportunity to observe your species on their first deep space venture has proven irresistible.
—"DEAR DOCTOR"

As Archer prepared to set sail for the final frontier, it occurred to him that an alien physician with a background in intergalactic medicine could be an asset in his crew. Thus Phlox, a Denobulan from the Interspecies Medical Exchange, came to serve on *Enterprise*—along with his menagerie of osmotic eels, Pyrithian bats, and sundry other slimy critters that Phlox says are good for what ails you.

A remarkably cheerful soul, Phlox doesn't seem to mind being away from his home for long periods of time. But if you had an extended household of three shared wives, four mutual husbands, and five children, you might like to get away for a few years too.

Key Phlox Episodes
- **"Dear Doctor"**
- **"The Breach"**
- **"Divergence"**

"I'm a physician, not an engineer!"
—Phlox, "Doctor's Orders"

HOSHI SATO (Linda Park), communications officer

> I was Jonathan Archer's first choice for this mission. Every inhabited world we come to is going to be filled with language. He needs me here.
>
> —"FIGHT OR FLIGHT"

Some people were born to explore the stars. Others prefer to observe them from their backyards. Hoshi is firmly entrenched in the latter camp, an admittedly strange attribute for someone who specializes in exolinguistics (the languages of nonhumans). Only the guttural sounds of Klingonese lured her from a secure teaching position at Brazil's Amazon University to a posting on the *Enterprise*. Hoshi was spooked by everything and everyone she heard/saw/met when she first arrived. By the time the *Enterprise* was doing battle with the Xindi, Hoshi established that she had "the right stuff." Her experiences on *Enterprise* ultimately allowed Hoshi to make fundamental improvements on the capabilities of the universal translator.

Key Hoshi Episodes

- "Vanishing Point"
- "Countdown"
- "Terra Prime"

TRAVIS MAYWEATHER (Anthony Montgomery), helmsman

Course laid in, sir.
—"BROKEN BOW"

Travis is a "space boomer," meaning he was born and raised on an interstellar cargo vessel. Everyone in the Mayweather clan works on the *Horizon* family freighter—except, of course, Travis, who felt that Starfleet offered more opportunities than intergalactic trucking. He's an excellent pilot, presumably one of the reasons Archer brought him aboard *Enterprise*. Unfortunately, the captain is pretty hands-on, and he's just as likely to pilot his own shuttlepod as allow Mayweather to do what he's trained to do.

Key Mayweather Episodes

- "Horizon"
- "Observer Effect"
- "Demons"

"Ever slept in zero g?"
—Mayweather, "Broken Bow"

"Somebody always dies."
—Mayweather, "Observer Effect"

RECURRING CHARACTERS

MAXWELL FORREST (Vaughn Armstrong), Starfleet admiral

Don't screw this up.

—"BROKEN BOW"

A senior admiral of Starfleet Command, Forrest oversees Archer's missions. He oversaw the NX development program and, several years later, gave the ultimate order that allowed Archer to take the NX-01 to the stars. Despite numerous conflicts with Ambassador Soval, Forrest ultimately sacrificed his life to save the Vulcan from a terrorist's bomb.

SOVAL (Gary Graham), Vulcan ambassador

We don't know what to do about humans.

—"THE FORGE"

Soval was once a key proponent of the ultra-cautious Vulcan policies that kept those immature, overemotional humans out of deep space (see Why Does Archer Hate the Vulcans?, p. 264). However, after he realized that members of his own government were a lot more misguided than the folks on Earth, he turned on his government to prevent interplanetary war from breaking out.

MAJOR ALIENS

Denobulans

On Denobula Triaxa, marriages typically involve multiple partners and large extended families. And if one of those partners wants to go outside of the family unit for a little "variety," that's okay too. With all that activity, it's a good thing Denobulans don't require much shut-eye; give them an occasional week of hibernation, and they're good to go for months. Although Denobulans are humanoid, with their prominent facial ridges and bifurcated foreheads you'd never mistake one for a human.

Suliban

Just your average sentient aliens until their homeworld became uninhabitable. Then they began wandering the space lanes, looking for a place to get a handout. They got more than they bargained for when they ran into a mysterious fellow from the twenty-ninth century (see Temporal Cold War, p. 263). This "Future Guy" (as the show's fans called him—the series never gave him a name) had a few little jobs to take care of in the twenty-second century, and he couldn't do them himself. So in exchange for their assistance, he gave the Suliban advanced technology and all sorts of genetic enhancements. It was a match made in . . . well, heaven is probably the wrong direction to be thinking.

The average Suliban looks kind of like the theoretical offspring of a human and a scaly chameleon. And if you think they look weird on the outside, you probably don't want to hear about what's been happening *inside* their enhanced chromosomes.

A Xindi-Primate, a Xindi-Arboreal, and a Xindi-Reptilian, three of the six kinds of Xindi.

SILIK (John Fleck), big-shot in the Suliban Cabal

Silik works for the guy from the future. His genetic enhancements allow him to crawl across the ceiling, slide under the door, and blend into wallpaper patterns. Wow! If that job with Future Guy doesn't work out, Silik might want to try out as a comic superhero.

Xindi

An alliance of five species from the Delphic Expanse: the Primates (who look like your average human), the Arboreals (slothlike humans), the Aquatics (underwater mammals that resemble manatees), the Reptilians (lizardlike humans), and the Insectoids (antlike beings). Although they all originate from the same planet and have the same goals, they differ in not-so-subtle ways when they have to decide on a plan of action. The Primates and Arboreals lean toward peace and diplomacy, the Reptilians and Insectoids believe in fighting for what they want, and the highly intelligent Aquatics tend to ponder issues for a long time.

Starfleet first became aware of the Xindi when the alliance attacked Earth on the advice of the Sphere Builders, a transdimensional race from another plane of existence. The Sphere Builders showed up in the Expanse after the Xindi civil war and warned the Xindi that humans would destroy their part of the galaxy. The Xindi believed them. It became Archer's job to convince the Xindi that the Sphere Builders were the real enemy—and the ones who actually planned to take over the Delphic real estate.

IMPORTANT XINDI

DEGRA (Randy Oglesby), humanoid

Degra was an engineer and a member of the Xindi Council. He designed the weapon that the council planned to use to destroy Earth and also the earlier prototype that wreaked havoc on Earth. After thinking about all the children who died in that attack, Degra—himself the father of two—came to regret the use of his weapon (think Robert Oppenheimer, father of the atomic bomb).

WHY ISN'T IT THE *U.S.S.* ENTERPRISE? All the other *Enterprise*s seen in *Star Trek* series or movies have included U.S.S. as part of their titles. Not Archer's ship, however. That's because *Star Trek: Enterprise* takes place prior to the founding of the United Federation of Planets—and only Federation ships use the U.S.S. appellation. Archer's ship carries the registration prefix NX, which means it's an experimental prototype.

Vulcans

During this era, most Vulcans think humans are odorous and immature. Turns out we remind the Vulcans of themselves long ago—and that scares them. That's particularly true of the Vulcan High Command. Because it's a period of repression and paranoia, Vulcans don't engage in many activities that are commonplace in other incarnations of *Star Trek*. The Vulcan mind-meld (see p. 11), for example, is forbidden; Vulcans who practice the technique are considered perverts. That includes the Syrannites, strict followers of Surak, father of modern Vulcan philosophy, who are hunted as outlaws.

It takes a brief civil uprising to turn things around. Well, that and Archer helping the Syrannites to recover and make public the *Kir'Shara*, Surak's original writings.

IMPORTANT VULCAN

T'PAU (Kara Zediker), future political figure

T'Pau is a fiery anarchist, part of the Syrannite movement that Archer and T'Pol get involved with on Vulcan. A century later, she will be the much more respectable matriarch of Spock's family (see p. 12).

Klingons

Humanity encounters Klingons for the first time in a cornfield in Montana. They don't hit it off—and things go downhill from there. Archer does his darnedest to be nice to them and even helps save them from their own folly after a disastrous attempt to enhance their genetic structure triggers a specieswide epidemic (see Why Do Some Klingons Have Bumpy Foreheads and Some Don't?, p. 257).

WHY DO SOME KLINGONS HAVE BUMPY FOREHEADS AND SOME DON'T? Fans have been waiting for the answer to this question for decades, but the Klingons do not discuss it with outsiders. Here's why.

Remember Archer's experience with the Augments? No? (See Who the Heck Are the Augments?, p. 264.) Although Archer dispensed with them, word spread to the Klingon Empire. The Klingons were concerned that human Augments might provide Starfleet with an advantage. So they got their hands on some of those embryos from Khan's time and used them to alter the DNA of Klingon test subjects. *Voilà*—Klingon Augments! They had greater strength, more intelligence . . . and smooth foreheads, just like humans. Unfortunately, they were dying like flies. And so were millions of other Klingons, because the Augment genes had somehow paired up with a nasty virus and become airborne, spreading the mutation far and wide.

The Klingons kidnapped Phlox and forced him to help them find a cure, which he ultimately did, with a little help from Archer. However, the cure took away all the fun aspects of the enhancements—the superstrength and intelligence—and left behind only the unsightly social stigma of a smooth forehead. That's why a large percentage of the warrior populace—including all the Klingons that Kirk encountered in *Star Trek*—came out of the incident sans bumps.

Now you understand why the forehead debacle is as embarrassing to the Klingons as the mullet hairdo is to us.

Blue man group—Andorian style.

Andorians

You may recall this blue-skinned species from *Star Trek* (see p. 16). Andorians live up to their reputation as a passionate, violent people, which may explain why they have such a hard time getting along with the dispassionate Vulcans, to the point of occasional warfare. Their relationship with humans, on the other hand, flowered during Archer's time and evolved into an interspecies alliance that was, at times, stronger than the one between humans and Vulcans. Those antennae, by the way, are used for hearing and balance, and will grow back if lopped off (ouch!). Pack some warm clothes if you're going to the Andorian homeworld; it's always cold there.

SHRAN (Jeffery Combs), commander

Captain of the Andorian warship *Kumari*, Shran was xenophobic when he first met Archer (whom he derisively referred to as "pink skin"), but they became close allies and real friends. Their initial encounters often put the two men at cross-purposes, but they inevitably found that cooperation worked to their mutual advantage against the Xindi, the Romulans, and even the unethical members of the Vulcan High Command.

"You have no idea how much I'm restraining myself from knocking you on your ass."
—Archer, "Broken Bow"

THE MENAGERIE

Tellarites

Sure, you may know that the porcine Tellarites love to argue (see p. 15), but did you know that arguing is considered a sport on their homeworld? Or that the homeworld is called (surprise!) Tellar? Or that they consider canine a culinary delicacy? They're not a very pleasant or trustful species, and are especially suspicious of Andorians and Vulcans.

Romulans

The imperialistic Romulans like to set deadly booby traps in space when staking claim to new turf. And they'll happily foster rivalries and initiate blood feuds between species like the Andorians and the Tellarites in order to prevent them from creating (horrors!) an alliance with those annoying pacifists from Earth. Because Romulans feel that stealth is a major virtue, they prefer to do their dirty work from the comfort and safety of their homeworld. That's why they created a remote-controlled drone ship that could be operated from Romulus and attack their enemies' ships without implicating them. The drone ship was a marvel of technology. It had an auto-repair system and an advanced multispatial emitter system that allowed the ship to mimic the appearance of nearly any other vessel. Pretty neat, huh? Too bad it got destroyed when Archer and his allies figured out what was going on. The Romulans were sneaky creeps, even back in Archer's day.

TEN ESSENTIAL EPISODES

1. "Broken Bow" Written by Rick Berman & Brannon Braga.

Ninety years after Zefram Cochrane's warp flight triggered first contact with the Vulcans, the human race ventures into deep space with Captain Jonathan Archer at the helm of the *Starship Enterprise* NX-01.

This exciting two-hour pilot showcases the series's thematic potential: a determined captain with a fire in his belly to explore the final frontier, a challenging relationship with our Vulcan "allies," and humankind's first encounter with the Klingons.

2. "Shockwave, Parts I and II" Written by Rick Berman & Brannon Braga.

When the *Enterprise* is blamed for the destruction of a colony—an event that time-traveler Daniels says never happened—Daniels takes Archer into the future to protect the timeline, only to see his efforts backfire.

Time-travel stories are, by nature, complex—that's what makes them so provocative and entertaining. This two-parter provides our first hint that Archer is a pivotal figure in Starfleet history.

3. "Cogenitor" Written by Rick Berman & Brannon Braga.

Trip's discovery that an alien visitor to the ship is treated as little more than a slave provokes him to teach the being to think for itself—with tragic results.

This twist on the Pygmalion myth is an outstanding example of what Star Trek's *storytellers do so well—transform a tale about alien behavior into relevant commentary on human social values.*

"You're good at building things. I'm good at blowing things up." —Reed, "United"

4. "First Flight" Written by John Shiban & Chris Black.

Archer reminisces about the early days of the NX test program, a time when he and a rival competed for the honor of being the first human to break the warp 2 barrier.

It's The Right Stuff *meets* Star Trek *in this tribute to the pioneers who make space travel a reality.*

5. "The Expanse" Written by Rick Berman & Brannon Braga.

A mysterious alien probe attacks Earth, killing millions of people. Archer convinces Starfleet that he must take *Enterprise* into a dangerous region of space to find the culprit.

This season finale concludes two years of traditional space exploration and sends the Enterprise *crew into new territory: a season-long mission that pits them against the considerable hazards of the Delphic Expanse and the Xindi who inhabit it.*

6. "Twilight" Written by Mike Sussman.

An injury destroys Archer's ability to form new long-term memories and renders him incapable of commanding the *Enterprise*. As a result, the Xindi are able to destroy Earth and wipe out humanity throughout the galaxy.

This action-packed story that also touches the emotions confirms that survival of the human race really does *depend on Archer's success in defeating the Xindi. Fans responding to a poll conducted by the network indicated that "Twilight" was their favorite episode of* Enterprise.

7. "Similitude" Written by Manny Coto.

Archer and Phlox find an unorthodox way to save Trip's life, but it requires them to take the life of the being responsible for the cure.

Captain Tucker welcomes his injured friend back to *Enterprise*.

Is it moral to take one life—even that of a clone—to save another? A hotly debated twenty-first-century issue receives the Star Trek *treatment in this episode (another fan favorite), which doesn't suggest easy answers.*

8. *"Kir'Shara"* **Written by Mike Sussman.**

Archer, T'Pol, and the Vulcan dissident T'Pau bring the *Kir'Shara* before members of the Vulcan High Command, forcing them to recog-nize the errors of their militaristic ways and step down from power.

A three-part Vulcan arc concludes with this episode, which brings Enterprise*'s previously intractable Vulcans more in line with their pointy-eared brethren in subsequent* Star Trek *series. With the discovery of the* Kir'Shara, *an artifact that reveals Surak's original writings, Vulcans adopt a more open-minded way of dealing with out-siders . . . and their own people.*

9. **"In a Mirror, Darkly" Part I: Written by Mike Sussman. Part II: Teleplay by Mike Sussman. Story by Manny Coto.**

Jonathan Archer's "evil twin" from the mirror universe commandeers a powerful starship that the Tholians have snatched from the future and uses it to carry out a daring power grab.

Enterprise *visits everyone's favorite alternate universe in this grimly entertaining tale, which features lovingly re-created ships, costumes, and sets from the first* Star Trek *series.*

"If you're going to try to embrace new worlds, you should try to embrace new ideas."

—Phlox, "Broken Bow"

10. **"Terra Prime" Teleplay by Judith Reeves-Stevens & Garfield Reeves-Stevens & Manny Coto. Story by Judith Reeves-Stevens & Garfield Reeves-Stevens & Andre Bormanis.**

As humans and aliens gather on Earth to discuss forming a "Coalition of Planets," a radical human isolationist group called Terra Prime threatens to destroy Starfleet Command unless all aliens immediately depart from Earth.

This powerful episode could have served as the series finale, with each member of the senior crew getting the opportunity to contribute something dynamic to the whole, and Archer demonstrating the qualities that will cause history to remember his name.

THE HISTORY OF THE FUTURE, PART 1. Sometimes Archer and his crew don't learn important stuff about the aliens they meet. Even though they have several run-ins with the Romulans, they never learn what the species looks like. They confront a large-lobed species in "Acquisition" but never catch its name: Ferengi. And they don't know enough to run like hell from those mysterious pasty-faced thugs that most viewers know as the Borg.

Why do they miss such important details? Because history—at least *Star Trek* history—won't allow it. Previous series have established that humankind doesn't figure out what the Romulans look like until Kirk meets them in the twenty-third century. And humans won't be able to recognize a Ferengi (or even a Borg, for that matter) on the street until Picard faces those unique adversaries.

Que sera, sera.

NOW HEAR THIS! *Enterprise* takes place about 150 years from now, beginning in the year 2151. That means the show is set *before* all the other *Star Trek* series, even though it was produced *after* all the other *Star Trek* series. It's a prequel, so if you've seen any of the other *Trek*s, you already know lots of stuff about the Alpha Quadrant that Captain Archer hasn't a clue about.

THE "SPOCK'S BRAIN" AWARD. "These Are the Voyages" . . . is the *Enterprise* episode that most alienated its audience. How? By relegating the familiar crew to second-banana status in their own series finale.

A MACO private places Hoshi's safety above his own.

WHAT IT IS . . .

WHO OR WHAT ARE THE MACOS?

MACO stands for Military Assault Command Operation. It's an elite group of specially trained soldiers comparable to the various Special Forces of our era's U.S. military (think Green Berets). A contingent of MACOs is assigned to the *Enterprise* to assist on the mission into the Delphic Expanse. These are not Starfleet personnel—they're highly trained military grunts—which is why they wear camouflage uniforms instead of the standard *Enterprise* blue jumpsuits. As *Enterprise*'s tactical officer, Lieutenant Reed has turf issues with MACO commanding officer Major Hayes.

TEMPORAL COLD WAR

This conflict, which takes place across both time and space, primarily involves a mysterious entity from the future who has recruited members of the Suliban species to alter history by disrupting the timeline in Archer's era. Fortunately, Daniels, a time-traveling Starfleet agent from even farther in the future, is on the case to foil the efforts of the Suliban. Other time-traveling factions mess with Archer at various times, but frankly, even we can't keep track of them all. We suspect our timeline may have been altered.

WHO THE HECK ARE THE AUGMENTS?

Remember Khan, the genetically engineered villain from *Star Trek*'s "Space Seed" (see p. 29)? It turns out some genetically engineered embryos were left over from Khan's era. A scientist named Arik Soong (ancestor of the Doctor Soong who later would create *The Next Generation*'s Data) brings them to term, propagating a gang of superhumans that Soong refers to as Augments. The Augments then try to start an interstellar war.

PRIMARY COLORS

The color-coded cording on the crew's costumes corresponds to the colors of Kirk and company's (costumes . . . uniforms: gold for command, blue for science, red for ship services).

Got it? Now try the one about Susie selling seashells at the seashore.

SPEED MATTERS. The *Enterprise* NX-01 is the first of a new generation of starships capable of reaching warp 5. That's a big deal to Starfleet. At warp 2, only eighteen inhabited planets are within a year's travel from Earth; at warp 5, that number increases to ten thousand planets! Slower ships can't travel to really distant star systems and back again within a human's lifetime, which tends to affect enlistment rates. Think about how long it took Columbus's crew to travel to and from the New World. Would *you* have signed up?

WHY DOES ARCHER HATE THE VULCANS? The Vulcans have been hanging out on Earth ever since pioneer Zefram Cochrane made his first trip into space in a warp-powered vessel (p. 236). Yet they still haven't shared their advanced technology with us because they say that humans aren't ready. Jonathan Archer believes those delaying tactics prevented his father—who worked on warp engines for more than thirty years—from seeing his own engines fly. This, understandably, ticked Archer off. His subsequent friendship with T'Pol, and a "meeting of minds" with Surak, the father of Vulcan philosophy, helped rid Archer of the chip on his shoulder.

THE HISTORY OF THE FUTURE, PART 2. Historical complications don't surround *every* significant species encountered in *Enterprise*, so the show is free to reveal more of the Tholians than we ever saw in *Star Trek*'s "The Tholian Web" (p. 36). Turns out they're not only crabby but actually kind of crablike from the neck down.

We learn that Orion men are a lot bigger than the sexy Orion females who charm viewers in Kirk's time. But size isn't everything. Orion females use their intoxicating hormonal appeal to call all the shots with the men of their world . . . and other worlds too.

Enterprise also reintroduces us to the Gorn and even to the mirror universe. It's practically *Star Trek* old home week. Except for the lack of tribbles.

EPISODE SYNOPSES

Season One

1./2. Broken Bow

Ninety years have passed since Zefram Cochrane's groundbreaking warp flight resulted in humanity's first encounter with beings from another world. Those aliens, the Vulcans, have taught humanity a great deal; they are skeptical about our readiness for space exploration. After a Klingon courier's ship is shot down over Earth, the Vulcans' arguments against allowing Starfleet to launch the first warp 5 starship are overruled. With untested technology and a quickly assembled crew, Captain Jonathan Archer prepares the *Starship Enterprise* NX-01 for a mission to deliver the injured Klingon back to his homeworld. At Vulcan Ambassador Soval's insistence, the crew includes Vulcan Sub-Commander T'Pol as an adviser. Only days into the flight, chameleonlike aliens invade the ship, intending to kidnap the Klingon. The crew identifies them as Suliban, a genetically altered species engaged in a Temporal Cold War. T'Pol argues that Archer shouldn't get involved, but the captain finds that remaining neutral is easier said than done.

3. Fight or Flight

As the crew of the *Enterprise* learns the intricacies of deep-space exploration, it comes upon a vessel floating immobile in space. Searching the vessel, the team discovers that someone killed the crew, apparently to harvest body parts. Communications officer Ensign Hoshi Sato attempts to send a signal in the language of the dead crew to inform their people.

4. Strange New World

Tucker, Mayweather, and several other crew members spend the night on the surface of an idyllic planet to study its nocturnal life. As darkness falls, a fierce windstorm sets in, disrupting communication with the ship. The crew take refuge in a cave, where they begin to see mysterious figures. When T'Pol claims that her scans reveal no life signs, the others accuse her of secretly meeting with the creatures. As fear and suspicion grow, Tucker threatens the Vulcan with a phase pistol.

5. Unexpected

A cloaked Xyrillian ship with malfunctioning engines is detected hitching a ride behind the *Enterprise*'s nacelles, where it is draining plasma from the *Enterprise*. Archer sees the situation as an opportunity and offers assistance by sending Tucker to the ship to help with repairs. As the engineer adjusts to the Xyrillians' reptilian environment, a female engineer, Ah'len, introduces him to her culture, including a game that enables them to read each other's minds. After the ships go their separate ways, Tucker notices an unusual growth on his wrist. Doctor Phlox diagnoses it as a natural Xyrillian side effect of Tucker's condition: the male human engineer is pregnant.

6. Terra Nova

Enterprise travels to the planet Terra Nova to search for a human colony that lost contact with Earth seventy-five years ago. Detecting dangerous levels of radiation on the planet's surface, Archer leads a team down and finds the colony's structures deserted and decaying. As Archer attempts to communicate with a

The ambitious mirror universe Archer delights in the futuristic starship's power.

group of humanoids living in a cavern, a barrage of gunfire wounds Reed. The away team is forced to retreat to the ship, leaving the injured Reed behind. T'Pol establishes that the cave dwellers are human descendants of the original colonists, but the Terra Novans have no desire to be reunited.

7. The Andorian Incident

Stopping at P'Jem, an ancient Vulcan monastery, Archer, T'Pol, and Tucker are taken prisoner by Andorians. The Andorian leader, Shran, accuses Archer of conspiring with the Vulcan monks to invade the Andorian homeworld. On *Enterprise*, Reed attempts to contact the captain, but Shran answers, telling Reed not to intervene or his colleagues will die. Using an old transmitter hidden in the monastery, Archer contacts the ship, and he and Reed formulate a plan.

8. Breaking the Ice

As Reed and Mayweather collect mineral samples on a comet, a Vulcan ship approaches *Enterprise*. Despite Archer's questions, the Vulcan captain declines to state his reason for being there. Privately, T'Pol confesses to Tucker that the ship has come to take her back to Vulcan. Reed and Mayweather continue their work, setting off several small explosions, which unexpectedly cause the comet's path to shift.

9. Civilization

On a planet with a preindustrial society, the *Enterprise* crew detects an antimatter reactor that shouldn't be there. Visiting the city in disguise, Archer discovers that the local people are afflicted with odd lesions. After determining where the reactor is hidden, the captain is accosted by an attractive female apothecary, Riann, who accuses him of causing the plague. Archer befriends Riann but can't prevent her

from seeing an arriving alien shuttlecraft. Riann is shaken by the sight, but not nearly as shaken as when they discover a massive underground drilling operation whose harmful emissions are causing the lesions.

10. Fortunate Son

Enterprise intercepts the Earth cargo freighter *Fortunate*, damaged by Nausicaan pirates. First Officer Ryan reluctantly accepts Archer's help. Having both grown up on cargo ships, Mayweather and Ryan compare memories. Meanwhile, T'Pol finds biosigns of an injured Nausicaan on the freighter. Ryan admits to holding a prisoner, and then he traps Archer and his team in a cargo compartment and sends it into space. Archer knows that Ryan hopes to use his prisoner to track down the Nausicaan pirates. If he succeeds, future freighter crews will suffer from his actions.

11. Cold Front

A disguised Suliban sabotages a conduit on *Enterprise*, but the disconnected wiring actually saves the ship from being destroyed. A crewman, Daniels, tells Archer that he isn't a Starfleet member; he's a soldier from nine hundred years in the future. Daniels claims he's come to stop a Suliban named Silik from altering history. Archer finds Silik, but the Suliban claims that *he* isn't the one who wants to alter history.

12. Silent Enemy

An unidentified vessel drops out of warp near the *Enterprise*, refuses to respond to hails, and warps away. A short time later, the alien vessel returns, scans the *Enterprise*, fires its weapons, and again immediately leaves. The attackers return a third time, knocking out the ship's warp drive, main power, and weapons. Adrift, the crew can do nothing as invaders board the ship. The captain realizes that this is a stronger enemy than his crew is prepared to face.

13. Dear Doctor

The *Enterprise* crew comes across the Valakians and learns that an epidemic is slowly killing their people. Agreeing that Phlox may be able to help them, Archer sets course for their planet. The doctor meets a second, less advanced race, the Menk, which has never contracted the disease. As he studies the two races' immune systems, Phlox learns that the primitive Menk have an untapped capacity for learning—and that curing the epidemic afflicting the Valakians will bring up unanticipated moral and ethical issues.

14. Sleeping Dogs

The *Enterprise* crew is surprised to discover that a disabled vessel containing several life signs is sinking into the atmosphere of a gas giant. T'Pol, Reed, and Hoshi board the vessel and find a group of unconscious Klingons. Reed knows that the warriors would rather die than face the dishonor of being rescued, but he refuses to leave without attempting to offer aid. One of the Klingons regains consciousness and steals the shuttlepod, stranding them to the very fate they were trying to save her from.

15. Shadows of P'Jem

Blaming Archer and T'Pol for the destruction of the P'Jem monastery, Soval arranges for T'Pol to be reassigned to Vulcan. Archer decides to make good use of T'Pol's last days aboard *Enterprise* and asks her to accompany him on a mission to the planet Coridan. They are abducted by Coridan soldiers rebelling against their government, which is controlled by the Vulcans. The Vulcan ship arrives, and its captain insists on taking charge of the rescue. Tucker and Reed go to the surface, but they too

are abducted—by Andorians—and soon find themselves in the line of rebel/Vulcan crossfire.

16. Shuttlepod One

As Tucker and Reed run tests on one of the shuttlepods, an unusual jolt disables the sensor array and communications system. Landing on an asteroid, the pair is shocked to discover debris from the *Enterprise*'s hull. Believing their crewmates dead, Tucker and Reed fly their disabled shuttlepod toward a subspace amplifier, hoping they can send a distress signal. With only hours of air left and subzero cold pressing in on them, the two stranded officers have little hope for survival.

17. Fusion

Archer and T'Pol are surprised when Tavin, the captain of a civilian Vulcan ship, explains that he and his crew are on a pilgrimage to explore and reintegrate their long-suppressed emotions. T'Pol is skeptical, but at the urging of Tolaris, one of the Vulcans, she agrees to forgo her nightly meditation. As Tolaris predicted, T'Pol dreams, and she's disturbed that the dreams are of a provocative nature—about Tolaris. Later, Tolaris convinces T'Pol to let him guide her through her emotional awakening by using an ancient technique known as the mindmeld.

18. Rogue Planet

As Archer and a team investigate the surface of a "rogue" planet, they learn that they aren't the only ones visiting this wild place. Hunters, the Eska, are stalking prey they call "wraith," as they have for generations. After Archer has an encounter with a wraith—a sentient shapeshifter that chooses a form from a poem Archer recalls—the captain realizes that he must do whatever he can to stop the hunt.

19. Acquisition

Tucker emerges from the decon chamber to find the entire *Enterprise* crew unconscious while a quartet of large-eared alien thieves bicker about the items they intend to steal. As Tucker watches, the thieves awaken Archer with a hypospray and demand that he tell them the location of the ship's vault. Meanwhile, Tucker manages to awaken T'Pol, and together they work to set a trap.

20. Oasis

While salvaging supplies from a derelict ship that's reputed to be haunted, the crew jokes that perhaps they should calibrate their sensors for "ghosts." But before long, T'Pol sees the reflection of a figure—even though her scanner shows no biosigns. Following the figure, she and Tucker come upon a group that has been stranded for three years. They have kept their biosigns hidden so that raiders won't finish them off. As Archer gets to know Ezral, the ship's engineer, and Tucker gets to know Ezral's daughter, Liana, they discover that details of their saga don't add up.

21. Detained

Mayweather and Archer awaken to find themselves in a cell, surrounded by Suliban. They learn that the facility isn't a prison; it's an internment camp, run by the Tandarans. Colonel Grat, the Tandaran in charge, explains that the humans are there because they trespassed, but if genetic tests prove they aren't Suliban, they'll be released. Archer learns that the Suliban prisoners are not part of the Cabal; they're victims. The captain undergoes a change of attitude, which Grat doesn't like. Suddenly, Archer's incarceration is about to become long-term.

"I'm following orders." —Hoshi, "Terra Prime"

22. Vox Sola

First contact with the Kreetassans doesn't go well, since Hoshi can't decipher their language. The crew can't understand why the aliens grew so indignant at being served a meal. As the angry aliens leave, a fibrous, weblike creature leaps into the *Enterprise*'s airlock before it seals shut. Archer, Trip, and Reed respond to a panicked call from Cargo Bay 2, where several crewmen are trapped in the creature's tendrils. Reed escapes, but the creature captures Trip and Archer. Reed and his team hit the creature with a burst of EM radiation, but as the creature writhes in pain, so do the captive crew. Phlox surmises that the organism is absorbing their nervous systems into its own, so harming it could also kill their own people.

23. Fallen Hero

At Starfleet's request, the *Enterprise* extradites Vulcan Ambassador V'Lar from the planet Mazar, where she had been accused of criminal misconduct. A Mazarite ship approaches, its captain demanding that V'Lar be brought back for questioning. When Archer refuses, the ship fires on *Enterprise*, so V'Lar volunteers to return to Mazar for the crew's safety. Archer orders the crew to continue. Now under attack by three Mazarite ships, the captain's only hope of survival is to outrun the more powerful vessels.

24. Desert Crossing

Archer and Tucker help repair a ship belonging to a charismatic alien named Zobral, who then invites them to his desert planet. The chancellor from Zobral's planet contacts *Enterprise*, claiming that Zobral is a terrorist. Zobral tells Archer that his people are being oppressed, when suddenly the chancellor's cruisers attack Zobral's village. Archer and Tucker retreat into the desert, where they must survive the attacking ships and the extreme heat.

25. Two Days and Two Nights

Embarking on a well-deserved shore leave on the pleasure planet Risa, Archer hopes to relax with a good book, until he meets a beautiful woman, Keyla. The evening seems ripe with romantic possibilities, but when their conversation turns to the Suliban, Keyla reveals that she is a Tandaran, and Archer suspects their meeting wasn't an accident.

26. Shockwave, Part I

When Archer's crew inadvertently triggers a massive plasma explosion that destroys a colony of three thousand six hundred people, Starfleet cancels the ship's mission. As the crew heads back to Earth, Daniels, a time traveler from the future, appears and tells Archer that historically the explosion never happened. This can only mean that factions in the Temporal Cold War are bent on sabotaging Archer's mission. Daniels's attempts to help Archer reestablish the correct timeline seem to make matters worse.

Season Two

27. Shockwave, Part II

Unaware that Archer has traveled to the thirty-first century with Daniels, where both men now are trapped, Silik and his Suliban followers commandeer *Enterprise* to search for the captain. Ambassador Soval assumes that the captain has disregarded Starfleet's orders to return to Earth and insists a Vulcan vessel be sent in pursuit. In the future, Daniels realizes that by removing Archer from his own time, he actually created the catastrophe that he was trying to prevent.

28. Carbon Creek

While celebrating her first year as an *Enterprise* crew member, T'Pol tells Archer and Trip about the actual first contact between humans and Vulcans, which she alleges took place years earlier than Earth history states. In 1957, an ancestor of T'Pol's accompanied three other Vulcans who were investigating the launch of Sputnik. They were forced to make an emergency landing outside of Carbon Creek, Pennsylvania, and to find ways to fit into the local society while keeping their identities secret.

29. Minefield

As *Enterprise* enters the orbit of an uncharted planet, explosions from an orbital mine damage the ship—and another mine attaches itself to the ship's hull. Reed dons an environmental suit and heads out, hoping to disarm the mine. When a spike jutting from the weapon injures Reed and pins him to the hull, Archer joins him. While the captain works to save his crewman and the ship, a vessel decloaks nearby and demands that *Enterprise* leave immediately or be destroyed. T'Pol confirms that this species—Romulans—mean what they say.

30. Dead Stop

Seeking repairs after a confrontation with the Romulans, the *Enterprise* responds to a jumbled message mentioning a nearby repair station. When they arrive, the crew detect no life-forms, but the fully automated facility scans the ship and immediately begins to make the needed repairs in record time. Archer is suspicious—it all seems too good to be true.

31. A Night in Sickbay

Archer doesn't know how he offended the Kreetassans again, but after unsuccessfully negotiating for a plasma injector, he and his dog Porthos are forced to leave empty-handed. Unfortunately, while on the surface, Porthos picked up a pathogen and the dog is forced to spend the night in sickbay. Archer decides to stay in sickbay as well, giving him a chance to comfort his pet, observe the doctor's nocturnal rituals, and discuss the cultural differences among humans, Vulcans, and Kreetassans.

32. Marauders

Hoping to replenish their supply of deuterium, the crew visits a small mining colony. The colony's leader, Tessic, agrees to an exchange but insists that *Enterprise* leave the area within two days. A Klingon ship enters orbit, causing Tessic to panic and insist that Archer and his people hide. The captain soon realizes that the Klingons are forcing the colonists to give them the best deuterium. Angered by the situation, Archer devises a way to help Tessic's people teach the Klingons a lesson they'll never forget.

33. The Seventh

T'Pol is assigned a secret mission by the Vulcan High Command: capture a Vulcan smuggler named Menos who escaped from T'Pol many years ago. Archer, Mayweather, and T'Pol soon find and capture him. But once she has the fugitive in custody, T'Pol begins to recall repressed memories. Although Archer insists that Menos is manipulating her, T'Pol can't help but wonder if she has apprehended an innocent man.

34. The Communicator

After Reed loses his communicator on an alien planet, he and Archer realize that they must return to recover it. Unfortunately, the planet's military leaders find the communicator, which they believe is a weapon. The pair from the *Enterprise* is discovered and suspected of belonging to a rebel group: the Alliance. Struck by their odd look, General Gosis orders medical tests, and when he learns the humans are a different species, he orders them executed.

"Vulcan children are never late with their sehlat's dinner." —T'Pol, "The Forge"

35. Singularity

During the two days it will take to pass through a trinary star system before reaching the black hole they want to study, the *Enterprise* crew looks forward to completing some personal tasks. T'Pol soon notices that each person's task has become an obsession. Eventually, T'Pol determines that radiation from the star system is affecting the crew. In order to escape, the ship must pass dangerously close to the black hole. Unfortunately, T'Pol can't pilot the ship alone, and no one else on the ship is in any condition to help her.

36. Vanishing Point

To avoid a pending storm, Hoshi is forced to beam up from a planet's surface via the transporter. After beaming, Hoshi begins to feel unsettled. First it seems that her fellow crew members are ignoring her; then she discovers that her hands can pass through solid objects and her image in the mirror has become transparent. Making things worse, a group of aliens has infiltrated *Enterprise* and is planting explosives, but Hoshi has no way, in her invisible state, to alert the crew.

37. Precious Cargo

Archer offers to help a pair of Retellian cargo pilots by letting Trip repair their stasis pod. The pod contains a young female. Trip discovers that the woman's wrists are bound—she isn't a passenger; she's a prisoner. One of the Retellians attacks Trip, and the ship takes off with the engineer aboard. Trip learns that the prisoner is Kaitaama, a member of the royal family of Krios Prime. But rather than expressing gratitude, Kaitaama is combative and resistant, even when Trip comes up with a plan to escape the Retellians' ship.

38. The Catwalk

Before crossing a wave front that emits deadly radiation, the crew offers passage to a trio of aliens. Trip suggests that the safest place for everyone to take shelter is the heavily shielded, cramped catwalk that runs through the warp nacelles. As the days wear on, tensions run high among the crew and the aliens. And when the matter and antimatter injectors inexplicably come online, endangering everyone in the catwalk, Trip goes to engineering to shut them down. But once there, Trip discovers that aliens seem more interested in stealing the ship than in keeping its crew alive.

39. Dawn

Trip's shuttlepod is forced to land on a nearby moon after an Arkonian pilot fires at him. The pilot follows him down and prevents Trip from contacting *Enterprise* for help, trapping both of them on the desolate moon. Archer mounts a search for Trip, but an Arkonian ship orders him to leave. T'Pol warns Archer that the Arkonians are very territorial and hostile, but the captain refuses to leave without his missing crewman. The Arkonians admit that they also have a missing crewman. As dawn approaches, the surface of the moon quickly will reach a temperature that neither man can survive.

40. Stigma

At an interspecies medical conference, Phlox hopes to learn more about an incurable disease from attending Vulcan doctors—without revealing that he is treating T'Pol for the disease. Pa'nar syndrome affects only Vulcans who have committed the unnatural act of mind-melding. T'Pol fears that if the Vulcan High Command learns that she has Pa'nar syndrome, they'll relieve her of her duties, despite the fact that she contracted it when she was

assaulted by the Vulcan Tolaris. Unfortunately, the Vulcan physicians quickly see through Phlox's interest in Pa'nar, making T'Pol's fears likely to come true.

41. Cease Fire

The Vulcans and their longtime adversaries, the Andorians, begin fighting over ownership of a small planet. After Andorian Commander Shran takes three Vulcans hostage, the Vulcans call for a cease-fire. Shran insists that Archer act as mediator, but Soval is skeptical of the human's abilities. Shran's lieutenant, Tarah, is equally skeptical, considering Archer's close association with the Vulcan T'Pol. As Archer, T'Pol, and Soval approach the disputed planet, someone fires at their shuttlepod and they're forced to crash-land in the middle of a battle.

42. Future Tense

The *Enterprise* discovers a mysterious futuristic vessel adrift and brings it into the cargo bay. Suddenly a Suliban ship appears, demanding the vessel be turned over. The crew manages to chase the Suliban off. A visit to Daniels's old quarters turns up what appears to be a schematic of the mysterious vessel in his database. Archer realizes he must keep the vessel away from the Suliban, who would take it apart and reverse-engineer it. Another vessel appears, this one belonging to the Tholians, a xenophobic species. The Tholians demand the futuristic vessel be given to them, and the Suliban return with the same demand.

43. Canamar

Archer and Trip are mistakenly identified as smugglers and placed on a transport headed for an Enolian penal colony known as Canamar. On *Enterprise*, T'Pol quickly proves their innocence, but before they can be released, Kuroda, a menacing prisoner, breaks free and kills the transport's pilot. Archer volunteers to fly the craft and attempts to convince Kuroda that he can be trusted. Meanwhile, the Enolians ignore T'Pol's pleas and dispatch ships to destroy the transport. Aboard the vessel, Archer realizes that Kuroda plans to kill them all.

44. The Crossing

The *Enterprise* crew encounters a huge ship unlike any they've ever seen. A portal opens and the larger vessel "swallows" their ship. As Archer, Trip, and Reed take a shuttlepod to explore the interior of the behemoth, an apparent wisp of smoke invades Trip's body for a few seconds. Trip claims that he is unaffected, but it becomes obvious that an unknown entity has appropriated his body. As similar entities take over other crew members' bodies—and T'Pol finally learns the truth behind their body snatching—Archer, T'Pol, and Phlox discuss options for returning the entire crew to normal.

45. Judgment

Charged with conspiring against the Klingon Empire, Archer is thrown into a cell and assigned a Klingon advocate named Kolos. During the trial, the captain meets his accuser, Duras, former captain of the *Battlecruiser Bortas*. Duras claims Archer ordered the attack because he was harboring fugitives. Archer insists that Duras's account isn't accurate. If he loses, he'll be executed. And if he wins—he'll spend the rest of his days in the frozen wastes of Rura Penthe.

46. Horizon

Mayweather takes a short leave to visit his family on the *Horizon*, the cargo vessel where he spent his childhood. But going home again is never easy; Mayweather learns that his father recently passed away. His brother, Paul, now in charge of the *Horizon*, resents that his sibling deserted them to join Starfleet. The true test of their blood

ties comes when a ship attaches an explosive device to the hull and demands that the crew surrender its cargo—and the ship as well.

47. The Breach

During a mission to evacuate a group of Denobulan geologists from a planet that has been taken over by a militant faction, Mayweather is injured, leaving Trip and Reed to rescue the Denobulans. On *Enterprise*, a badly injured Antaran evacuee named Hudak refuses to be treated by Phlox because his people and the Denobulans have long been enemies.

48. Cogenitor

As *Enterprise* prepares to study a hypergiant star, the crew makes first contact with the Vissians. While the crew befriends these cordial aliens, Trip becomes intrigued by one nameless individual. Referred to as a "cogenitor," its apparent sole purpose is to help a Vissian couple become pregnant. This third gender is treated like a possession. But when Trip discovers that the cogenitor has the same mental capacities as the other Vissians, he encourages it to learn, despite the fact that interfering with the Vissian culture could have disastrous results.

49. Regeneration

On Earth, scientists discover two cybernetically enhanced bodies buried in an Arctic glacier and thaw them out. The strange beings abduct the scientists and their transport vessel. After being ordered to find the transport, the *Enterprise* receives a distress call from a Tarkalean freighter that is under attack by the transport, now oddly modified. The crew is able to fend off the transport, but the Tarkaleans have been injected with nanoprobes from the cybernetic species—and one of them injects Phlox. The altered transport targets

Enterprise, and an ominous transmission informs them that they will be assimilated, and that "Resistance is futile."

50. First Flight

Learning that A. G. Robinson—his old rival from the NX program—has died, Archer reminisces about the time he and Robinson were competing for the honor of being the first to break the warp 2 barrier. Robinson is given the assignment—a blow to Archer, since his father had designed the engine. But when the experimental craft NX-Alpha explodes, the Vulcans proclaim the engine faulty and put the program on hold. Disregarding the Vulcans *and* Starfleet, Archer, Robinson, and a newly assigned engineer, Trip Tucker, join forces to prove the Vulcans wrong—by launching an unauthorized flight in the NX-Beta.

51. Bounty

Archer is abducted by Skalaar, a Tellarite bounty hunter, who plans to turn him over to the Klingons for a reward. When a rival bounty hunter damages the Tellarite's ship, Archer convinces Skalaar to free him so they can make repairs. Archer learns that Skalaar wants the reward to buy back his cargo ship, the *Tezra*, which was confiscated by the Klingons. Skalaar learns that the *Tezra* was cannibalized for its parts. Devastated, the Tellarite knows that he still has to give Archer to the Klingons—or else he may end up dead.

52. The Expanse

Millions of people are killed on Earth when a probe cuts a swath of devastation from Florida to Venezuela. As *Enterprise* hurries toward Earth, Silik abducts Archer and informs him that the attackers are the Xindi, and they believe humans will destroy their homeworld in the future. Silik says the Xindi have an even more powerful weapon. Armed with this infor-

mation, Starfleet orders *Enterprise* to travel to the Delphic Expanse, home of the Xindi. Fitted with new weapons and added military personnel, the *Enterprise* sets off into the unknown on an all-new mission: save Earth.

Season Three

53. The Xindi

Aided by a group of Military Assault Command Operations soldiers (MACOs) newly assigned to the *Enterprise*, the crew searches the Delphic Expanse for the Xindi, the mysterious aliens that attacked Earth. When Archer and Trip finally track down one of them at a mining complex, he refuses to give them any information—unless they help him escape. Archer reluctantly agrees, and as they make the arduous journey through the facility, Archer learns that there are not one, but five distinct Xindi species, all in conflict with one another. The five species have united to form a council for the sole purpose of killing all humans and destroying Earth.

54. Anomaly

In the Expanse, the ship is rocked by destructive spatial anomalies that leave *Enterprise* without weapons or warp capabilities. Then Osaarian pirates attack the ship, killing a crew member and stealing weapons and supplies, but leaving an injured individual named Orgoth behind. While the *Enterprise* tracks Orgoth's ship into the anomalies, they pass through a cloaking field and come face-to-face with a large sphere. Inside are many of the goods stolen from *Enterprise* and an even more valuable Xindi computer database.

55. Extinction

After discovering a Xindi landing pod on a junglelike planet, Archer, T'Pol, Hoshi, and

Reed contract a virus that changes their DNA, making them develop bizarre alien characteristics. T'Pol manages to contact Trip on the ship, but her altered colleagues take her hostage. Even as Phlox attempts to develop a cure, a vessel hails *Enterprise*, demanding that the infected members of the crew be destroyed before the virus can spread and cause an epidemic.

56. Rajiin

The Xindi council argues about how to deal with the Earth ship advancing into their space. A Xindi-humanoid scientist named Degra ultimately prevails by insisting that continuing work on the weapon he is building is more important than taking immediate action against *Enterprise*. Meanwhile, the *Enterprise* crew visits a bazaar, where Archer seeks to obtain a formula to synthesize trellium-D, a substance that can protect the crew from the Expanse's anomalies. While there, Archer helps a woman named Rajiin escape from her captor. Once Rajiin is aboard, she betrays the crew's kindness by taking scans that will help the Xindi create a deadly bioweapon.

57. Impulse

Responding to a distress call from the Vulcan ship *Seleya*, *Enterprise* enters an asteroid field that is made even more treacherous by the Expanse's spatial anomalies. When Archer, T'Pol, and their landing party board the *Seleya*, they note that the Vulcans had tried to line the ship with trellium to block the anomalies' effects. Suddenly, they're attacked by a group of Vulcans, now zombie-like and homicidal. The team struggles to evade the Vulcans, but soon T'Pol begins to display violent symptoms just like them.

58. Exile

Hoshi has a vision of a mysterious telepathic alien named Tarquin who claims to be willing to help the crew find the Xindi. Archer reluc-

tantly agrees to escort his communications officer to Tarquin's planet. Once there, Tarquin says he understands their mission and believes he can find the superweapon the Xindi are building, but only if Hoshi stays while he researches the weapon. Meanwhile, T'Pol and Archer discover a second giant sphere in the Expanse, leading them to suspect there may be a way to chart a course around the destructive spatial anomalies that the spheres produce.

59. The Shipment

The *Enterprise* travels to a planet where one of the Xindi factions manufactures kemocite, a substance required for their superweapon. Archer befriends Gralik, a Xindi-Sloth plant manager, who knew nothing of the council's plan to destroy the people of Earth. Unfortunately, Archer may have arrived a little too late; Degra and the Xindi-Reptilians have arrived to pick up the kemocite.

60. Twilight

Twelve years in the future, the Xindi have succeeded in destroying Earth and have wiped out every human outpost they've managed to find. One small enclave survives: on a distant world, T'Pol cares for her former captain, Jonathan Archer, whose mind is ravaged by parasites from outside of normal space-time. Phlox arrives with good news—he thinks he finally can destroy the parasites. The procedure can be done only on *Enterprise*, now under Trip's command. Phlox and T'Pol realize the procedure may have the potential to undo the events of the past twelve years, saving Earth and the human race. But the Xindi have tracked down *Enterprise* and will arrive long before the operation is complete.

"Math is just another language."

—Hoshi, "Observer Effect"

61. North Star

The *Enterprise* crew is shocked to discover a colony of humans living on a planet in the Delphic Expanse. Their settlement is similar to a town from America's Old West. Archer soon learns from a schoolteacher, Bethany, that the humans were brought there as slaves by the Skagarans. The humans eventually rebelled against their Skag captors and turned the tables on them, preventing them from going to school or owning property. Bethany feels sorry for them, and she takes Archer to one of her secret nighttime sessions where she illegally teaches the Skags.

62. Similitude

Trip is badly injured during a warp core breach, prompting Phlox to perform a controversial experiment to save the engineer's life: create transplant tissues by cloning a symbiot of Trip. The symbiot, dubbed Sim, matures, and the crew comes to see him as a real person. They realize that taking Sim's life in order to save Trip's is a prospect that will affect them more than they had anticipated.

63. Carpenter Street

Time-traveler Daniels alerts Archer that a trio of Xindi-Reptilians have traveled back in time 150 years to Detroit, Michigan. Disguised, Archer and T'Pol follow the Xindi, and they discover a man named Loomis supplying unconscious human bodies to the Xindi so they can collect blood samples. Realizing that they are building a bioweapon, Archer pretends to be unconscious and lets Loomis deliver him into the Xindi's hands.

64. Chosen Realm

Enterprise is commandeered by the Triannons, a group of aliens who believe that the Expanse's mysterious spheres are sacred objects. Their leader, D'Jamat, plans to use *Enterprise* as a weapon against heretics who don't follow his religion. When D'Jamat decides that the crew has desecrated the spheres by flying through their cloaking barriers, he insists that Archer chose one of his crew to be put to death.

65. Proving Ground

The *Enterprise* crew follows a signal from a device that Archer planted in a canister of kemocite. The ship sustains damage in a dense field of spatial anomalies. Suddenly an Andorian vessel helmed by Commander Shran appears and offers assistance. The crews of the two ships join forces. They find where the Xindi are running tests on prototypes of the superweapon. Unfortunately, at a crucial moment, Archer finds that Shran's interests and his own are not identical.

66. Stratagem

After the *Enterprise* captures a Xindi ship, the crew realizes that one of the occupants is Degra, the mastermind of the Xindi superweapon. Phlox learns it is possible to erase Degra's most recent memories, so he and Archer devise a plan to trick the scientist into revealing the weapon's location. Pretending that the two of them have just escaped from a Xindi-Insectoid prison where they've been held together for three years, Archer attempts to convince Degra to trust him.

67. Harbinger

An alien recovered from a drifting ship refuses to tell Archer why he was attached to monitoring equipment. He admits he's from a transdimensional realm and is participating in an experiment he knows nothing about. When the alien escapes, Reed and MACO leader Major Hayes must set aside their long-simmering hostility while they work together to track him down.

68. Doctor's Orders

As the only crew member immune to the effects of a transdimensional disturbance that *Enterprise* must pass through to reach Azati Prime, Phlox puts everyone else into a comatose state and runs the ship alone for four days. At first he enjoys the solitude, but as time passes he begins to hear and see increasingly peculiar things.

69. Hatchery

While investigating a damaged Xindi-Insectoid vessel, the *Enterprise* discovers a hatchery containing Insectoid eggs. One of the egg sacs sprays Archer with a strange liquid that Phlox determines to be a neurotoxin. Although he seems unharmed, the captain becomes oddly concerned about the hatchery and the eggs—more concerned, in fact, than about the survival of his own ship.

70. Azati Prime

Arriving at Azati Prime, the site of the Xindi superweapon, the *Enterprise* learns that the weapon is located under the surface of the planet's large ocean. Studying scans of the weapon, Archer devises a suicide mission that he is determined to carry out himself. Time-traveling Daniels appears and whisks Archer four hundred years into the future to show him another destiny. The Federation, explains Daniels, needs Archer to live past this day, to keep the Sphere Builders from influencing the Xindi. Once back in his own time, the captain returns to his suicidal plan. When he arrives at the underwater site, the weapon is gone—and Archer is taken prisoner by Xindi-Reptilians.

71. Damage

Archer is released by the Xindi, and returned in a Xindi-Aquatic pod to the *Enterprise*, which has been badly damaged. The captain of an Illyrian vessel negotiates for supplies but cannot provide a warp coil. On the Xindi pod, T'Pol finds an encrypted message hinting that Degra wants a meeting. Unfortunately, without a warp coil the ship can't reach Degra's location—forcing Archer to make a choice: abandon his mission, or abandon his humanity by stealing the Illyrians' warp coil, stranding their ship in the Expanse.

72. The Forgotten

Finally able to meet with Degra, Archer and T'Pol offer evidence that the beings that built the mysterious spheres are responsible for the war between the Xindi and Earth. But convincing Degra isn't Archer's only pressing problem—a powerful Reptilian ship is approaching rapidly, and if its crew manages to notify the Xindi council that Degra is consorting with their enemy, all hopes for an alliance will be off.

73. E2

As *Enterprise* heads toward the meeting that Degra has set up with the Xindi Council, it encounters an *NX*-class Starfleet vessel. It's the *Enterprise*. The ship's captain, Lorian, tells Archer that if the crew tries to take the subspace corridor to get to the meeting, Archer's *Enterprise* will be thrown back in time 117 years. Lorian's crew members are the descendants of Archer's crew. They've come to show Archer an alternate way to rendezvous with Degra.

74. The Council

Archer finally meets with the Xindi Council and presents his evidence that the builders of the mysterious spheres are the Council's real enemies. Three of the five Xindi species believe Archer, but the Reptilians and Insectoids refuse to listen and the meeting dissolves into chaos. The Reptilian commander, Dolim, secretly meets with one of the Sphere Builders, who promises Dolim that if he eradicates human-kind, the Reptilians will dominate the other Xindi species. Meanwhile, T'Pol, Reed, and Mayweather take a shuttlepod into the heart of a sphere, hoping to extract its memory core. On *Enterprise*, Degra tells the captain that the council has agreed to delay deploying the superweapon; however, he is murdered by Dolim. The Reptilians and the Insectoids steal the weapon—and kidnap the one human they know is proficient enough to break the weapon's launch codes—Hoshi Sato.

75. Countdown

On the Xindi-Reptilian ship, Dolim tortures Hoshi, forcing her to decipher the launch code to deploy the superweapon. Meanwhile, Archer and T'Pol find that damaging a specific sphere may disrupt the Sphere Builders' space-altering plans. *Enterprise* battles with the Reptilian and Insectoid ships, while Dolim heads for Earth to destroy humanity. Hoping that he can disable the weapon from the inside, Archer follows Dolim in Degra's ship, leaving the slower *Enterprise* back in the Expanse.

76. Zero Hour

In the Delphic Expanse, the *Enterprise* crew fends off an attack by the Sphere Builders and attempts to disrupt their hold over the Expanse. Aboard Degra's ship, Archer, Reed, and Hoshi frantically work to stop the Xindi superweapon from launching. Suddenly the captain again finds himself transported into the future by Daniels. The time traveler urges Archer to let someone else complete the mission, but Archer refuses to listen. As the Reptilian vessel attacks Degra's ship, Andorian Commander Shran's ship unexpectedly joins the fight, giving Archer his chance to board the superweapon. Unfortunately, Dolim also beams into the

weapon, where he confronts the captain. As the weapon approaches Earth, it overloads, leading to a huge explosion. Afterward, Archer is nowhere to be found.

Season Four

77. Storm Front, Part I

Mourning the apparent death of Archer, the *Enterprise* crew finds that their ship has time-traveled to the year 1944 during World War II. However, there are some discrepancies between history and what they are witnessing: the Nazis have invaded America and are in control of the eastern seaboard. Unknown to his crew, Archer is alive and in the same time frame. Initially captured by the Nazis, who are led by a nonhuman SS officer, Archer escapes and hides with resistance fighters. On *Enterprise*, time-traveler Daniels reports that the Temporal Cold War has escalated into a huge conflict, with fights occurring throughout the timeline. Daniels warns T'Pol that *Enterprise* must stop "him"—but falls unconscious before he can explain.

78. Storm Front, Part II

In the altered 1944 timeline, Archer finds himself working with his old nemesis Silik to stop Vosk—the alien that already has wreaked havoc upon Earth's past—from completing the time machine that will return him to his own era and further inflame the Temporal Cold War. At stake: the lives of Archer's crew and every living being on Earth—past, present, and future.

79. Home

Returning to Earth after their yearlong mission in the Delphic Expanse, the *Enterprise* receives a hero's welcome. Despite the mission's success, Soval accuses Archer of not having tried hard enough to save Vulcan lives in the Expanse. Meanwhile, T'Pol and Tucker travel to Vulcan. T'Pol's mother, T'Les, quickly discerns that the two are in love, although *they* don't seem to be aware of it. T'Les has been forced out of her academic post because of T'Pol's decision to stay with Starfleet. However, if T'Pol agrees to marry her ex-fiancé, Koss, his family will help her mother.

80. Borderland

A band of genetically enhanced superhumans known as Augments hijacks a Klingon bird-of-prey. Starfleet assigns the *Enterprise* to capture them. Archer reluctantly takes along the scientist responsible for the Augments' existence, Doctor Arik Soong, paroling him from prison. As *Enterprise* follows the Augments into hostile territory, several crew members are beamed off the ship and sold into the Orion slave market. Archer attempts to rescue T'Pol, and in the ensuing chaos, Soong tries to escape. Aboard the stolen bird-of-prey, the Augments discuss plans for finding their missing "father," Soong.

81. Cold Station 12

In his efforts to find Soong and the Augments, Archer heads to Trialas, the planet where Soong raised the Augments. He discovers the scientist's plan: to raise thousands more Augments from the genetically altered embryos stored at a medical facility, Cold Station 12. Attempts to hide the access code that will allow Soong to take possession of the embryos are foiled when Malik, an Augment, threatens to kill Phlox. Malik can't resist one final stab at humanity; as he and the other Augments leave Cold Station 12, with the embryos, he initiates the release of a deadly pathogen that will kill everyone.

82. The Augments

Aboard the stolen bird-of-prey, Malik usurps leadership of the Augments from Soong, who finally realizes that he no longer controls his "children." After Malik imprisons Soong, the scientist manages to escape in a shuttlepod and calls upon Archer for assistance. Now the unlikely team must work together to stop Malik from destroying an innocent Klingon colony, which could incite a Klingon/human war.

83. The Forge

A bomb set by a zealous Vulcan sect, the Syrrannites, kills Starfleet's Admiral Forrest. This prompts Archer and T'Pol to follow a coded map across the Forge, a desolate Vulcan desert, in search of the sect, whose members include T'Pol's mother, T'Les. Meanwhile, Trip and Phlox discover they may be looking for the wrong Vulcans. To prove their theory, Trip must convince Soval to perform an unsanctioned mind-meld on a security chief from the bombed Earth Embassy. On the Forge, T'Pol and Archer encounter a man who has a connection to the dawn of Vulcan civilization.

84. Awakening

Archer and T'Pol make contact with the Syrrannites. The sect's leader, T'Pau, distrusts them until she realizes that the living spirit of Surak, the father of Vulcan philosophy, has been transferred into the human captain. Meanwhile, V'Las, head of the Vulcan High Command, orders the planet's military to bomb the Syrrannite camp. This prompts Soval to team up with the *Enterprise* crew. Soval reveals a disturbing secret to Trip: V'Las's plans include attacking Andoria in order to start an interstellar war.

85. *Kir'Shara*

Under fire by V'Las's troops, Archer, T'Pol, and T'Pau cross the desert to deliver a Vulcan relic, the *Kir'Shara*, to the High Command as proof that the Syrrannites are not traitors. Trip and Soval must convince the Andorian commander and the Vulcan commander not to fire on each other. Archer hopes the *Kir'Shara* will convince members of the Vulcan High Command to stop a Vulcan/Andorian war.

86. Daedalus

The *Enterprise* crew is happy to assist Emory Erickson, the inventor of the transporter, as he conducts experiments to advance transporter technology. After the scientist directs the ship into a dangerous area of space, it becomes evident that Erickson has lied about the true nature of his mission.

87. Observer Effect

Two aliens secretly inhabit Reed's and Mayweather's bodies in order to observe human behavior. Trip and Hoshi return from a routine expedition—but it's evident that they've contracted a deadly, highly contagious virus. After Phlox places the pair in quarantine, the curious observer aliens transfer themselves into their sick bodies to experience illness. When Hoshi goes into cardiac arrest and Phlox finds he can't handle the medical equipment alone, Archer lends his assistance, disregarding his own exposure. As Archer awaits his fate, the observer aliens reveal their presence. When they state that they will not save Trip's and Hoshi's lives, Archer finds it difficult to believe that they're as advanced as they claim to be.

88. Babel One

While escorting Tellarite Ambassador Gral to the neutral planet Babel for a meeting with his planet's trading rival, Andoria, *Enterprise* answers a distress call: an Andorian ship has been destroyed, apparently by a Tellarite ship. The survivors, including Archer's old acquaintance Commander Shran, are furious, but Gral insists that his people are innocent. *Enterprise* is then attacked by what appears to be an Andorian ship. The crew gives chase and manages to catch up with the vessel, which inexplicably sits motionless in space. Trip and Reed board the vessel, but a quick search reveals that no one is aboard.

89. United

Reed and Trip are trapped on the mysterious ship that T'Pol deduces is a Romulan vessel that can be masked, making it look like other vessels. This may explain why *Enterprise* was recently accused of destroying a Rigellian vessel. With the Romulans staging attacks throughout the area, T'Pol devises a plan to expose them. However, it will require the cooperation of a number of Tellarite and Andorian vessels. Unfortunately, the tension between the two has led to tragedy: Shran's partner, Talas, dies after being wounded in an attack by a Tellarite. Shran angrily challenges Gral in a fight to the death, but Archer, hoping to salvage a coalition between the species, takes the Tellarite's place.

90. The Aenar

On board *Enterprise*, T'Pol reveals that the masked Romulan ship is a drone, controlled by a pilot from a remote location via telepresence. Andorian scientists recognize that the highly telepathic pilot's distinctive brain wave patterns belong to an ice-dwelling Andorian subspecies, the Aenar. Traveling to Andoria, Archer and Shran approach the Aenar, who surmise that the drone pilot might be Gareb. Jhamel, Gareb's sister, accompanies them back to the ship, where she agrees to test a telepresence unit that Trip has constructed. It may be too late. The Romulans now have *two* drone ships, and they're targeting *Enterprise*.

91. Affliction

The *Enterprise* returns to Earth for the launch of a new starship, the *Columbia*, and for Trip's transfer to that ship. Unexpectedly, Phlox is abducted and taken to a Klingon research facility where he's ordered to stop a virus. Meanwhile, a mysterious man approaches Reed with an assignment that will require his deceiving Archer but may be the only way to save Phlox's life. Leaving Earth, *Enterprise* pursues the vessel that hijacked Phlox, only to find that it's been destroyed. Suddenly a group of fierce human-like aliens boards *Enterprise* and sabotages many of the ship's systems. The crew manages to capture one of the intruders who, despite his appearance, seems to be Klingon. In the research facility, Phlox is shocked to discover that a Klingon's genes have been modified with Augment DNA. The Augment genes have mixed with a virus and developed into a deadly airborne plague—one that may destroy the entire Klingon race.

92. Divergence

With *Enterprise*'s engines sabotaged to explode if the ship drops below warp 5, the crew requires the assistance of Trip Tucker and the *Starship Columbia*. At the Klingon facility, Phlox and a Klingon scientist discover that there may be a way to stop the virus—but it will destroy any of the benefits the Klingons would have gained from augmentation. Plus, they'll have to live with the disfigurement of looking like humans, with smooth foreheads. Klingon Fleet Admiral Krell's preferred method is much more direct: wipe out the entire planet where the research facility is located.

93. Bound

Archer agrees to a business proposal made by Harrad-Sar, commander of an Orion ship. He presents the captain with a gift: three extremely sexy Orion slave girls. Soon the crew begins acting strangely: the men grow preoccupied and aggressive, and the women are oddly listless. Kelby, the ship's new chief engineer, goes so far as to sabotage the ship's engines. Phlox determines that the Orion women have exposed the ship to a very potent pheromone. Curiously, only T'Pol and Trip are immune to the effect, so it's up to them to stop Harrad-Sar from taking over the ship.

94. In a Mirror, Darkly, Part I

In the mirror universe, Jonathan Archer, first officer of a warship named *Enterprise*, proposes to his superior, Captain Forrest, that they head for Tholian space to investigate a ship that's rumored to contain advanced technology. Forrest dismisses the idea, so Archer has Forrest thrown in the brig. T'Pol frees Forrest, but he finds that Archer has locked the ship's controls onto their destination, and his superiors want Archer's plan to proceed. Archer briefs the crew that the vessel, *U.S.S. Defiant*, is from another place—a parallel universe—and another *time*—one hundred years in the future. Forrest sends an assault team, led by Archer, to the *Defiant*, while secretly telling T'Pol to make sure he doesn't come back alive. The *Enterprise* is surrounded by a group of Tholian vessels that weave a complex web of energy streams around the NX-01—which suddenly explodes.

95. In a Mirror Darkly, Part II

Archer and his crew see the *Enterprise* explode in the deadly Tholian web. However, they manage to use the futuristic *Defiant* to fight their way out. Perusing the *Defiant*'s computer, Archer and Hoshi read about their parallel universe counterparts. Archer is disturbed to learn that his alternate is a starship captain and revered explorer. After saving the imperial starship *Avenger* from a rebel attack, Archer becomes enraged when the ship's commander, Admiral Black, says that he'll recommend Archer for a promotion for having captured the *Defiant*. Knowing that the Empire will take the *Defiant* away from him, Archer kills Black and announces that he plans to seize control of the Empire.

96. Demons

Humans, Vulcans, Andorians, and other species are meeting at Earth's Starfleet Command Headquarters to form a coalition of planets. Suddenly, a dying woman bursts into the conference and presses a vial containing humanoid hair into T'Pol's hand. Phlox determines that the hair belongs to the daughter of T'Pol and Trip—but T'Pol has never been pregnant. The dead woman is a member of Terra Prime, an underground movement whose goal is to restore Earth to a society of humans only. Determining that a Terra Prime base is located in a mining colony on the moon, T'Pol and Tucker infiltrate the colony in search of the mysterious baby. They're captured and taken before the movement's leader, John Frederick Paxton. With *Enterprise* in pursuit, Paxton launches the mining facility—actually a large ship—and heads for Mars, where the passionate separatist commandeers a huge weapons array and aims it directly at Earth.

97. Terra Prime

Broadcasting from Mars, xenophobic leader John Frederick Paxton addresses the people of Earth. He displays the image of a half-human, half-Vulcan baby—a clone he's created from T'Pol's and Trip's DNA—as an example of how

> *"Every species we run into seems to be gunning for us. We may as well paint a giant bull's-eye on the hull."* —Tucker, "Anomaly"

humanity's genetic pool will be polluted. Then he gives his ultimatum: all nonhumans have twenty-four hours to leave Earth or he will begin firing, beginning with Starfleet Command Headquarters. On Earth, Nathan Samuels attempts to hold the interspecies coalition together, while Archer takes a small team to Mars to stop Paxton. On *Enterprise*, Hoshi prepares to destroy the weapons array if Archer's mission fails. Archer reaches the array and overpowers Paxton, and discovers that the paranoid bigot has locked the firing sequence. Archer can't stop it from firing at Earth.

98. These Are the Voyages . . .

From his twenty-fourth-century vantage point, Commander Jonathan Riker watches a holodeck re-creation of a key moment in Federation history when the *Enterprise* NX-01 heads back to Earth. Suddenly, Captain Archer receives a message from his friend Shran, who says that former associates have kidnapped his daughter. Disregarding the possibility of being late for the ceremony, Archer and his crew go to Shran's assistance. After successfully rescuing the girl, the crew and Shran say good-bye and go their separate ways. But as *Enterprise* resumes the trip to Earth, the kidnappers board and demand to be taken to Shran—or they will kill Jonathan Archer.

WHO IS PORTHOS? Porthos is Captain Archer's pet beagle. The dog is named after a character in the novel *The Three Musketeers* by Alexandre Dumas (his littermates were named for the two other musketeers). The original Porthos loved wine, women, and song; *this* Porthos seems to love only cheese—but then, he *is* a dog.

Note: **Bold** page numbers indicate main discussion.

EPISODE INDEX

R

S

Slaver Weapon, The, 51

Sleeping Dogs, 269

Soldiers of the Empire, 148

Someone to Watch Over Me, 200

Sons and Daughters, 150

Sons of Mogh, 143

Sound of Her Voice, The, 153

Space Seed, 17, 29

Spectre of the Gun, 36

Spirit Folk, 203–204

Spock's Brain, 35

Squire of Gothos, The, 28

Star Trek Generations, 233–34

Star Trek Nemesis, 242–43

Star Trek: First Contact, 236–37

Star Trek: Insurrection, 239–40

Star Trek: The Motion Picture, 215–16

Star Trek II: The Wrath of Khan, 218–19

Star Trek III: The Search for Spock, 221–22

Star Trek IV: The Voyage Home, 224–25

Star Trek V: The Final Frontier, 227–28

Star Trek VI: The Undiscovered Country, 230–31

Starship Down, 142

Starship Mine, 98

State of Flux, 182

Statistical Probabilities, 151

Stigma, 273

Storm Front, Part I, 279

Storm Front, Part II, 279

Storyteller, The, 132

Strange Bedfellows, 156

Strange New World, 265

Stratagem, 277

Sub Rosa, 101

Suddenly Human, 88

Survival Instinct, 201

Survivor, The, 50

Survivors, The, 85

Suspicions, 98

Swarm, The, 188

Sword of Kahless, The, 142–43

Symbiosis, 80

T

Tacking into the Wind, 157

Take Me Out to the Holosuite, 154

Tapestry, 74, 97

Taste of Armageddon, A, 29

Tattoo, 184

Tears of the Prophets, 153–54

Terra Nova, 265–68

Terra Prime, 262, 283

Terratin Incident, The, 51

That Which Survives, 38

Thaw, The, 187

These Are the Voyages . . . , 83

Thine Own Self, 101–2

Things Past, 146

Think Tank, 200

Thirty Days, 198

This Side of Paradise, 17, 29

Tholian Web, The, 36

Threshold, 185

Through the Looking Glass, 140

Ties of Blood and Water, 148

'Til Death Do Us Part, 156

Time and Again, 181

Time Squared, 83

Time to Stand, A, 149–50

Time Trap, The, 51

Time's Arrow, Part I, 95

Time's Arrow, Part II, 95

Time's Orphan, 153

Timeless, 175, 197

Timescape, 99

Tin Man, 87

Tinker, Tenor, Doctor, Spy, 201

To the Death, 144–45

Tomorrow Is Yesterday, 28

Too Short a Season, 80

Transfigurations, 87–88

Treachery, Faith, and the Great River, 154

Trials and Tribble-ations, 146

Tribunal, 137

ACKNOWLEDGMENTS

We wish to thank the creator of *Star Trek*, Gene Roddenberry, along with the producers who were the driving force behind the saga's subsequent eras, Harve Bennett and Rick Berman. And we extend our gratitude to the hundreds of writers, actors, and filmmakers who have evoked magic over the past four decades.

We owe unbounded attribution to the reference book writers who allowed us (knowingly or not) to take advantage of their great works while assembling this volume: Allan Asherman, Larry Nemecek, Marc Okrand, Michael and Denise Okuda, Stephen Poe, Judith and Garfield Reeves-Stevens, Paul Ruditis, and Jill Sherwin. Our deep gratitude to Tim Gaskill, Marc Wade, and the rest of the former team at STARTREK.com for the quality information at that site, to Konrad Petter, formerly of Paramount Home Entertainment, for providing desperately needed materials that aided our research, and to John Van Citters at CBS Consumer Products for keeping us in line. Thank you all.

Thank you to Margaret Clark, our fearless editor at Pocket Books, for your articulate commentary, critical support, and patience, patience, patience, and to book designer Richard Oriolo—your artistic eye makes us look good (once again). Also at Pocket Books, thank you to Marco Palmieri and Ed Schlesinger. Together you stand as the best *Star Trek* publishing team on Earth, bar none.

Thanks to our friends Andrea Hein, Terri Helton, and especially Pam Newton for believing in this project. And to Neil Newman for inspiring it, even though we're sure he has no idea that he did. Thanks, too, to Liz Kalodner, Risa Kessler, Jason Korfine, Margaret Milnes, Rod Roddenberry, and Dave Rossi. Finally, thank you to Gary Berman, Lori and Gordon Chapek-Carleton, Marian Cordry, Jeff Erdmann and Joyce Kogut, Judi Hendricks Stott, Devra Langsam, Jan Linder, Dan Madsen, Adam Malin, Joe Marconi, Dave McDonnell, Scott Shannon, Paula Smith, Joyce Yasner, and dear Amanda Ruffin, who would have loved this.

TERRY J. ERDMANN & PAULA M. BLOCK